KINDRED

Kindred Book One

NICOLA CLAIRE

Copyright © 2012, Nicola Claire
All Rights Reserved

The stunning artwork for the paperback covers in this series was created by Tithi Luadthong.

This book is a work of fiction. The names, characters, places and incidents are products of the writer's imagination or have been used fictitiously and are not to be construed as real. Any resemblance to persons, living or dead, actual events, locales or organisations is entirely coincidental.

All rights are reserved. No part of this book may be used or reproduced in any manner whatsoever without written permission from the author.

ISBN-13: 978-1482032505

ISBN-10: 1482032503

❀ Created with Vellum

ABOUT THE AUTHOR

Nicola Claire lives in beautiful Taupo, New Zealand with her husband and two young boys.

A bit of a romance junkie, she can be known to devour as many as half a dozen books a week if she drinks too much coffee. But her real passion is writing sexy, romantic suspense stories with strong female leads and alpha male protagonists who know how to love them.

So far, she's written well over 50 books. She might have caught the writing bug; here's hoping there's no cure!

For more information:
www.nicolaclairebooks.com
nicola@nicolaclairebooks.com

ALSO BY NICOLA CLAIRE

Kindred Series

Kindred
Blood Life Seeker
Forbidden Drink
Giver of Light
Dancing Dragon
Shadow's Light
Entwined With The Dark
Kiss Of The Dragon
Dreaming Of A Blood Red Christmas (Novella)

Mixed Blessing Mystery Series

Mixed Blessing
Dark Shadow
Rogue Vampire (Coming Soon)

Sweet Seduction Series

Sweet Seduction Sacrifice
Sweet Seduction Serenade
Sweet Seduction Shadow
Sweet Seduction Surrender
Sweet Seduction Shield

Sweet Seduction Sabotage
Sweet Seduction Stripped
Sweet Seduction Secrets
Sweet Seduction Sayonara

Elemental Awakening Series

The Tempting Touch Of Fire
The Soothing Scent Of Earth
The Chilling Change Of Air
The Tantalising Taste Of Water
The Eternal Edge Of Aether (Novella)

H.E.A.T. Series

A Flare Of Heat
A Touch Of Heat
A Twist Of Heat (Novella)
A Lick Of Heat

Citizen Saga

Elite
Cardinal
Citizen
Masked (Novella)
Wiped

Scarlet Suffragette Series

Fearless
Breathless
Heartless

Blood Enchanted Series

Blood Enchanted
Blood Entwined
Blood Enthralled

44 South Series

Southern Sunset
Southern Storm
Southern Strike (Coming Soon)

Lost Time Series

Losing Time
Making Time
Stitching Time (Coming Soon)

The Sector Fleet

Accelerating Universe
Apparent Brightness
Right Ascension
Zenith Point

The Summer O'Dare Mysteries

Chasing Summer
Sizzling Summer (Coming Soon)

For Tony:
My kindred.

DEFINITIONS

Accord – A blood binding agreement, often between two parties of equal power; cannot be broken.

Alliance – A word of honour agreement; has varying degrees of binding, some alliances cannot be broken.

Blood Bond – A binding connection between master and servant, requiring the exchange of blood to seal. It can only be broken by someone more powerful than the master who created it. A blood bond establishes a close relationship between the blood bonded. The master provides safety and protection, the servant offers obedience and loyalty.

Bond – The connection between joined kindred Nosferatu and Nosferatin; reflects the emotional and psychological relationship. Enables both parties to find each other over distance; to perform whatever is required to get to that person, overcoming any obstacle; to direct thoughts to each other; to feed off the life force of each other. It is always an equal exchange.

Command – A directive given by a Master vampire to one of his line. It requires *Sanguis Vitam* in order to enforce obedience. It cannot be ignored.

Dream Walk – A Nosferatin power, enabling the Nosferatin to appear in a different location. The Dream Walker is invisible, cannot be sensed or smelled, and only heard if they talk when in this realm. They can, however, interact and be harmed. The only exception to a Dream Walker's invisibility is another Nosferatin. Two Dream Walks in a 24 hour period results in prolonged unconsciousness once the Dream Walker returns to their body. A very rare power.

Final death – The true death of a Nosferatu. There can be no survival from the final death.

Glaze – The ability to influence another. It requires direct eye contact and *Sanguis Vitam* to insert the influence. Usually a Nosferatu skill, allowing a vampire to influence a human.

Hapū – (Maori) Tribe; sub-tribe – e.g. the Westside Hapū of Taniwha is the local Auckland sub-tribe of New Zealand Taniwha.

Iunctio – (Latin). The Nosferatu connection and governing power. All vampires are connected to one another via this supernatural information exchange highway; enabling sharing of rules, locations of safe havens and hot spots to avoid. It is powered by both Nosferatu and Nosferatin *Sanguis Vitam*, but is operated by the Nosferatu in Paris. There are twelve members of the *Iunctio* council, headed by the Champion. The *Iunctio* is tasked with policing all supernaturals throughout the world.

Joining – The marriage of a kindred Nosferatu with a kindred Nosferatin. Upon joining the Nosferatu will double their *Sanguis Vitam* and the Nosferatin will come into their powers, but for the Nosferatin, their powers will only manifest after reaching maturity; the age of 25. The joining will also make the Nosferatin immortal. A symbiotic relationship, should one member of the joining die, the other will too. Without a joining, the Nosferatin would die one month past their 25th birthday. The joining also increases the power of the *Iunctio* and Nosferatu as a whole.

Kaitiaki – (Maori) New Zealand shapeshifter (Taniwha) name for Nosferatin. Meaning protective guardian of people and places.

Kindred – A Nosferatu or Nosferatin sacred match, a suitable partner for a joining. To be a kindred there must exist a connection between the Nosferatu and Nosferatin; only those suitably compatible will be kindred to the other.

Line – The family of a Master Vampire, all members of which have been turned by the Master, or accepted via blood bond into the fold.

Master – A Nosferatu with the highest level of *Sanguis Vitam*. There are five levels of Master, from level five – the lowest on the *Sanguis Vitam* scale, to level one – the highest on the *Sanguis Vitam* scale. Only level one Masters can head a line of their own. Some Nosferatu may never become Masters.

Master of the City – A level one Master in control of a territory; a city.

Norm – A human unaware of the supernaturals who walk the Earth. They also do not have any supernatural abilities themselves.

Nosferatu – A vampire. The Nosferatu turned towards the Dark, when their kin, the Nosferatin turned towards the Light. They require blood to survive and can be harmed by UV exposure and silver. They do not need to breathe or have a heartbeat. They are considered the undead.

Pull – The Nosferatin sense of evil. Guides a hunter to a Dark vampire; sometimes, but not always a rogue, who is about to feed off an innocent.

Rākaunui – (Maori) Full Moon.

Rogue – A vampire no longer controlled by a master, full of evil and Darkness, feeding indiscriminately and uncontrolled.

Sanguis Vitam – (Latin) The Blood Life or life force of a Nosferatu. It represents the power they possess. There are varying degrees of *Sanguis Vitam*.

Taniwha – (Maori) New Zealand shapeshifter. Dangerous, predatory beings. The Taniwha have an alliance with the Nosferatins.

Turned – The action of changing a human into a vampire.

Vampyre – Old term for vampire; used rarely in modern language.

*"There is so much light in this world,
we only have to open our eyes to see."*
Lucinda Monk

1
NIGHT, NIGHT, SWEETIE

I knew things weren't quite going according to plan when his fist connected with my jaw. The pain sent a sharp stab up through my skull; making me grit my teeth, hear bells ring inside my head, and causing my vision to blur. But, for the life of me, I couldn't understand why. Never one to dwell too long on the morose, I decided the best course of action was to come out guns blazing. As I don't actually own a gun, I settled on a taunt instead.

"Is that the best you've got?" I managed to squeeze out between my still clenched teeth.

I shouldn't have been antagonising the nasty stinking creep, especially as I was still down on all fours spitting blood out of the side of my mouth, but I just could't help it. Call me a sucker for punishment; it's just how I worked. Never let them see fear, that was my motto. So far, it had worked.

Not so sure about that today, though.

"Oh, sweet Hunter, you think your witty repartee will distract me?"

Why did all the bad guys sound so freakishly prim and proper all of a sudden? Where had the good old *take that, you bitch* gone? I liked the simplicity of an evil bad guy dropping his H's and missing his T's. It just went with the territory, *you know wo' I mean, Luv?*

And there was the foot again, straight into my ribcage. I heard the crack this time; it sounded like a gunshot in the alley we were in. It reverberated around the brick walls on either side - or was that just inside my head? I couldn't tell, but breathing was suddenly a challenge. Oh God, though, it hurt. And how did this upstart get the drop on me? I mean, it all seemed so easy.

There he was, down the far end of the dark alley, against a dirty brick wall, like all good evil vampires should be, with his arm casually over the blonde's shoulders, looking into her eyes and mind fucking her, fangs down and glow on. It should have been a walk in the park; he was distracted, about to get his fill, nowhere to run, but somehow here I was on the ground struggling to inhale, and there he was with a cocky grimace and the upper hand. What the...?

"They told me you were stronger than this; more clever too. Hmm, I guess they were wrong, my sweet. You are nothing but a little girl playing *Buffy the Vampire Slayer*. Where is the big bad Hunter I have heard so much about, hmm? Where indeed?"

Where indeed, sweetie? That was just what I was thinking. Not trying to be egotistical or anything, but usually, my hunts went a hell of a lot better than this. And usually, I didn't have to battle more than one bloodthirsty vampire in a night. This, however, was the third numbskull vamp to cross my path trying to feed off the innocent. I'd have to ask Michel about this influx of careless vampires, eating in such a public way, disregarding all of his rules when entering his city.

That's if I could get out of this little encounter alive. So far, the jury was still out on that one.

I rolled onto my back, feeling the wet muck of the alley seeping in through my light chiffon blouse. The stars were out tonight, no clouds in the sky from the earlier downpour, almost a Full Moon, but not quite. Old Evil Face was slowly stalking closer; if you could call it stalking. It was always more of a glide with the older vamps, and this one was about 150 years, judging by the power level oozing off him like thick syrup. I could almost reach out and touch it, so thick and sweetly smelling. With a hint of rot underneath.

I had to stall him, get back on my feet. He'd disarmed me as soon as I had approached; a simple flick of his wrist, a magical brush against my fingers and the stake was gone. It was now down the far end of the alley, by the entrance, where all of a sudden, not a single soul was walking by. Go figure. Not that I'd want a Norm to get involved in this, but I did kind of feel alone right then. Even just the sound of late night "clubbers" would have been welcome, but no such luck.

Still, I hadn't honed my skills over the past two years without arming myself with more than one weapon. I shifted slightly to my right, casually slipping my left arm into my belt at the top of my skirt, all the while making full eye contact with Fang-Face.

"You seem awfully sure of yourself," I hedged. "What makes you think this isn't some trap?" I watched him stalk ever closer; so slow, so predatory, so sure.

He glanced over his shoulder quickly at that, though. I must have managed to ruffle his feathers or cape. It was enough of a distraction to slip my little silver knife out of its sheath at my waist and hide it behind my wrist and arm.

"I don't think so, Hunter," he sneered. "You work alone. I know a lot about you; you could say, your name is on the Most Wanted List of my kind. An all-points bulletin. We even study your moves."

Huh? It was just one of those nights for surprises, I guessed. I didn't know I was that popular amongst the otherworldly nasties, but there you go.

"It's always nice to be recognised for my efforts," I replied while lying perfectly still and taking small shallow breaths to ease the pain. It was just a constant ache now, no longer that sharp stabbing pain as though a rib was about to pierce the side of my skin.

He noticed, of course; they always do when you're injured. Something about the predator in them. They sense the weak; they sniff out the pain to use it against you. I'd have to time this just right. One shot and one shot only.

There was one thing you can count on when it came to vamps, though, they were arrogant sons of bitches. This vampire might have known all my moves or thought he did, but he wouldn't believe for a moment that I could succeed in using them on him; could succeed in getting the drop on him. I was betting he'd be wrong there. Pride before a fall and all that.

He leant over me, fangs obvious in the glint of the moon streaking down the alley above us. There was a fat drop of blood hanging off the right one, threatening to spill on my shirt. He'd either bitten himself accidentally, or more likely, he did manage to get fang to neck on the now unconscious blonde in a pile over by the dumpster. Bastard!

"I'm going to enjoy teaching you a lesson, Hunter," he whispered as he moved in for the strike.

"That's what they all say," I countered as my arm arced gracefully across the front of him. I knew I couldn't get the heart from the angle I was at. That wasn't what I was aiming for, but that beautiful face of his would certainly feel the silver as it sliced into his cheek.

A howl rent the night air. An intense sound of anger and guttural, visceral pain. He sprang back against the far wall, with his hand covering the slash from his left ear to mouth, already healing, despite the silver of the knife. It took a lot to damage a creature of the night permanently.

I used the distraction and distance to get to my feet, not as ladylike as I would have liked, but hey, no one was watching. Well, no one who mattered. Old Sweetie Pie hadn't taken his eyes off me for a second. They could be very focused when they needed to be.

"You shall pay for that!" he spat. "I've been holding back, toying with you, but no longer, Hunter. The game is up."

Indeed, it was. We began slowly circling each other, me with my now somewhat pitiful slender silver knife, him with his fangs which only seemed to be getting bigger and longer the more I looked at them. Oh, what big teeth you've got, I thought hysterically. Losing it now was not an option. Luckily for me, since my first encounter with a vampire, my strength at resisting their spell-binding gaze had increased. To such a point that only the rare higher level master vamp had any effect on me. This guy was only a level four on the *Sanguis Vitam* scale; strong, but not strong enough. So, I could look him in the eye when I said, "Right back at ya, Sweetie." And then I forced a grin.

I've always felt confidence in a retort could only be achieved when making direct eye contact, somehow the effect is lost when you have to look at your shoes.

He came at me in a flash. I was expecting it, but still, they could move, and you wouldn't even see them coming. Especially when they wanted to and this chap had had it with me. Anger poured off his skin in waves. I only just managed to raise the knife enough to glance the sleeve of his shirt and knick the skin ever so slightly - I might as well have been a mosquito for all the good it did - but his arm crashed against the side of my face, throwing my head and body around and against the hard and unforgiving brick wall. I tasted blood and felt my vision blur again, but the hit hadn't been a straight hand punch, thankfully.

I used the momentum of springing back off that solid mass of brick and concrete to roll away and under his approaching bulk, sweeping out my leg as I passed him. It only made him stumble, but still... go me!

He rounded on me in that lightning speed. But I rolled to the left, closer to the entrance of the alley, making what would have been a killer blow, into a somewhat lesser one. Pain in my back erupted like a burst balloon, shooting up my spine into the base of my head. I thought my back would snap; it was so bad. Tears started rolling down my face, my fingers tingled and then went numb. Now, I was mad.

I rounded to face my killer. No way was I going down without a fight. He grinned; a typical evil bad guy grin, all teeth and smirk. He hardly had a scratch on him. Some reputation I've got. I took a step back, towards the entrance and light, towards the safety of a crowd. He cocked his head as though to say; you think you can make it?

I couldn't, and we both knew it, but I could reach my stake. I moved; right before he flew through the air towards me. I rolled head over heels, transferring my knife to my left hand and picking up my stake with my right as I sailed over it. All those hours play-fighting with my best mate Rick's shapeshifter Hapū was paying off. I landed in a crouch; half twisted towards him. It wasn't perfect, but it would have to do. His arms came out around me, his head and face over my left shoulder, he grabbed my hair and jerked my head to the right, lifting me off my feet. I felt a few hairs come loose, and my back was screaming for release, but his hold was slack, not crushing. Stupid. Never lower your guard.

I twisted with the pull of my neck, not resisting it. I brought my right arm across my chest and up under my left armpit, directly towards the vamp's chest. The angle wasn't great, but it was close enough. As soon as he felt the silver of the stake breach his skin and enter his chest wall, he froze. I took my advantage and pushed the baby home.

There was a sickening, squelching sound as the stake slid further in, resting on the edge of his heart. His arms fell away, no longer responding to his commands and he crumpled backwards towards the ground. I went with him, twisting around to face him completely, not letting my grip on the stake release, or the stake move anywhere but further in. Lying on top of him, looking into those red-rimmed glowing eyes, I twisted the stake minutely, feeling the moment it touched the chamber of his heart.

His eyes widened slightly, a look of utter incredulity on them. I smiled and said, "Night, night, Sweetie" as the stake finally sunk home. For an instant, nothing happened, and then I was face first in a pile of dust, coughing and choking on vampire residue.

I rolled away, grasping my side, trying to stop the racking cough from tearing my already tender ribs further apart. Finally, after several minutes, I managed to control myself and slowly sat up.

It took a moment for me to get my bearings. There was still a low-level humming in my mind, the last of the vamp's *Sanguis Vitam* seeping into the night, but there was no other indication of power in the vicinity. I took as deep a breath as I could manage, then hauled myself over to the blonde.

She was coming around, groaning. There was a slight mark on her neck, not deep; he hadn't managed to penetrate her vein fully. Thank God. "You'll be all right now," I said. She opened her eyes and looked at me.

"Who the hell are you?" she demanded, speech a little slurred.

See, here's the thing: When a vamp glazes you with his gaze, he can have you thinking any number of things. Hell, he could make you jump off the Harbour Bridge if he wanted to, but most of the time, they're not that inventive. It's usually a vision of utter happiness if they're kind, or in Sweetie Pie's case, a feeling that you're drunk and just having a quiet moment in the alley to yourself. Waking up and finding a dishevelled female leaning over you is not the most pleasant of visions, even if you think you're smashed.

I pulled back. "There's a taxi stand down the street by McDonald's," I said, indicating the direction with a nod of my head. "You fell over, must have been a good night, huh?"

She struggled to her feet, still glaring at me, but started to take a shaky step away. I wanted to reach out and help, but vampire induced psychosis is not something you can easily get involved with. The glazing just didn't allow it. She'd be all right, though, no real harm done.

Me, on the other hand, I ached. From head to toe. I hadn't been that badly beaten up for months. This was going to take some getting over.

I dusted down my skirt and straightened my blouse. No rips, cool. And was just reaching for my stake and knife when I heard the humming and felt the low-level power of a baby vamp nearby. Only young, less than 50 I'd say. Easy on any regular night, but tonight was shaping up to be unusual. You never knew.

I spun around to face it, stake out and knife ready to go. Shane Smith walked round the corner of the alley and stood ten metres away. He smiled his shy smile and thrust his hands deep into his pockets. His shock of curly white hair caught the glint of a street light, his pale features in contrast to his black attire; regular wear for members of Michel's inner circle.

"Hey, Shane," I said as I sheathed my knife and pocketed my stake. "What's up?"

Shane had been turned no less than thirty years ago, by none other than Michel Durand, the Master Vampire of Auckland City. He was now serving his time as Michel's gopher; the vamp who took messages and parcels where they needed to go. He was a weakling, as far as vamps went and always would be. But I liked him; I couldn't help it. I felt sorry for the guy. Who knew you had to give up your soul *and* live forever like a doormat when offered life for eternity. He was a sorry excuse for a vampire, but he meant no one any harm.

"The Master wishes to see you," he said with a small, tentative smile.

I sighed. "Now Michel knows I'm not one of his puppets to order around, so why don't you just go and tell your *Master* that I'm busy tonight."

"Aww, come on, Luce! Ya know I can't return to him without ya, he'd have me for dinner; he would."

Unfortunately, as melodramatic as that sounded, he would. Michel might be one of the nice guys, but he was a Master Vampire in charge of a city, albeit a city in the antipodes; he had to be strong and ruthless when it counted. I had no doubt Shane would get it for my refusal to *attend*.

Another sigh and another subconscious flattening of my skirt and shirt. "OK, let's go see the Master," I said as I strode past him into the night.

2
MASTER KNOWS BEST

Michel owns a number of nightclubs and bars throughout the city. All the Masters of Cities throughout the world seem to be in the same business. I guess it's easy to conduct your affairs from an establishment that only gets going after it's dark. The one Shane led me to this evening was called *Sensations*. If I didn't know it was vampire owned, I'd have liked it. It had a certain charm and was very subtle in its overtures towards the nightlife. And I'm not talking your average club scene either. Some of the bars around, even ones Michel owns, are a bit camp, to say the least. It was a surprise vampires weren't out of the coffin yet, everyone seemed to be into fang.

Fantasy at it's best. Unfortunately, I knew better.

Sensations was just off K' Road; Karangahape Road to those from out of town. But not down the red light end of the street, up near Queen Street and the more reputable establishments. It had an ornate plastered concrete façade painted in black, with large double sided dark wooden doors. The windows were all blacked out and the overall effect, far from being too dark and foreboding, actually gave off the appearance of sophisticated chic.

There was always a bouncer on the front door; tonight it was

Bruno. Yeah, clichéd I know, but that's his name, has been since well before the Napoleonic Wars. He wasn't one of our allies, that was for sure, I somehow doubted that he was even one now. All muscles and broad shoulders, he was an impressive sight. Of course, that's the point of a bouncer, isn't it? To intimidate, but to also look damn fine in their tight fitting black jeans and tee. Bruno wore it well.

He nodded to us both as we passed the queue to get in and turned to open the door. "Lucinda Monk, long time no see." His sharp eyes made a slow, graceful trip from my head to my toes, then back up again. "Good to see you."

His smile didn't fool me, though; Bruno wasn't one I'd like to meet alone in an alley. Not exactly a bad guy, but not OK either. I never put my back to Bruno if I could help it.

"Yeah right, Bruno. Wish I could say the same."

See, that's me, all bad attitude. Scare the boogie men off with my smart mouth. That'll work.

Inside the club was all plush upholstery, lush furnishings in muted colours, dark wood, not imitation, but the real stuff, substantial but sleek. Smoking's not allowed in public premises anymore; they made that illegal some time ago, thankfully. So it didn't have the old world feel of smoke filled rooms and sweat soaked people. The air conditioning was on and although not super cold; it was fresh and pleasant. That's Michel for you, creates a pleasant environment even in a place where you intend to get drunk.

The place was, of course, packed, any establishment owned by Michel would be. Especially if he was known to be in attendance and I didn't doubt for a moment that the people here knew just that and hoped to catch a glimpse. Michel was *the* bachelor of the city. Everyone wanted a piece of him.

They could have him, for all I cared. I just wanted to go home and take a steaming hot shower and ease my aching body into bed. It had been a hellishly long night.

Shane walked straight past the people milling around the comfortable couches and sitting at the cosy two seater tables, past the first and main bar, to a door marked private at the back. He punched a number into the security control, careful to hide his hand movements from any prying eyes. Couldn't have the master's privacy interrupted by an over enthusiastic groupie. And then he held the door open for me without making eye contact.

Hmm, what's he trying to hide? Never good when the nice ones couldn't even look you in the eye. I squared my shoulders and marched down the long, thin hall. My feet didn't make a sound on the plush carpet, but I knew Michel could tell I was here. Hell, I could feel him, no doubt he could do the same back.

I didn't bother knocking on the door to his office. Shane had stayed back by the door to the bar area, hadn't even bothered to follow me to Michel's door. *Sensitive much, Shane?* I shook my head to clear the thought and turned the handle to the door in front of me.

Power rolled along the floor and caressed up my body, sending tingles through my centre and goose bumps along my arms. I don't know how it is for others like me, but I've always been able to judge a vampire's age and level by their *Sanguis Vitam*. Michel is about as high up as they go, a level one Master. There may be stronger vamps out there, but I doubt it. Michel is as big as it gets here in New Zealand anyway, I've yet to meet a vamp who comes even remotely close.

I swallowed visibly and pushed past that wave of pure, unadulterated joy Michel's *Sanguis Vitam* had over me and strode into his lair.

"Knock it off, would you!"

"Ah, Lucinda, ever the lady I see." Michel smiled wickedly, his rich voice curling around my stomach and his vivid blue eyes trailing over my face. Devouring every feature, as though he was starved for a glimpse of me. "I thought you may have missed me and needed a little reminding."

"Very funny, Michel, but could you can it for a bit? I can hardly draw a breath." The only way to deal with a vampire is to be direct, anything else and they take it as an invitation to play. Playing with Michel was not a good idea.

Instantly the power that had enveloped me, stroked me and whispered sweet nothings against the sensitive skin on the side of my neck was gone. I missed it already.

In its absence, Michel was looking at me intently. He wasn't breathing. Sometimes they do that if they forget to cover, or can't be bothered. I guess Michel and I were passed that pretence; I knew he was a vampire the moment I met him. Likewise, he knew what I was. I only wish he'd tell me.

"You are hurt," he said and was suddenly in front of me reaching for my cheek. I hadn't even seen him move. I mean not a flash, a sound, a sensation. Not a thing. *Whoa.*

He stroked the side of my face, tracing the bruise lightly that had started to puff out and stretch my skin. His hands hardly touched me but left a searing sensation. Not pain, but something else, as they traced the marks on my face, neck, arms and down the sides of my body, to rest on either side of my hips.

It's not often he catches me by surprise, I've got good at anticipating his moves, but he's not usually this outrightly obvious in his affections for me. Flirts a little, sure, but to be so intimate, so quickly upon my walking in his office was new even for him.

I realised I'd been holding my breath. I slowly let it out, and as I did, I also noticed I was no longer sore. There was a dull ache, a sense of fatigue that had been there before, but the pain on my cheek and in my back had gone.

"Wh..what did you do?" I stammered. *Go the smooth talker, me.*

Michel visibly shook himself, just a small movement, but he was breathing again, human looking, almost. He took a step back and smiled. A coy smile that managed to light up the deep blue of his eyes. It was shockingly mesmerising.

"You were hurt, my dear. I could not have that." Each word was articulated perfectly, as though he was fighting not to let his French accent show, straining to remain very English.

"You heal people now?" It would be good to know, if I ever found myself in a similar situation, or worse like I had done tonight.

"Only when the desire is strong, it would seem." I'm not quite sure what he meant by that, but I let it go.

He moved back around the other side of his desk and slid down into his seat. A smooth movement like a sleek cat reclining in the sunshine. Of course, there'd be no sunshine for Michel, if he could help it. Vampires don't like the sun; it tends to give them a fatal sunburn.

His eyes hadn't left me. Actually, I had the distinct impression they were still devouring me, but I chose to ignore that too. It didn't pay to let the mind wander on those trains of thought, best to stick to business.

"So, you requested my presence. Here I am."

He smiled, this time it was full of an amused knowledge, as though my presence here was nothing but expected, a foregone conclusion. With the smile his eyes lit up like a shining light, all shades of blue possible, swirling together in a hypnotic movement that made me struggle to pull my gaze away.

"Have a seat, my dear. We have much to catch up on."

I'd rather have stayed standing, somehow remaining on my feet so I could make a quick getaway seemed prudent. But it's difficult to argue when you're so tired you're swaying. Besides, Michel was not one to take no easily. I had first-hand knowledge of that.

I threw myself into the overstuffed armchair opposite his desk and felt my body relax at the luxuriant feel of the upholstery and softness of the padding. It was made to fit my body.

He must have noticed because he tried to hide a smirk by reaching for a bottle of wine on his desk and pouring two glasses, which I hadn't even seen until that moment. He stood up and came around the desk to offer me one. No reaching over obstacles for this guy, nothing but the height of manners would do.

I took a good look at him as I accepted the offered glass, no longer befuddled by his power. I allowed my eyes to trail the length of his beautiful body as he turned back towards his seat. At 6'2" he was all lean muscle and tall, tightly coiled, controlled strength. His shoulder length dark brown, almost black, hair shone in the low lights of the room. It always seemed to catch my attention, no matter how hard I tried not to notice its beauty. His profile was chiselled. Firm jawline, high cheekbones, long lashes that swept his face and a straight, almost regal, nose. All giving the appearance of strength and power, wrapped up in an oh-my-god imposing façade.

He wore a dark expensive Armani suit, almost black, but not quite. The staff may have to wear black, but the Master gets to diversify. The jacket was made to fit perfectly; he had it unbuttoned with a white

Pierre Cardin shirt showing, gold cuff links at each wrist and a sleek dark blue pinstriped tie. The tie was slightly loose; that would be the extent I had ever seen Michel allow himself to slum it where his clothing was concerned. He looked every inch the self-made millionaire bachelor. Handsome, intelligent, at ease. I could appreciate the package, even if I didn't want to undo the wrapping.

He inclined his head as if to say, *you done?* You could never surprise a Master of his level.

I'm a big girl now, I resisted the urge to blush.

"So, what did you want to catch up on, Michel?" I said as I sipped my wine. Cabernet Sauvignon, no doubt from his winery. I didn't know for sure, but I couldn't help thinking Michel was one of those characters out of a fantasy novel. Accomplished, sophisticated and omnipresent. The truth was a little more realistic. He bit people to drink their blood. Otherwise, he would grow weak and die. I kept reminding myself of that whenever my mind decided to take a vacation from reality.

He sipped his wine and asked, "How was your evening?"

I had to smile then. "You're asking me about my evening?"

"I would like to know, my dear, that you are well and happy. I'll start with your evening and then progress from there. Or perhaps you would like me to - how do you say? - cut to the chase? If so, then why not come a little closer, there's room enough for two on my chair."

The last was said with that knowing smile he so often wore in my presence, the words wrapping out to surround me, making a shiver run down my spine. He could tell it was taking all of my self-control and whatever supernatural blocking power my body possessed to refuse the invitation. Man, he was playing for keeps tonight.

"Very funny. It was eventful, how was yours?"

"Eventful, how?" He didn't even bother acknowledging my question.

I put my glass of wine down on the desk, careful to stand it on a placemat that happened to be waiting in exactly the right spot. "I killed three vampires who were preying on innocent lives. One was a level four Master."

"The bruises and fractured rib." He said it as a statement, not a question. *How had he known a rib was fractured, even I wasn't sure of that?*

He looked momentarily distracted, not his usual controlled self. "Is there something you're not telling, Michel? What's with all the activity lately? The lack of manners on your turf?"

His eyes flashed a strange purple, as though the blue was fighting the red that glows when vampires are emotional; be it anger, hunger, lust or pain. Someone was encroaching on Michel's turf, but who would be so bold? And reckless.

He shifted, a small movement, barely noticeable, but I was finding myself more and more in tune with Michel's minute mannerisms lately, a development I was trying fervently to ignore. The slight repositioning of his body made me think he had suddenly decided something, made a choice and I would soon benefit from that change of heart. "What I am about to tell you must not leave this room, Lucinda. Do you understand? Not even to your shapeshifter friend and his kin." His *Sanguis Vitam* was climbing again, caressing my skin, but not as beautifully as before, this time it crackled with hidden meaning; small pinpricks of pain were scattering up my body, stealing my breath.

I swallowed, I knew what Michel was capable of, even if part of me believed he'd never use it against me. Another part, that insistent voice that never stopped its internal monologue, kept whispering, *run.*

"Of course," I answered, but it wasn't in my usual voice, there was a slight crack. It was also a little too high. Damn it; I hated Michel seeing me weak.

The power abated abruptly, and he sat back slightly. A look of regret briefly touching his perfect features, to be replaced with the neutral mask he usually wore.

"There has been some rumblings in the *Iunctio* of late. At first, I thought nothing of it, but it has traversed the seas and landed upon our shores. A group of vampyre who flout the rules, who wish to take over the night completely."

He couldn't mean what I thought he meant, could he? I didn't dare say a word, he didn't look in the mood for interruptions, so I sat still as a statue waiting for him to continue.

"The revolt was thwarted in London; a similar one barely got started in New York. I had thought we were far enough from the centres of power to avoid attention, but it seems even I cannot keep some things hidden from the *Iunctio*."

The *Iunctio* Michel was referring to was the vampire connection all vampires felt to one another, it was also their governing power. Not just a network as such, more like an information highway. A bit more sophisticated than tom-tom drums and a whole lot more supernatural. Somehow they communicated as a whole to one another. You could hide things from the *Iunctio*, you could drop out for a time, but sooner or later, if you're the undead, you hooked up to the mainframe so you knew what was hot and what was not. The *Iunctio* rules the vampires. It is their law.

That's how they had avoided discovery for so long. Let's face it, with vampires being the "in" thing right now and with modern technology the way it is, even glazing every human in a hundred kilometre radius around a vampire hot spot would not be enough to hide them. So, the *Iunctio* kept them abreast of rules and regulations, hot spots to avoid and places to congregate for protection. They also, on occasion, stepped in to reprimand and control. That part of the *Iunctio* was run by the council. I'd never met an *Iunctio* council member, and I hoped I never would.

He looked back at me, his eyes had been wandering to a different place as he had spoken of the vampire connection, who knows, maybe to the *Iunctio* itself for a brief view, they were centred on me now, however. "You should be careful for a short while, my dear. Take extra precautions. Now would not be the time to rush with foolhardiness down dark dead-end alleys."

He knew where I had been tonight; why did that surprise me? It shouldn't have.

"This is your war, Michel, not mine. I've still got a job to do. No matter how many rogue vamps enter the city, they can't just chow down willy-nilly on my neighbours."

He winced slightly at my terminology. "But that is where you are wrong, my dear." He said it with what sounded like regret, as though he'd had a part in what he was about to tell me, as though it was all his fault.

"It is you they seek, Lucinda. It is you they hunt."

3
UNBELIEVABLE FAIRY-TALES

Well, that was a turn up for the books.
"Yeah, right." My usual answer to the incredulous. "What on earth would they want with me?" I mean I know I kill the odd one, but come on, they deserve it. They break the rules even the *Iunctio* sets, let alone law abiding humans who run this country. They know what they're doing, and they know the consequences. Hunters like me exist for a reason; we may not number in the hundreds, but we're around, here and there. The chances of getting a stake through your heart in a Master controlled city such as Auckland was acceptable if you broke the rules.

"Hunters have been preyed upon for centuries, my dear. It is nothing new. I had hoped, however, to keep your success here in Auckland a secret a little longer." He seemed a wee bit angry at that last comment, as though this was a dent to his pride. The Master of the City unable to control his mob.

"Of course, I could protect you." His eyes met mine with a challenge. A challenge he knew I would not accept.

"You can get off that bandwagon, Michel; you know the answer. I am not yours, nor will I ever be." Michel had been trying to claim me as his since I arrived in Auckland, fresh off the farm two years ago.

"Ah, but the benefits, they could outweigh the negatives, my dear." Again with the power, this time in places it had no right to be. I didn't miss the innuendo.

I shifted in my seat. I hadn't meant to, I didn't want Michel to see the immediate effect he had on me, but I couldn't help it. It was a natural movement, like breathing, one I just couldn't control. Of course, he knew and smiled. "You want it, Lucinda, be truthful. You want this as much as I do."

Arghhh. His voice was caressing me, his power enveloping me, before too much longer I'd be a blubbering puddle on the floor.

"No," I managed to get out in a puff of breath. "No!" Much more adamantly.

He looked momentarily surprised and then just as quickly regretful, followed again by that implacable mask.

"No fair, Michel. You promised no mind games."

"I did, didn't I? I am sorry, Lucinda, it seems where you are concerned my control is somewhat lacking."

Yeah, ri-ight. Master vampire loses control over young woman covered in alley muck. I doubted it, but I wasn't going to argue. The power had stopped, the room was back to normal. Always a roller coaster of sensations with Michel, usually decadent and delicious. Never really liked themed parks much.

"Look, thanks for the heads up, but it's business as usual for me." No response, no change to the mask he wore, no power level fluctuation, just that preternatural stillness vamps could muster when required. It was a bit creepy.

I swallowed. "Um, it's late, and I'm tired, so thanks for the chat and wine, but I gotta go." Eloquent, I know, but my mind was miraculously elsewhere. I needed to find something out, and I could only do that at home in front of my laptop.

He rose in one fluid motion and smoothly came around his desk to me. It all happened so quickly I hadn't moved from my comfortable spot in the armchair, but slowly enough for me to see his muscles move, the line of his body curl. Of course, it was on purpose.

He reached his hand out to me, and I took it, who wouldn't? Letting him pull me up to a standing position to face him. I momentarily thought it must be interesting for Michel to have a human look into his eyes willingly. Even those under the glaze fight the instinct on a basic level. I didn't fear him that way. He had never tried to glaze me. And I'm thinking, but not quite sure, that his glaze would be unable to hold me for long, just like his power. Somewhere along the way, God had given me natural vampire repelling skills. My luck.

"It has been a pleasure, my dear, as always." I doubted that too; I had seen frustration in those big blue eyes briefly while we talked. He always had trouble hiding all of his emotions from me. A small part of me reluctantly acknowledged that maybe it was intentional, his way of appearing more human and therefore more appealing. You could never trust a vampire. "I shall escort you out."

It wasn't necessary, but Michel rarely lets me off the premises without a personal escort. He undoubtedly didn't want me staking any wayward vamp on his dance floor on my way out. Bad for business.

He didn't let go of my hand, slowly caressing the back of it with his thumb as we emerged from the private sanctum through the door to the club. Strangely, it was comforting, rather than annoying. I would allow him this moment I decided. I attempted to hide my smile at my obvious pathetic mental denials of my emotions. The sooner I was out of here and away from him, the better.

As expected, every eye was on us as we traversed the club. They were of course on Michel, and he knew it. The odd glare was thrown my way by jealous women. They should thank me; I was occupying the monster on their behalf. But still, I liked that he held my hand and not theirs. *Bad, bad me.*

At the front door, he stopped and turned towards me, leaning in to brush both my cheeks with his lips. This was as close as I usually let Michel get. I put it down to his heritage, they all kiss-kiss cheeks over there, don't they? He hesitated over my left ear and whispered, "The offer will always stand, Lucinda. Your safety is guaranteed with me, all you have to do is acknowledge that you are mine." His thumb had not stopped caressing my hand, and although there was no evidence of his *Sanguis Vitam* rolling off him, I felt weak at the knees. My breath suddenly caught in my chest and my heart beat a staccato rhythm in my ears. His eyes, when he pulled back, were looking right into my soul. Was that possible? Vampires don't have souls do they, can they even recognise another?

The moment stretched to an almost embarrassing length of time, and then the door opened, and Bruno appeared. Thank God for Bruno.

Michel smiled, lighting up those impossibly blue eyes. "Good night, my dear, safe journey."

I just nodded like some stupid Kewpie Doll and walked out the door past Bruno. His smile said it all.

Finding a taxi home had been easy. If there's one thing Auckland is good at; it's taxi's on every corner after dark. It's as though we humans have subconsciously banded together to provide a lifeline amidst the turbulent waters of the undead.

My apartment is my sanctuary. I had toyed with the idea of flatting with others when I first arrived in Auckland, but I'm not good with regular humans. It just takes a lot of effort, you know? So, I found myself a one bedroom apartment on the ground floor of a complex with only eight homes. Low density is always so much nicer. And being on the ground floor offers perks. Height doesn't stop the otherworldly nasties; you could be twenty stories up, and a vamp could just fly there. But on the ground, I can escape through a window and not break *my* neck. You have to think of these things when you're a farm girl from the sticks, and I'm guessing my natural anti-supernatural skills had already kicked in, unbeknownst to me, when I was perusing potential flats.

It's a one bedroom place, compact but not small. Coming from the farm, I thought it would be impossible for me to live inside a box. But I chose this apartment as it was at the end of the row, farther away from the sounds of traffic on the street, but with windows on the end facing out to the large expanse of lawn out the back. Of course the view is kind of ruined by the communal clothesline, but still, I can see green and the sun comes through from late morning 'til evening.

My bedroom is off the main room. That's where the lounge, dining and kitchen reside, with a bathroom off the kitchen. It's a box, but it's nicely done. I entered my bedroom and stripped off. Shower first and then on to business. Before I left for the bathroom, I switched the computer on. It's on a desk in the corner. One thing about my personal space is it's big. Spacious, that's what the real estate agent said when she showed me through. I think she was exaggerating, but there is space to have a small office set-up in the corner and not feel cramped.

By the time I came back from the shower, the laptop was all go. Wrapped in a robe, I plonked myself down in front of the glowing screen and brought up my web browser.

The internet has been my friend for a long time now. It provides a necessary service. One I could not imagine my life without these dark-filled days, but it wasn't always that way. It wasn't until my first run-in with the undead that I latched onto to the power of the Net. That first introduction to the creatures of the night had been only a couple of days after arriving in Auckland to start my new job at the bank. I had no idea what he was, but before I knew it, this creature was in my face, his eyes glowing a strange soft red, the humming a crescendo of voices in my mind. My heart beat like a jack rabbit running at a hundred miles an hour. My inner monologue started jabbering away in a frantic no-nonsense kind of way. It hasn't stopped since. *Run, run as fast as you can, get away from this creature while you still have your Light intact.* Yeah, my inner monologue said *Light*. Freaky huh?

I don't know what happened next; it's all a bit of a blur, but I do remember there being a bright light; so white and crisp and clear. And the next thing I knew I was running as fast as my 5'4" frame could carry me. Somehow, I got away.

So, after that run-in with the undead, I did a bit of research, turning to the never ending information highway of the World Wide Web. Of course, all I found on the internet was the usual stuff of legends; garlic, silver, holy crosses and all that. Some of it is right, but some of it is just the over-imagination of a literary brain. Garlic, for instance, just a myth. But silver, that's the big baddie right there. The vamps and ghouls can't stand it. Even the shapeshifters try to avoid it if they can. Crosses, unfortunately, have little effect, other than the scorn that appears on the face of the vamp you're shoving it at.

So, I started searching for my unique skills. The humming I had heard, the recognition of power and the evil stench coming off of the thing that had attacked me and that strange bright white light. It's surprising what you can find on the net when you enter the right combination of search words. It took several goes and several weeks of surfing in the evenings - no way was I going outside after dark - when I stumbled upon a website. It was password protected, which was a clue in itself, but even the best-protected websites have a way in. Not that I would have a clue how to do that, but one of the guys in my best friend Rick's shapeshifter family, Josh, is excellent at hacking things. And I mean *excellent*.

I'd already met Rick by this time; he's a kickboxing instructor at my local gym. Fitness is a compulsion with me. I've always belonged to a Gym, so I joined Tony's Gym as soon as I arrived in Auckland. When I mentioned in passing that I wanted to get onto a password protected site, he put Josh on it.

One evening at my place, three jumbo pizzas later and I was in. A fair exchange Josh had said. I think I lucked out, though.

The website is set up by a group of people just like me. As far as I can tell. They're careful what they put up there. I mean they're not stupid, they know the site can be hacked if the hacker is good, so they still take care. But it is the first stop on the freaky-supernatural-antenna-person's radar when info is needed. Since Josh hacked into the website for me, I've become a legitimate member. Now, I no longer need to break and enter. Now, I have a password.

I entered my login now and brought up a forum. There were five others on-line. Quite a lot for this time of night. I mean New Zealand, if you don't know, is half way around the world, so when it's night here, it's daytime elsewhere. My compadres are usually tucked up in bed after a hard night's killing, or more likely, at work in their "day jobs" at this hour, so I was a little surprised.

My hand hovered over the keyboard, trying to think of what exactly to write. There are rules if you want to belong to this club. Careful scripting of questions and answers was mandatory, or you got locked out. I couldn't afford that, so I took care before I hit enter.

I typed in *How busy have you guys been lately?* And hit enter.

There was a five-second delay before Nero answered, he's based in, surprisingly, Egypt. For some strange reason, Egypt's a little hot-spot for vampires, who knew with all that sunshine.

Busy and you?
More so than usual. What's the goss?
They'd long ago got used to my language skills. We Kiwis abbreviate anything.
Can't talk here, meet us at the usual in 30 minutes.
Strange, but not unheard of. Clearly, our site was being monitored.

The usual is a satellite phone with a scrambler. Not all of our kind has one; satellite phone's cost an arm and a leg, and they can't be used all the time. What with big brother watching, even with a scrambler, means it's usually a last resort. And to top it off, we need to hook into a teleconference type arrangement, which has to be initiated by one of only a couple from our group. I guess they're the oldest and wisest, I've never asked. Nero's one of them. I've only talked about four or five times before on the phone, and they were only minor initiation type conversations.

There's no way I could afford a satellite phone with scrambler on a bank teller's salary, but it was a gift. I guess from Michel, but I never asked. It just appeared on my bed one night after I'd been out hunting, there was a residual of power left in the room, a signature so to speak. No card to say, *here you go, have one on me,* just the quiet humming of a high-level vamp. Usually, I can tell if it's Michel, I just know his signature, but this vamp had taken the time to conceal his scent. I don't know why, but I still thought it was Michel.

It never occurred to me at the time how he had entered my home. The old myths of them needing an invitation are correct. But he's never been back in again. I've never invited him and I never will.

Half an hour can seem like an eternity when you're waiting on answers, but finally, the satellite phone buzzed. I answered and entered my code, the one that changes weekly. You have to log in to the website before the end of the week to make sure you grab the code. I'd only missed it once, and I'd had a call the next day from one of the group, simply telling me the code and hanging up. I heard the static of other live lines now as my hook up to the conference had been accepted.

"Kiwi here," I said into the mouthpiece. Kiwi is my handle and if you don't know, a native flightless bird of New Zealand. It's one of our icons, our symbols, and I feel very connected to it. I'm proud to be a Kiwi.

A warm, luxurious voice said, "Nero welcomes Kiwi," followed by acknowledgements from Yankee, Islander, Citysider and Smurf. Don't ask me where they get their handles from; it's a personal thing.

"So, you've had some trouble too?" Nero's voice again, distinctive in its thick northern African accent. He never tried to hide it, neither did I.

"Yeah, it's been chronic. Three in one night and one a level four master."

"Much the same as here. Crawling out of the cracks in the pavement they are." This time Citysider. I guess he's from London, but I'm not sure.

"Why the sudden increase in activity?" Me again.

"It has been foretold that this would occur." Sometimes Nero talked like this, like all of what we do is from some bad B grade movie and he's the director influencing the scene. I guess Nero's quite old, but sometimes, just sometimes, he sounds like he's as old as Michel.

"What do you mean, Nero?" This time Yankee had piped up. No disguising that accent.

"We are entering a difficult time, my friends. Our people are in danger."

"Being hunted you mean?" I asked, thinking back on what Michel had said.

"Hunters have been preyed upon for centuries, my dear. It is nothing new."

"Yes, our kind have always been hunted, as we hunt them. We must be vigilant. Spread the word to your comrades, should you meet them, but do not mention this on the site. We are being watched from every angle and must remain calm. We overcame their dominance once; we will again."

"There were more of us back then, Nero." Islander's thick southeast Asian accent filtered through the line. "We are but the remaining few of a dying race. What can we do?"

You see, here's the thing. Often these guys allude to things. Things that I guess I should know about, but have never had the guts to ask. It's as though they all belong to the exclusive part of our club and I'm missing the link, or the invitation, to enter. It was high time I swallowed my pride and got some answers. I was just about to voice some of the questions that have long been on my mind when Nero suddenly barked.

"Disconnect, we have been breached. Stay strong Nos-"

The line went dead. All connections gone. I wasn't even listening to static.

To say I was stunned was an understatement. So many questions were swirling around inside my head. The obvious: *Why were we suddenly being hunted, why now?* The old and faithful: *What am I, other than a hunter, to these creatures?* And the unfamiliar: *What had Nero been about to call us?* He had said Nos- before being cut off, but I knew there was more to the word than those three letters.

Reluctantly, I switched my laptop off. I was so tired, despite the spike in adrenaline, I couldn't keep my eyes open. It was as if as soon as Nero uttered those three letters, my body began to relax into the safety of sleep. But I knew even in sleep; we were not truly safe.

At least, I never seemed to be.

4
SWEET DREAMS

The dream started as it always did, on a hill overlooking my parents' farm. Familiar, yet not. The lambs with their little tails wagging were in the distance drinking blissfully from their mothers. Oh, how I loved watching those tails waggle when I was young. Just like a puppy, they were in joyful, rapturous happiness snuggled into the safety of their parent.

I guess it was how I always felt when these dreams came visiting; safe. Oh, I knew they were of Michel's doing. But still, a sense of safety always stole my heart when I was here, despite the thought that Michel created this vision.

"You look sad, *ma douce*." For some reason, his French accent and mannerisms were not hidden in this other realm. He lowered his disguise, like a mask, when here. Letting me see him bare.

"It's all changing. Can't you feel it?" I asked without turning to face him.

"Sometimes, change is for the good, *non*? Perhaps it is time."

I turned then, to look at his face, to try to decipher his meaning. Of course, facing him here is always hard. Like his accent, his attire is different in my dreams. Almost as though this is the Michel he would want me to see on a daily basis, instead of the prim and proper upstanding businessman of the city. He was wearing casual dress pants, still elegant but not stuffy, with a dark blue long sleeved shirt, open at the neck with his sleeves rolled up. The pants hugged his hips and the length of his legs like a glove, and the shirt set the colour of his dark blue eyes off to a "T". I could see his bare chest through the opened buttons at the top of his shirt. The desire to reach out and touch his perfect cream coloured skin was electrifying.

"There're so many questions, and somehow I think you would know the answers, wouldn't you?" I looked into his eyes, daring myself to fall into the swirls of blue and indigo that lived there.

"Yes." One word, nothing more.

"Then why don't you tell me?"

He smiled then, a slow smile that made his face glow in the sun that reached us. Yes, in my dreams Michel could stand in the sunlight. Maybe another trick to make him appear more human, who knows. All I knew is I loved the sun dancing along the cream and golden skin on his arms. How he must miss it.

"Not here, *ma douce*. Come to me when you are ready, and we shall talk."

"I'm ready now." I'd had enough of hiding from the truth. I had known for some time that there was more to me than meets the eye. Obviously, the supernatural magnet and being in-tune with the vampires had been a hint, but deep down, I knew there was more. I had known it from the first day I met Michel.

It had been a couple of days after my first intrepid meeting with a vampire. There was a sudden summer storm, and deep black clouds had rolled in to cover the city. Not unheard of in Auckland, if you know anything about this city, you'd know it has a high rain count. Even in the heat of summer, rain continues to fall.

I was at work. Still my first week at my new job - Business Banker for the Bank of New Zealand in Queen Street, a job I was so proud to have landed - talking to a customer across the counter from me. He was from one of the local businesses, making his daily deposit. I'd counted his coins by hand already and was just running the notes through the counting machine when I sensed a presence.

You see, here's the thing. You know I said vampires don't like the sun, they try to avoid it and all that. Well, yeah, they do, but it's not impossible to go out in daylight. If there's enough cloud cover and they're not in direct sunlight, and they're a mega-master level vampire, they can get away with it. Hell, for all I knew, there was a lot more that Michel could get away with, he just didn't care to show me it all at once.

So, there he was, standing just inside the doorway to the bank. I could see how tall he was against those coloured strips they have on the door jam, to tell you the height of a fleeing bank robber. Well, he wasn't fleeing, and he came up to the red. Over six feet tall. He just stood there and looked at me, this strange look on his face. But the thing was, it was as if no one else could see him, just me. The customers all walked around him. Not up to him or through him, or anything like that. Somehow they knew to avoid him, but they still didn't acknowledge him. Which was strange, because he glowed, not obviously, but in some ethereal way, where you couldn't take your eyes off it. It was just so compelling.

My customer was chattering away about the latest trend in fashion this season and hadn't noticed my statue-like appearance. Lucky. It wouldn't have been good to stand out on the first week in the new job. And suddenly Michel was in front of me, across the counter. I had no idea where my customer had gone to and when I glanced down at my hands, the counter was bare. The completed deposit slip sitting on its shelf, my terminal screen back to the new customer page. Somehow I had lost several minutes; I had no idea how.

Michel smiled at me. It was open and friendly, yet there was more to it than that. I couldn't open my mouth; I couldn't breathe. I knew beyond a doubt that he meant me no harm, but I also knew my life had changed and that this being across the counter was to blame. It was at that moment that I knew for certain that I was different. That there was more to me than being a girl from the farm and a bank teller in the city. But I also knew, somehow, as though Michel was telepathically telling me, that I was special. Special to him.

I know, I know, it sounds a little hokey, but what do you expect dealing with a more than five-hundred-year-old vampire. And that's the thing, all of a sudden Michel let me see. He let me feel his power, his age, his intentions. He let me see him. And you know what? It didn't scare me. At least not then. It felt like....well, it felt like home. Weird didn't even cover it.

As quickly as he came, he was gone, and I was left shaking from head to toe like a leaf.

You don't forget your first encounter with a Master Vampire; I certainly won't forget Michel.

I looked at him now, waiting for him to answer. "Are you so sure you are ready, *ma douce?*" he asked with that knowing smile. It irritated me, that smile. But it was all him, nothing I could do to change that. There was no point getting upset about it; he'd only smile more. Like a bloody Cheshire Cat.

He was right, though. I wasn't ready to face him here; he had too much control in this place. But in the real world, I could resist. Another visit to *Sensations* was on the books it seemed.

He had known my answer before I gave it, with the shake of my head. He slowly reached up to trace the outline of my face with the fingers on his right hand. The shot of fire that went through me felt real, burning in my veins, spreading throughout my body. I shuddered a breath out and fought the urge to lean into his hand. It's only in these dreams that I let him get this close. In reality, when I get summoned to his club, I rarely let him more intimate than a kiss on the cheek, or my hand in his. But here, I don't know; it just seems safer, not real. As though I can allow that part of me, the part that longs for him despite what he is, free reign.

It's all an illusion. These dreams may not be a reality, but they are real. When I wake, I will still feel Michel's touch, still smell his expensive cologne around me, on me, still hear his whispered words inside my head. And he will remember too. He makes sure I know that. That he visits in my dreams, that he is there.

So, why do I let him get so close here and not in real life? It's amazing what the mind can tell you. It can shelter you from the harsh light of day and have you believing any number of falsehoods. I let Michel close in my dreams because, although they are real, they are still to my mind, a dream.

He made a move closer, intensity and conviction in his eyes I hadn't seen before. As though he would test me this time, see how far I would let him go. But although I longed for his touch, dreamt of it, a part of me was distracted. Fancy that, a luscious dream with a gorgeous male giving me his undivided attention and my mind was wandering? Who would have thought?

Then it dawned on me why. There was banging in the background. A hard thumping. Fist against wood. It took only a second to latch on to that sound and the world around me on the hill above my farm vanished. The last thing I saw on Michel's face before he disappeared and the farm we were standing on shattered, was complete and utter frustration.

I woke in my bed to an insistent and loud banging at my door.

If you've ever gone to bed with fatigue after a marathon, or the dull ache of a too exuberant exercise routine - or in my case post a fight with three vampires in one night, one of them a level four master - and only had five hours sleep, then you'd know what I felt at that moment as I rolled out of my bed and stumbled to the door.

The clock on the bedside table said 10:00. I don't do 10:00 on a Sunday normally.

I reached for the door with a grimace at the light that poured in through the frosted glass window. You'd think I'd be more careful, opening my front door to an unknown and persistent banging. But I've long gotten over my fear of the average human and the undead wouldn't step foot on my doormat. I've known for some time now, that Michel has put a protection on my property. No vampire or ghoul would dare step on a millimetre of this land. My neighbours don't know it, but they've got the safest building in the city. Besides, where-ever it is that Michel rests during the day.

Anyway, I knew that sound. It was the ever cheerful banging of a wound up shapeshifter ready for some fun. I opened the door, reluctantly taking in the fresh-faced exuberance and endless electric energy of my best bud. His brown hair was in disarray, short spiky tufts of it standing out at odd angles like he'd run through blackberry bushes backwards. His soft brown skin glowed in the morning sun, and every well-toned muscle on his medium height body was defined in detail by a tight fitting white muscle shirt and hip hugging camouflage cargo pants. His feet were bare.

"Rick," I croaked in greeting and turned back towards the kitchen and the coffee machine. Need coffee now.

"Whoa. You look like death warmed up." His chocolate brown eyes twinkled with unrestrained mischief.

I glared at him for that one.

"Tough night huh? On the streets, or in the dreams?" he asked with one eyebrow raised.

Rick knows about me. Everything. It was just too hard to hide it. Especially when the vamps started circling when we were out on the town one night, and I had to flash silver. Silver, which as a shapeshifter, he tries to avoid. We decided then and there, to be honest with each other.

You can imagine the look on my face when he first changed in front of me on my living room floor. He'd warned me by then of course. But still, if you haven't ever witnessed a Shifter change, then it's bound to have an effect. And it's not as though his alter ego is a pleasant sight. Rick's a Taniwha. That's pronounced *Tan-e-far*; a native Shifter to New Zealand. They are considered dangerous, predatory beings. With the razor-sharp serrated teeth, large round beady eyes - the colour of their human eyes remained with them through the change to Taniwha; they just became more sinister - and four-inch long claws on both front and back legs, you can see why.

They have sandpaper skin, covered in small scales, grey on their backs with a white stripe down their fronts. The scales, along with their long, spiked tail, are designed to provide thrust and aerodynamic speed. They are shark-like in their Shifter appearance and characteristics. Although capable of running on all four clawed feet, they can move as a bipedal. Larger than their human form, Rick had taken up most of my lounge when he first shifted for me. But aside from the magic required to make the shift, his bulbous head, no neck and thick tree-like stumped legs and arms were what caught my attention the most. The size of him and the size of his very sharp serrated teeth that is.

"Both," I said as I prepped the coffee machine. I love my coffee.

Back on the farm, it had been a stove top espresso maker, but here in the city I splashed out and got myself one of those fang-dangled uber expensive flash jobbies. You know, the kind that grinds the beans, froths the milk and even milks the cow? Yeah, it's a weakness I don't mind others knowing.

I grabbed two mugs out of the cupboard. Both covered in pictures of bright red lipsticked lips with fangs and a blood dripping message that read: *Bite Me! It's Monday*. What can I say, I'm a sucker for a good novelty shop.

Rick jumped up on one of the barstools at the kitchen counter. "Come on, 'fess up. What's happening?"

I sighed as the coffee machine poured frothy milk over two steaming mugs of espresso and handed Rick his across the bench.

"Three last night and one was a level four master." I was getting used to saying that, even though it still sounded foreign to my ears.

You may think that vampire hunters spend every night hunting the undead. But that's the thing, very few vampires stray from the *Iunctio's* rules nowadays. It's odd to have so many in one night. I usually manage one or two each week, but they're spread over the entire week, not in one night. And how do I find them? Well, when evil comes calling in my city I just know. It's like a homing beacon or something. I just know they're here and I find them. Usually, but not always, when they're about to bite into an innocent. Nothing like getting hands-on proof you're doing the right thing.

"Wow, that's busy. Why the action, ya think?"

"Um, I'm not exactly sure why, but Michel reckons it's something to do with me." I dared a glance at him across the top of the steam coming from my mug. He just looked at me expectantly, waiting for me to elaborate. "He mentioned something else. Something about a group of vampires who *wish to take over the night completely*. Does that mean anything to you?"

Rick shook his head from side to side slowly. "Nah, not a thing, but let's back up a bit. Michel reckons it's something to do with you. What's that about?" Rick, being a shapeshifter, is well aware of what Michel is. Shapeshifters and Vampires don't normally live so closely together, but Auckland's a little different. They say it's the Ley Lines, those invisible lines interconnecting various psychic hot-spots around the world. Well, Auckland, for some unknown reason, is the Grand Central Station of all those Ley Lines. The supernova of all coming and goings on the supernatural plain. So, even though it's not common when these two supernatural creatures do co-exist, the vamps are on top of the food chain, and the shapeshifters know it. So, Rick knows what Michel is and is afraid of him. Clever boy.

"Apparently, my status as a Hunter comes into it, but I'm not altogether sure how. There's another thing, I got on the site last night and had a pow-pow with the others. It's happening everywhere; we're all being inundated with careless and aggressive vamps. There was something that Nero said; that didn't make any sense to me at all. Something about this happening to *our kind* before and we prevailed, or some such guff. You know Nero, he's so melodramatic."

Actually, Rick didn't know Nero, but he knew what I meant. I'd conveyed enough of my conversations with the Egyptian over the past two years for him to get a picture of what he was like.

Rick shrugged. "So, what are you gonna do?"

"Well, pay another visit to Michel, get some answers and then, I suppose, do what I do best. Kick some vampire butt." I grinned at him and swallowed the rest of my coffee.

"Cool." Ever the relaxed Shifter. "Well, with that settled, get dressed. Celeste has been gunning for you to come visit for months, so get going we're having a party." He got up and ushered me into the bathroom to get ready.

There was just no arguing with a shapeshifter.

5
HAPŪ PRIDE

Celeste is a member of Rick's Hapū. New Zealand shapeshifters don't run in Taniwha packs; they run in a Taniwha *Hapū*. She's youngish, about two years older than me; that would make her 26 and the mother hen to the younger members of Westside Hapū. They call themselves that, but there's no Eastside Hapū, or Southside or whatever, it's just them. They are the Hapū of the city.

Shapeshifters aren't as prevalent as vampires and certainly not as widespread as Ghouls. Celeste is as close to a best girlfriend as I have. We get on, we laugh together and can share the odd joke at the expense of the guys, but she's still a little aloof. I'm not Hapū, and I never will be. My inclusion in their world is purely at the insistence of Rick. The others tolerate it, the guys especially - hormones! But, the girls, in particular, are wearier. It goes against their scaly skin to disclose who they are.

I guess a bit like a vampire.

The Hapū have lived in Auckland for decades. Maybe even longer than the vamps. New Zealand's not that old. The *Maori* have been here a while, but the white man, the *Pakeha*, only arrived in the early 1800's. The *Treaty of Waitangi* was signed in 1840; that's really when New

Zealand as we know it today was formed. So, Taniwhas and vampires have not been here centuries like in Europe or elsewhere.

The Hapū lives out in Whenuapai, the west of Auckland City. They own several hectares, which is slowly being encroached on all sides by urban sprawl, but they'll never sell. Their roots are too deep. The land is heavily wooded and well fenced. No one strays onto Hapū land accidentally. They can get away with it because they're right next to the Air Force Base. All that menacing barbed wire fencing looks legit.

The woods, of course, offer up enough coverage to run freely at Rākaunui, or Full Moon. Taniwhas, like any other shapeshifter, are compelled to change in light of the Full Moon. They can change by desire at any other time of the month, but they cannot refuse the pull of the moon. The Hapū does venture further afield when the need arises; when they have to stretch their legs now and then. But mainly those who work for a living in the city, like Rick, stay close to the land, the woods and their home. It takes Rick at least an hour, if not more, to get to the gym from home. I couldn't stand that. Why live in a city and travel like a country bumpkin? My work is five minutes away if I take the car - which I don't, parking's a bitch in downtown Auckland - but only ten or so if I jog.

Today, being a Sunday, the trip was much quicker. We turned off onto Hapū land after only 28 minutes on the road. I immediately rolled down my windows and inhaled the smell of the trees. It's always so peaceful to come here, not anything like my farm of course, but something akin to it. I figure it's all the trees and nature. You do miss that in the city if you're used to it. No lambs wagging their tails here, though, they wouldn't last past the first Rākaunui.

The crunch of gravel under the tyres slowed as we rounded the final corner to the main houses. There's about a dozen or so in the centre of the land, a bit like a settlement. It used to be called a *Pa*, a Maori hill fort, but you can't make out the rise now with the woods so thick. Maori blood runs deep in Westside Hapū. It's not always obvious; they're not all brown skinned, but it's there, strong and true.

Celeste greeted us on the doorstep as soon as we arrived. Tall and thin, with waist length long brown hair and deeply tanned skin. She's beautiful in an exotic dancer kind of way. After a few hugs all round, bone crunching, bear hugs that is - they are very tactile Taniwhas, part of being in a Hapū I guess - and I was part of the gang again.

"It's been too long, Luce," she squealed, actually squealed. I think I may have cringed.

"Leave off her, Cel." Rick shoved at her in what seemed a gentle move, but she ended up spinning round like a top.

"Oi, creep! You're asking for it."

Then it was on, just like that. You get used to it, well kind of. They play-fight a lot, the Taniwhas. It's just in their natures. They don't have to shift to do it, they tend to stay in human form, but it can be rough. I soon realised there was a lot they could teach me when I first visited their land. I've been a regular member of the fighting sessions since. You don't learn how to street fight dirty at Judo or kickboxing lessons, but you sure pick up a few helpful hints from Taniwhas.

I took a resigned seat on the swing bench on the veranda. I was still not up to a full-on fight after last night. The combination of lack of sleep, invaded dreams and you guessed it, three vampires in one night, one of them a level four master, had taken its toll. But, I didn't have to watch it alone for long. Mary slid into the seat next to me and started swinging her legs, while her twin brothers, Joe and Rocky - don't ask me where he got that name from, maybe he chewed on rocks when he was young - jumped into the fray.

I glanced at Mary; she's only 12. Not fully grown by Taniwha standards, but quite capable of holding her own in a fight, be it in human form or Shifter. Taniwhas are raised tough from birth; there're no namby-pamby sit-on-the-sidelines characters in the Hapū. Each and every one of them is a finely tuned killing machine. Just because they look like you or me most of the time, does not mean they can't kick your arse when they feel the need.

Still, Mary didn't look like she was up for a demonstration on juvenile Taniwha prowess. "Not joining in, hun?" I asked.

"Naw, can't be bothered. They've been at it all weekend. It's Rākaunui tomorrow."

Oh yeah, I'd forgotten. Not a good idea to be on Hapū land when it's Rākaunui. Even the days leading up to it can be a bit tetchy, but when that Full Moon rises, it's a different world altogether.

I'd never been near the guys at that time of the month, but Rick's told me all about it. You know, no secrets and all that. The testosterone goes crazy, the urge to fight impossible to ignore. The only solution is to shift and run. Run with the wind and the Hapū and the moon; it seems to be their elixir. Without it, they'd all be homicidal maniacs I think. And I hang with them? Well, they're not always like that.

The group had moved the fight further from the house now, into a clearing in the middle of the settlement. The older Taniwhas were out doing whatever it is older Taniwhas do, but a few more of the younger guys came out to watch and egg them on.

I think Rick was winning, but I couldn't be sure. Even as humans these guys can move fast. Not vampire fast, but fast enough to cause a bit of a blur. After tumbling head over heels for several rotations, they'd settled into a bundle of limbs and fists and snapping mouths. Not Taniwha snapping but cursing snapping. Taniwhas have no problem with swearing; I guess that's where I pick a lot of my language skills up from. I'm spending way too much time with the riff raff.

Finally, Rick had Celeste pinned. She growled a little at the proximity of his face. I couldn't blame her; I'd be put out to be pinned by all that barely contained male strength and dominance. Like me, Celeste does not like being out of control.

He just smiled down at her, taunting her. "You give up?"

She bucked trying to move him. The other guys, Joe and Rocky, had backed off. They knew this was between Celeste and Rick, no one else. I noticed something then that I hadn't noticed before. Electricity in the air between them. For some reason, I felt something at that. It wasn't supernatural, just human in every way. I felt a little jealous.

Which was ridiculous. Rick is my mate, a friend, nothing more. But the look that passed between them in that instant should have been private, not on display for all this crowd to see. I didn't feel comfortable seeing it myself. But that's Taniwhas for you, affection, for want of a better word, in public, is the norm.

Celeste cleared her throat, a blush slowly creeping up her delicate bronzed features, making her exotic dancer looks shine with a sensuality I hadn't noticed before. The slightly uncomfortable cough was enough to shake Rick out of the moment, and he slowly rose up off her.

"You can never beat me and you know it," he said with a lower voice than usual.

"In your dreams, deadbeat," came her reply, as she dusted herself down and walked stiffly back towards me, shoulders back, head held high. I couldn't help smiling to myself, Celeste was, for all her shark-like characteristics, all woman. None of us liked being shown up.

"Come on," she said as she climbed the veranda steps towards me, "we've laid a Hangi. We're feasting this arvo."

A *Hangi* is a traditional Maori method of cooking. The food is wrapped in tin foil - it used to be big leaves, but modern technology has far reaches - and is laid on hot stones, then buried under dirt. It's left to cook for several hours. This one would have been started before dawn.

The food when retrieved is succulent and tender, like nothing you've experienced before. And there's usually heaps of it. Enough to feed an army or in this case a ravenous pre-Rākaunui Hapū of Taniwhas. I love it. I can't deny, but I can never stomach as much as the others. I'm a bird in comparison.

"Need a hand?" I asked as I followed Celeste inside.

"Na, she's right mate. Just come and have a natter while I prep some salad."

Celeste lives with her mum. Her dad died several years ago. Cancer I think. Even Taniwhas have to face mundane ailments. Her mum must have been out with the other elders because the house was quiet. Bare wooden floors led into the kitchen, the heart of the home. The kitchen bench was covered with salad ingredients and cakes and Pavlova for dessert. It was going to be a feast all right.

"So, how's it going in the city?" Celeste refuses to believe she lives in the city. To her, the small parcel of wooded land around her home was proof positive that she was a country girl. I didn't have the heart to correct her.

"Busy. Complicated. You know how it is?" I replied while slipping into a seat at the bench to watch her work.

"Complicated? That wouldn't have something to do with a particular Master of the City, would it?"

I don't usually go into much detail with Celeste. I consider her a friend, but we're not as close as Rick and I. Still, she is the only girlfriend I have and even hardened vampire hunters need to vent occasionally.

I let a frustrated breath out. "He's..." I paused trying to put into words the tumble of emotions Michel seemed to be able to elicit from me, "...persistent, aggravating, superior." The list could go on, but I stopped before I got totally carried away and admitted more than just the negative emotions he managed to create in me.

She laughed. It seemed to be way more knowing and understanding than I had expected. "He's a male, Luce; they really can't help throwing their weight around. It's ingrained in them since birth. See a beautiful woman, make her yours. It's a compulsion they can't deny."

"So, we should just accept it? Let them bang their fists against their chests and roar like Tarzan?" I asked, incredulously. No way would Celeste go for that. Shapeshifter or not, she was a strong-minded twenty-first-century woman.

"Hell no, mate! You use it to your advantage. You let them *think* they own you, but you defy them at every turn. My mum always says, a woman should play hard to get. No man wants an easy target."

I wasn't so sure I could play anything with Michel. He was the enemy. The idea of getting close enough to play sent an unwanted shiver of pure terror, mixed with a smidgeon of excited anticipation, down my spine. It was probably all a game to *him*, but I liked to think that the attachment of my head to the rest of my body was something more serious than just a game. I could never forget he was a vampire, that evil lurked inside him, no matter what façade he chose to wear.

A couple of hours of casual girlie chatter had passed before Rick came in the house with some platters. I hadn't realised how much I had needed a girl-to-girl talk. Celeste was a breath of fresh air. Even though Rick had won the battle - for all intents and purposes, fair and square - out in the yard, I was now beginning to think that maybe Celeste had planned it that way. The way he looked at her now, as he walked into the kitchen, was one of pure possession. There was simply no other word for it; he thought he'd won a prize and yet I knew now that Celeste would be a prize that bit back. I had to admire her; she was reeling him in, and he didn't even know it.

If only I had that kind of self-confidence, that womanly awareness. I shook my head at that idiotic thought. Why on Earth would I want to seduce Michel? I might as well slit my wrists and wait for him to drain me dry.

"Here you go," Rick said as he placed the platters in his hands on a spare space on the bench. "The others have arrived, and they're all over at the Hangi."

I helped them both pile the salads and desserts onto the platters and then carried them out to the picnic table in the shade of an old Pohutukawa tree. The Hangi was off to the side already getting unveiled; the heady smells of deeply cooked meat and vegetables wafting through the air. My stomach rumbled in anticipation. God, Hangis were the best! I said hello to Celeste's mum and Rick's family, then I made my way over to the Hapū master. I was on his land; I needed to acknowledge the gift of his hospitality. It was never a good idea to ignore formalities around Taniwhas; they may fit in like normal people, but they were not. Piss them off, and they'd make sure you didn't live to regret it.

Jerome, Westside Hapū's Alpha, is built like a proverbial brick outhouse, he's all muscle and bulk, with a little padding around the middle just because. With a slightly rough, coarse brown beard and curly, grisly brown hair, you'd think him more a bear than a Taniwha. But those dark chocolate brown eyes held the wisdom of his lineage. Even in human form, they looked a little shark-like. He's always been very friendly and polite to me, though, but I wouldn't want to piss him off. He hadn't become a Hapū master of the only shapeshifter Hapū in Auckland by being weak.

"Hey, Jerome. Thanks for having me over for dinner."

"No prob, mate. You know you're always welcome on our lands." A very generous offer considering the Hapū 's desire for privacy and one I wouldn't forget to be thankful for when in his presence.

"I hear you've been having a busy time of it lately?" His gruff voice was quiet, just loud enough for only me to hear. He was a big guy, looked a bit of a brute from afar, but his voice would have you think of a gentle giant, rather than an outright ogre if you didn't already know he was a Taniwha.

The question didn't surprise me, though. Jerome knows what I am, or at least as much as I do, I think. As Hapū master not much gets past him. It occurred to me then that maybe he knew a little more. I took a deep breath in and fortified my resolve. If I wanted answers, I would have to face the music first.

"Yeah, it's getting hot in town all of a sudden. Have you heard anything that might help explain it?"

He huffed a little and ran a big oversized hand through his beard. "Actually, I thought it was about time to tell the youngin's a story or two tonight. You might like what you hear."

I wasn't sure if that was true. Hapū stories, or lore, were fascinating, but how anything to do with me could be wound up with shapeshifter legends was a mystery. Still, if Jerome said it was worthwhile listening in, then I would.

A bonfire was lit. Even though it was almost full winter, it was still quite warm in Auckland. The bonfire was more for show and ambience than necessity, though, I think. We all grabbed plates, piled high with delicious pork and puha, salad and more veggies. Mine was enormous, brimming at the edges, but nowhere near as big as the others and I knew they'd go back for more.

I sat down next to Rick, and we leant into each other, a sense of familiarity and friendship settling between us. I slipped a glance at Celeste; she was watching us closely, but just offered a smile when my eyes met hers and then turned her attention to the rest of the Hapū. I wasn't sure how Celeste felt about Rick and me. I knew we were just friends, nothing more, but Celeste had apparently laid a claim on my best mate, and I briefly wondered if I was now in the way. How do Taniwhas deal with unwanted opposition? It didn't bear thinking about. I pushed those uncomfortable thoughts aside and settled into enjoying the company, food and feeling of being with people you loved.

Jerome's voice started out quite deep and resonant, a little otherworldly too in the flickering light of the fire. After a plate that full, I almost wanted to drift off to sleep listening to it. A gruff, but warm bedside story voice, one made to ensure a sense of safety and peace. Not something you would expect a shapeshifter to possess at all. But I forced my eyes open and sat up a little straighter, to ward off sleep. I had a feeling, from what Jerome had said, that this bedside story would be significant. Besides, never miss a chance to educate myself, me.

"In the beginning, there was only us. We were the chosen ones of the Long White Cloud. We roamed the land from the top of *Te Ika-a Maui* to the bottom of *Te Wai Pounamu*. The North Island and the South were our Hapū's right, our land. We shared that right with the people; we lived along side them as one, we fought with them when needed. We were blessed with such a beautiful and plentiful land.

"Then came the *Nosferatu*. They did not share the land as we did, they took it. But we endured, we hid, we took refuge in the forests, on the desolate plains, away from towns and villages. We made our life alone, without the people, without the *Nosferatu*.

"Finally, word reached us that another had arrived on our shores. A kindred spirit, a guardian of the people and places, a *Kaitiaki*, but not from our kind."

He looked at me as he said this and I felt goose bumps rise along my arms. The crackling of the fire was the only sound of the night. The heat I felt in my face had nothing to do with the flames though and everything to do with the Taniwha who stared at me with deep brown, almost black, eyes. I had a feeling he could see right through to my core, to the deepest, darkest, most secret places within. To places, I didn't even know existed, let alone knew what they hid.

"They were here to protect the innocent, their powers as great as those of the night. They fought hard and long and finally the night was ours again. All of ours.

"We returned to the towns and villages, to our fellow countrymen. We heeded their call. They had vanquished *Nosferatu's* hold on our land, but they could not stay.

"They left one of their kind behind. To safeguard against the creatures' return. The *Nosferatu* would come again they said and alone the *Kaitiaki* would fail. Too strong the pull of the Dark night. They asked for our allegiance in return for our land's freedom, and a pact was sworn. Whenever the *Kaitiaki* should call on us, we will fight along their side. We would be proud to serve."

He smiled at me then, a friendly smile laced with something else - sadness. I tried to return the smile but failed. Rick rubbed my arm, where the goose bumps had risen and one by one the Hapū began to stir and talk and laugh with one another. Life returned to normal, from the other plane of folklore fantasy.

My life, I felt, would never return to normal again.

Nosferatu were, of course, the vampires, then what did Nero mean when he started to call us *Nos*-?

6
GOTCHA!

No matter how I tried to make sense of it all, I still came up blank. It had been great catching up with Celeste. Having a girl-to-girl talk and seeing the cubs play fighting after the Hangi was entertainment plus, but my thoughts the next day were completely consumed with Jerome's story. There was no denying what he had been trying to convey to me through that tale. The Taniwhas and hunters like me had worked side by side at one time fighting the Nosferatu, the vampires. And there still existed a treaty or pact, that Jerome believed bound the Hapū to me, to this day.

But, despite my wayward musings on shapeshifter legends, work called. I did my best to ignore the growing uneasy feeling that life was changing and I was just along for the ride. Sometimes, I wondered just how much control I had left. Since moving to Auckland, so much of my life had been turned upside down. Michel was at the centre of that turmoil, that spiralling tornado of supernatural events that was sucking me inexorably in. He represented not only the evil I now was exposed to, but also the reason why my life was fast becoming a mess.

And then, of course, I felt drawn to him in a way I had never felt to another before. Reconciling what he did to my pulse rate when near and what he represented to my day to day life was impossible. I chose, for now, to just ignore it and concentrate on work. Denial could be a wonderful thing.

I'm usually the second to arrive at the branch, after the manager. He gets there at the crack of dawn, but that suits me fine, I wouldn't be able to get in if he hadn't done the usual checks beforehand. Once the signal is set, you know the poster is facing the right way in the front window of the branch, you know it's safe to approach, he's not being held hostage by gun-wielding robbers.

If my life outside of work was spiralling out of control, at least my days at work were pretty much the same. From when the front doors open, until the close of banking business at five. I grab my float from the safe out back, count it and place it in my drawer. I log on, open up my float on screen and I'm good to go. I'm the branch's chief business teller. The others do everything from opening accounts, average customer deposits and withdrawals and foreign currency exchange. Me, I just deal with the big guys.

Queen Street is the centre of business here in Auckland City, and my branch is right in the thick of it. I'm busy at the moment my sign says *Queue Here* until I tally up my float and store it back in the safe at the end of the day.

I like my job; there's something so familiar in counting coins and notes and adding up cheques. The only variant is the customer, and I know all of them by name now. It's such an opposite from my nighttime gig; I relish it. In the evening, I never know when the pull will happen, what I will face and how it will end. But at work, I know. I know exactly what will happen.

Apart from today.

I felt them before I saw them. It was sunny out, so I was a little confused to start with. But when they entered the sliding doors at the front of the branch, and I could see they were dressed head to toe in thick black coats, sunglasses and hats, I knew they had taken the vampire version of *Slip, Slop, Slap* to the extreme. However, covering up so heavily is pretty much a no-no in a bank. You could only make it worse if you were wearing a ski mask.

I knew these guys weren't here for the money, though. Evil reeked from every pore. I almost choked on it, it was so strong and pervasive, seeping past the customers before me and slipping up my nose. I tried to breathe through my mouth, but then I could only taste it, and that was ten times worse. It wasn't the evil of a human criminal however, these guys were on a whole other plane.

There were three of them. Two standing either side of the doors, like Mafioso bodyguards, backing up the boss. The boss was big, over six feet looking at the strips of colour on the door jam. He walked slowly towards the end of my queue, which thankfully wasn't very long. The thought of my customers getting in the way of this vamp was not a pleasant one. When he reached the end of the line, he just stood there, patiently, like a normal customer waiting their turn. There was absolutely nothing normal about this. He'd taken his glasses and hat off, so I guess even bad guy vamps don't want to set security off and he just stared at me with a hungry look on his face.

In between dealing with those few customers in front of me, I took the opportunity to assess this new threat. He had a scar down his left cheek. It must have been made before he was turned because an injury like that would have healed in a vamp, especially a vamp with *Sanguis Vitam* off the scale like this one. I'd guess 250 years old and a level two at least. He didn't try to hide it; he could see its discomfort on my skin by the look on my face, and he was enjoying it.

Finally, I finished with the last customers in front of me, frantically thinking if I could just put up the *Sorry, I'm Closed* sign and see if that worked. I don't carry any silver at work. No stake, no knives. It's just never occurred to me that I'd need it in broad daylight. Not here in Auckland. Even the Ghouls are well behaved under the direct light of the sun. But I guess I'd have to change that philosophy from now on.

He approached the counter in the usual vampire glide. His skin was pale white, the epitome of Hollywood vampire complexion. Vampires keep pretty much their skin colour from before they were turned, the only difference being a paler version when they haven't fed for some time. His hair hung over his forehead in a greasy hunk of black - another stereotype, not all vamps have dirty, scraggly hair - the contrast against his skin though was startling. He leant on the counter, letting out a breath of stale, metallic smelling air and it took every ounce of my effort not to pull back and show my fear.

His voice was surprisingly musical, for such a big hulk of a guy. He casually said, "You're going to leave now. Tell your boss you're sick and have got to go home. Don't talk to anyone else, meet us right here, in front of the counter. And Hunter, don't bring silver."

Just like that, no please or thank you. No, we're gonna kill everyone if you don't comply. Just a simple statement of fact. He wasn't even trying to glaze me, but when the threat was made - and it was a threat, no two ways about it - I glanced at Tom & Jerry at the doors. One had his hand on a semi-automatic rifle under his coat, and the other was glazing one of my colleagues, making her laugh out loud. I knew then what they'd do if I refused.

The threat was implicit. Don't comply and we'll mess with your bank. I looked around at the other tellers, at my supervisor at the back. The manager was shaking hands with his latest appointment, and it dawned on me how many lives would be affected. There were over twenty customers in the branch too, all of them with wives or husbands, kids or loved ones. All of them important to someone else.

Me? I'm just one person. Sure my Mum and Dad would miss me, but that would be it. They'd survive, they've got the farm to keep them busy. I briefly flashed on Michel but quelled that thought. I wasn't that important to a Master Vampire; he'd find another obsession no doubt.

So, I nodded. Closed my till drawer, withdrew the key and walked back to my supervisor. It didn't take much convincing for her to let me go. I must have looked like shit. My mind was reeling for an escape plan, but it just kept coming up blank. Maybe, just maybe, they didn't mean me any harm and just wanted a quiet chat.

Yeah, ri-ight.

By the time I made it to the front of the branch, where Tom, Jerry and Scar Face were waiting, my knees were knocking, my breath was hitched, and my heartbeat was thundering in my veins. There was simply no way to hide that level of fear. The vamps would have been able to smell it a mile off. They didn't say anything, though, just nodded to each other and walked me out of the bank and my daytime sanctuary, between them.

The hats and glasses were back on, but I noticed our side of the street was in shadow, so I guess that helped. A black van pulled up in front of the bank, typical bad guy get-away vehicle. No markings, dark windows, nothing distinctive. I noticed it was being driven by a human. I couldn't help thinking; *Huh? Team effort eh?*

Tom got in the front; Jerry opened the sliding side door, and Scar Face nudged me forward. There was nowhere to go, too many people on the footpath, too many innocents could get hurt, and I'd never had to take on three vampires at once. And certainly none as powerful as this bunch. So, I just got in and sat on the bench seat in the rear.

Jerry sat on the bench seat in front, taking up most of its bulk and Scar Face squeezed in next to me at the back seat. I felt like a sardine in a can. If it weren't for the *Sanguis Vitam* that rolled off them in menacing waves, I would have cracked a joke. My timings not always the best, but we live and learn.

No one said anything for the entire ride. They didn't blindfold me, they didn't threaten me, things were looking up. We left the CBD and headed towards Parnell, at the top of Parnell Rise we turned down a winding side street. Cars were parked on both sides of the narrow lane, so the driver took it easy, slowing the van to a crawl. Mustn't scratch the vamp's car.

Finally, we pulled up in front of an old warehouse. Parnell's not known for its warehouses; it's more a trendy urban café style haunt. Older houses are made over to look old, but new. The warehouse was no exception. It was old but freshly painted in modern colours. Huge pot plants out the front, on either side of the large roller garage door, had Cabbage Trees in them. They didn't make me feel tropical in the slightest.

The roller door did its thing, rolling up noisily and the van inched forward into a courtyard. The finality of that roller door closing behind us made all my hope disappear. I was stuck now; there was simply no escape.

Jerry jumped out and held the sliding door open Scar Face shuffled, wedged, and awkwardly squeezed his bulk out between the seats and the van walls, to stumble to his feet on the concrete floor of the courtyard. If this guy wasn't careful, he was going to make me laugh.

We walked across the covered courtyard to the front door of what was obviously the dwelling on the premises. As soon as the door opened, I doubled over in pain. Doors don't usually contain vampire power; they're a pretty flimsy wall when it comes to the supernatural pull or effect of *Sanguis Vitam*.

Obviously, the vamp above us wanted to time things just right and make sure I knew he was there. Show off.

The power abated slightly, enough for Scar Face to grab my arm and hoist me forward up a thin staircase to what was bound to *not* be the Energiser Bunny despite the prickles of *Sanguis Vitam* that rolled across my skin. It was more than I had ever faced before. More than even Michel. I swallowed a lump in my throat. *Dear God, what did they want to do to me?*

The vampire who owned all that unbelievably strong *Sanguis Vitam* was waiting in the room we entered and was tall and well dressed. His style was a combination of luxuriant casual, oozing an easy sexual appeal. Could I see the sexual appeal despite my now outright fear? Hell yes! He wanted me to, so I did.

He was wearing expensive jeans, which as you'd expect fitted him like a second skin. His chest was bare where his black shirt gaped open to his navel, showing an expanse of muscular skin, unblemished and in a honey gold colour you could almost lick when you looked at it. His eyes were green, an unexpected colour for a vampire. And his sandy blonde hair short, above the collar, another unexpected. Vampires usually had longer hair, a throwback to the good old days no doubt. They could cut it and regrow it, but for some reason, it was their fashion faux pas.

"Welcome, Lucinda Monk."

Like everything else about him his voice dripped sex. It wrapped around me like a luxurious coat and sent shivers down my spine. I couldn't help feeling that this was going to be tedious if our entire conversation was going to wreak havoc with my innocence. I felt an uninvited blush rise up my cheeks.

The power abated abruptly as if he could read my mind.

"Forgive me; I can't seem to help myself it would seem." So similar to Michel, hadn't he said something like that?

"Please take a seat, be comfortable." When I hesitated, he said, "I only wish to talk. For now." The *for now* kind of ruined the reassurance he was going for.

I took a seat in a chair across from him, as far as humanly possible away from where he stood leaning back casually against the wall, legs crossed at his ankles, arms in his pockets. He was a poster boy for GQ Magazine, an absolute god. He was so gorgeous, but despite all that beauty, I wasn't fooled. He nodded to Scar Face, who turned and left with a quiet click of the door. I guess you don't need a bodyguard around a petite unarmed female when you're master of death.

And that's the thing. I could feel the evil floating off the goons who had collected me from work, but this guy, he was hiding it well. All I got was the now muted sense of his *Sanguis Vitam*, untainted, yet also un-anything. With Michel I could feel the good in his power, it's kind of like reading someone's aura I guess, although I'm not very good at that. But with Michel, I can sense his aura or goodness; it's all gold and light. This guy though was just a void. *What are you hiding, buddy?*

When he didn't immediately say anything, I thought I might as well jump right in. In for a penny, in for a pound, so they say.

"Why am I here?"

"I wish to make an offer. You have been in the company of such an exclusive lot you need to realise your potential, broaden your horizons, so to speak." He smiled at me then, a stunning smile that lit up his eyes making the greens so vivid it was almost blinding. But it wasn't my Michel's smile; there were no blues or indigos there. I mentally shook myself at that thought, but then stopped. If thoughts of Michel could dispel whatever this vamp tried on me, then so much the better.

When I didn't respond, he went on. "You are wasted here, Lucinda." He stalked across the room toward me in a sensual glide, all hips and legs and muscles rippling. He leant over my chair and looked me in the eye, his hand resting on the bottom of my chin to tilt my face slightly upwards. His touch was warm and yet cool. I could feel a slight tingling where his thumb stroked my face. "I offer you the world."

Something inside me, something akin to my inner monologue, but not quite as insistent, spoke in my mind. *Stall. Stall for time, drag this out as long as you can.* I could only assume that when this conversation was done my life would be over, that's why my voice was telling me to stall for time. To what end that would accomplish I did not yet know, but I had faith I'd think of something. I'm pretty good at thinking on my feet.

I cleared my throat and pulled back slightly from his grip. He let me, for now. "What exactly are you offering?"

His smile widened, it looked more genuine than before. His earlier effort had obviously all been for show; this one was natural. My question was apparently what he wanted to here.

My inner voice growled.

"First, let me introduce myself," he said as he perched on the arm of my chair. *Too close, too close!* My inner monologue, the insistent one, shouted. I shoved the voice aside and hid my emotions as best I could. When you've been around vampires as long as I have, you learn to suppress your facial expressions, to hide anger or fear or any of those other unwanted emotions. If not, it could lead to an instant death. It's not easy if the emotion creeps up on you unexpectedly, but when you're braced and on high alert like I was right now, then it's possible. Just.

"I am Maximilian; my friends call me Max."

"What do your enemies call you?" It was out before I could stop myself. I mean, come on, the guy had left himself wide open for that one!

He smiled a sly smile this time. "They call me Death." *Spooky much?*

I swallowed and shifted a little further away in my chair. He laughed at that and threw back his head. A delightful manly chuckle that warmed me up inside.

"I mean you no harm, Lucinda. On the contrary, I wish for a joining. I would not have my servant injured in any way."

"Servant?" I raised my eyebrows. He lowered his.

"Has *he* not told you?" And then more to himself, "Could it be?" He stood up quickly at that and paced the room. Go figure, a vampire pacing?

"There is much to tell you, but we do not have time. Not here. Will you come with me willingly?"

Stall! Do not let him move you from here. Keep him talking, delay him at all costs. This time my inner voice almost shouted, I had to use every ounce of control in me to not openly wince. What the?

"Um, I...I'm not sure what you're offering." And then seeing his eyes darken ominously added, "I want to go with you, really, but I just need, I mean, I haven't eaten all day, and I'm feeling a little weak. I don't suppose...?" I let the question hang in the air, hoping he'd accept my piss-poor attempt at subterfuge.

He was already at the door. "Tony, bring us some food". He hadn't raised his voice, so Tony, whichever one of the goons he was, was nearby. Vampires do have great hearing, but still, they need to at least be in the same building.

"You shall eat and then we shall go." He returned to his chair across from me. At least that was an improvement.

I glanced around the room, taking in my predicament, for all the good it would do me. I couldn't tell what time it was, the windows were shuttered closed, and I don't wear a watch, but I guessed it was about four in the afternoon by now. Maybe even as close to five. The bank would be closing, the sun getting lower in the sky. Maybe travelling at night would be better for him too, that's why he had acquiesced so easily to my request.

"I plan for an equal joining, Lucinda. More than you could hope from him. You will participate in all my endeavours right beside me, where you can be seen, admired for what and who you are."

Somehow that didn't have the desired effect on me I was guessing he was after. Just then Tony, Scar Face - who would have thought the goon had such an appropriate Mafioso name - came into the room with a bag from McDonald's. I could smell the French fries, and I wasn't in the slightest bit hungry. Being held captive by an uber-powerful Master Vampire and told you will be *joined* to him in *all* his endeavours tends to unsettle the stomach somewhat, but I had to carry on the pretence.

I smiled slightly at Tony. His power level was well under check in the presence of his Master, but his returning grin told me just what he'd do if the Master weren't there.

"That will be all, Tony." Max/Death, whatever, gave Scar Face a glare that could have frozen a snowman. To Tony's credit, he didn't hang around.

I pulled the French fries out of the bag and began nibbling on them. Max watched with quiet intrigue. "You are stunning," he said, with a hint of sexual desire that coated his every word.

"I'm eating a French fry. How is that stunning?"

He smiled wryly. "I had heard you often spoke without thinking. I shall teach you restraint. You may never need worry about that fault again."

Fault? I kinda liked the way I have independent thought. My inner voice purred. Huh?

I decided just to nibble on another French fry rather than answer that statement out loud.

"You will like my home. It is in a much better climate than here," he said conversationally. His eyes never left me as he spoke. The green gaze felt weighted, as though every moment he looked at me, he owned more and more of my soul.

I hadn't missed the innuendo of his statement, though, that his home had a nicer climate than here. I couldn't help defending my adopted city, but I kept my retort internal, no point pissing the Master Vampire off. *You mean the swamp, that is Auckland? I like it, buster, it's my home. Don't knock it.*

"There will be many occasions for you to use your powers when they fully manifest. I lead a busy Court."

"Court?"

"Yes, somehow the intricacies of Vampire Court life have been lost on most of today's vampires. I run a traditional Vampire Court."

I was sure I did *not* want to know what traditional meant. I'd take my Master of the City running a nightclub any day.

"Just where do you live, Max?"

I think he liked hearing me say his name, he positively glowed. "Far from here. You need not worry yourself with the details."

So much for *right beside me* and *an equal joining*.

"So, um, what is it like to be joined exactly?" I had no idea what *joining* meant, but I wanted to keep him occupied. If asking questions did that, then I would feign interest.

He stood up and prowled towards me. His eyes glowed a slight red, which was quite disconcerting. Not just for the fact that he was expending power right then, but because green and red, they don't mix so well. I couldn't move, my hand half way into the bag of fries, my breath a little laboured. He held my gaze, not entirely glazing me, but trapping me like a deer in headlights. I could not have looked away if my life depended on it and it probably did right then.

Power rolled off him in waves, intermittently giving me sensations of pleasure, quickly followed by spikes in adrenaline full of fear. His intention was clear; he wanted me to know how easy it was to affect me, control me. At a simple thought, he could have me groaning in bliss or screaming in terror. He stood not half a metre away and watched as wave after wave of conflicting sensations washed over me.

The sensual feeling of flesh on flesh. The heat of a body moving in mine. The crest of a wave, making my breathing come in pants and a small moan escape my lips. Golden pools of lava centring in my soul. Then abruptly, before I could completely crest that wave of desire, sharp, hot stabs of pain. Excruciating jabs of knife-like slices across my skin. Tearing flesh, rendering skin apart. Hot blood soaking my clothes, running down my body and pooling at my feet. Then promptly the flesh on flesh all over again. The utter contrast of sensations making my body shake, my voice cry out in alarm and my mind scream for it all to end.

I'm not sure how long I sat there, completely and utterly at his mercy, but the images and sensations that he conjured in my mind and body will stay with me for life. How he could have me longing for his touch, begging with my eyes for release one minute and then fighting bile in my throat and straining not to wet myself another, is beyond me. A true monster lurked beneath that stare.

Finally, when perhaps he had bored of the enterprise, he smiled, and his eyes returned to their normal shade of green. He stepped forward and knelt down in front of me. He reached for my hand, the one not still hovering over a now semi-cold French fry and stroked the back of it with his thumb. "Don't you see, Lucinda? The power we could share. What is mine is yours, what is yours is mine. You shall have my power, as I shall have yours. Together we shall be stronger, fiercer, more powerful than any other that walks this earth today. You *are* to be mine, Lucinda. We shall rule the world."

I didn't know what to say to that. The thought of having anything to do with the power that had just engulfed me, tortured me in both pleasure and pain, repulsed me. I felt sick to the stomach. *Was he insane? Did he think I lusted after his power?*

I was just searching for something to say, something that wouldn't offend and then invoke the wrath of this being when I felt him. Michel. I wasn't the only one to notice; I guess that was the point. Couldn't he have just snuck up on the bad guy, though? I mean, pride before a fall and all that.

Max was on me in an instant, my head in a vice-like grip. His left arm around my neck holding me securely, his right gripping the top of my head in a position that meant all business. The French fries forgotten at our feet. I didn't breathe.

There were loud shouts and a few thuds from downstairs and then the door opened ever so slowly into the room.

The landing was bare.

I couldn't hold my breath any longer, but I didn't want to make a move. Finally, after what felt like an eternity, Michel appeared in the entranceway.

I let the breath I was holding out and felt a deep-seated sense of pure joy at the sight of him. No mind control, no forced emotion, this was all me.

I shouldn't have counted my chickens so soon.

7
THUNDERBOLTS AND LIGHTNING

Sanguis Vitam crackled around the room like lightning. The hairs on my arms stood out, sharp stabs of pain danced across my skin as flashes of energy swirled through the air. Neither vampire had moved, but the world was a hazy glaze of impulses. My eyes ached at the bright lights, but I couldn't close them. I was trapped, not just by the steel hold of a vampire's arm around my throat, but by the tangible power growing in the room. And it was growing.

Michel took a step towards us, and I felt like I had been punched in the stomach. I let a whimper out involuntarily, but neither vampire noticed, too wrapped up in the power play that was unfolding between them. Blue and indigo swirled with purple and red in those eyes across from me. I had never seen Michel like this before. Was I scared? Shit-less. But, I also felt an undeniable pull towards the vampire who stood outlined in the door to the room.

Suddenly, as soon as I acknowledged in my mind that pull, I felt I could move. I struggled against the arm that held me in a vice-like grip. The movement momentarily distracted Max and Michel pounced.

It wasn't so much a pounce, as the flight of a dangerous animal leaping through the air. His fangs were down; I hadn't even seen them move. A feral look crossed his beautiful face, but far from detracting from its stark beauty, it seemed to make it even more frighteningly incredible. My eyes were fixated on the being that hurtled through the room towards us, everything seemed to slow down, but yet was happening in lightning quick speed.

Max flung me from his grip to face his attacker without hindrance. I sailed through the air and crashed into a side table in the corner, the lamp splintering against the wall above me and shards of glass raining down to scratch on my face and arms. The air was pushed from my lungs by the impact, and I struggled to breathe.

In the middle of the room, the two vampires were a blur of intense light. Bright yellows and blues, greens and reds, all swirling together in a hazy ball of energy. I could feel it, I could taste, I could hear it. But I could do nothing to stop it. I was sure that this was the night I would die. It was inevitable, I could see no end to this, so evenly matched were these two master vampires. They would destroy themselves and take me with them.

Suddenly the ball of energy burst and Michel was thrown through the wall into the next room. Plasterboard shattered, chairs and a bookcase went flying until he came down in a heap at the far end of the next room.

Max was already on me, lifting me up like a rag doll and bringing his face towards my neck. His fangs were out, and his head was cocked, ready to go in for the kill. My whimpering had started again; I couldn't help it. His grip on me so tight I felt his fingernails breaking skin and blood starting to trickle down my wrist. His eyes glowed that horrible green and red, his face was contorted in a ghastly grimace of anger. His lips brushed the side of my neck, and I felt his fangs pierce the skin.

I screamed.

Then, all I felt was air beneath me as I fell, again, towards the couch on the other side of the room. At least it was a couch and not the table, I thought briefly, before hitting its solid mass and realising that it probably made no difference at all. My body broke the back of the couch and wood from the frame sliced through my side. I grunted as I came to rest on my side against the far wall. I reached down to just above my left hip to staunch the flow of blood that had started there.

You see, the thing is, when vampires fight each other, there are always human casualties. If you happen to be in the vicinity of where a vampire loses his rag, then it's lights-out baby. They are a tornado at best, a supernatural one and a combination of a volcano and earthquake at worst. Their power electrifies the air; their energy can pierce human skin. Forget about your mind being squashed by all that controlled fury; your body won't stand up against the physical onslaught of their combined assault.

There are always casualties when vampires fight. Just my luck I was the only human in this building with two master vampires out for the kill.

Michel and Max were circling each other now. The *Sanguis Vitam* hadn't abated, but they had slowed down their pursuit of each other's throats. It was like watching an intricate dance, deadly but compelling.

"You think you can beat me, Durand?" He said Michel's surname like it was a particularly distasteful piece of food. "You know you cannot. You are not strong enough."

Michel smiled, a cunning, knowing smile. "Ah, but it has been a long time since we last sparred, Maximilian. Time for my powers to grow, unnoticed."

Far from looking fazed, Max just shrugged. "I do not feel it, my old friend."

"Then you have not been paying attention."

The air began to hum with elevated power and Michel started glowing, like the first time I laid eyes on him at the bank that storm covered day. The humming escalated to a crescendo in my mind, the power crashed against my chest in a crushing wave. I felt pinned against the wall, unable to move or breathe. Lights had started to flash before my eyes, but I couldn't tell if it was to do with the battle which had resumed in front of me or the fact that I couldn't draw breath. Or maybe it was due to the blood loss that I had suffered. The pool of blood at my side was startlingly large.

I couldn't see what was happening, but I could hear it and feel it. The sound was deafening, the whole of central Auckland would have heard it. It was a combination of jet engines whirring and metal screeching, along with trees breaking and thunder booming. There was no longer any witty repartee between the two vampires; it was all a physical onslaught, and I couldn't see who was winning. If there was going to be a winner at all.

At last, after what felt like an hour, but was probably only a mere few seconds, the crescendo of noise reached its pinnacle. A blinding light filled the air, and everything froze. And I mean everything. Particles of dust hung in the air like magic, fragments of furniture were suspended in their fall towards the floor. There was no sound, no hum, nothing. Just a void.

The last thing I remember, before darkness completely enveloped me, was the shadow of a man standing over me. No features were discernible, just the outline of a large and imposing figure.

I didn't wake with a start; it was more of a gradual thing. At first, I could sense movement, like the slow rock of a boat, or the feel of tyres rolling over a road and also the sensation of warmth around me. It blanketed me, cosseted me and then I felt a chest rising and falling against my head. Heard the heartbeat, steady and constant. The sound of a car engine, an indicator ticking. I opened my eyes slowly, blinking in the dark that surrounded me, registering the low glow of lights from the front of the car's dashboard, the occasional headlight beam sweeping past of oncoming traffic.

There was just enough ambient light to make out whose arms I was being cradled in. Whose chest my head rested against.

"Michel." It was a whisper, but he heard it.

"You are awake, *ma douce*." A statement. His eyes held a strange look, one I hadn't seen before. Was it relief? It was gone before I could fully register it. "We are almost there, my dear. Rest now; you are safe."

And with that, the darkness enveloped me again, this time with a blissful sense of safety and warmth.

The next time I awoke, I was in bed. A large four poster bed with white gauze curtains hanging loosely at the corners tied back by a pale blue band of satin. The mattress was deep and moulded to my body, the covers thick and luxuriant, in a deep navy damask which matched the curtains on the floor length windows to my right. They were closed.

I gingerly sat up in bed and momentarily felt the world tilt. I took a breath to steady myself and waited for the sensation to pass. Slowly, the world righted, and I swung my bare legs over the side of the bed. I was in a nightshirt; white cotton, loose and down to just above my knees. I had nothing on underneath. This made me blush slightly for some reason. I had no idea how I had got here. I had no idea where *here* was.

I stood up and walked over toward the curtains. Surprisingly, I didn't hurt anywhere. I reached for my left side and only felt smooth skin beneath the fabric of the nightdress. I quickly grabbed the hem of the shirt and lifted it to see pale and unblemished skin. Michel, no doubt. I guess I'd have to thank him.

I was just reaching for the curtains when the door opened, and a woman walked in. She was greying and slightly plump, maybe 60 or 65 years old. She was human. She glanced up and smiled.

"You're out of bed? Fantastic, the Master will be pleased." She had a slight English accent. Maybe from Kent, I'm not sure. But it was friendly, and I immediately liked it.

"You must be hungry. Shower first and dinner afterwards I think," she said as she went to another door, I hadn't noticed, to the left.

"Dinner? What time is it?" My throat was dry, and my voice came out in a rasp. I tried not to cough. The woman rushed over and handed me a glass of water from the bedside table.

"There, there, child. You've had a busy night. You were in quite a state when the Master brought you in."

I took the glass and swallowed the cool water down; instantly I felt relief. She took it from my hands and returned it to the table. "It's seven in the evening. The Master will be rising soon."

I must have slept the whole day. A whole friggin' day. Whoa. The woman bustled me towards the bathroom and handed me some fresh clothes from inside the door. "Have a nice hot shower and then come down to us. We'll be in the den, no doubt, third door on the right at the bottom of the stairs." With that, she was gone.

I showered quickly; I didn't feel entirely safe to be caught in the nude in a strange bathroom and dressed in the borrowed clothes. Tan skirt and white blouse not my normal attire, but it would do. The house, I discovered, was modern. The bannister of the stairway a sleek metal, the flooring a pale polished wood. Artwork adorned the walls of the stairwell. Jazz prints in gold frames; a saxophone, keyboard, bass and clarinet. The gold frames looked subtle against the cream of the painted walls.

It had a surprisingly airy feeling to it, not the sort of place you'd think a vampire would be comfortable. The windows in the bedroom had heavy drapes, but those on the landing and now downstairs were just big expanses of glass. The view was spectacular, despite it already being dark. Lights of a town, I didn't know where, sparkled across an expanse of water. A lake perhaps? The lights were a magical orange colour, so delightful in the distance.

I counted the doors and entered in the third. Michel was reclining on an overstuffed couch. He was casually dressed in black trousers but had on an open-neck light blue shirt. It would have matched his eyes when they chose to display a paler shade, had they been open. Instead, he had his hand resting on his forehead, as though he was suffering from a headache. The woman was sitting reading in an armchair off to the side, she looked up and smiled as I walked in. There was an older man standing by the large, unadorned windows talking to Bruno softly. No doubt the woman's husband. They both turned as well. The man smiled, Bruno just nodded.

"Lucinda." His voice was so soft, curling around me, pulling me to him, irresistible and lush. Deep blue eyes met mine. I don't know what people, or vampires, see when they look at me. I'm not very tall, 5'4", not that pretty. I'm trim and athletic; I like to keep fit and being short you need to work at it. I have shoulder length mousy brown hair. It shines and is dead straight, but that's about the only saving grace. It's a bit thin, I think. I would have liked something a bit thicker, but we take what we're given. I do have good skin, though, lightly tanned, never really worried about pimples or the like when I was a teenager. Must have been all that clean farm air growing up. But, looking at Michel's face right now, I could have sworn he saw something, someone, different from what I do. There was a look of utter longing in his eyes; it almost bowled me over.

He recovered himself, it seemed reluctant and motioned to the seat beside him on the couch. Despite having had practically a whole night and day's sleep, I was too tired to fight him right now. It wasn't a physical exhaustion, more an emotional and mental one. If I was honest with myself, I was tired of pushing him away. I knew that would change, though. You couldn't keep a good girl down for long.

The couch faced the window where the older man and Bruno stood. I could see the twinkly orange lights in the distance, the reflection of them coming back towards us on the still waters of the lake.

I sat down, as far as I could away from Michel. Habit.

"Where are we?"

Michel placed his arm along the back of the couch towards me. Despite having sat down as far away as possible from him, he took up an awful lot of that couch. His hand was able to pick up a strand of my hair and play with it in his fingers. Oh boy.

"My holiday home in Taupo."

I laughed, I couldn't help it. "You fly-fish?"

He chuckled too. "There is more to Taupo than the Trout, my dear." And he swept his other arm out to indicate the view from the windows. "Sometimes I need a break from the city, and I come here. Kathleen and Matthew take care of it when I am city bound."

Kathleen, the woman who had checked on me in the bedroom, shuffled forward in her seat and stood up stiffly, as though she had aching bones. "Time for some dinner, I think." She smiled and left the room.

"What happened?" I glanced at Michel; he was watching me, leaning back on the sofa, quite relaxed. "Is..." I swallowed, "Is Max still alive?" I know technically vampires are meant to be the undead, so not alive, but with the really old ones, like Michel, they can make themselves seem just as alive as you and me. Heartbeats, breathing, blinking, they can even keep their body temperature close to normal. Easier when they have fed, but not impossible when hungry either. Asking if a vamp is *dead* dead, just doesn't sound right, so I don't bother anymore.

I think Michel kind of likes that. The appearing more human thing again I'm guessing.

"Alas, yes."

I bolted upright on the sofa. "What do you mean *yes?*" I asked, my heartbeat hammering along like a freight train, I resisted the urge to look over my shoulder. Michel leant forward and cupped my face in his hands.

"*Ma douce*, you are safe, do not fear him."

"I'm not sure anyone is safe from... him." I wanted to spit out a curse, to call Max something horrid, but words failed me right then. There were no phrases bad enough to cover what I felt for Max. I sat back on the couch a little defeated. Michel hesitated, as if waiting for me to spring forward again, to say the words that were so obviously on my mind, but then he slowly reclined and continued to play with my hair.

"It was unexpected that he would show himself here. I must apologise, my dear, had I known he was in our city I would have protected you better."

The part of me that likes to think the best of people wanted to say it was OK, that he couldn't have done much in the light of day. But that other part of me, the one that was becoming more and more prevalent the longer I lived in this new world of mine, was angry at Michel. Of course, I hadn't really counted on him coming to my rescue, but because he did in the end, I couldn't help feeling he should have come a little sooner. Then I wouldn't have had to feel what Max made me feel, see what he made me see. I still couldn't stop the images playing like an old movie reel over and over across my eyes whenever I close them. I may never go to sleep again.

I sighed and rubbed my temples, leaning forward in my seat, running my hands through my hair. Michel moved his arm back into his lap and watched. "I am sorry, Lucinda. He is very strong, attacking him in daylight would have been disastrous. I could not risk losing you. I am, unfortunately, not omnipotent."

I nodded. Being angry at Michel really wouldn't help, not now anyway.

"I have questions."

"And you shall have answers, but first you eat."

And as if on cue, Kathleen came in with a tray of food. She placed it across my lap; lamb and baby veggies with a fruit jus. How did she know? I may have loved those little lambs and their waggling tails back on the farm when I was young, but I'm a farmer's daughter through and through. Give me a succulent lamb chop any day over a veggie burger. There was wine on the side, two glasses. She filled them both and handed one to Michel. Vamps may need blood to exist, but they won't pass up the odd glass of Merlot or Cab Sav when offered.

Bruno came over then and whispered in Michel's ear; he nodded, and the big man left the room. Matthew walked over to his wife, and they both bid us good night, I guess it was just the boss and me then?

The food smelled divine; I could feel saliva filling my mouth. My stomach decided to make a rather loud grumbling noise at that moment. Michel laughed. "Are you just going to stare at it, my dear, or should you not heed the call of your body and eat?"

I'd never eaten in front of Michel before; it was kind of nerve-racking. I mean, would he be disgusted at my eating solid food, or would it remind him how hungry he was and make him want to bite into something equally as succulent, but definitely not on the menu? Time to find out I guessed.

It tasted as good as it smelled. It didn't take long for me to forget all about the big bad vampire sitting to my left and devour the whole meal. When I finished, it was Michel who lifted the tray and placed it to the side. He also refilled our glasses again with wine. He settled back down on the couch facing me, reclining like royalty waiting to be served. I twisted in my seat so I was facing him.

He did look stunning in the low light of the room, very comfortable and at ease. This really was his home? He sipped his wine and waited for me to start. For some reason, I couldn't face the big questions right away. I mean, I wanted to know what it was about me that was in such hot demand and all, but I was also a little scared of the answer. I'd build up to it.

"This doesn't seem like a vampire's house?" He raised his eyebrows at me. "All the glass," I added, indicating the floor to ceiling, wall to wall expanse of glass in front of us.

He smiled and reached over his shoulder to the side table, picking up a remote control unit. After pushing a button, a slow whirling noise started in the walls, then a plain concertina wall came out from either side and proceeded to close over the glass completely. "Oh," I said.

"Every window in the house has one, set to a timer. They close right on sunrise each day." Michel pushed the button again, and the windows were revealed in all their splendour.

He sipped more wine and waited. It's not often you could call a vampire patient, but Michel was the epitome of patience right then. Somehow he knew how difficult it was for me to ask these questions, he wasn't rushing me; he was quite happy to wait and let me get there on my own. I would have preferred a little help.

I took another sip of wine for fortitude. "What am I?" I didn't even look at him when I said it; I couldn't bear to see pity or sympathy or even anything else for that matter.

Michel moved closer and took my free hand in his; his thumb stroked the back of my hand in a familiar pattern. "You are a remarkable young woman. Strong, capable. Beautiful." I pulled my hand free and stood up. I didn't need his flirting right now, nor his compliments, I needed the truth.

"Come on, Michel, give me a break. I deserve better than this. I almost got killed in your little power play last night. It's obvious you've got a beef with Max. This isn't something new, but here I am, slap bang in the middle of it. What's changed and what's so damn *special* about me?"

He had been leaning forward on the sofa when I stood and hadn't moved an inch during my little speech. He shifted back in the seat now however and gazed up at me. Another sip of wine. *Drag it out why don't you?*

"Centuries ago our races lived side by side, similar to how we exist with the humans today, but there was full disclosure back then. Your kind knew what we were and likewise, we knew who you were. We were made to work together. We are of the same ilk. We are designed to have you by our side. Some abused this relationship, however. Choosing to treat their kindred as servants, as a means to an end. That abuse led to a rift and finally your kind could contain themselves no more.

"We parted ways, yours into hiding, ours into the cities. It is only in the past 200 years or so that your kind has resurfaced again, out of necessity, but still not in the numbers of before. We vampyre brought it on ourselves. We hunted with abandon; we fed without pause. We were accountable to no one, not even ourselves.

"Then, with your elders' help, we re-established the *Iunctio*. It had never really been destroyed, just neglected. Part of what powers the *Iunctio* is from your kind, with their re-emergence we were able to fortify the *Iunctio* and bring it back into what it was meant to be. Rules were set. Safety precautions for humans, fall back positions for vampyre, strict guidelines for our kind. It works, in a fashion. Nothing is perfect, my dear, but it is what we have."

He sipped his wine again. I just stood there, staring at him. I couldn't even put into words what was going through my head. I wanted answers, but now I had even more.

"Unfortunately, with the reappearance of your kind, comes the Maximilian of ours. He and his kin, have tried to secure one or two of your brethren overseas. But once you reach maturity it is harder of course and what he offers is not to everyone's liking. When I found you, became aware of you, I did everything in my power to keep your identity, your success as a hunter, a secret from the *Iunctio*, in the hopes it would give you the time needed to reach maturity."

"I am mature."

He smiled. "Of course, my dear, without a doubt, but the maturity that I speak of for your kind is not considered until age 25. You are three weeks off your 25th birthday, is that correct?"

Huh? "Yeah. What happens when I turn 25?"

"You come into your powers in full, of course." And before I could get the words out, he raised his hand in a placating manner. "Do not ask me; I do not know the full extent of your powers. It differs for each of you, but it will be similar to those of mine and my brethren. You will be stronger. Not quite to our level, but enough to protect yourself. You will become faster, nearly as fast as I. You will also possess psychic powers of some description; the ability to control your environment, for example, or influence those around you."

Wow. He must have seen the look on my face because he leant forward and continued. "There is a catch." There always is. "Your powers were never meant to exist without a vampyre at your side. Without a joining... you will die." He said it softly, as though he didn't want me to feel the punch those words held.

He'd failed.

"When? How long have I got?"

"One full turn of the moon. One month from your 25th birthday." He looked intently at me, no sympathy or pity in his eyes, just a strength, a conviction that that would not happen.

"But, but...that can't be right. What about the others I talk to on the website? They've never mentioned this. They're all older than me. This can't be right; maybe it's changed?"

Michel stood then and smoothly walked across to me. Still no pity, only a hint of sadness in the depth of those rich blue eyes.

"They will have had a joining, my dear. They will have a vampyre they trust, someone of my kind, they have pledged their life to. I am sorry. I know this is not what you wish to hear."

I just looked at him, standing there in front of me, those strong, handsome features, not offering a hint of pity for me to rage against, not offering anything other than understanding.

"What am I, Michel?"

"You are Nosferatin, my dear." He pronounced it *Nosferat-een*, lengthening the end.

I didn't hear if he said anything else after that, I felt so very tired all of a sudden. So, so tired. The last thing I registered, was the world tilting on its axis and the floor approaching fast.

8
NOSFERATIN

"Wake up, *ma douce*. Wake up."

I was lying in Michel's arms, on the floor. He was cradling my head in his lap and softly stroking my cheek. The first thing I saw when I opened my eyes was his face. Slight edges of concern were showing in the corner of his now indigo eyes. I shifted abruptly away and scuttled backwards towards the armchair.

He looked a little defeated and sighed.

"What did you do to me?" I demanded.

"When you know how, the word can have power." Seeing the look of outrage on my face, he quickly went on. "I did not use it to harm you, my dear, simply to see what you're reaction to it would be. It seems you sleep." He cocked his head at me then, raising an eyebrow delicately and smiling slightly. "Perhaps, you seek sleep for pleasure, *ma douce?*"

The implication, I could only guess, was obvious, he visits me in my dreams. In my dreams, I feel safe.

"Well, that's just grand! Now any old vamp can cast a spell on me with the name of *my kind*, and I'll fall asleep at their feet, ready to be dinner."

"It doesn't quite work that way." He looked a little contrite at that.

Oh great, what next? "Only those who are suitable as your kindred vampyre can wield its power and only a response appropriate to *that* vampyre will be elicited." He shrugged, as if to say, that's just the way it is and went on, but gritted his teeth slightly. "I suspect, should Maximilian be suitable - which he no doubt is, his power level would indicate a good match - your response to him voicing that word would be different. I'm hoping it would involve silver."

I shot him a glance at that. "Will he always have that hold over me?"

"No, when you choose a kindred vampyre and join with them, that power will cease for all others."

My mind was reeling. *Too much info! Too much info!* I could feel a thumping headache coming on. This was *way* too much. I belonged to a *race* of kindred vampire people, with powers! But, I would die if I didn't *join* with a vampire. Not just any vampire, but one that has the power to make me sleep, or whatever, simply by saying my race's name.

Why the friggin' hell me?

"What's in it for you? What's in it for the Nosferatu? You wouldn't want someone who has the ability, the power to kill you, so close. Surely?"

He sat back down on the couch in a languid movement. It was obvious he was doing it for my benefit. I swallowed visibly and briefly shut my eyes. It wasn't as though I didn't appreciate the performance; it was just not wise to fall under the effect his act created.

"*Au contraire*, my dear. You are in fact a prize, to be sure. With a kindred Nosferatin at their side, a vampyre will double his powers. The Nosferatin empowers the Vampyre; the Nosferatu empowers the Hunter. Symbiotic, the relationship. One cannot live without the other."

"Huh. But you won't die if you don't join with a Nosferatin?"

"No." And then silence.

I started pacing; I needed to think.

"But, you would be immune to your kindred vampyre's powers, unless you allow them. They would have no hold over you, in the psychic sense, at least. That is a bonus, is it not?"

That was a bonus, a vampire who couldn't fight back. "So, I could *join* with a vampire and then stake them?" A thought formulated in my mind. Maybe, if I was forced to, I could join with Max and then stake him in his sleep. End of story. Good night bad guy.

"Not impossible, but unlikely." When I stopped pacing and raised my eyebrows at him, he went on. "The relationship is symbiotic. You kill your kindred, and you die."

"Well, that sucks. What's the point of being able to resist their power if you can't use it to kill them?" Crap.

He smiled. "We are not known for stupidity, Lucinda; my kind would not have formulated such an alliance if it favoured just you."

We locked gazes then. There was no power coming from him when he said it; there didn't need to be. Vampires at the top of the food chain and all that.

OK, so I could take the hint, but I wasn't giving up, though. This was the first time I'd had the chance to find out what I was, what I really was. I wasn't going to waste the opportunity.

"Where did we originate from?"

He relaxed back into his seat slightly, the dangerous topic of death to the Hunter had passed. "History is unclear on this point, but it is believed that at the beginning we were of one kind."

I interrupted. "One kind?"

He just spread his hands as if to say *what do you think I mean?*

My mind was doing the whirly-gig thing again. I could hardly breathe. I think I may have even been panting.

"If...if we were *one kind*, does that mean..." I mimed fangs into my neck with my fingers.

He laughed. "No. When we parted ways, the Nosferatin went into the Day, the Nosferatu; the Night." And when he saw the look of incomprehension on my face, "In this instance Day and Night do not refer to a period of time within one cycle of the Earth's rotation. They refer to Good and Evil. Light and Dark."

Huh? So does that mean Michel thinks of himself as *evil?* I'd file that little piece of information away for later, I thought.

OK, so we were technically the same race when we started out - I didn't really want to acknowledge that, but it was centuries ago, before New Zealand even existed, evolution and all that - but now we were practically against each other. I mean I'm designed to kill bad vampires. But then, I also feel *at home* when I am with them. *How does that work?*

Back to basics, I think.

"So, just to recap. I die if I don't join with a vampire before one month past my 25th birthday. But I get powers, and that vampire's powers have no hold over me any longer, but *he* will double his own. And if I kill him, I die. That about right?"

"Yes."

"What happens if I die first?"

He paused then, didn't shift his gaze, just rubbed two of his fingers together as if calming himself, as they rested on his crossed knees.

"They would die too."

That didn't make sense. Why would a vampire limit himself to a mortal's lifespan just for a double load of his powers? And then it hit me. Like a tonne of bricks. "I would become immortal, wouldn't I?"

Softly. "Yes."

Good grief. Death at just 25, or live forever tied into a *joining* with one of the undead. The guys I'm built to hunt. One of the guys that can only survive on human blood and can kill with the flick of their wrist. Fuck!

"This is a lot, Michel. A hell of a lot to take in, in one hit."

"Usually, a Nosferatin elder would impart this knowledge to you. Nosferatin runs in the family's bloodline. The firstborn holds the Nosferatin gene and becomes the Nosferatin, the second holds the knowledge and passes on the gene to the next generation. Your parents, your natural parents, died, did they not?"

His eyes held sadness when I looked at them. Sadness for me. I didn't want to acknowledge his compassion, he was a vampire, vampires don't care.

"Yes," I whispered. I didn't talk about my biological parents with anyone. They died when I was only a baby. In a car accident, driving the Arthur's Pass, from Greymouth to Christchurch. My Aunt and Uncle, on my mother's side, raised me as their own. They're my Mum and Dad.

"Your father," Michel answered before I had even formulated the question. Which one of my parents was Nosferatin?

"How do...?"

"I had to be sure, my dear. It has been so long since I have encountered a Nosferatin, there are not many of your kind left, I'm afraid."

My father. My Aunt and Uncle, my Mum and Dad for all intents and purposes, they cut off all contact with my father's side. I'm not exactly sure why, but I think there was a falling out of some sort. My Mum had always told me that they were different. I just thought she had meant they weren't Anglicans.

OK, so this sucked. It sucked big time, but I'm not the sort of girl to play the victim. I'm not into that damsel in distress crap at all, so this was not going to get the better of me. Besides, I had a reputation to uphold and despite how nice and caring and all *let's work together and be friends* crap that Michel was spouting right now, he was still one of the bad guys. Maybe not evil personified, but a *vampire* all the same.

I know, I know. It had occurred to me too. I was going to have to choose a vampire to *join* with, or let myself die. Part of me and I admit it was just a very small, very teeny part, was considering the *let's just see what happens* if I say no road. But, the thought of having to choose a vampire was still hovering in the back of my mind.

I grabbed that thought and shoved it deep, deep down inside. I'm not usually the one for denial. I mean when I met that first vampire, I didn't curl up in a ball and cry for mummy. No, I started researching and arming myself with as much knowledge as I could. I am not a push over. But I am practical. We still had a mega-master vampire out there gunning for my soul.

"OK, so, there's still a lot I want to know, Michel, about all of this... this crap, but," I took a breath, "it can wait. For now." I looked directly at him, daring him to say otherwise.

He just smiled. "Of course, my dear, of course. Whatever you say. But, you will have to face facts soon, Lucinda. And the sooner, the better, to save your life."

Trust Michel; he couldn't just agree. He had to have the last word. I tried not to let anything show on my face and took a seat in the armchair opposite him.

"Max," I said.

"Yes, indeed." Michel took another sip of wine. Ever the casual sense of ease, despite having to talk about an evil piece of shit like Max. "He is proving troublesome. And he is a threat to you."

"Can he force me to join with him."

"Yes, I dare say he could. Quite easily, in fact."

"How so?"

"His *Sanguis Vitam*, unfortunately, is greater than mine. He is close to 900 years old."

Whoa. I knew he was off the scale powerful, but I had never heard of a vampire living that long before. Usually, a stake through the heart would see to that. No vampire had, that I was aware of, managed to live to such an age without attracting attention from a Hunter. Or at least a few vampire enemies gunning for their final death. How had old Maximilian survived?

"That's old."

I considered telling Michel that I was unable to gauge Max's age or power level, that he had appeared as just a void to me when I was with him, but I didn't want to admit that fault. And it did feel like a fault to me. For some reason, Michel's respect of my talents was important to me and not just because it's always good to keep up appearances with the bad guys.

"Why has he not just followed us here?" I asked.

Michel looked a little uncomfortable at that question. "You are safe here, my dear, do not fear."

"No. That's not an answer, Michel. Why has he not come here?"

"I do have a few tricks up my sleeve, Lucinda. I have masked us sufficiently for now. He cannot sense where we are."

Now, call me a sceptic, but I wasn't buying it. I'd got pretty good at reading Michel by now. Most vampires of his power level can hide their true feelings well. And ordinarily, he's pretty damn good at it. But lately, I've noticed, I can sense more than usual from him. I can almost feel what he's feeling. Spooky, huh?

"I'm not buying it."

"Buying what?" He tried for the innocent look and on anyone else it may have worked, but I was getting a bit angry now.

"Stop being the evasive *Master* and just cut to the chase. Why. Is. He. Not. Here?"

Michel sighed and started rubbing his forehead. "I am too tired to fight you on this, my dear. Last night took a lot out of me."

I felt momentarily alarmed. Michel had never shown any signs of being anything other than fighting fit. Ever. I guess I wasn't reading him as well as I thought I was.

"Are you OK?" I regretted it as soon as the words were out of my mouth. Stupid. Don't let them see you care. I didn't really. I'm just a nice person; that's all. *Really*.

He smiled that damn knowing smile again. "Thank You. I shall be fine. I have fed."

I so did not want details. Luckily, he wasn't giving any.

"So?" I ventured, a little less aggressively. "Why's he not here?" Never let it be said that I don't follow through on something. A bit like a dog with a bone. I don't let things go easily, and I wasn't giving up on this, just yet.

The mood, however, changed. Power filled the room.

"Oh God, Michel. I thought we were through with this.?"

"It is a question I am unwilling to answer, right now. I suggest you drop it."

Maybe there is a limit to Michel's patience after all. Maybe the animal that is vampire deep inside him, just can't be contained. But I got the distinct impression that he would fight me on this, despite him saying he was too tired to do so.

The silence stretched out awkwardly between us. I was damned if I was going to speak first.

But then, I'm not a vampire, and I can't do that preternatural calm they do. That sitting absolutely still, not breathing, not blinking, not anything. I sincerely hope I can never do that.

Rather than give in, because I admit it, I can be stubborn when I try, I just stood and left the room. A breath of fresh air wouldn't go astray right now.

There was a large expanse of perfectly trimmed lawn in front of the house, towards the view of Lake Taupo and the township. It stretched out about 20 metres or so and then disappeared, I'm guessing over a cliff face. I had the impression we were up quite high. I decided to walk to the edge to see.

Along the sides of the property, leading towards the cliff, were trees. Acacias, Cherry, even a Pine or two. A mixed bag, but they all seemed to work together nicely, providing privacy and protection from the wind. As I made it to the edge of the lawn and confirmed my suspicion that there was indeed a cliff there, straight down to the water, I noticed movement out of the corner of my eyes. It was only then that I sensed his *Sanguis Vitam*.

Man, my mind was distracted right now.

A vampire came out of the trees to my left. How long he'd been watching me, I could only guess. He wasn't in a hurry. Just sauntered up and stood next to me looking at the view.

"Hi, Bruno."

"Luce. Getting a bit of fresh air?"

"Mm-hmm. What are you doing out here?"

"Sentry duty. You don't think the Master would have the place unguarded, do ya?"

I quickly looked around to see if there was movement anywhere else. "You won't see them, or feel them for that matter. They've been told to hang back and give you space."

"Give me space? Since when?"

"Since you walked out on the Master just now."

Great. Michel was giving me space. How considerate.

"So, why are you disobeying him?"

He smiled at that. That evil smile he can do so well, the one he uses if you piss him off outside one of the clubs he's bouncing at. I'm sure it scares the pants off Norms, but I can take it.

"I have different orders."

OK, I'll bite. "What would they be?"

"If I tell you, I'd have to kill you." A twinkle in his eyes.

"Sure, somehow I don't think the *Master* would appreciate that." I'd call his bluff on that one.

He chuckled. "I'm your guard. I go where you go from now on."

Oh no. That was not what I wanted to hear. *God damn Michel, I was not a child to be babysat!*

Bruno must have sensed my anger, hell it couldn't have been hard, I was boiling in it. He stiffened slightly and said, "What did you expect, Luce? You are in danger, and he can't watch you 24/7, he is the Master of the City."

"I don't expect him to *watch* me at all! I am not his property to take care of!" I was fair shouting by now, my fists in balls at my side, my heartbeat thumping a staccato rhythm in my chest.

He looked at me as if I was mad. It didn't help my temper one bit. "But you are *his*, Lucinda. He would not let you be harmed." He said it as if it was special, a gift. I should be lucky to have the Master of Auckland City claiming me as his own. Yeah, ri-ight.

All at once Bruno turned swiftly towards the house. "That will be all, Bruno." He was gone, so quickly I didn't see him move. There one second, gone the next. Poof.

I could feel Michel standing right behind me. My back was stiff, shoulders rigid. My nails digging into the palms of my hands, drawing blood. Then a wave of peace washed over me, almost making me drop to my knees. I fought it, I really did. I so did *not* want him to be able to do this to me. Tears rolled down my cheeks. I don't know why I was crying. It could have been the anger, but part of me reluctantly acknowledged it was my disappointment. Disappointment at Michel using his powers on me again. I thought we had passed that.

All at once he was in front of me, brushing those tears away with his hand. It felt warm and soft and oh, I did not want him to stop.

"*Ma douce*, please do not cry." His voice cracked ever so slightly, the French lilt unmistakable.

"Why do you do this?" I looked at him, his eyes a deep blue and indigo swirl.

"I cannot help it. You are in pain."

"I was angry, Michel. That's different. I should be *allowed* to be angry at you."

"Yes, you are right." His hand was now holding the side of my neck, caressing it softly just below the ear. He brought his head down and kissed my forehead, lips lingering on my flesh. "I am so sorry, Lucinda. Truly I am."

"Then why do you do it?"

He sighed. "I am connected to you in a way I have never been to any other before. The pull is so strong; I cannot fight it."

"Cannot? Or will not?"

He smiled a rueful smile. "You know me well, my dear."

"I am not yours, Michel." No harm trying to reiterate the obvious.

"Oh, but you are."

"No."

The tears were still coming, why couldn't I stop them? I hate crying, it's all puffy eyes and snotty nose and completely and utterly unattractive. I do *not* cry in front of people. Ever. But for the life of me, I couldn't stop crying now. Because I knew, I knew he was right. From the moment I first saw him in the bank that wet, cold, cloudy day. I knew he was mine too.

All of a sudden I realised his power was no longer there, it hadn't been for a while. Perhaps he'd even pulled it back as soon as I challenged him. All I knew was I felt bereft, and then quickly the anger returned.

I took a step back and struggled to calm my breathing. Michel looked pained, as though he hated seeing me upset. *Well, get used to it, buddy.*

"What are we going to do about Max?" Business as usual, see? I can be professional.

"We strike before he has a chance to regroup."

Now we were talking.

It was only later that I realised that he had won this round. He hadn't answered my question of why Max hadn't found us at this house.

9

TRUCE

It didn't go exactly to plan. Michel had located where Max had retreated to, but when some of his vamps did a reconnaissance trip, to scope the place out, he had fled. Less than 48 hours after the battle Max had vanished.

More and more of Michel's vamp underlings came and went, keeping him abreast of what was happening in the city and throughout the country. At least that was one thing Michel could say, even though he was Master of a two-bit city in the south Pacific, far away from the big boys, he has actually got the whole country to himself. He doesn't have to share with another master controlled city.

You see, New Zealand's not that big. We've got about four million people, 30 million sheep and several hundred vamps. There's Taniwhas dotted here and there. Rick's Hapū aren't alone, but they don't mix well together. It's a natural instinct to fight. Top dog and all that. We've got an untold number of ghouls, but they stick to Auckland, they don't like open spaces for some reason, so travelling out of the city's a bit of a no-no for their kind.

Vamps can roam. There's a few down in Wellington and maybe even on the South Island, but they keep a very low profile. It's a lifestyle choice not to hunt in a city the size of Auckland or larger.

They've basically shunned their natural instincts. Not impossible, but it takes control. You don't usually find a rampaging vamp anywhere other than Auckland here. The ones that choose to live elsewhere are pretty tame.

So, it didn't take long for Michel's men to scour the country and come up empty-handed in their search for Max. He wasn't here; he'd left our shores to regroup. Just as Michel had feared.

We hadn't been quick enough.

Michel insisted that we stay at the holiday home while they searched. He had covered at the bank for me, having one of his vamps glaze my supervisor into believing I had a few days leave owing. I wasn't happy about that. I find glazing akin to assault. There's no defence of it, but I couldn't help thinking at least that was one thing I didn't have to worry about. Bad me. I couldn't stand the thought of losing my job, though, it was my lifeline to reality. The only thing that kept me sane.

Rumours on the *Iunctio* were concerning. There were indications that Max was garnering support overseas. Some very strong and powerful vampires were rallying to his cause. He had them believing that I was *his* and that Michel had usurped his position with me. I don't know what was more frightening, the fact that they believed him so readily, believed that I could *want* to be with that man, or the fact that they were older Master Vampires. Either option scared me.

After three days of looking at the view from the windows of Michel's holiday home, I'd had enough. I had never been very good at sitting still and just relaxing. My vacations have always been back on the farm, helping Mum and Dad with the sheep, fixing fences, feeding lambs. I don't do reclining by the pool with a magazine.

Besides, even though I couldn't feel the pull of my hunter instincts, I knew that didn't mean that there weren't any wayward vamps out there taking advantage of my absence from the city. I was just too far removed from the source to feel it here. The need to hunt was overwhelming.

Surprisingly, Michel did not fight me on it. We all returned to Auckland five days after the battle in Parnell. Nothing was said, but I didn't for a moment believe that Michel had lowered his guard and allowed me to walk away from him, back to my apartment and life, without leaving Bruno somewhere hidden in the shadows. I couldn't fight him on that one, but if Bruno stayed out of my way, then I'd stay quiet. For now.

Waiting on my doorstep was the familiar round of gifts. Flowers, cards, a basket with stuffed bunnies and chocolate cats. Must be a shapeshifter joke. I couldn't face the entire Hapū's affections right now. I needed to get physical. So, after the usual rounds of catch up housekeeping, I headed to the Gym.

Grabbing a backpack with my toiletries, change of clothes and my silver, I was set. After being taken at the bank in broad daylight, I wasn't risking it ever again. Silver would be with me 24/7 from now on; I'd learned my lesson. I headed toward the gym. If I were lucky, Rick would be there and spar with me for a bit.

Tony's Gym is in an old brick building, two stories high. Painted a lighter shade of grey with a red trim, it kind of looks like an old fire station from a distance. There's not much parking to speak of nearby, but I don't have a car anyway, so it doesn't bother me. Some of the other patrons grumble a bit about it though.

The kick boxing area is on the second floor, towards the back. Although an old building, it's all modern and refurbished inside. Air conditioning makes it pleasant in the heat of an Auckland summer. It wasn't hot out now, but not cold either. Usual Auckland temp.

I found Rick sparring with a client. I popped my gear away and donned my gloves. I watched their moves from the corner of my eye as I warmed up at one of the bags hanging a few feet away. It wasn't long before Rick had worn the poor guy out. He looked a newbie, all flailing arms and awkward kicks. Nothing landing where they should.

Finally, Rick let the guy go. I couldn't help smiling at the relief on the chap's face.

"Hey, Luce! Didn't know you were back."

I'd been in touch with Rick, of course, told him where I was and not to worry. The Hapū had heard about the battle in Parnell. Every supernatural being had been aware of the power force unleashed that day. Hence the gifts waiting on my doorstep.

"You up for a round, or did that guy wear you out?" I asked, a small smile playing on my lips. Shapeshifters, never wear out.

"Yeah right! Come on, let's see if you've gone soft on me."

Rick's been my kickboxing teacher ever since I came to Auckland. All shapeshifters tend to work in a physical role, or labour intensive environment. All that testosterone I suppose. He held back when we first met, but it didn't take him long to see I could keep up with the big boys. It was only when I'd passed all his "tests" in the ring, that he let me meet the Hapū. Even well behaved Taniwhas can be dangerous. He wanted to make sure I could fight if needed.

We quickly fell into an easy routine, in the quiet, yet echo sounding kick-boxing area of the Gym. I'd feint, he'd counter until finally, we started to connect. It felt good to land the first punch, followed swiftly by a semi-circular kick, but Rick was expecting it and jumped lithely out of the way. He rounded on me with an uppercut, but missed as I dodged and came back with a back kick. Got him good with that one.

It went on like that for a few minutes and then I really found my pace. By the time we finished our fifth three minute round, he was puffing and had marks all over his upper and lower body. His short, usually spiky, light brown hair was limp against his head and his T-Shirt clung to his muscles like glue. I'd slayed him. He looked a little surprised.

"What have you been eating, Luce? Man, you haven't fought like that before." He rubbed his jaw where I had landed a great flying-punch.

"I just needed to let loose a bit. Sorry if I got carried away," I offered as way of an explanation to his bemused and slightly shocked expression.

He looked at me a little strangely then and said, "I don't think that was it, Luce. You've never been that strong before. Honest, it's not my pride talking here, although that's taken a bit of a hit. Um, has something happened?"

When I looked at him with total confusion on my face, he went on. "You know, has Michel done something to you already?"

I felt my stomach drop. "He... he couldn't do anything without me knowing." I wasn't sure of that, but I had been clinging to it throughout my entire stay in Taupo. I still wasn't sure what exactly Michel was capable of. He may have let me get closer than any other human around, but he still held a few things close to his chest. I didn't, for a moment, think he wasn't capable of a shit load more supernatural things than he had been letting on. Michel was a consummate actor, sometimes I thought he was just playing me. I really hoped he hadn't been the past five days.

Rick could see the look of distress on my face, so didn't push it. "Yeah, well, just a thought that's all. You were pretty strong."

We got changed and had a coffee at the café downstairs. Neither of us mentioned it again, but it was festering in the back of my mind, my subconscious just wouldn't let it go. My life was changing all around me, and I couldn't stop thinking Michel was to blame.

Rick brought me up-to-date with all the happenings with the Hapū. He turned a little red in the cheeks when he told me he and Celeste had had an official date. Surprisingly, I was happy for him. Not a hint of jealousy. Great!

By the time I left him for his next class, I felt good. My muscles had had a good workout; I'd caught up with my best friend, and he was happy and content with his new girl. If only my life would sort itself out that easily.

The sun had started to set as I headed in the direction of my apartment. I'd made it perhaps a dozen steps when I felt it. That undeniable pull. Something evil was lurking in my city, and it was about to strike.

I shouldered my pack and started running in the direction of that force, like being pulled on a string, or by a magnet. I didn't need to see where I was going, just follow my instincts. It felt good to go at this speed, legs pumping and arms swinging. The desire to face what was there was so strong, so deep within, it felt as though it was just a part of my soul.

I shot down Nelson Street and out onto Customs Street. He was in Britomart, near the train station. As I got closer, I slowed to a jog. I realised, the nearer I got, that he wasn't just close to the train station, he was actually down on one of the platforms. Usually my pull will tell me what rough location the evil is at, but it is only when I get closer, that an exact image of where they are appears to me. I paused to stash my backpack in a locker and grabbed my silver, surreptitiously hiding my stake inside my shirt and my sheathed knife in the top of my jeans.

Humans were everywhere, end of the day, businesses closed, but bars opening up all over the CBD. It was a Friday too, so it was busy. *What was this vamp thinking?*

I casually walked towards the down escalator, checking around for any surprises. After seeing a human driver for the goons the other day, and how much Michel relies on Kathleen and Matthew, I wasn't naïve any more. It had never occurred to me that vampires would work so closely with humans. I mean I'd seen the groupies at *Sensations* and other vampire haunts. I knew they existed, but I could not for the life of me understand why they would assist the vampires. Even Kathleen and Matthew had puzzled me. They referred to Michel as *The Master*, like he was their master too. Yet he treated them as more than employees, open and not afraid to show how tired he was after the battle. He trusted them. I'd never witnessed a vamp lower their guard around humans like that before, especially one as powerful as Michel.

The evil vamp was on the outbound platform, a train had not long left, so still fifteen minutes before the next arrival. I'd better get a move on, though. He wasn't trying to hide from me. He was expending a little *Sanguis Vitam*, cloaking himself from humans across the tracks on the other platform, but that was all. He wanted me to find him. That scared me more than I wanted to admit.

I chose nonchalance as the best approach. Never let them see your fear. I walked casually towards him and his captive. A young guy, about 19 or 20, dressed for a good night out on the town. I didn't think he'd bargained for this kind of excitement. The vamp grinned, he might as well have been saying, *come here, little Hunter, come let's play*.

"What's up, deadbeat?" I asked conversationally.

His eyes flashed red. There was no other colour that I could see. Maybe black, but nothing remotely human. The red looked wickedly stark against his porcelain white skin. He didn't have a blemish on him. He would have been about 25, my age, when he was turned. Judging by his power signature he was about 100 now. Not young, but not old either. Handsome, with a haughty look to it. Slightly wavy dark brown hair, down past his shoulders. This vamp was a traditionalist.

"Hunter. You took your time." Not an unpleasant voice, but not the kind you want whispering sweet nothings in your ear, that's for sure.

"I was busy."

When he just smiled at me, just stared with those nasty red eyes and didn't say a word, I thought to hell with this. "So, you gonna eat that guy or what?"

He thought that was amusing. I'm glad someone was having fun. What the hell was going on here? He reeked evil, he had a human glazed in his arms and his fangs were down, but he was just standing there like we were having a conversation over the dinner table.

I withdrew my stake.

He growled at that. Oh goody.

"I have a message for you, Hunter."

"Well, I knew you weren't here just for the sights."

"The Master wants to offer a truce."

Oh, I got it, this was one of Max's slaves, sent to offer the hand of friendship. I didn't think so somehow.

"What? He couldn't be bothered visiting in person?"

"He thought it would attract too much attention."

No shit, Sherlock.

"He wanted you to have time to *digest* his offer without interference." The *digest* was said as though he was rolling a titbit of food around his mouth, savouring the taste. Yum.

"OK, so spill. What does Max want to offer?" It's not that I wanted to enter into a bargain or truce with Max, but this was taking too long. The platform had already started to fill up with a few people down by the escalators, and the next train would be here any minute. Party goers, ready for a night out on the town, would be pouring out in droves. I had to move this along.

"He asks for your hand in joining."

Man, this guy was a one sentence kind of dude. "Aaaand?" He wasn't telling me anything new, but I was sure there'd be more to it.

"If you come willingly, without any struggle or resistance, he will spare your city."

"Spare my city?" OK, we were making progress, but still, *come on already!* I mean a threat to my city was kind of to be expected. He wants me, Michel doesn't want to let me go, Michel owns this city. I could do the maths as well as any six-year-old.

"If you resist, he will unleash the *Jinn* on your people. Your city will not know Light ever again."

Wow. Two sentences.

The *Jinn* is another name for ghoul. It is believed that ghouls originated in the Middle East. Some people thought ghouls were devilish genies, but most of today's modern supernatural beings don't go for that. The term isn't often used nowadays, but now and then you meet an older vamp, and he just can't help himself. This vampire wasn't old, but his boss was. I was betting he was reciting his message word for word.

"Well, thanks for the offer. I'll take it under advisement." I shifted the stake in my hand. His eyes flashed on the movement.

"You would be a fool to refuse. My *Master* does not take no for an answer lightly."

"And I don't go for blackmail, so we're even. Now, let go of the kid, and let's get on with this."

For some reason, I didn't think he was betting on fighting me. I got the distinct impression he thought he'd deliver his message, grab a bite to go and head on home to Max. I'm betting Max knew this was a suicide mission from the get-go. You don't waste your best man on a message delivery service.

He dropped the young guy, who without any physical or eye contact from the vampire, or any long term command, scuttled away with an inborn natural urge to flee. Good for him.

I took a step forward. I wanted to get him off the platform, away from the crowd which would descend on us in all too short a time. There was a darker area off to the side. A maintenance corridor. That would do.

He stepped back at my approach. Go the big bad hunter, me! But quickly resigned himself to the situation. The mask back on, he flashed fang and crouched ready for battle.

"If you've got anything else to tell me, now would be the time. Wouldn't want to deliver only half of your master's message now would you."

He growled, a low guttural growl, like a big cat, or rabid dog. "You have 48 hours to comply. Two nights, on the third night he will return for you."

"See, that wasn't so hard, was it?" And I sprang forward and down, with my left-hand punching into his gut and my right following through with the stake. Of course, I may have been a bit faster in the ring with Rick than normal, but Rick's almost human. Taniwhas are tough and all, and have a bit of speed, but nothing compared to a vampire and this vampire was getting his mojo on now.

I suspect, his orders were *not* to kill me, but harm me? That, he could probably get away with and not meet the final death back home.

He slapped me away like an annoying fly. I sprawled out on the floor, spinning as I came to rest, nearly knocking over the maintenance trolley that was shielding us from other people's view. I didn't stay down for long, jumping back onto my feet in a swift motion. He sprang, but I had already moved managing a slash along his arm with the stake.

He grunted but controlled himself well. Not loud enough to attract attention yet, but I needed to end this. The less the average Norm knew about vampires, the better. My usual kills were in isolated places; alleys, junkyards, behind dumpsters where no one wanted to get too close to that smell. This was as public as I had ever got and it made my stomach churn. I did not want some old biddy or lost toddler to walk in on this.

He came at me low this time, his eyes a blaze of red, his power level trying to accumulate, but having little effect on me. I could hear the humming, but it wasn't touching me at all. I smiled at his grimaced face and leapt over the top of him in an acrobatic somersault. Play fighting with the Taniwhas had taught me to think outside of the box. Somersaults, flips, rollie-pollies, whatever it took, you used. As I passed over his back, I pushed the stake home.

Usually, it's easier to stake a vampire in the front, through the intercostal muscle between the fourth and fifth ribs. That's right above the heart and the most direct route to that organ. But, it's not impossible to have success through the back. The only thing you need to watch out for is the scapula. Depending on the positioning and angle, this can get in the way. Today, though, my luck held. I pierced the heart and felt the blade slide home.

My momentum took me further, so I had to let the stake go, but by the time I landed it was buried in dust.

I stayed still for a moment to catch my breath, then realised the humming hadn't stopped. My stake was still over a metre away, could I reach it in time?

I hadn't even moved a muscle when the source of the all that thrumming *Sanguis Vitam* came into view.

10
L'ESPERANCE

He sauntered along as though he owned the place. He probably did. At least he ran the city, from an undead point of view. Dressed in his usual near-black Armani suit, crisp white shirt and today, a burgundy tie. I preferred the blue; it looked better with his eyes, I wasn't gonna tell him, though. Michel just smiled at me, his lazy, sexy smile, as I stood and dusted myself off.

"My dear, that *did* look like fun."

"What are you doing here, Michel?" I bent down to pick up my stake, but I didn't miss the way his eyes followed my every movement. They looked particularly happy when I was leaning down waving the dust off my weapon. I stood upright again quickly.

"I was in the area; I thought I would say hello." He shrugged as he said that, somehow making the movement seem elegant and quite practised.

I laughed at that outright lie. "Since when do you slum it with the rest of us?"

"The rest of us, Lucinda? Could it be that you count yourself among my kind at last?"

I rolled my eyes and ignored the question. "Are you keeping an eye on me, Michel? Didn't trust Bruno?"

"On the contrary, my dear. I was merely in the area and heard all the fuss." He waved his hand around as he said *fuss*. A casual movement intended to look relaxed and at ease no doubt. It worked. I still didn't believe it though.

"You can cut the bull, Michel. We were hardly making a sound and his power level was practically non-existent."

He stilled and looked directly at me. "I can sense *you*, Lucinda. It was *you* I heard."

Oh. That was a little creepy, but anyhoo. "I don't need a bodyguard. I don't need you breathing down my neck."

"Are you sure about that?" he whispered into the silence between us and suddenly he was breathing down my neck, but not in any way I had intended. My body gave an involuntary shudder. "It could be quite enjoyable you know." His voice stroked my skin at the base of my head, like a molten liquid of pure bliss, it rolled over my neck and around my shoulders, then down my chest and threatened to go further. I stepped away and turned to face him, but was finding it hard to control my breathing.

"You promised no more mind control." My words were a little breathless, giving me away.

"I'm not using my powers, Lucinda." He looked at me, as though trying to convey a message, willing me to understand. Whatever it was, I didn't get it. Give it to me straight or don't even bother.

When I didn't move or say anything, he asked, " Have you eaten, my dear? Perhaps you would accompany me to dinner?"

OK, being invited to dine with a vampire is bit scary, even one you halfway trust, like I do Michel. "My dinner or your dinner?" I couldn't help it; I had to ask.

He laughed. "You are welcome to watch me feed, my dear, but I dare say you would not like it."

"I'd agree with you there."

"Oh, not for the reasons I suspect *you* have." Did I really want to know? I raised my eyebrows anyway. This uncontrolled body movement thing was going to get me into trouble.

"When we feed with willing donors, it can be a very pleasurable experience."

My cheeks flushed with heat at the way he said that, all sensual innuendo and more.

He smiled slightly at my discomfort and then straightened his features into a more serious look. "I would like to take you to dinner, Lucinda. Would you care to accompany me, please?"

Maybe it was the please, maybe I was just hungry, but before I could stop and think about it, I said yes.

L'Esperance is in Viaduct Quay, overlooking all the super yachts in the marina. It's strictly a table by appointment only kind of place. I could understand the appeal to Michel; this was a five-star restaurant and all, but the cutlery was usually pure silver. It didn't faze him in the slightest. He wasn't eating anyway and obviously did not fear any of the patrons picking up a butter knife to have a go.

I did feel a little out of place in my jeans and pale blue shirt, though, but I had luckily placed a cream cashmere jersey in my pack before leaving home, and that draped over my shoulders provided me with some sense of encouragement.

The waiters fussed over us as soon as we arrived. Whether they knew *what* Michel was, I couldn't say, but they definitely knew *who* Michel was. A table was quickly made available, much to the disgust of a couple trying to get in without a booking at the door and champagne was brought out as soon as we sat, without Michel even having to ask.

It was all a little overwhelming.

After giving my order; Hauraki Gulf Snapper, wakame, gnocchi, watercress, tua tua and mussels - I am quite capable of branching out from lamb when given the opportunity - I took a sip of my champagne, trying not to sneeze from the insistent bubbles against my nose and levelled my gaze on the unnaturally beautiful vampire opposite me.

"What's the occasion?"

"Can I not court you in the old fashioned way, Lucinda?

I scoffed at that. "Somehow I don't see you as the roses and chocolate kind of man."

"Would you like roses and chocolates? I can arrange it." He raised his hand slightly as if to call the attention of a waiter; I batted it back down. He just smiled.

"Are you going to tell me why you were at the station just now? Can you even admit that you're shadowing me, trying to protect me?" I asked.

"I had thought you might give me some credit for not intervening at all. You have no idea how hard it was for me to stand back and just watch. Enjoyable on so many levels, but difficult all the same."

"You watched the whole thing?"

"Practically, yes."

Well, that was an unusual sensation. I'd never really had an audience before. Part of me wanted to ask, *Did I do OK? How did I look? Bad ass?* But I mentally chided myself as soon as the thoughts entered my head.

"You are amazing when you fight." He said it with such respect, reverence even, it sent a little shiver down my spine.

"I don't need your protection, supervision, whatever you want to call it. I don't want it. It has to stop." When in doubt, just stick with what you're good at. Maybe after saying it a certain number of times the miraculous would happen and he'd comply. A girl can only dream.

Michel sat there looking at me, almost as still as a vampire could be. But he was in public, so I could still see his chest rise, the pulse at the base of his neck move. He was keeping up pretences even when he didn't want to. Finally, he moved to sip his champagne.

"I am sorry, Lucinda, but that is not possible." Before I could even voice my many objections to that statement, he went on. "I am what I am. The urge, the *desire*, to look after you, is deep within me. Please understand, this is unusual for me too. I am... not used to this kind of emotion. I am afraid, I do not quite know how to behave."

He actually looked abashed. Go figure. I shook my head slightly to clear the image from my mind. What was he saying? Could he not help feeling this way, was it really not a game he was playing? Part of me and I admit, it was a very loud, very noisy part, wanted to believe that. But I am a vampire hunter by birth, and I still couldn't find a way to completely trust this man in front of me.

"You could try to resist, Michel."

He simply looked at me, no emotion at all. Not a word. Not a blink.

OK, so that wasn't an option. But... "We can't continue like this. I will begin to resent you." Hell, I was borderline resenting him now, but I knew if this continued, this constant interference, constant checking up on me, I would begin to despise him. And really, if I was truthful with myself, he was too big a part of my life to let that happen.

Finally, he breathed and reached for his champagne glass. My meal arrived at that point, smelling and looking delicious, so he didn't say anything straight away, but once the waiter had left and I had started tasting bits and pieces off my picture perfect plate, he said, "It will get easier, my dear."

I swallowed a mouthful of succulent fish. "What do you mean?"

He leant forward. "If we were to join, the emotion, although remaining within me, will be easier to control."

"How so?"

"Well, you will then be mine of course."

"Is that suppose to clarify things for me?"

He sighed and looked decidedly grumpy as if this should all be abundantly clear to me already. "At the moment, you are only mine by desire, not by fact." He looked as though he really, *really*, did not want to disclose that little bit of information.

Oh, I got it. All that *you are mine, Lucinda* crap was just him *wishing* for it to be so.

He spoke unexpectedly then, as though he might as well keep going now that he'd admitted his deepest, darkest secret. His voice was low, so no one but I could hear. It surrounded me and bathed me in its warmth. "The alliance our races formed so long ago, provided for this urge to protect one's kindred Nosferatin prior to their maturity. It intensifies the closer your 25th birthday comes. It is a fail-safe, you could say. Designed to bring us together. Together, is how we are meant to be. That is why, of course, your death on failing to join with a vampyre is also necessary. There is a chance that you would not choose to do so otherwise." He looked at me ruefully then.

Well, that made sense. "But, why do we *have* to join?"

"And therein lies the rub, my dear. We may have parted ways all those many centuries ago, but we were once kin. The power that resides inside us comes from *both* of us. Separate, our powers weaken, together it re-establishes the true bond. Vampyre have been losing their powers for some time now, we have felt it, we knew it was inevitable, but your kind had disappeared. Abandoned the alliance, chosen to forgo their powers and their life, for their peace."

That was so sad; I felt my heart break at what my ancestors had chosen to do. The enormity of their decision astounded me. I suddenly lost all appetite for the sumptuous meal in front of me. How could I eat when my people had chosen death for their first born?

"Do you not feel your power increasing when around me, my dear?"

Huh. I had noticed that from the moment I saw Michel in the bank, I became stronger and quicker, not vampire quick of course, but definitely faster than I had ever been on the farm. And recently, that had intensified two-fold. Hadn't Rick mentioned how much stronger and faster I was in the ring after spending five days with Michel?

"We are meant to be together, Lucinda. Can you not feel it too?"

And you see, even though there was this enormous part of me that knew just how bad and evil and wrong vampires are, there was also a part of me that wanted with every being of my soul to make them better. If it couldn't be by culling those beyond reproach, then it was by standing by them and trying to influence them toward the light. Heck, my name even meant *Light*.

All my battles with Michel had been over his vampire ways and my insistence that he could do better. I saw the good in Michel, but it was also laced with bad. However, I knew beyond a doubt that he could fight that side of him given a chance. Was I the chance he needed? Did I even want to be?

I chose to not answer his question; it felt a little rhetorical anyway. Instead, I asked, "Is that why Max and his cohorts are trying so desperately to get me and my kind? Their powers are diminishing?"

"That is exactly why, my dear. The older the vampyre, the more powerful; the more powerful, the more they have to lose. Maximilian and those like him, are too powerful for their own good."

"Why were you able to beat him the other day?" I think I already knew the answer, but I wanted to hear him say it.

"I did *not* beat him, merely stalled for more time." For some reason, his use of the word *stall* triggered a memory in me, but I pushed it aside as he continued. "But I understand your meaning. My strength has been increasing, the more time I spend with you. It will reach its full potential when" - seeing the look of questioning on my face, he amended what he was about to say - "*if*, we join."

"Is that why you're spending time with me now?" I said it evenly, but it wasn't at all what I was feeling inside. Doubt. Confusion, a little more than usual. Despair.

He leant forward and took my hand, rubbing the back of it with his thumb as he always does. I didn't feel any power roll off him, but I felt that familiar sense of tingling and warmth, gradually making its way up my arm and down my body. How did he have such an effect on me?

"Not at all, *ma douce*." Maybe it was the French accent which crept in, the use of his intimate pet name for me, the name he only ever used in my dreams until recently, or maybe it was just my deep-seated longing for it to be so, that allowed me to believe him.

The waiter came at that point and removed my plate, Michel did not release his hold on my hand, but continued to stroke it softly. I couldn't face a dessert, all that sweetness when we were talking about such depths of horror that my world now contained. But, the night was still young and there was much to be achieved if we planned to face Max prepared in two day's time. And let's face it, I was *not* going to go willingly as he had requested.

Coffee, the perfect solution. I have never seen Michel drink coffee, only various types of wine. As a liquid, I understood that he could, I just thought perhaps he didn't like its taste, but he ordered one now, whether to keep me company, I didn't know, but I kind of liked it. Coffee is my elixir; all should enjoy it.

Of course, his selection was a long black, the traditional coffee choice for connoisseurs. Hell, for all I knew he probably was there when they discovered coffee beans in the forests of Ethiopia or some such place way back when.

When the coffee came, he didn't pop sugar in, just sipped it delicately, as is. Me? I opted for *sweetener* and stirred my frothy milk with abandon.

"So, my dear. What did our little friend want with you at the station?"

Ah, the true meaning behind our dinner date perhaps? He obviously hadn't been close enough to hear what old deadbeat had delivered; he was curious. Understandable.

I gave him a quick recap of the message and threat. Comply and go with Max willingly, or watch as he used ghouls to feast on my city.

You see, ghouls do feast. They're meat eaters. Actually, they could be called carnivores as it's all they eat, but ghouls prefer their meat as close to living as possible. Of course, they have *feasted* on human flesh on many occasion in the past, but in today's world, they usually behave themselves. The odd one might break into a morgue or such, but that's about as close as it gets. It doesn't stop them from pretending, though, and now and then a ghoul will scare a human, but the thing is, on the whole, they're a lot like you and me. They have jobs, communities. Hell, I've even had a ghoul taxi driver on an odd evening. When out and about, they tend to explain their dining preference as being on *The Atkins Diet*, most people just go with the flow.

But the real problem is, ghouls can be called by a vampire to do its bidding. They don't like it of course, but they have little choice in the matter. The fact that Max had threatened to use ghouls was a real concern.

Auckland has a thriving ghoul population, well thriving in the sense that there's at least fifty or more. That's a lot for ghouls, and even though it doesn't sound so intimidating, 50 ghouls could do a lot of damage in one night. They can be lethal.

Of course, I wasn't expecting Michel's response to this threat, I should have, but I'd lowered my guard, yet again. Stupid.

"Two can play at that game," he mused, a calculated look stealing over his features.

"Oh, no you don't, Michel! You cannot use ghouls to do your bidding." My voice must have risen, because I suddenly felt *Sanguis Vitam* electrifying the air around me, blocking any of what I said from those nearest our table. It hadn't really hurt, but it did feel like a slap in the face. On more than one level.

"Perhaps, we should continue this conversation elsewhere." He rose and came to offer his hand.

I stared at it for a moment, refusing to give into the blush that was threatening my cheeks and then simply ignored the offered hand and walked past him to the exit of the restaurant and into the night.

11
GUTS AND GLORY

A few minutes later he came through the front door and joined me on the sidewalk. I glared at him. He didn't apologise, I hadn't expected him to, hoped for, but not expected. He offered me his arm and said, "Shall we walk?"

It wasn't a request, but I gave him a good hard look before admitting we still had more to discuss. Pushing my anger and humiliation aside, I carefully laced my arm in his.

He felt hard and strong against my forearm; he pulled me a little closer, so we were shoulder to shoulder. I could feel the warmth of his body along the full length of mine. His hand stroked the back of mine as it was laced through his arm, his entire presence so near sent shockwaves down my side. I don't think I had ever voluntarily been this close to Michel before for any extended period of time. I fought the thought that it felt so good so hard, but I don't think I was winning.

We walked past all the crowds of people milling around the waterfront bars, past the upmarket stores and on down towards the ferry terminal and its ornately moulded concrete building.

Downtown was busy, as it usually is this time of night on a Friday. People laughing and shouting, walking arm and arm as we were. We blended in so well. No one would have suspected we weren't human. *Had I actually just thought that?*

We crossed the road at the intersection and headed up Queen Street, passing souvenir shops, late night fast food joints and closed businesses and banks on the way. Finally, Michel spoke. "He will use our ghouls against us, as well as those he brings to our shore. We can not allow that, my dear."

I knew what Michel was saying, but I still had to believe there was another way to combat Max. Lowering ourselves to his level was unacceptable. Michel being the vampire that he is, could not see that. I had to make him understand. The only way I could think that that may ever happen was to make him meet a ghoul in person.

You see, vampires may be able to control ghouls to do their bidding, but they have absolutely nothing to do with them ordinarily. They actually shy away from them and pretend they don't even exist. Sure they set rules in their master owned cities for *all* supernaturals, including of course ghouls, to adhere to, but they don't choose to get to know them. They consider them like dirt on the bottom of their shoes most of the time, and when needed, just a means to an end.

Ghouls, on the other hand, detest vampires with a bitter hatred. They welcome the anonymity the vampires give them and cherish the fact that most of the time they don't even register on a vampire's radar. I don't blame them, who would like the thought of a vampire having that sort of control over your actions and life should he choose. A bit like how I was feeling right now, so I could relate to their cause.

"I think you need to meet someone," I finally answered.

He turned his head slightly toward me and raised his eyebrows in a questioning manner. Me suggesting that he should meet someone had been unexpected, I think. I'd like to believe I could do that from time to time - surprise him.

"I have a friend who might be able to help us, but you have to promise to be on your best behaviour, Michel. And I mean Absolute. Best. Behaviour. Got it?"

He seemed intrigued at that, a small smile curving those full red lips, a little glint in his eyes, different shades of blue swirling in their depths.

"Of course, my dear, of course. Anything you say."

Why was I beginning to believe he was playing with me again?

Pete is one of my contacts. A vampire hunter has to have their ear to the ground occasionally, just to keep tabs on what's happening or potentially could be happening, in their city. Pete is my man. He's a ghoul, of course, and ghouls are particularly good at finding information. If they don't know what you're after, then they'll find out for you. Period. They have a reputation to uphold after all. But, their currency isn't cash. If you want info from a ghoul, you have to provide info back in return. And they'll only offer up info that warrants the level of info you have given them too. They like to consider themselves the gateway to knowledge in any given place. Pete was the head honcho of knowledge in Auckland City.

He runs a sports bar in Newmarket, just off Broadway, behind all the trendy fashion shops. It's called *Guts and Glory*. The Norms don't get the joke, but I kind of like it. Poetic, don't you think? He keeps it crisp and clean, who would have thought a ghoul with a hunger for raw meat would like a clean floor in his bar, but he does. Glasses sparkle, coasters abound. You *don't* want to start a food fight here. It would cost you an arm and a leg; literally. I don't think he'd have anything remotely like the champagne we just had with dinner; it's beer or beer all the way. If he really likes you, he'll spot you a pack of peanuts on the side.

The big flat screen plasma TV was playing a re-run of an All Blacks rugby game when we walked in. I couldn't tell who they were playing. Australia? South Africa? I always get those two mixed up. A few people were watching it, but most were just enjoying each other's company and ignoring the commentator altogether. The volume wasn't loud, just enough for those hardcore rugby fans at the front to be able to hear over the conversations throughout the pub.

Pete was in his element, behind the bar, cleaning glasses with a fluffy white cloth as he talked to a couple of guys at the counter. Ghouls. There were about six of them here throughout the room, all visibly stiffening when we entered. I was going to have to win Pete over quickly with my unexpected companion in tow.

"Luce. Long time no see. I see you brought a guest."

Pete doesn't beat about the bush. Ghouls are straight forward, no bull kind of guys. I guess that's why I like them. None of this innuendo crap and complicated games that I constantly get with the vamps.

He'd stopped cleaning and put both the fluffy white cloth and tall schooner glass down behind the counter, both his hands were resting on the counter top, balled in fists. OK.

"Hey, Pete. Good to see ya. Can I have my usual?"

"You can. Not him. I won't serve his kind in my bar."

"You do not have what I desire, *ghoul*," Michel practically growled.

I sighed, this was going to be tougher than I thought.

"Sit down, Michel," I said tugging him into the bar seat beside me. I was surprised he let me do it, so was Pete by the look on his face. Maybe Michel was trying to stick to his promise to be good after all.

"Pete, I guess you know Michel?"

Just a nod. Short, to the point. That's my boy.

"Michel, this is Pete. He runs the place and has his ear to the ground."

Michel slowly inclined his head, his eyes a slight purple colour in amongst the blue. Great.

The formalities over, Pete filled the schooner glass he had just been cleaning with some draught beer and pushed it across the bar top toward me. I like my lager pale. I took a sip quickly to calm my nerves.

Although ghouls are particularly straightforward creatures, it's best not to rush into things too quickly with them. They like to banter a bit, although I was picking Pete would be happy to forgo that ritual if it meant Michel would leave sooner. A vampire in his bar was probably not good for ghoul business.

"So, heard anything handy lately?"

He picked up another glass and started cleaning, never moving his eyes off Michel. "Things are heating up, but I'd guess you'd be aware of that, wouldn't you, Luce."

"What kind of things, Pete?"

"Now come on, Luce, you know the deal. Scratch my back, and I'll scratch yours."

Michel growled at that, low enough that only the three of us could hear over the noise in the bar. I put a hand on his sleeve to calm him, he immediately took hold of it with his other and started softly rubbing the back of it lightly with his thumb. Pete paused in his cleaning duty and stared at the motion. I fought a blush. Men.

Carefully removing my hand from Michel, who now wore a slight smirk, I used it to play with the condensation on the side of my schooner of beer as though it was the most important thing right then. Better to look busy, I guess.

OK, Pete didn't want to beat around the bush, so right to it then. "There's a war brewing, Pete and we need your help."

"Yeah. So you say. Give me something I can work with."

All right, so I had spent the entire trip over here in the taxi trying to formulate a plan, one that wouldn't put me in the centre of this scenario. But right now, I figured the truth was all Pete was going to go for. If I wanted him to trust me, and by extension the vamp that was feigning casual disinterest by glancing around the bar right now next to me, then I'd have to pull out the big guns. Unfortunately, the big guns were probably going to get me into more trouble than it was worth.

"It's over me."

He stopped looking at Michel then and turned his undivided attention on me.

"Why?"

Michel casually moved his arm to rest behind my shoulders, he didn't touch me as such, just left his hand on the top of my stool's back. I'm not sure if he was encouraging me, discouraging me, or just letting the world know *I was his*, but I'd started this, so I might as well finish it now too.

"A vamp named Maximilian wants me as his own, and he's threatened to use ghouls against the city if I don't comply."

Michel's arm abruptly left my chair. Oh, so I guess it was *discouraging me* then. Oops.

The thing is, I know Michel wanted that whole *using the ghouls* thing kept on the hush so that he could use the ghouls without their knowledge, but that was the reason for bringing him here. I did *not* want him to use the ghouls without their consent. I wanted to find a way to get them on board willingly, and Michel needed to be here to agree to it.

"Why does he want you, Luce?"

Now two can play at the bartering information thing; I certainly wasn't going to offer up anything else if I could help it, without first getting something to go on from Pete. I wasn't new to this game after all.

"No. Your turn. What have you heard?"

He smiled an appreciative smile. I think the ghouls don't like their informational sources to be pushovers. Always do business with people you respect.

"There's a bunch of ghouls in Sydney on the move. Unheard of really, that's why it got my man's attention. Couldn't find out what they were up to, but the intention seemed clear. They're on the hunt, and it's not in their own backyard."

"How many?"

He was obviously in a generous mood or my information was worth more than I had thought, because he answered straight away, "One hundred, maybe more."

Shit. One hundred ghouls were practically a dozen legions of soldiers; SAS, Green Beret, Navy Seals, combined. This was *not* good news, and I felt, rather than saw, Michel stiffen ever so slightly at it.

"That's big. You think they're coming here?" I asked Pete.

"What do you think, Luce? You tell me, would your Maximilian go for Aussie *Jinn*?"

"He's not my Maximilian," I answered automatically. "And yes, he would."

"Then, you've got a big problem, haven't you? And that observation was on the house. You want anything else, pay."

So, the moment of truth. I took a deep breath and jumped right in. "We want your help to fight them. We're asking for your help." I hoped he got the inference, *asking* not commanding.

He did. Nothing gets past Pete. His eyebrows raised and he returned his attention to Michel. "So, vamp. You asking?"

Now, here's where I actually held my breath, because as much as I wanted Michel to understand the right thing to do here was to get permission, consent, whatever, I also knew he was a vampire and vampires by nature don't ask, they take.

He smiled, a brilliant flash of teeth with an ever so small hint of fangs. God, typical. "It would seem my Lucinda is trying to tame me." I didn't miss the *my Lucinda* part, but I still wasn't breathing, so I let it pass, for now. He turned and looked at me, blue swirls lighting up his face, I could so easily have melted into them. His hand reached out and stroked my cheek, the backs of his fingers gliding down my left side, sending tingles through my entire body and causing an involuntary shiver. I froze. Even if I hadn't already been holding my breath, I would have stopped right then and there. He inclined his head to me in a small nod of acquiescence, not breaking eye contact and said, "I ask for your help, ghoul."

I let my breath out, trying not to show the relief and joy at what he had said. This was more than just being on *absolute best behaviour*; this was Michel letting me know he could meet me halfway. In some things, he could agree to do the right thing. When I asked, he might just move a little closer to the light.

Pete was staring at us with his mouth slightly open, not blinking; I'm not even sure he was breathing. He pulled himself together when Michel returned his attention to him across the bar.

"How can I trust you?"

"You would have my word, however," I cringed slightly, " it would require a certain amount of my influence over you to be allowed, so that you are not used by Maximilian against us. My influence would mean he could not sway you at all."

"No." Emphatic, implacable, no.

My heart felt crushed. To come so far and be halted now by the brick wall of mistrust was not going to happen. "What would it take, Pete, for you to trust him?"

He swallowed, this was probably the one opportunity that he had never been presented with, but had always craved. The chance to negotiate with the vamps on equal footing. To have something worthy of negotiating at all. I could almost see the cogs turning in his mind.

"We would want an accord. Permanently giving us freedom from your influence and those of vampires in your city, under your control."

I knew Pete was asking a lot, but I also knew with my whole heart that he wouldn't settle for anything less. The problem was, Michel didn't have to do this. He didn't have to show his *nice* side and then also give the ghouls a free run for as long as he remained master of this city. He could simply compel them to do his bidding now and save himself the grief of not having them when needed in the future. I had absolutely no idea how this would play out. I was asking a lot of him and I didn't know yet if I was worth *that* much to him to warrant it.

Michel didn't hesitate for long, he simply raised his arm and a stainless steel knife, which had been sitting on the counter behind Pete, came sailing to his hand. He quickly sliced the centre of his palm. He wasn't threatening Pete; he actually agreed to his request. An accord in the supernatural world is made through sharing blood. A slice in one palm, another in the opposing accord member's palm, then a simple handshake. There's just something binding about vamp's, shapeshifter's and ghoul's blood; the accord can't be broken. I guess I can also count my blood in with that category now too.

The knife didn't surprise me, I've seen Michel use his telekinesis before, but his relatively quick agreement to the accord sure did. He must have noticed the look on my face because he leant in and said so softly only I could hear, "You do not think I had not seen this coming, do you, *ma douce?*"

He stood then and reached his hand across the counter top towards Pete. Pete hesitated, still baffled by the turn of events, then reached forward and took up the knife, sliced his own hand and clasped Michel's. Michel spoke his side of the accord, "I will ensure all ghouls who reside in my city shall be free from influence from me and mine, for as long as I am Master of this City." Pete replied. "I will ensure all ghouls aid in this coming battle with the vampire Maximilian and allow influence from the Master of this City to prevent intrusion from any other vampire on our will."

It was done. I felt a wreck. The roller coaster of emotions from watching this unfold had exhausted me, but we were one step closer to meeting Max with what could be success.

We left the bar not long after that. They may have just made an unprecedented accord, but Michel was still not welcome in the ghoul's bar without unease. I thanked Pete, paid for my beer - no way I was letting Michel jump on that one - and we walked out into the early morning darkness.

It was now 3 am, and I was bone weary. I needed to get some sleep because I had a plan for tomorrow and wanted to be at full function to carry it out. Michel hailed a cab, and as one slid to a stop at the kerb, he stiffened slightly and turned his head to the side. His eyes blazed purple and then he straightened.

"Forgive me, my dear, but I have matters I must attend. I must part with you here, but it has been a most *eventful* evening. I thank you whole-heartedly."

His eyes sparkled, and he reached for my hand, bending to place a kiss on the back. With that, he was gone. I didn't even see which direction he had flashed away to, it was as though he had evaporated into thin air.

The spot he had kissed on the back of my hand, however, glowed with warmth and the tingles it had sent through my arm and into my body didn't stop until I was tucked up in bed and had fallen fast asleep.

12
PROMISES KEPT

I woke with a groan and rolled over into a spot of sunlight that was filtering through almost closed blinds onto my bed. Glancing at the bedside clock, I realised I'd had about six hours sleep, not enough, but there was no way I could have returned to my slumbering now.

I lay there for a while trying to determine what it was I was feeling. Anxious? Uptight? Angry? All of the above, but underlining it was a sense of disappointment, Michel had not visited me in my dreams. I sighed and pushed that thought aside as I hauled myself out of bed and stumbled towards the bathroom.

Half an hour later I was dressed and sitting at my kitchen bench hugging a hot cup of coffee. I couldn't stomach breakfast, only one more night until Max returned, but coffee I could never forgo. The usual Saturday morning noises were filtering through the walls and windows of my apartment. Mrs Cumberland, my next door neighbour, was calling to her four cats to come in for breakfast and Sally from upstairs was hanging out her washing on the clothesline in the back yard. I could see her through the kitchen window struggling with her sheets, as a soft winter wind kept whisking them around.

I felt infinitely sad all of a sudden. These were people I barely knew, just enough to say hello and share a word or two with, or in the case of Mrs Cumberland, occasionally feed her cats when she was away from home visiting her daughter in Whangarei. Yet all of them meant something to me, and I could be about to bring down the wrath of a powerful vampire into their midst. The only thing I could think of doing was telling them to stay home on Sunday night, convincing them to stay indoors. Michel's protection on our building would hold, but only as long as he was alive.

After washing out my mug and putting it away, I slipped into my grey leather boots. I sold my soul for these boots; I love them like they were my babies and grabbed my stake and knife. I slipped the knife into my short black skirt and the stake inside my faded denim jacket. I liked winter; Auckland can be a melting hot pot of humid air most of the year, but summer was most insufferable, meaning concealing a stake was damn near impossible. But in winter you could get away with a jacket, sometimes anyway and hide your weapon inside. It was a bit colder today, so I was wearing black tights under my mini skirt, but a short sleeved black tee on top. The thing is, even though I'm a kick-ass vampire hunter and all, wearing jeans or pants is just not my style. I far prefer skirts, it's just who I am, but they do have to be short and allow for movement, hence the tights. No one wants to be flashed by a 5'4" ball of fury.

I knocked on Mrs Cumberland's ranch-slider and watched as she plopped Fluffy, or was it Snowball, down to shuffle over to me. Mrs Cumberland and I have a deal, I look after her cats when she goes off gallivanting around the country, almost twice a month I'll have you know, and she lets me borrow her car. Borrowing someone's car is a big responsibility, they've got a lot invested in that one possession, but Mrs Cumberland is a sweetie, and she's never once given me a speech about taking care not to scratch the *Corolla*.

"Morning, Mrs Cumberland. How are you today?"

"Fighting fit, Lucinda, fighting fit. What have you got planned today, dear, do you need the car to visit that young man of yours?" As sweet as Mrs Cumberland is, she refuses to acknowledge my denials that Rick is *not* my boyfriend. She took one look at his lithe body and muscular frame and fell in love. No one else would be good enough for me in her eyes. So, I gave up correcting her after about the twentieth time; it just wasn't worth the effort.

"Yeah, I'm off visiting. Do you need the car today or is it OK if I borrow it?"

"Not a problem, dear, I'll grab the keys." When she returned with them in her arthritic old hands and handed them over, she said, "You give that man of yours a big kiss. He's a keeper, Lucinda, a keeper."

I just laughed and thanked her and made my way to her dark blue car at the front of the building. There's just no reasoning with the old lady.

I always like the drive out to the Hapū's land. The North-Western Motorway had started to get busy, lots of cars exiting at St Luke's, there's good shopping there. But once past that off-ramp it was free flowing and with the radio up it didn't feel like much time had passed until I was turning off on Brigham Creek Road and winding my way through Whenuapai to Rick's.

The sun was higher in the sky when I pulled up in the clearing of the main group of houses. I couldn't see anyone, but that didn't mean they weren't around. I switched the engine off and listened to the tick, tick of the cooling motor for a moment, glancing around the area. I knew, even before I had shut the door to the car, that I was in trouble. There wasn't any sound, shapeshifters can move silently if they wish, but I had just felt the prickle of hairs rising on the back of my neck when he pounced.

I went flying through the air but managed to twist my body, so I landed in a half crouch, and then I spun to meet my attacker. Josh was a blur of motion as he came at me in a low movement, wrapping his arms around me and rolling me over in the nearby grass. We tumbled for a couple of feet and then with a quick elbow to the ribs, I managed to jump out of his grasp and spin around to place a nice kick towards his torso. He was too fast and grabbed my foot pulling me towards him. I twisted my body and with the momentum that created, used my other leg to counter his grip. I heard him grunt as my foot found his chest and he let me go.

See, the thing with Taniwhas is, they play fight when showing affection. I knew Josh wasn't trying to hurt me; he was showing how pleased he was to see me, but they do fight for the win. It might be love of a kind, but it's going to leave bruises.

He was already standing and ready for attack, but I didn't give him time. My strength and speed had increased recently, with all the time spent with Michel, and Josh hadn't seen me for a while, so the look of surprise on his face was priceless when I sprang at him and pinned him to the ground. I held him down with my forearm across his throat and my legs pinning his arms to his sides. He tried to buck, but I was too strong for him. I grabbed his thick brown hair, securing his head to the ground and leant my face down to his ear and whispered, "You're out of your league, sunshine." Then growled. Not a vampire growl, but an intimidating sound nonetheless.

His eyes bugged out a bit at that, his breathing rapid and a little uneven. We stared at each other for a full minute before we heard the slow clapping from a crowd that had come out to watch the action. The twins were hooting and shouting obscenities to Josh, all about his lack of masculine abilities and he reddened slightly.

I thought that might be my cue to get off, so I jumped up in one swift motion and held my hand out to him as he lay in the dirt. He paused, a brief look of uncertainty crossing his face, one I was a little saddened to see and then grabbed my hand and came to stand in front of me. Awkwardly, he gave me a soft punch to the shoulder and said, "Good to see ya, Luce, long time no see."

Joe and Rocky came bounding over at that point and grabbed me in a bear hug, or is that Taniwha hug? They jumped up and down, shaking me in their grip like a rag doll. "Hey, quit it would you!" I shouted, but there was a smile on my face.

Rick came running over from his house and clasped me too; it was one big hug-fest. It's great to be loved. I glanced up over Rick's shoulder and spotted Jerome. He had a strange look on his face, contemplative, but when he noticed me looking at him, he just smiled and waved and went back to chopping some firewood by the shed.

After everyone had calmed down and gone back to whatever they were doing before they heard my car and scampered into hiding, Rick and I sat on the swing seat over by Celeste's. She was out at the moment, but due back soon, he said. He got a wistful look on his face when he mentioned her; I grinned at that.

I always thought that I wouldn't want to share Rick. He's my best friend, we do everything together, but my life has become so complicated lately, that I haven't wanted him to be pulled into the whirlpool that is devouring my world. Seeing him a little removed, in bliss with Celeste, someone I had a lot of respect for, had me surprisingly relieved. Who would have thought I could be so magnanimous?

We spent the next hour catching up, but my mind was elsewhere, and he could tell. My stomach had started churning over what I was about to do, and my concentration on the conversation had been waning.

"Luce? Luce? Are you even listening?" He didn't say it angrily, but more with concern, his eyes crinkled in worry at the edges.

I sighed. "Sorry, Rick, I'm just a bit wound up over everything right now, and I really need to talk to, um, Jerome, OK?"

He nodded, his eyebrows furrowed in query. For the first time ever, I didn't want to spill my guts to him. I needed to get this over with Jerome and talking about it with Rick was likely to get me sidetracked to the point of not completing the real reason why I came out here at all. I hugged him and stood up, brushing myself down, my usual calming move before facing a daunting prospect.

It's not that I am afraid of Jerome, not really; he is a little rough around the edges, but he's only ever been a gentleman to me. Welcoming me on Hapū lands, greeting me with respect and open friendship, but what I was about to ask of him was a lot. And a big part of me so did *not* want this to happen, but I saw no alternative. People's lives were on the line. My city was threatened.

Rick watched me walk over to Jerome, who had stopped chopping wood to wipe his brow with the hem of his checked shirt and take a swig of water from a bottle. Even in winter here in Auckland, you can work up a sweat in no time.

Jerome nodded in greeting as I approached and screwed the lid back on his bottle, placing it to the side on a stump of wood he used as a table. He looked at me, as though he was assessing me, but didn't really smile. There was sadness in his eyes I hadn't seen before. Was everyone as down as me right now?

"Hi, Jerome," I said quietly. For some reason my voice and courage seemed to be failing me, he picked up on it and smiled reassuringly.

"Hey, Luce. Come and have a seat." He indicated a couple of deck chairs out on their own under a gnarled old Rimu tree.

The chairs creaked as we both sat down and the wind swirled a few of the tree's needles at our feet around in mini tornadoes, then abated.

Neither of us said anything, to begin with, content on watching the younger *mokopuna* play fighting in the distance. He could obviously sense my reluctance to start the conversation, so he took the lead, bless him.

"I knew it wouldn't be long until you came to me. I've felt the change for some time now."

I looked at him then, unsure of what he was saying, but aware his choice of words mirrored mine. I had been feeling like everything had been changing too.

"Lucinda. It has been a long time since my kind has had anything to do with yours, but we have not forgotten our *kupu taurangi*, our promise to you."

"You said the other night at the *Hangi*, that the Taniwhas would fight along my kind's side, should we ever ask?"

"We would be proud to serve."

I wrung my hands together. "What I'm asking is dangerous, Jerome. Some of your people may get hurt," - I swallowed - "killed even." My voice barely a whisper, but he heard.

"We have always known this time would come. We have been lucky, Luce, to have had so long to thrive and grow unhindered, but from a young age, our *mokopuna* are made aware of our pact with your kind. They have been schooled from birth to be ready. You need not worry that we cannot, or will not, heed your call. This is what we have lived for. The chance to return the favour your kind did us so long ago."

I looked into his dark brown eyes and saw he meant it. Unflinchingly. "How did you know it would be soon."

He laughed out loud at that. "From the moment Rick brought you to us. If the *Kaitiaki* had returned, then our time was due. Besides, your powers have been growing stronger and stronger, most noticeably so today."

Huh. Even the Taniwhas had been able to see it. I guess it was all the time I spent here. Jerome didn't miss much, being the Alpha of the Hapū. I had always thought he was a little removed, though, polite and welcoming, but never having more than a few words to say to me and never being in my company for long. I guess he'd been watching from the sidelines, though. That's a shapeshifter thing. They hunker down in the undergrowth and watch.

"So, when do you need us?" he asked softly.

"Tomorrow night, in the city. The vampire we fight wants me, and he's going to use any method possible to succeed. He has 100 ghouls from Australia and an untold number of vampire. Michel has made an accord with our ghouls, and here I am, asking you to honour ours." I smiled ruefully, and Jerome reached out and took my hand. His hands were rough and calloused, not the smooth fine hands of Michel. These were working hands, unafraid of getting dirty, but they were reassuring all the same. "We will be there."

I wasn't sure where "there" would be, but it was a safe bet it would happen in and around the CBD. I didn't think Maximilian would fly in, Ghouls don't do aeroplanes, it was more likely they would come ashore at the docks or wharves downtown and head up towards K Road. That's the centre of vampire business in Auckland, Vampire Central and that's where Max would expect to find Michel and me.

I looked out across the expanse of lawn and gravel area where my car was parked and noticed Celeste was back, sitting on the swing seat with Rick. My heart ached at the thought that these fine, strong, but caring people, could get hurt because of me. All of this was because of me and it killed me slowly inside to know it.

"We are strong, Lucinda," Jerome said, almost reading my mind, as he stood from the chair. "We will be all right."

Somehow, I wasn't so sure.

I bade everyone farewell then. Jerome wanted to call a Hapū meeting and get everyone prepared. I didn't want to be there when they heard the news, see the looks on their faces as they learnt of what

I had asked them to do. Cowardly, I know, but I needed to protect my heart from any more damage than it was already receiving in droves.

I headed back to the city in silence. I couldn't face music; there was too much static in my mind. I was just pushing open the front door of my apartment, after returning the keys to Mrs Cumberland and making her promise to stay indoors tomorrow night, when I felt it.

A vampire had been in my home.

13
WHAT A BITCH

He hadn't tried to hide his signature, on the contrary, the *Sanguis Vitam* reached out and grabbed me, wrapping tendrils of his scent along my arms, neck, body and legs. Power tingled over my skin in a caress, the scent intoxicating, enveloping me in a molten lava of bliss. I took an involuntary step inside.

If I didn't know better, I'd have thought Michel was marking his territory like some determined and possessive dog. His power and scent were everywhere. I glanced towards my bedroom; nothing seemed disturbed, but I was guessing the power signature had not left my bed alone. Over on the dining room table was an enormous bouquet of flowers. Bright orange roses, more than a dozen. He knew my favourite colour, and from teenage years, I knew what orange roses meant: Desire. The flowers filled the room with a further scent, slightly fruity and deeply floral. The colour sprang around the room, lifting my cream on cream interior and making a glow extend across the lounge.

Michel never did things by half. I sighed and tried to push that distracting scent and sense of power aside, pulling up any shields I could muster to block those feelings evoked out. I stomped over to the table and snatched up the folded note resting in amongst the blooms.

The writing inside was in a flowing and neat style, slightly old world. No one alive today would have this type of penmanship.

If you are not too busy, ma douce,
 I would delight in your company tonight.

The note was on *Sensations* letterhead. I guess I was being summoned. I had to admit, reluctantly, though, that this beat Shane Smith as a message delivery service any day. Michel was improving.

I'd spent the better part of the day at Whenuapai with the Hapū, but there was still another hour or so before sunset, so I freshened up and grabbed a bite to eat. Even with a churning stomach, you get hungry sooner or later if left long enough. And I really wasn't sure if I'd make it back home 'til the wee hours tonight, there was going to be a lot of preparation going on, I didn't doubt it.

Once I was all satisfied, I checked my pockets. I grabbed a second stake from the case under my bed, tonight just felt like a second stake kind of night, and headed out the door. Still plenty of time to take a leisurely walk towards *Sensations* and be there in time for vampire start of business day.

It's not that I was overly eager to come running on Michel's command, I was just practical. Delaying it would only frustrate him, and although we had come a long way from the good old days, Michel was still not one to be left waiting. I wasn't sure my new status as *my Lucinda* would grant me much protection on that.

Surprisingly, Shane Smith was bouncing on the door when I walked up. No queue at this time of night, people would be freely able to get inside, but Shane is not your bouncer type of physique. He's a little skinny on it and most definitely doesn't have the snarl. So he looked more than a little out of place.

He smiled openly when he saw me walk over. *Oh, Shane, when would you ever grow up and be a big vampire?* I smiled in return, though, you just can't help it with this guy, he's so sweet.

"Good evening, Luce. The Master's waiting inside." I didn't really need to know that, but Shane was trying to be professional and competent in his new role as doorman.

"Thanks, Shane, have a great night," I said as I walked past into the darker lighting of the club. The room was about quarter full, even the vampire groupies don't turn up 'til later, so it was a small crowd of local daytime Saturday business owners checking out Happy Hour at the club.

There was another vamp on the door to the private area out the back. Dillon Malone was of Irish descent and a regular in Michel's group. About 200 years old and reeking power. Other than Shane Smith, Michel's vampires were usually impressive on the scale of vampire power. I'd seen him around but not had much to do with him; he was more of a satellite in the Durand power structure. I was guessing Michel had called all of his vampire *protégé* close right now. There'd be more vamps in the CBD than normal this weekend, all of them out to protect Michel to the end.

He inclined his head and opened the door without a word. I was expected, so it wasn't a surprise. But the wall of foreign *Sanguis Vitam* that greeted me in the hallway to Michel's office was, and it was not at all friendly.

I swallowed hard and pushed against the barrier the power had made, it whipped around me, making my hair lift off my shoulders and my short skirt fly up in a sad attempt at imitating Marilyn Monroe. It started nipping at my sides, my arms, my legs and I felt myself hunch over to protect my stomach and chest.

It was unrelenting and continued for a good five minutes before I heard Michel's soft, but firm voice say, *"Che è abbastanza, Alessandra. Avete fatto il vostro punto."*

It didn't stop straight away, but lingered in a caress that left my nerve endings screaming for release, sharp and brutal in its pursuit of a response. When it finally abated, I almost stumbled to the floor. *What the fuck?*

I took a few deep breaths in and straightened up, brushing my skirt back down and trying to flatten my now tangled and birds-nest of a hairdo. Great, I looked like I'd just rolled in a haystack on the farm. And not in a good way.

All right, so I was warned. Whoever, or whatever, was in the office with Michel wasn't playing nice. But there was also more than one power signature there, so my heartbeat did rise just a little at the thought of facing more than one of that powerful and unforgiving force. I braced myself and put on my best vampire hunter smirk as I walked through the door.

Michel was sitting in his chair behind his desk, in his usual dark suit, white shirt and this evening, midnight blue tie - had he picked up on the look I gave the burgundy one? He looked relaxed and at ease, actually quite comfortable, but that may have had something to do with the tall, blonde female vampire resting on the arm of his chair and draped sinfully over his shoulders.

She was stunning. Her hair was a long golden mass of softly wavy tresses, reaching passed her waist and bouncing slightly as she cocked her head at me. She was wearing a blood red slinky dress, which moulded to her gorgeous figure like a second skin. The hem of the dress was well up past her knees, exposing a large amount of deep cream porcelain skin on her perfectly smooth thighs. She had on matching red high heels, dangerous in their three-inch glory and was softly running her hands through Michel's hair.

I felt like a child in comparison.

I hated her at once.

To the right stood another vampire, male, cream-coffee coloured skin, deep dark brown almost black eyes and long black hair, tied in a clasp at the nape of his neck. He was leaning nonchalantly back against a bookshelf, in tight black jeans and a black tee-shirt. All of which did a wonderful job of showing off his muscular and graceful physique. He wasn't smiling but he was watching me with an intensity that reached my core.

On the far left, sitting in an armchair, was another male vampire. This one had a shock of red hair, but was dressed much the same as old black jeans, his hair tied back, his rugged, but somehow handsome, face open in a smile. I didn't trust it. I didn't trust any of them, the power that rolled off them toward me was almost suffocating. It took every ounce of my anti-vampire Nosferatin skills to stand up straight and not blanch at the waves of *Sanguis Vitam* against my body.

All right then.

Never let it be said that I can't hold my own with the big baddies of the night. No self-respecting vampire hunter would let a bunch of the undead threaten them, at least they wouldn't dare show any fear on the outside. I was damn sure these fangers weren't going to get the better of me. I was angry at Michel, angry at him for letting me walk into this ambush, so I grabbed that anger and wrapped it around me like a shield. The moment I did, I felt a deep-seated sense of strength inside me build into a crescendo and suddenly felt my own power lash back out at the vampires in the room, Michel not excepted.

The two male vampires stiffened visibly, old slinky bitch gasped, then re-schooled her features into a sneer. Michel didn't move a muscle, despite my knowing he had felt it too.

"She has claws, *caro mio*," the female vamp purred in Michel's ears.

Michel didn't say a word in reply. He was looking at me coolly, no softening of emotion showing in his face. It was almost as though my Michel had gone away somewhere and left an imposter in his place. I felt a deep ache in my heart at that, then I mentally straightened my shoulders and glared back at him.

The vampire on the right, all golden coffee coloured skin and deeply delicious eyes came forward and reached out to shake my hand. No fast movements, mustn't scare the powerful and angry vampire hunter. "I am Enrique, *Señorita* Monk. It is a pleasure to meet such a fine Nosferatin." He said it like Michel does, lengthening the end, with a strong Spanish accent and also with a subtle cloak of power. He was looking for a response; he got it.

My stake was in my hand and heading towards his chest before I had even realised it. Michel just smiled, the red-haired vampire whipped the stake away, and Enrique took a casual step back. It took a mere split second for all of that to unfold; I hadn't even got a breath in. No one had touched me at all. No one looked like they wanted to.

"Intriguing," the redhead said as he flipped the stake over in the handkerchief in his hands, he had a soft Scottish lilt. "I don't think I'll try that trick. Enrique, you have more courage than sense."

"It is appalling," old slinky slut spat. "How dare she?" She was still wrapped over Michel's chair, but she had stiffened and did not look happy. No change there then.

I wasn't going to apologise, but I felt I had to stand up to this group or it would head south pretty quickly. "I'll make a deal with you all. You knock off the power, and I won't stake you."

Enrique laughed, old redhead decided to join him. "I like her, Michel; she has spunk."

"Indeed," said the Scot.

The *Sanguis Vitam* in the room abated, all except slinky. The men returned to their previous places, redhead delicately placing my stake on the far side of him, away from me. I wouldn't be able to reach it without first going through him, but I did have another in my jacket. So I just smiled.

"Lucinda. You have been introduced to Enrique; this is Jock." Michel indicated the red-headed Scot, who inclined his head with a respectful nod. "And Alessandra." He reached up and stroked her arm not taking his eyes off me. She sniffed delicately in acknowledgement of the introduction, but only glared at me. I returned it with equal vehemence. "They have agreed to fight alongside us, with their own."

What it would have taken for Michel to strike a bargain with three other level one master vampires such as these, I did not know. But I was sure it would have been an expensive exchange, one that he would no doubt have cause to regret in the future if he survived. Michel knew he was not strong enough to take Max and his cohorts on alone; he needed support, and it needed to be fierce. I didn't doubt that those in the room weren't up to the task. But part of me was also deeply scared that they were here at all, and in the case of Alessandra, a little threatened as well.

"So, we have met her. Now let us continue in our talks." The woman practically purred as she stroked Michel's arm with one hand and waved a dismissive hand in my direction with the other. "She does not need to remain."

I simply walked over to the only other empty armchair in the room and plonked myself down with a thump, not very ladylike I know, but I was making a point. "I think I'll stay thanks."

She glared at Michel and me petted her arm. "It is for the best, Alessandra, that she remain. She is integral to our plans, after all."

Michel's petting wasn't having the desired effect as she bristled and her power level rose, swooshing out towards me, making it hard to breathe. I blocked it, as best as I could and through gritted teeth said, "Knock it off, bitch and let's talk business."

OK, so it was probably not the wisest thing to say to the most powerful female vampire I had ever met, one who obviously had a thing for Michel and did *not* like me stepping in on her territory, but I had just about had as much of this woman as I could take and anyway, time was of the essence and all.

"I think the young hunter is right, Alessandra," Enrique piped up. "Perhaps a little foolhardy, but surely you can understand her lack of diplomacy is due to age."

Great, back to feeling like a child again. Thanks.

Alessandra just flashed her long delicate fangs at me and returned her attention to Michel. She knew it wouldn't scare me; I'd seen too many to make me even blink, but it was a reminder of who she was and that I shouldn't forget it. As if.

Jock cleared his throat, I don't think he really needed to, it was more a habit than anything else and said, "So. We're quite certain they will approach from the docks and proceed towards us here, is that right?"

"Yes, my informant is quite solid on that," Enrique said. "I think we can trust him. Maximilian has a vessel 50 miles off the coast, in deep waters, waiting to enter when the deadline to his request has been reached. It won't be doing the ghouls much good, all that motion on a rolling boat, but they will recover quickly once they reach land."

You see, even though Maximilian is an evil bastard I wouldn't trust as far as I could throw him, he had given me 48 hours and he would abide by that, or as close to it as he could. We may not have had an accord, a blood binding agreement, but a vampire is, among other things, true to his word, when a challenge has been set. It's something so deeply within them, from centuries of having to survive against mankind's pursuit of them. Without a strong sense of morals, albeit deeply cruel and sadistic morals, at times, they would not have been able to survive. Wiped out before the Reformation no doubt.

Jock continued to summarise the plan for tomorrow. "They will be met by your ghouls, Michel, at the wharf?"

"Yes. I will also have some of my own nearby to relay information on their progress to us. They are outnumbered, but they will delay their march into the city as best they can."

"Where will *we* meet them?" Enrique this time.

"Here. We can contain them quite well within this building, minimise their spread throughout the city."

"It is not the city that you should concern yourself with, *caro mio*. Protecting innocents is a waste of your time."

Why didn't it surprise me that the bitch would be old school? Michel simply inclined his head and replied in an even tone, "It *is* my city, *dolce*."

She smiled a sickly sweet smile and continued to stroke his hair. "As you wish, *caro mio*."

I was getting a bit sick of all this lovey-dovey endearment crap going back and forth between them; it really wasn't doing any good for my foul mood. It was high time to enter into this conversation; I was never very good at being just a spectator.

"We'll also have the Taniwhas."

Everything went dead quiet, you could have heard the old proverbial pin drop, it was so still. Not a vampire moving, breathing, you know their preternatural calm, but thrumming behind it a foreboding sense of threatening power. Oh great. I reached into my jacket to feel the familiar shape of my spare stake to calm my rapidly climbing heartbeat.

"Whatever do you mean, Lucinda?" Michel's eyes pierced mine in a not at all friendly stare. I forced myself not to swallow and took a steady breath in, while never looking away from the challenge in his deep blue and indigo swirling eyes.

"They have agreed to fight alongside me." I thought it best not to say *alongside us*, I had a strong sense that that would not be welcome for some reason. I hadn't realised that there was bad blood between the Taniwhas and vampires, but obviously, something was not quite right in this room right now, and I didn't want to chance my luck.

"Your hunter has been doing things behind your back, *caro mio*," she said it in a teasing purr, but the undercurrent of tension in the room ratcheted up a notch or three.

Michel abruptly stood and the *Sanguis Vitam* rolling off him was unfathomable.

"Leave."

The vampires were a blur as they streaked out the door, I stood to leave as well, assuming the command was for all of us, but Michel growled, "Not you, Lucinda. You stay."

He stalked toward the door and shut it swiftly then waved his hand in a movement in the air, power rippled from the motion outwards around the room. He had sealed us in, nothing we said, or did – and I swallowed deeply at the thought of that – could be heard or felt outside these walls.

I was trapped. And the vampire before me was *not* happy.

14
YES OR NO

Michel turned slowly from the closed door and looked at me. He visibly calmed himself with a deep breath in. He didn't need to breathe to survive, but sometimes that old familiar feeling of it could be a balm, I suppose.

"You should take more care, *ma douce*. Alessandra does not like competition. She would consider it a joy to take issue with your impertinence."

Of all the things he could have chastised me over and oh I knew he was chastising me, I hadn't expected that. Even the use of his pet name for me again, did not assuage the slight ball of fear I felt at the look of him. His eyes were blazing the most incredible purple, a colour I was only too aware of as being a sign of his barely controlled power.

He stalked closer to me and came to rest not a bare foot away. The smell of him in the closed space between us was heady; I fought to keep myself under control. Now was not the time to lose it with a very angry vampire in front of me.

He suddenly reached up and stroked my face with the backs of his fingers on his right hand. "What have you done, *ma douce*? Entered into an agreement with the Taniwhas?" His eyes flashed as he said Taniwhas, but were soon back to just a deep blue with flecks of indigo. He was controlling himself well.

"I only reconfirmed an old alliance, Michel. This is my city too."

A brief smile fluttered across his lips and then was replaced with a more firm expression, but I got the feeling that the storm had passed, he wasn't going to lose his temper with me now. Thank God.

"You are always so full of surprises. I should not have expected otherwise. Shifters?" He let a little laugh out. "First you make me sell my soul to the ghouls and now you bring Taniwhas into it. Do you have no care for my reputation at all?" The smile was back, a mock look of shock on his face. I couldn't help it, I smiled too.

And then I pushed him away. "What was all that power crap about? You didn't even stop her!"

He looked aggrieved. "Surely you understand the necessity for me to remain impassive, implacable, in front of equals of my kind?" He took a step toward me, but I mirrored the action with a step back. His face fell, followed by a return to his usually well controlled mask of calm. "You are *mine*, Lucinda and as such you do not have a right to challenge my guests or me, nor do you receive special treatment just for being my kindred immature Nosferatin."

"Immature?" I spluttered. How dare he?

"You know what I mean!" Equally as outraged, the anger returning to his features, the power starting to accumulate around him. "You are not considered mature until you turn 25 and come into your powers in full, until then, you are a servant and nothing more."

"Damn you, Michel! I am no-one's servant!" I glared at him then. Without even thinking about what I was doing, I pulled my spare stake out of my jacket and took a step towards him.

Purple eyes flashed at me as he moved so quickly I didn't even see the blur. Instantly he was behind me breathing down my neck. "You mean to use that on me, my dear."

I swirled around to face him with the stake half raised. He'd gone, moved somewhere else. I spun in a 360 trying to see where he was. Nowhere. I was alone in the room, or so it seemed. I slowly glanced up at the ceiling, I did *not* want to see him doing a bat impersonation, but you never know. Nope, not there. After a full minute of looking about me like some demonic bubble head toy, I gave up and lowered the stake.

Instantly he was in front of me, I swear, just appearing out of thin air. He thought he had me, I could tell. He wore that smirk, you know the one that says: *You gave up? Silly little girl.* But he hadn't counted on the years of play fighting with the Taniwhas. I sprang forward and just as the realisation hit him I noticed a look of surprise, but I had already slid between his legs feet first, before seeing anything else register on that beautiful face and came up behind him, stake resting against the back of his suit jacket, not piercing material or skin, but digging in all the same. Hell, even I was surprised at the move. Go me.

Of course that sense of triumph didn't last long. He vanished and reappeared over my shoulder, one arm around my upper body pinning my arms, the other stroking my head and hair, his fangs against the softest part of my neck sending shockwaves of pleasure down my body. "If you want me dead, my dear, I suggest you follow through when you get the chance, I will not lower my guard again." His voice was pure silk, teasing my senses. I struggled against his hold. "Tsk, tsk, you do not take losing well, do you, my little hunter."

"I. Am. Not. Your. Little. Hunter." My voice was even, strong, despite my heartbeat thrumming through my entire body. He would have been able to hear it; he certainly could feel it in the pulse at the base of my neck where his lips rested and his fangs lightly dug in.

He laughed at that, a throaty masculine sound I felt right through to the depths of my being. "You are feisty; I shall enjoy our joining immensely."

Now, I know to a vampire, this little exchange we'd been having, had been nothing but a bit of fun, something to make the blood pump, to get the juices flowing, so to speak. And it was abundantly clear to me right now, from the feel of Michel's hard length against my body, that he was enjoying this immensely, but I was really angry with that last comment. So much so, that a sense of real calm had stolen over me, shielding me and hardening my heart.

So, this was how it really was? I had no choice in this, he had decided it for me and to top it all off, he thought I was nothing but an annoying *immature* problem to boss around and command at will. I felt hollow inside. In all my previous imaginings of working alongside Michel, I had never considered this depth of betrayal. It had never crossed my mind that he would be so cold, so mechanical. Stupid. Stupid. Me.

I turned abruptly from him and he surprisingly loosened his hold, letting me go. I ran to the door of his office. I had no intention of remaining in this room with him, my heart trampled all over the floor. Before I could even get my hand on the handle, he spun me around and pressed me against the wood of the door. His body moulding into the length of mine, warmth wrapping around me and surrounding my senses, his smell making my mind go to mush.

"Wh... what are you doing?"

"What I should have done a long time ago," he husked, and his mouth met mine in brutal possession.

His skin was hot against me, his fingers holding me rigid at my sides. Slowly his tongue parted my lips and I tried to turn my head, he growled and brought his hands up to my face, caressing the sides and turning me back towards him. I couldn't think, I could hardly breathe, he felt so good, so right, but I so did not want to give in to him. He was the enemy after all. But my body was on automatic, I felt slightly removed from the scene playing out in front of me, and then he gently bit my lip and the flood of sensations that that brought was overwhelming. I whimpered and his body responded to that sound, pushing closer, lips moving from mine to cover my face and neck. Without even realising it I had moved my hands up to his hair, feeling the silky length of it through my fingers, revelling in the shine that glinted in the lights of the room.

His mouth found mine again and this time I didn't fight it, I let him in and gave every ounce of myself back. He groaned against me, pressing his leg between my thighs. I had no idea where this response of mine was coming from, where this hunger and need originated, but I couldn't deny it any longer. I couldn't fight it anymore. And I couldn't get enough of him. I was practically crawling up his body, clutching at him, devouring him with an intensity that would have shocked me if I paused to consider just who I was doing this with. He met my demand with one as fierce as his own. Stroking my sides and kissing my ears, neck, face, and upper chest. I couldn't feel a spot on my entire body where he did not reach me.

I had never felt this level or strength of longing before, this need so deep it felt a part of my soul. I'm not a prude, I've had boyfriends in the past, mainly when I was a teenager back on the farm. Rolling in the hay has featured in my youth, but nothing, *nothing*, compared to this. I felt as though I would simply die if I didn't get closer to him.

Michel swiftly picked me up and carried me to a large couch in the corner of his office and lay me gently down onto it. He just stood there a moment and gazed down at me, devouring me with his look. The need I felt, reflected in his eyes. He licked his lips and knelt down beside me, then began kissing my neck, my clavicle and towards my breasts. His fingers finding my nipples through my shirt, making them rise with one swift tease of his thumb, swiftly followed by his mouth and tongue through the thin material of my top. I arched my back towards him, but he continued to move his hands down my side exploring through my clothes with those deft fingers, distracting me from my movements.

He reached the bottom of my skirt and brought his hand back up under it to rest on my rear, kneading with his fingers through my tights. His eyes, when he returned from investigating my breasts, were alight with purple swirls, deeper than I had ever seen before. I experienced a moment of panic which faded as soon as his lips found mine again. His upper body pressing me into the couch, his hands stroking, kneading in places they really shouldn't have been, but were crying out for his touch anyway.

When he started to remove my tights I felt a sense of clearness break through the fog of my desire, snapping me awake, reluctantly from a blissful dream. I started pushing against him, at first unable to make a dent, he was so strong and too aroused to notice, but I managed a half hearted plea. "Michel, stop."

He didn't, but kept kissing and nibbling and stroking. I almost let him keep going as I swiftly returned to that haze of pleasure, but a small part of me was still trying to take back control, and I managed a much firmer, "Stop!"

He heard me that time and pulled back, the desire and lust in his eyes flabbergasting. "Stop?" he asked breathlessly. "You could not be so cruel, *ma douce*." The accent undeniable. But he didn't make a move to come closer, his hands stilled at my sides, his face flushed.

When I didn't answer or pull him closer, he rose quickly and stepped away. He turned and walked to the far wall, as though he couldn't bear looking at me. I felt momentarily hurt until his husky voice, slightly broken, said, "You had best straighten yourself up if you wish no further pursuit of this pleasurable activity tonight. The sight of you lying there so ready, so inviting, is too much even for my self control, my dear."

I hesitated briefly and then quickly sat up and brushed myself down. It took a bit of straightening, things had gotten a little twisted and out of place, but I had myself looking respectable by the time he turned back around. There was still a purple glaze in his eyes, a slight flush to his features. I dreaded to think what I looked like.

He stood still and looked at me, a rueful smile on his face.

"Your anger has long been my aphrodisiac, *ma douce*. There is nothing more desirable than a woman who can stand up for herself. You are beauty personified when in a rage. I would not have you any other way, but you must take care," - he chuckled then- "not only from my fervent advances, but from those like Alessandra, who would devour you in a much more unpleasant way."

I swallowed. I couldn't find a coherent sentence in my head; my emotions were tumbling so beautifully inside my mind. He walked over, all sensual glide and lithe movements. I licked my lips before I could help myself. He groaned as he knelt in front of me and reached for my hands.

"You want this as much as I do, Lucinda. It calls to you too. Why deny it, we are meant to be together." Husky, inviting, reeling me in.

"I am not your servant, Michel." I was unbelievably relieved to have found my voice again and didn't even mind that it cracked a little at the end.

He stroked my face, my neck. "Your scent calls to me, *ma douce*, like a beautiful wine."

"That isn't an answer, Michel."

"I wasn't aware you had offered a question."

"Why do you call me your servant and then tell me with such passion we are meant to be together?"

He looked me in the eyes, his own blue and indigo, forcing out the deep purple of before, but haunts of the colour remained. "I am what I am, Lucinda. We vampyre are extremely territorial. The exchange with Enrique and even Alessandra to a certain extent, had all but released the beast within. You could never be my servant and my heart knows this, but my vampyre mind does not acquiesce so easily."

My heart skipped a beat. My throat was suddenly dry. Was this even happening? Part of me knew I should be addressing the *I shall enjoy our joining immensely* bit, but a stronger part was simply pushing that aside. The part that purred and reared its head in longing when I looked into his eyes.

"Of course, we could make things so much more uncomplicated, *ma douce*."

"Uncomplicated?" Did I really want to know?

"You could join with me now and even as an immature Nosferatin you would warrant respect from my guests and equal standing in the room. Your protection would be assured."

"And no doubt your powers would come into their bonus straight away?"

"Yes. I would be the most powerful vampyre here. But you would be safe."

"Would I have my powers?" I couldn't believe I was actually contemplating this after everything we had just been through; there was still so much I didn't understand and time was running out. I felt a little panicked at the thought.

"No." He looked sad; I'm sure it was just for show. "Your powers would not arrive until your 25th birthday."

I just stared at him, but he went on not fazed. "Of course, it may also be enough to dissuade Maximilian from his claim and prevent him from starting a war on our lands. He would be a fool to come against me when I have a Nosferatin at my side."

I chose to ignore the *a* Nosferatin part and concentrated on the rest. "Do you really think that that would stop him? He's just off our shores and gone to a lot of trouble. It would be embarrassing for him to step down, wouldn't it?"

"He would be a fool to continue, but yes, it would be unlikely he could step down, so far along this path already."

"There's one more thing you haven't mentioned, Michel. I would be as weak as I am now."

"You are not weak, *ma douce!*" he interjected.

"You know what I mean. If things go wrong, I wouldn't be able to protect myself, not as well as if I had my powers anyway. He could still kill me."

"I would not let it happen!"

I reached up and stroked his face, that beautiful face so full of conviction and something more, something that I had not allowed myself to see before, but refused to acknowledge even now.

"If I die, Michel, and we are joined, you die. I will not tie you to me until I can protect myself sufficiently."

I hadn't even realised that was what I felt, but as soon as I said the words I knew. I could not place Michel in such a position. The thought of him not going on, not living in this world, was too hard even to contemplate. If things did go wrong tomorrow and I did die, at least I would leave this world knowing that Michel still lived.

He just looked at me with utter devotion in his eyes and pulled the palm of my hand to his lips. He kissed it softly and tingles of excitement threatened to wash all over me again. When his eyes lifted to look into mine, purple swirled in their depths.

"I will protect you with my life, *ma douce*, forever."

I didn't doubt it. Despite everything I thought he was, I could see it there, written so plainly on his face, in his eyes, in the way he held onto me so fiercely. But I was also aware of what he would gain out of a joining with me and no matter how much I didn't want to face it, Michel would be powerful when - *God did I just say that?* - if, we joined. And would he still be the Michel I know now when given that much power at his command? I wasn't so sure. I saw that momentary look of hunger on his face when he mentioned he'd be more powerful than any other in our land, more powerful than those vampires he has invited to join our battle, yet worked so hard to not show any weakness in front of.

It was thoughts like these that made falling into his arms so much harder.

The night had passed far quicker than I imagined and after leaving me alone for a moment to check on things in the club, Michel returned with some food and liquid refreshment for me. I wasn't naïve enough, or stupid enough, to pretend he hadn't *eaten* too, I just didn't want to know about it. The practical side of me knew he needed to be fighting fit for tonight, when he rose to face my abductor and that was why I perhaps agreed to his suggestion that I stay at the club with him for the day.

Amazingly his argument that we would both benefit from the proximity of each other and therefore be stronger when we faced what came tomorrow made complete sense.

The guest vampires had been secured in lodgings on the premises and he led me to his chamber. I felt a little nervous to be entering the daytime resting place of a vampire. He assured me this was one of many he had throughout the city. Why was I so nervous, when I had spent almost a week in the same house as him in Taupo, I wasn't sure. It may have had something to do with the fact that during the day in Taupo he had quietly gone to his "room" and I had never seen where it was or what it looked like, but now I was faced with a king sized bed in a sumptuous room full of dark colours and rich fabrics. No coffin in sight, go figure.

He closed the door behind us and locked it. The loud click of the multiple deadbolts securely closing made my heart skip a beat. He paused, looking at me standing stock still, then proceeded to slowly take his jacket and shirt off, making sure that every move was a seductive motion. Swiftly followed by shoes, socks, belt and trousers, all the while keeping direct eye contact with me, daring me to blush. Finally, he was just left in his boxers, and I could not look away from the splendid sight of his body. The urge to reach out and trace the lines of his tantalizing muscles was excruciating.

He smiled a languid inviting smile and said, "I promise not to bite."

Somehow that broke the spell. "Knock it off, Michel. We're just staying close, that's all, OK?"

"Of course, my dear, of course. Anything you say." And he threw himself on top of the bed covers like some Italian gigolo and patted the space next to him with a wicked grin.

God help me.

I took my jacket and boots off, but stayed in my tights, skirt and top and quickly climbed under the covers. He laughed, throwing his head back in pleasure.

"Are you laughing at me, Michel?"

"*Ma douce*, you are adorable. Such a delight."

I wasn't sure if I should be angry at him just then, but my stomach was still churning in nervous lumps so that when he suddenly lifted the blankets and crawled in next to me, I almost choked.

He pulled me to him before I could protest and kissed the top of my head. "I will not steal your virtue, *ma douce*, we both need rest. Well at least, not tonight. However, I cannot promise to be such a gentleman when presented with a similar opportunity in the future." He nuzzled my neck and softly kissed me behind my ear. I made a pitiful half-hearted vow to myself, not to give him the opportunity again.

There was no way in hell I could fall asleep like this, though. His nearly naked body pressed along the length of mine; his arms wrapped around me, his breath on my skin. My heart was leaping from my chest; my own breath was shallow and constricted.

"I will help you fall asleep, my dear. Will you allow it?"

I nodded against him, he wrapped me even closer in his arms, resting my head against his upper chest. I could hear the beat of his heart, and then I felt the warmth of his power envelop me, sending a shiver down my spine, but before it could build to anything else, a sense of utter calm stole over me.

The last thing I heard as I drifted off to blissful sleep was Michel whispering softly against my neck, "*Ma belle petite lumière, la raison de mon existence.*"

15
ONLY IN MY DREAMS

The dream started in the field above my parents' farm, as it always does, but this time everything felt so much more real. The colours were vivid, the greens of the grass after a winter downpour leapt up and met me, the blue of the sky; a deep azure interspersed with tufts of white clouds scuttling across its expanse. I almost felt like I could reach up and touch one. The sun filtering through the sparse clouds was bright and warm against my bare arms and face. There were daffodils all over the fields, something that didn't happen in real life, but made the paddocks dance and sway as if they were alive. The lambs were in the distance, waggling their tails as usual, but this time I could hear the odd bleat, the wind in the nearby trees, the sound of the river behind me out of view, water trickling over rocks and rushing against boulders. I had never heard those sounds in my dreams before; it had always been a soft shushing in the background, a sound you could contribute to these things perhaps, but never be really sure.

I was dressed differently too. Usually I was in my normal attire, short dark skirt and top, but today I was in a flowing white dress, the bodice close against my skin, the slight breeze coming over the hill making the long and draping material of the skirt swish around my legs, my feet were bare. The material was soft and smelled like new laundry, clean and fresh, there were the most intricate little designs embroidered all over it, and when I looked closely, I could see flowers, bees and butterflies, all small but with hints of orange in them. Not visible from a distance, but close up giving the dress a detail and depth beyond imagining. I couldn't stop touching those designs, running my fingers over and over them. My hair was slightly longer too, and the wind lifted it softly and moved it around my shoulders like a caress.

And then, I heard him, the soft footfalls through the grass, overriding all other sounds until all there was, was just his breathing and my heart beating.

"Do you like it, *ma douce?*"

"It's beautiful. Why is it so different?"

"We are together; everything is more."

"It is still your creation. A part of you."

"It is a part of both of us, but I have made it, yes."

"Thank you." And I meant it. Even if it was more than my farm ever was, I had needed to see it tonight, needed to touch my roots and centre my soul. Nothing calmed me like being on the farm, and this, even a dream, was a balm to my ragged nerves, an elixir to the terror that had been building at what we were about to face.

"It is my pleasure, *ma douce*. I would give you the world."

He was beside me now, looking out at the view. He was wearing casual black trousers and a black t-shirt. I'd never seen him in a t-shirt before; it seemed too casual for him. But when I turned to face him and my hands reached up of their own accord and touched his chest through the thin material of the top, I realised why he had chosen it. I could feel every line, every curve of his firm body. The material almost insubstantial as I ran my hands over his torso, down the flat plane of his stomach and around the sides to his hips, then just continued to move my fingers all over every part of him. He closed his eyes, but didn't stop me, his breathing shallow and controlled, but I could tell he was fighting it.

I took a step closer and felt the warmth of him roll towards me, wrap around me and send shivers down my spine. The overall sensations all tumbling together were electrifying, it caught my breath. So many feelings were running through my mind, my body, I was quickly losing control of myself. I did not want to stop touching this body. Ever.

I closed my eyes and licked my lips, trying to get myself under control. This was just a dream, but it felt so real.

His hands touched my cheek and softly stroked the side of my neck. "Do not fight it, *ma douce*. This is right." His words whispered against my mouth.

I parted my lips involuntarily, and he took the opportunity without hesitation. Warm lips met mine, wet tongue enveloping my own, wrapping around it and filling my mouth with such warmth and my body with such desire. His right hand had moved down to the centre of my back, and he pulled me close to him, his body moulding into mine. I could feel his fingers kneading and stroking my back through the thin material of the dress.

For some reason, I was crying, or at least tears were slowly trickling down my face. Michel kissed each one in turn, with small soft movements, down my face and onto my neck. He found my sensitive spot on the side of my throat above my pulse and sucked gently on it. The sensation was extraordinary, sending a violent shudder through me. He groaned.

"How is it that you fill me with such longing, such desire, even in a dream, *ma belle*? I cannot get enough of you."

Right back at ya buddy, was the only thought I had before falling once again into a delightful cloud of bliss. I didn't argue when he gently manoeuvred me to the ground, lying on his side beside me, his body against me, his leg slightly over one of mine. We were kissing again, and the crescendo of heat inside me was reaching the most delicious parts of my body. Without even noticing he had moved, his hand was on my bare skin under my skirt, softly moving up my calves, stroking behind my knees and kneading along my thighs. The wind against my bare legs was warm and far from distracting, just added to the plethora of sensations rolling all over my body.

He hadn't stopped his persistent kissing of me either, finding every spot on my face and neck that would send the most fervent impulses through me. Combined with what his hand was now doing, in my most intimate place, which I had only now just realised was uncovered, was thrilling, exhilarating. I guess it was his dream creation; he could have me wearing, or in this case not wearing, anything at all. I, surprisingly, did not feel exposed, I simply relished the sensations he was causing, building a deep and lush heat right down inside me with the deft movement of his fingers.

My body was arching up towards him, it had a mind all of its own, it wanted more and I couldn't have stopped it even if I had wanted to. For some reason, this being a dream made it feel that much safer. That I could do this without all the hindrance of reality and what that entailed, I was just letting go and *so* wanted this never to stop. His thumb had found the spot that made me whimper, my breath catching and the heat sky-rocketing. He didn't stop, he was relentless in his pursuit of my satisfaction, stroking and probing, but pulling back when I was near the peak, only to start again when I had come back down. The roller coaster of heightened sensations was so intense, sending my heartbeat into overdrive, my pulse thudding in my neck beneath his kisses.

He groaned against me at the increase of the beat. I felt his fangs come out and scrape along my neck, but my mind was concentrating elsewhere as my body rode his fingers, trying desperately to get as much of him as I could inside me. It wasn't enough, not nearly enough. This time he didn't pull back, but let me ride the wave of desire, lust and heat that had built, through to completion. My body shuddered violently as he held me close while I climaxed, whispering sweet words I couldn't understand in my ear.

It felt like it went on forever, but then I began to be aware of Michel against me, his hard length pressing into my side, his rapid breathing, not quite as fast as mine, against my neck. I could feel his heart beat, his warmth, I could smell his scent, intermingled with mine and it was intoxicating. The heat had already started to build again inside me.

I sat up slightly and rolled him over onto his back. He didn't fight me, but the look in his slightly widened eyes almost made my heart stop completely. The purples and blues so vivid against the cream of his skin and the flush of his face. I undid his trousers and reached in to hold him. He threw his head back and moaned, the length of him swelling even further under my touch. I stroked and fondled his shaft, moving my fingers down to the soft skin of his scrotum, where he managed a whimper I had not ever expected hearing from him and then back up to his thick length. I repeated this again, getting more whimpers and shivers through his body in response. I decided it was time to take a closer look and bent down to lick him. He stiffened, and the hands at his sides tightened into fists, one hand grabbing grass and ripping it out of the ground.

I smiled to myself then; I had never thought I could have the great Michel Durand in such a state, in such a vulnerable position, allowing himself to be pleasured without thought for his safety or for the calm and professional demeanour he works so hard to portray. I decided I liked it very much. I was certain he liked it too when I took the tip of him into my mouth and sucked gently. He groaned and lifted his head to look at me, but before he could get a word out I pushed him back down. "Stay." This was my moment, and I was going to enjoy it. He looked momentarily surprised; I don't think he was at all used to being bossed around. He threw his arm over his face and started muttering, no doubt curses, in French as I returned my attention to his beautiful body and that most responsive part of it.

He tasted salty but delicious, the taste calling to me in a way I had never experienced before. I couldn't get enough of it, licking, sucking, stroking and when I accidentally scraped him with my teeth, he actually screamed out. I thought at first in alarm, but soon realised it was pleasure. I started to increase my speed and the length of my stroking, all the while licking and sucking and interspersing with nibbles. He was practically writhing on the ground under me and then all of a sudden, he had moved, flipped me over and was between my legs.

I felt his hard tip against the entrance to me, pressing but not entering, he looked down at me with such longing, hovering there; then he slowly started to move himself up the length of my opening, sending wave after wave of pleasure through me. I reached up and grabbed him, attempting to pull him closer. I needed him closer, I wanted him inside me, there was nothing I wanted more in this world than that.

Just as he groaned and swore softly, I felt him shift to enter, and the world fell away.

I heard myself scream, "No!" and felt the air leave my lungs as I crashed against a hard concrete floor. What the?

I was having trouble catching my breath, my heart still on its mad pursuit of leaping out of my rib cage, my body screaming for release and coming up with a gaping, gnawing hole, where there should have been warmth. I shuddered as my mind tried to wrap itself around this new reality. I was no longer with Michel, I was on a cold, unforgiving floor and watching me with amusement was the one vampire I so did *not* want to see right then.

"Did I interrupt something?" Max smiled, a slight smirk twitching the edge of his mouth. "It looked like it had been fun."

I attempted to straighten myself, surprised to find I was still dressed in Michel's dress. But knew my eyes were wide, my face was flushed and slightly sweaty, and my heart was still thundering in my chest, all of which Max was aware of and looked like he was relishing right at that moment. I fought a blush unsuccessfully rising up my cheeks.

"You are a little vixen, aren't you, Lucinda?" Something in the way he said it, did not make me feel safe. If Michel could do to me what he just did in a dream, I didn't doubt that Max could either and by the look on his face right now, he was contemplating it. I had to distract him.

"What are you doing here?" My voice was steady, even if my heartbeat wasn't.

He still wore that smile on his face, his lips curved in a sly smirk, his eyes devouring me. They took in every inch, from my flushed face, down my neck, over my rapid pulse, the dip between my breasts, the rise and fall of my chest and down the length of me. As though he was seeing me completely bare, laid out for him to enjoy. I was so glad for the flimsy material of the dress that was covering me; I could not imagine what it would be like to face Max naked.

He completely ignored my question. "You are a feast for the eyes, Lucinda, but I think I'd prefer to see a little less material overall." And suddenly I was sitting there in a red lacy teddy, the cold of the concrete biting into my knees and shins as I knelt on the floor. The lace of the teddy was scratchy against my bare skin, nothing as soft and luxurious as the draping material of the dress had been, the colour gaudy, even against my slightly tanned body. I felt like a cheap hooker waiting for my client to tell me what he wanted. The feeling so removed from only a moment ago.

He prowled towards me, like a sleek jungle cat, dressed in black jeans and his trademark open shirt, again black. I quickly jumped to my feet to better greet that hunger in his eyes. He stroked my cheek and jaw and then grabbed my head and pulled it backwards in a sudden movement that sent a sharp pain down my spine. His lips grazed over my pulse in my neck, and for the life of me, I couldn't slow it. I was beginning to realise just what an enticement a rapidly beating pulse was to a vampire. He softly kissed my neck, licking with his tongue.

I didn't want to feel anything other than anger and repulsion at this man. I didn't want to respond, I wanted to stay stiff and rigid and still, let my non-movement show my distaste, but my body had other thoughts. Or perhaps Max was influencing me, and I melted under the attention his mouth was giving me, even as my mind was screaming against the assault. He purred and whispered, "Your scent is delicious, Lucinda, I do not think I can contain myself any longer, I must taste you, I must have you. I cannot wait."

My mind was frantically reeling, searching for a coherent thought, this couldn't be happening, I couldn't let it happen. I had to think of something to stop this. *Wake up!* I shouted at myself, *Wake up you idiot!* It didn't work, he just kept kissing and licking with his hand gripping my arm, his fingers digging into my flesh, his body pushed against mine. I only then registered the wall at my back, it hadn't been there before. Max had me pushed up against it, his body firm against mine, his grip on my head unrelenting, baring my neck to his lips, mouth and teeth. He thrust his leg between my own, spreading them, kneading his thigh over my sensitive parts.

It was rough and ugly, and I did not want it, but my body kept doing things of its own accord. My hands were suddenly in his short, thick blonde hair, running my fingers through the roughness of it, pleasuring in the feel of it against my skin. He growled in appreciation.

"We will be so good together, Lucinda. Like molten fire, our passion will ignite the world."

Some part of me registered that this was all wrong, that the green eyes looking at me with such ferocity were not good, but filled with evil. That this was not a vampire I wanted to lead towards the light, that this was not *my* vampire at all. He had stopped kissing my neck, where I was sure a bruise would form from his rough nips and nibbles, and looked me in the eye. I held my breath.

"Now, my little Nosferatin, let us play." And he bared his fangs.

Finally, I felt the veil of his influence lift; I felt my power centre in my body and the tingling created by his touch disappear. I looked back at that expectant face and with all my strength pushed against that rock hard chest and cried, "No!"

Max went flying across the room and landed in a heap on the concrete floor. He was up in an instant, fangs down, eerily red glow ringing the green of his eyes. He snarled. "You shall pay for that, Hunter, your city will pay dearly for your defiance."

He sprang towards me, flying through the air in slow motion. I had barely a chance to register the feral look in his face, the unnatural grimace, and raise my arms in protection when the world fell away again so abruptly that my stomach was left behind.

I woke to someone shaking me roughly, my head lolling around on my shoulders, my neck screaming from the movement and the ache radiating from its side.

"I'm awake, I'm awake," I mumbled.

Warm arms embraced me, almost crushing in their need to be around me. "*Merde, ma douce!* I could not reach you. I thought I had lost you. Don't *ever* do that to me again." There was such naked rawness in Michel's voice it made my heart ache.

"I don't plan to," I croaked and then realised I was going to be sick. I pushed him aside and ran to the bathroom, heaving up the remainder of my late night snack. I didn't stop until I had ejected everything inside me and was dry retching into the toilet bowl. I vaguely registered that vampires had toilets before I started giggling uncontrollably. The giggles increasing until I started hiccuping. Whoa, what was wrong with me?

Michel appeared beside me with a wet cloth to wipe my face and knelt down next to me on the tiled floor, rubbing in circles on my back. "It is all right, *ma douce*, you are safe. It is over."

I leant back against him as the hiccoughs slowly subsided and my body began to relax its rigid stance. He reached up and grabbed a glass filled with water off the countertop and handed it to me. It was cool and refreshing and eased a little of the rawness in my throat, washing away the aftertaste of sick. I was exhausted, spent and was aching from head to toe. My stomach a raw knot of ugly fists. My head pounding in unrelenting thumps. My neck so sore, I could hardly swallow past the pain. I reached up and touched the tender spot against my pulse. Michel noticed the movement and moved my hand aside. His *Sanguis Vitam* thrummed around the small room.

"He did this to you?" His voice was flat.

He'd obviously worked out that Max had taken me from his dream into another. Perhaps he'd known all along that it was possible, or perhaps it was the only explanation that fit, either way the anger rolling off him was tremendous. He gently stroked the spot where Max's fangs had grazed my skin; they hadn't penetrated, but I did not think I'd be so lucky next time. The bruises, however, were extensive as I stood to look in the mirror above the sink. Max had not been playing nice.

Michel turned me towards him and slowly lowered his own mouth over that spot. I tensed slightly out of fear, I couldn't help it, it was an echo of what had just happened with Max, but Michel stroked my arms and softly whispered, "Trust me." His lips glided over the bruises, and I started to feel a tingling sensation where they touched, within a minute the ache had gone, replaced by warmth and heat and blissful delight.

He raised his head to look at me, his eyes a purple and blue maelstrom of colour. I reached out and grabbed a fistful of his hair and roughly pulled him to me, claiming his mouth in a not so perfect kiss. He did not fight me, letting me devour him as the anger inside me subsided to be replaced by something just as strong, but so much sweeter. When he noticed the change in my body language, he took control of the kiss, slowing it down and turning it into a languid exploration of my lips, mouth and tongue. Then my eyelids, cheek, face, down my neck and over my clavicle, to the crease between my breasts. He sighed as he rested his forehead against my skin, nestled between my breasts.

"This is almost too much to bear," he murmured against me. "I do not know if I can find the strength, should I lose you." I stroked his head, running my hands over the dark silky smoothness.

From out of nowhere came the thought and before I had a chance to temper it, to consider exactly what I was feeling, I whispered, "You won't have to, I'm not going anywhere."

16
IT BEGINS

It was still daylight out, according to Michel, but the sun was not far from setting. His inner vampire clock telling him exactly when it would be safe to exit his chamber. Although Michel could venture out in the day, it did take it out of him, and he needed to conserve his strength as much as he could right now. I knew the club was enclosed, with no external windows to speak of, but I relished his reluctance to leave my side, despite the fact that he could have. We cuddled for a while on the bed, his arms so warm around me, his breath so soothing against my skin. Every move he made slowly replacing the images and feelings of my dream with Max with warmth and light and safety.

When I was more or less jelly in his arms, he kissed my nose and rose from the bed. Taking one look at me, he said, "Do not look at me like that, *ma douce*. It is difficult enough to pull away from you to dress." And when my expression of fervent desire didn't change, "Arghh, you are impossible! I need a shower. Cold, very cold, I think." He stalked off to the bathroom, making sure I could see his body ripple as he moved.

I covered my head with the pillow and lay there listening to the waterfall in the bathroom. I fought every instinct in me not to follow him and join him under that hot wet stream, trying desperately to push the images of slowly washing his body from head to toe from my mind. I was going crazy, and I knew it. I was so lost to him; I had no hope of pulling back. The slippery slope had already begun, and all I could do was watch in a dazed kind of horror, as I fell further and further into his arms.

A few minutes later he emerged from the dressing room, beside the bathroom, dressed in black trousers and a black shirt, sleeves rolled up. I was momentarily surprised not to see his trademark white shirt and tie, but the reason behind his change of clothing suddenly made me realise just what today would bring, and I had to the fight bile rising in my throat.

He came and sat next to me on the bed, reaching out to stroke a stray piece of my hair back into place. "There is a change of clothes in the dressing room, *ma douce*. I shall leave you to freshen up; my self-control not quite as good as yours". The twinkle in his eyes letting me know he had thought of me joining him in the shower too.

When I emerged from the chamber and followed the hall to the office, it was empty. I stopped long enough to pick up my second stake and slid it into the pocket of my new black jacket and then carried on to the club itself. Michel somehow had some of my clothes brought over from my apartment; I was going to have to break him of that habit. My apartment was my sanctuary, the thought that he had sent one of his people to my home grated, but I was also glad to be in familiar gear. Boots, leggings, black mini skirt and a tight black tee with the words *Make My Day* emblazoned across it. Whoever had picked the clothes out must have thought it a riot, but I just felt comfortable and at ease to be in my own hunter gear after last night.

When I entered the club, it was surprisingly full. At least a dozen vampires of various power levels dotted the room, most were keeping their power in check, but Alessandra reached out to stroke my arms with little electric shots. I waved my hand subconsciously, and the power abated immediately. She pouted. Dressed in a slinky dress again, this time black, her golden curls stood out in stark relief. I couldn't imagine how she would be able to move in that tight fitting long dress, but that was her problem.

Every other vamp in the room was in black, but they weren't the only ones here. Pete and a couple of ghouls were huddled in the corner, hunched over themselves, but rigid with a barely disguised sense of threat. They were not comfortable, but at least they were here.

Up by the bar were Jerome, Josh and Rick. I smiled broadly when I saw them, but it quickly left my face when I saw the look of accusation on Rick's. His fists were clenched, his jaw rigid. Jerome quietly put a hand on his shoulder and waved me over.

I hadn't seen Michel anywhere, but he suddenly appeared at my side as I approached the Shifters. Protective much? From the look of anger on Rick's face, I was actually glad of Michel's presence for a moment and then scoffed at the idea. This was my best friend; if he had a problem with me spending a night with a vampire, then he could say it to my face. I was a big girl, and I could fight my own battles. My shoulders straightened, and I lifted my chin, glaring back at Rick in defiance.

He wilted slightly, paused and then turned away.

Jerome patted me on the shoulder when I arrived and gave me one of his huge trademark smiles. I think he was trying to make up for Rick's behaviour, but it wasn't working. I still felt a little hollow inside at his harsh judgement and the fact that he had turned away. He couldn't even look me in the eyes now.

"So, it's all set, Luce," Jerome said. "We'll be down at the port with the ghouls and hold them off as long as we can." My stomach knotted at the thought of them being part of the greeting committee, but it made sense. Max had so many more ghouls than we had, our guys needed reinforcements, and the vampires would be busy up here.

I swallowed roughly past the lump in my throat. "Are you sure?"

"Absolutely. Those bastards won't know what hit 'em when they meet the wrath of our *kairakau*".

I just nodded. "It is best you go now, Taniwha. I thank you." Michel barely contained his power, his voice even and non-threatening, but Jerome would have felt the energy building and understood the reason behind it. And even though Michel was fighting to keep his vehemence under control and had even *thanked* Jerome, I couldn't help feeling he was being a tantrum throwing toddler over their involvement. It was needed, without it, his city could fall. But, that's the thing, the fact that Michel had to allow shapeshifters to be a part of the city's defence was undoubtedly a hit to his pride. He was struggling with that side of him, the least I could do was let him manage it in his own way.

"I'm not doing it for you, vamp. This is for Lucinda and this city. Nothing more." Jerome stood to his full height, an impressive 6 foot 3 inches, broad shoulders and large mass, even his slight chunky mid-drift didn't seem to detract from the overall appearance of his bulk.

Michel didn't waver, just simply said, "It is time."

With that the vampires in the room straightened and a handful streaked out the door, the ghouls headed in the same direction with Josh and Jerome turning to take up the rear. Rick took one last look at me, I took a step forward and felt a hand on my arm, trying to stop me. I shook it off and wrapped my arms around my best mate and held on tight. He stood stock still for a moment and then slowly relaxed and lifted a hand to my hair.

"It'll be all right, Luce. We'll be fine. You just stay out of trouble 'K?"

"She will be well protected, Taniwha, you need not worry."

Rick's head shot up at Michel's softly threatening voice. "Not all of the bad guys have yet to arrive, *vampire*," he spat. He kissed the top of my head, not letting his eyes leave Michel's and stormed out of the club. I felt desolate, alone. My best friend was heading off to face an untold terror, and I may not see him again. I tried unsuccessfully to stifle a sniff, my shoulders shaking with suppressed tears.

Michel hovered for a moment, then settled on sending me a wave of concentrated power, not allowing it to leak out into the room, but silently wrap me in an embrace that said he understood. By the time I had steadied my ragged nerves he was already in discussions with Enrique and Jock. Alessandra was standing to the side staring at me, her head at an inquisitive angle, a knowing smile on her luscious red lips. I flipped her the birdie and went to sit next to Bruno at the other end of the bar.

Bruno pushed a plate of food towards me. "Eat," he simply said. It consisted of toasted sandwiches, ham and cheese by the looks of it, and had been sitting there a little while, so was cool to the touch. Yum, nothing like cold toasties to fill the gap. I broke a bit of the crust off and nibbled it silently.

We didn't say anything to each other, but I felt quite safe sitting there next to him. He may have been expending a bit of power to make me feel that way, I could certainly sense something coming off him, but my mind was so distracted I couldn't focus on its intention. All I knew was I trusted him, at that moment, more than I ever could Alessandra and her little clique; that was for sure.

After a few minutes, Michel's voice floated across the room and wrapped around me. It wasn't loud; it didn't need to be, he directed it straight to me but didn't hide it from anyone else either. He might as well have been standing at my shoulder breathing down my neck, though. "Lucinda, come."

I stiffened, and Bruno softly said, so no one else could hear, "Don't show him up, Luce."

I swallowed my pride and walked toward Michel. Enrique and Alessandra watching my progress with interest. He turned and entered the private area of the club and went straight down the hall without pausing to see if I was following. I expected to see him turn into his office, but he kept going to his chamber and waited for me just inside.

My heart skipped a beat at being back in his room, but it soon steadied slightly at the look on his face when I finally stood before him. He was wearing a slightly pained expression, one I had not expected to see.

I went to him instantly and cupped his face with my hands. His arms enveloped me as he used his power to close the door behind us with a soft click, his lips found mine in a desperate kiss, full of so much emotion words couldn't fully justify; longing, desire, passion, and regret. That last one made me pull back slightly from his embrace.

"What's wrong?" I asked, fearing what he was about to tell me.

He led me over to the bed and sat down next to me. He seemed reluctant to talk, fighting a losing battle within himself. Finally, his deep blue eyes met mine and he said, "This is the safest room in this building. Reinforced walls, titanium door, multiple deadbolts. It would be impossible for someone to break in here". I silently thought with dread, *or break out*. He stroked the back of my hand and went on, "I cannot sufficiently protect you *and* fight him, I wish I could, but I simply can not." He was pleading with me with his eyes to understand. I wanted that look to be replaced with something else so fervently, but I also could not stand by, tucked up safe and warm and wait to be told of his fate and mine.

I settled on softly saying, "I am not entirely incapable of protecting myself, Michel."

He smiled sadly at me. "I am not strong enough to let you try, *ma douce*." Then as I felt his power engulf me and the world begin to tilt, his hard arms embraced me, picking me up and gently laying me down on the bed and his voice whispered in my ear a final plea, "Forgive me."

I didn't wake up, but I didn't sleep either. I was stuck somewhere between a dream world and reality, all misty murkiness and soft sounds. Slowly the noises became more distinct; growls and gnashing teeth, thuds of fists against mass, thumps of bodies falling, squeals of pain and roars of rage, interspersed with shouts of commands and the electrical crackle of power. Everything began to come into focus, the blur at the edges of my vision began to recede, slowly showing me the scene before me.

To the left was a tall stack of different coloured rectangular metal boxes; shipping containers. Stacked three or four high, reds, yellows and blues, with the brown of rust along the edges and spots of it showing through the peeling paint. Writing along the side in large letters said *Hamburg Süd*. I struggled to find my bearings; Hamburg was in Germany, where the hell had my dreams taken me? Then a ghoul ran past, followed by a streak of grey, scaly skin, shark-like muzzle bared in a grimace, long sharp serrated teeth going in for the kill.

A bang to my left made me spin around, a ghoul had another in a headlock, the eyes of the choked victim bulging out of their sockets, the gurgle of their throat being crushed so loud and unlike anything I had ever heard before. The ghoul attacking grunted as he twisted the head of his victim swiftly sideways, causing a sickening squelching and tearing sound to rent the night air. He dropped the body with a growl, lifting his head to sniff for scents. It was Pete. In a second he bounded off after another ghoul stomping towards him.

I was at the docks; somehow my mind was showing me what was

happening down at the port and the battle had already begun. I felt my heart start to race and my throat go dry. I looked down at myself. I looked normal, in the clothes I was dressed in before, substantial and fully corporeal, but those fighting around me didn't even glance in my direction. They couldn't see me at all. I took a grateful breath in. Then shuddered as a vampire bit into the neck of a Taniwha to my side.

The Taniwha yelped, and blood started trickling down its body, its eyes started glazing over to a whitish hue and the whimpering that had started got fainter and fainter. The four-inch claws frantically trying to get to the marauding vampire, but unable to find purchase at all. In less than sixty seconds the vampire had drained the Taniwha dry before I had even taken a step towards it to try to intervene. He dropped the Taniwha with a disgusted thrust away from himself and wiped the blood from his mouth with the back of his sleeve. When he lifted his face, I saw who it was. Maximilian.

He was still at the docks and had been caught up in the melee. He streaked off toward the lights of the loading cranes in the distance, where more vampires, ghouls and Taniwhas were fighting.

I hadn't taken a breath since the moment Max had appeared with the Taniwha in his grasp. I turned slowly toward where the Taniwha had landed, my heart in my throat. He had changed back into human form, so small and pale, curled in a ball. I took an unsteady step towards him, reaching out my hand, it was shaking I noticed distractedly, shaking like a leaf. I knelt down next to the pale body and went to touch him. I could feel him, my vision or dream or whatever the hell this was allowed me to feel, as well as hear and smell, all of which I wasn't sure I truly wanted right now. The male body of the now human looking Taniwha was lying facing away from me, so I gently pulled him over to get a closer look. His body flopped back against my legs like a rag doll. It was Rocky. Oh dear God, it was Rocky. Why hadn't I done anything to stop this? I can feel, surely I could have intervened, why hadn't I stopped this from happening?

I was crying uncontrollably, tears freely falling down my cheeks, great racking gasps threatening to break me in half. I had to physically hold myself together with an arm across my stomach, for fear of my body disintegrating into that raw anguish I could feel so deep down inside. *Not Rocky, not a kid.*

Finally, I pulled myself together and wiped the tears away from my face. I was here, I was alive, I was sure as hell going to see how far this vision would let me take this. I grabbed my stake out from inside my jacket, took one last look at my fallen friend, kissed my hand and placed it against his cheek and stood, resolve steeling my features and hardening my heart.

I ran as fast as I could towards the battle. No one saw me coming; no one heard my footfalls. The first vampire I encountered, I thrust my stake into his heart, feeling the reassuring and familiar sensation of it sliding home and finding its target, the sickening squelch as it tore through skin and muscle and then the rush of adrenaline as he burst into dust. Alri-ight! A vampire to the side turned suddenly, seeing his comrade in dust on the ground. He frantically looked around to see how it had occurred, unable to see or sense me at all. *I could get used to this.*

I circled around him; I could feel the uncertainty rolling off him in waves. My stake found its target through his back a second later, turning him to dust before he could even cry out a warning to his friends. I coughed a little as the dust settled around me and then set off to find my next prey.

Shifters and ghouls and vampires were in a mad thrashing of limbs and teeth and arms and growls. The night air was thick with the scent of blood, the sound of battle. Maximilian was off to the side fighting both a Taniwha and a ghoul. He was holding his own quite well, but the thought struck me, that this could be my chance. I circled the rest of the battle, coming up behind him as he struck out at the Taniwha, sending it flying through the air to land with a loud thud against a nearby container. I heard the crack of bones breaking and stopped short in my steps towards Max. I couldn't take my eyes off the fallen figure which had changed back to human form, long black hair draping over the female's shoulders. It was Celeste. My heart did a terrible thud- thudda- thud kind of missed beat. I was frozen where I stood, unable to look away, then I noticed, ever so softly, the rise and fall of her chest, the pulse rapid, but still strong, at the base of her neck. She was alive, barely, but alive. I reluctantly returned my attention to Max.

He was not there. Damn it. In the moment of distraction, whilst watching Celeste tumble against that container, I had missed him move. I frantically looked around to see where he had gone. Nothing. Nowhere. In fact, most of the vamps had vanished into thin air, leaving only four behind and one of those belonged to Michel. In my rage at losing Max, I dispatched the three foreign vampires quickly, letting my anger and frustration and heartache at the sight of all those fallen take me from one to the next in under a minute.

Michel's vampire looked alarmed but was trying to hold himself together. I stepped up to his ear and whispered, "Relax. You're safe. I'm not after you. Well, not tonight anyway." I have no idea if he heard me, because suddenly I was back in Michel's chamber and awake, all around me the sounds of battle seeping through the walls.

It was horrifying. I could hear the guttural growl of vampires, feel the crackle of power through the wall, the sounds of furniture and solid walls breaking, timber snapping, concrete cascading and windows shattering. It was louder than I expected, so much louder, like the sound was being piped into the room through surround-sound speakers.

I felt the weight of all that noise pushing against me, and although I had leapt up from the bed, I stumbled only a few feet away and fell to the ground, covering my ears and curling into a ball to protect myself. I realised I was rocking back and forward, back and forward and keening in a small high pitched scream. I tried to block the sounds out, but it took several minutes of failed attempts and fist banging against the floor before I was able to centre myself enough to detach. I could still hear everything, but the sounds were more muted and allowed me to breathe again.

I took a shaky step upright. Nothing happened. The noise still there, but controlled now, the world not closing in on me in a crushing wave. I took a deep breath in and walked over to the door. Naturally, it was locked, but by no locking mechanism that I could see. I felt around the edges of the shiny metal frame, unable to find purchase, or any indication of locks or even hinges. It was just a solid mass of metal, stuck inside another metal frame. I frantically glanced around the room, to see if there was something I could try and pry down the sides of the door. I rushed over the bedside table and quickly rifled through the drawers. Nothing, just paperback books, pads and flimsy ballpoint pens. I dashed into the bathroom and checked the cupboards there, nada. The dressing room was next; I flung clothes aside, emptied drawers and cupboards, but everything was just useless. Not nearly strong enough, nowhere near the right shape or size. I stifled a panicked whimper and reinforced my shields as the sounds from outside threatened to encroach.

Finally, I remembered my stakes and grabbed one out of my jacket. I ran back to the door and thrust it into the small gap on the side, the point of the stake going about 10mm in. Not much, but these stakes were solid, strong, moulded by a top silversmith in Egypt. Both of them gifts from Nero. I started moving the stake up and down the gap and then gently prying it sideways. Nothing was giving, so I tried the other side and then the top, standing on a chair and then the bottom. Nothing changed. Out of frustration, I slammed the stake as hard as I could into the side the locks should have been on and put all of my concentration into sending any power that resided in me towards the door, then twisted the stake as if to pry it open. I heard a snap, briefly thought I had succeeded, then felt my stake come away and watched its tip fall to the floor.

No friggin' way!

I couldn't help it, I screamed out in frustration and sunk to the floor with my back to the door and my head in my hands. I was trapped. Even if I tried to dig my way out through the walls, I knew Michel would have had the room lined, somehow, to be as strong as the door. It was useless. I felt useless. All I could do was sit here and listen to sounds of destruction and death coming from inside the bar.

Then I felt it. Michel's sudden fear, quickly replaced by searing pain. I was up on my feet screaming for someone to open the door in an instant, pounding against its solid mass until my hands were raw. All I could feel, though, was Michel's pain, interlaced with his desire to strike out, obviously at whatever or whoever had hurt him. He was full of anger, but he was having a hard time battling the pain, which was like fire through me, from the top of my head, right to the tips of my toes. My whole body felt like it was burning, so hot and raw and unfair. My heart was racing, and the sense of panic I felt was threatening to make me vomit. I realised I'd stopped banging on the door and was actually trying to pull strands of my hair out. I succeeded when a couple came away in my hand, stinging my scalp and making me separate myself briefly from Michel. I gasped, as soon as his emotions came flooding back in.

He was fighting the pain, and for a moment it felt like he was winning, his power level so great, it was thrumming through my veins, but it returned again with a vengeance. I couldn't take it; I was practically climbing out of my skin, my mind a raw mess of emotions, my heartbeat so loud I could hear it in my ears.

I began to concentrate on the sound of my heart, not trying to stop its rapid pace, but simply as a focal point to centre my mind. I felt like I was drifting away from reality, that this couldn't possibly be happening, that I hadn't seen a bright, young, lovable Taniwha die right in front of my eyes, or that Michel could possibly be hurting, dying right now. I could not believe it. I would not believe it.

I lay myself down on the floor on my side, curled up in a ball and just listened to my heartbeat, drowning out all other sounds of battle and all other sensations of Michel and just allowing myself to float there, not alive but not dead either. My body felt like it was just shutting down, the numbness that came over it a welcome relief from the pain and fear and heartache from before. I could stay like this forever. I could choose not to come back to this harsh world, that has such beautiful beings in it, amongst such evil. This felt right.

Then as I allowed myself that final move toward the blissfulness of nothing, the world changed around me and I was standing in the centre of the club, surrounded by fifty vampires, all in various forms of battle. The air was thick with vampire dust, but there was still so many. I looked down at my hands and found I was already holding my second stake. Another vision, just like before, I could hear, smell, feel everything, but no one could see or sense me. This was a gift I could not ignore.

I searched frantically for Michel, but couldn't see him anywhere. I couldn't feel him at all either, and that made me very, very scared. I could sense other vampires' *Sanguis Vitam*, but for Michel, there was just a void. Panic threatened me and my vision began to blur. I swallowed quickly and centred myself, reaching out my senses to hear my heartbeat and bring me back to the club.

As the room coalesced around me again, I tightened my grip on my stake and entered the fray. It was easy pickings. A small part of me felt like I was cheating, they had no defence. They couldn't hear me or see me. The first thing they knew of my existence was the feel of my stake sliding into their heart. But then I saw what they were doing to my vampires, and yes, I had a strong sense of Michel's vampires belonging to me. Well, at least, they belonged to my city, and I was damned if someone else was going to take out the vampires of my city without my consent. That was my job, and I so did not want to share.

I had dispatched about nine when I heard Enrique shout to Jock that something was wrong. *Wrong! Are you kidding? I'm helping you here.* But all Enrique could see was powerful master vampires being cut down in the droves and no reason for it happening. His fear blinded him to the fact that they were all Max's men and not ours. He had just taken out two vampires and had his back to the wall, scanning the room intently when I walked up to him and stood about a foot away, he didn't see me, didn't acknowledge me at all. I tentatively waved my hand in front of his face. Nothing.

"Huh?" I muttered under my breath.

"Who said that?" Enrique's eyes were wide, but his face had returned to its implacable mask. Show no fear.

Fancy that, he could hear me. Cool. "It's me you dolt. And I thought you'd be happy I was helping out. I have only been targeting Max's guys after all."

He let out a yelp and leant forward slightly. "Lucinda?"

"Got it in one," I said then turned and took out a vamp that had approached while Enrique was choking on his tongue trying to get himself under control.

"How are you doing this?" he asked as he started regaining his composure and scanning the room for approaching threats.

"Beats the hell out of me. Have you seen Michel?"

"No. I can't even see you." I rolled my eyes, of course he couldn't see me.

"Gotta go, more vamps to kill." And I ran in the opposite direction. I felt he was somewhat in control again, I didn't think the bad guys would get the drop on him now, so it was time to leave.

I spent the next twenty minutes taking out all but a few of Max's vampires in the room, making Michel's very nervous, but not exactly ungrateful of the respite. I did leave a few stragglers behind for Enrique and Jock to finish off. Michel's vamps and I'm guessing those of Enrique, Jock and Alessandra, were damaged and sore and we had lost quite a few, but I spotted Bruno and to my utter surprise, Shane Smith, so at least there was a bonus in there too.

But no Michel. Where the hell was he?

It dawned on me as I stopped to catch my breath, that I hadn't seen Alessandra or Max, for that matter, too, maybe they were where Michel was. I couldn't sense Michel, but I could sense everyone else, so I sent my spidey-sense or whatever the hell it was, out into the room and beyond, seeking them out.

I found them in the basement of the club, both of them, no-one else.

I dashed across the room and slammed into the door to the basement at the rear of the club. The stairwell was dark and dusty, not your usual dust either, the vampire kind. There'd been a battle here, a big one. I carefully stepped onto the stairs and watched as the thick dust swirled and puffed outwards away from my foot. I looked back at the steps behind me and in the light coming from the club could see my footprints as they descended the stairs. Creepy.

At the bottom of the stairs it was pitch black, but I could see light coming from the direction of Alessandra and Max's power, right at the end of the hallway. Michel had told me there were storerooms and vampire sleeping chambers off this corridor.

Remembering that old saying, *only fools rush in*; I decided to do a quick scan with my senses to see if anyone lurked off to the side hidden. They couldn't see me or sense me, but knowing my luck, they could probably find a way to kill me, so I wasn't risking it. Despite my heart and mind yelling at me to *Move it, Dammit!*

I couldn't sense a thing other than the pulsing power of those vampires ahead of me, so I quickly scurried along the hallway not giving a damn about the disturbed dust. I choked back a cough and peered in through the crack in the slightly ajar door. Alessandra and Max were facing off at each other, energy balls blazing, electricity filling the air. Michel was in a heap in the corner; I couldn't see him move, breathe, anything. Of course, that didn't really tell me much, vampires don't need to breathe, but it left me feeling shaky all the same.

The room was quite large, about the size of an average house's lounge, dining and kitchen put together, so that would make it three times the size of mine. There were two solid columns equally spaced in the middle, with support beams above to hold the floor of the bar up. Stacked along one side, covering the entire wall from floor to ceiling, were various boxes of top shelf liquor, surprisingly most of it was still intact. The room was otherwise empty of stock or furniture, either the storage space unused, or vaporised by the vampires now wielding an enormous amount of *Sanguis Vitam* at each other.

Alessandra's dress had been shorn off just below her butt, beautiful streamlined legs, going from here to Africa, for all I could tell - they were so long - were pouring out of the bottom of what remained of her dress. Her top was slightly ripped, but mainly OK and her hair only ever so slightly disturbed. This bitch just couldn't look bad anywhere, could she?

Max was sweating slightly and did have a quite a few rips in his shirt, his right sleeve having been completely torn off. There was blood all over his legs; I couldn't help feeling that some of that just might have been a friend's. I shook my head to clear it of that thought. He looked OK, but it was evident that he had been in a furious battle and only recently as some of the marks on his arm and cheek were only just healing over. Maybe Michel had managed to get a few strikes in before he fell after all?

I decided, while their concentration was on each other, I had to take my chance. I slowly opened the door, centimetre by centimetre, by the time I had it wide enough for me to slip through, Alessandra was on one knee, still battling, still looking frighteningly beautiful, but losing ground by the second. I slipped in and ran around the edge of the room to Michel. They didn't even notice the dust softly swirling in my wake.

I knelt down beside his body on the floor and gently reached out to touch him. He was warm. Thank God. And although I couldn't sense an ounce of power rolling off him, I could sense Michel was alive. I'm not quite sure how to describe it, but combined with the warmth, I just got a feeling of his presence, no power, just him, like a soul was lurking nearby. Weird doesn't even cover it.

I bent my head down to his ear and softly whispered, "Michel. Wake up. Michel, please don't be gone." My voice cracked a little then, which kind of sounded strange. If you've ever heard someone whisper and it cracks, you'd understand. Husky and squeaky at the same time. Not attractive.

He didn't stir, but I had the feeling the soul, or whatever the hell it was I could feel, did. I glanced over at Alessandra and Max. Max had taken a hit to the chest but was succeeding in his struggle not to go down. Alessandra had a look of intense fury on her face, but sweat was marring its perfection. She was working hard, and it was taking its toll. I quickly bent back down to Michel and tried again. "Michel, please. Please come back."

Now, I know what you're probably thinking, *why doesn't she just go and stake the big bad vampire while he's distracted by the bitch?* Unfortunately, it didn't even cross my mind. My sole focus was on Michel and getting him up and back, to me. Staking Max would have been great and all, but staking him without Michel around, was just not. And part of me feared that if I didn't get Michel's essence, soul, thingamajiggy back into his body right now, right this instant, it would all be over. I just couldn't contemplate anything else.

"Michel, please." I was begging now and practically crying, my eyes stinging from unshed tears, my throat raw and closing shut from emotion, my hands wringing in my lap. Of course, even if he were awake, he wouldn't have seen the distress on my face, but he could hear it. And luckily, that's all he needed.

"I am here, *ma douce*." I let a whimper out, I couldn't help it.

He sat up slowly, no colour in his face, his eyes a little glazed over.

Luckily Max was too occupied with Alessandra. I might not like the woman, but I sure as hell could appreciate the effort she was putting in right now, even if it was to save her own arse.

Michel took a deep breath in and his gaze focused on the battle crackling and sizzling in the room, I saw the purple swirls start to swim in his eyes, and I almost cried out in relief. Colour came back to his face, and he started to glow softly, like when I first met him that day in the bank. He stood slowly to his feet, not because he was still shaky I think, but because he didn't want to call attention to his movements, his eyes were fixed solely on Max.

I stepped away. I wasn't sure what was about to happen, but I didn't think my vision thingy would protect me from a direct hit, or at least, I didn't want to try and see what would happen if I got in the way of Michel's power. Michel raised his hand slowly, and I expected to see sparks fly or something, but Max simply fell to his knees. His head turned, and a look of utter incredulity spread across his features. So, he'd written Michel off, had he? He countered Michel with his own raised hand, both of them stretched out towards each other, Max's other hand raised towards Alessandra, but she was fading. Her head kept dropping down, and she'd jerk it back up and grimace.

Finally, when I could stand the tension no longer, Max smiled, flicked his wrists and simply disappeared. What the?

Alessandra immediately crumpled to the floor panting, Michel glanced casually around the room and then stepped over to her, resting a hand on her shoulder. She didn't even try to grab it in a possessive slutty manoeuvre, she simply hung her head and continued to try to catch her breath.

I made a move to walk toward Michel, then I felt it, the blur against my vision, the rush of sound fading past me and away and I let myself be dragged down into that nothingness that had brought me here, hoping against hope that it would take me back to my body. Waiting for the moment when sensation would return and I'd find myself on the plush carpeted floor of Michel's chamber.

But all I could feel was a void of nothingness that stretched on and on forever.

17
SLEEPING BEAUTY

I slowly woke to the sounds of something bleeping. I couldn't open my eyes or move my body and my hearing came and went for the first few hours. Every time it returned, there'd be the constant bleeping, not loud but persistent, repetitive, steady.

Finally, I started picking up other things about me, but they made absolutely no sense at all; the sound of birds, seagulls I think and wind whistling through the trees. The rustle of paper, the clink of a glass, the rush of waves against a beach. The humming of someone nearby, I couldn't make out the song.

Then I started to feel. The pull of something in the crease of my elbow, the weight of the blankets, the softness of the pillow which cupped my head and the soft warm hand holding mine, stroking the back of it with a thumb. Soft, warm and oh so comforting. I just lay there for a while revelling in the sensation. I decided it was time to see who was doing that to me, such a simple movement, but filled with so much care.

The light was harsh at first and I found myself blinking. The ceiling was a plain white, nothing special, a sunken light fixture in the middle, not directly over the bed. I turned my head towards the hand stroking mine and found Michel with his forehead resting on the side of my bed, his dark hair tumbling across the white coverlet on the mattress and butting up to my hip, one hand holding mine, stroking, the other resting across my legs. He didn't know I was awake.

I tried to say something, but no sound would come out, my throat was parched, so I opted for squeezing his hand instead. His head shot up and deep blue eyes, as deep as any ocean, looked into mine. He smiled.

"Tu es réveillés mon amour, mon précieux amour."

"English," I managed to whisper then licked my lips and cringed as my throat closed over completely. Michel quickly stood and reached for a jug of water, pouring some into a waiting glass, he held it to my lips and I sipped at it gratefully. You have no idea how much better I felt after that. I hadn't realised just how thirsty I was and how dry my throat had been and once that was dealt with, I felt a million times better.

But, Michel wouldn't let me get up straight away, he pushed the buzzer next to the bed and a human nurse came in. She fluffed around checking this and that out, taking my temperature, listening to my chest, flashing a pen light into my eyes and looking down my throat. I croaked out the *Ahhh*, but it seemed to satisfy her. She proceeded to remove a number of tubes from my arm, my nose and then one much lower. Once she was satisfied she had a quick word with Michel at the door and was gone.

I took the chance to sit up while his back was turned, swinging my legs over the side of the bed. The world tilted abruptly, and Michel caught me as I fell.

"Too soon, *ma douce*. You have been lying still for one week now; you need to let your body do this slowly."

One week? One friggin' week? No friggin' way!

He raised the back of the bed up halfway using a control on the side, hanging on a cord. It was kind of like those beds you see in the emergency room. He lay me back down gently, lifting my feet back onto the bed and perching on the side next to me.

"One week, huh?" I said, my voice sounding a little tinny, different, not quite yet strong, not mine. "What's that all about?"

Michel brushed my hair out of my eyes and let his hand trail down the side of my cheek. "You gave me quite a scare, *ma douce*. When I opened up the chamber at *Sensations* you were curled up on the floor. I could not rouse you. Nothing I could do could make you wake." He looked pained at the memory. "I had you brought here immediately and waited for you to stir."

He smiled then, a slightly wicked smile. "You do make a wonderful sleeping beauty, though."

Despite the unusual realisation that I had missed a week, totally slept through it, Michel was quick to bring me up to date on the events after I left the basement. It turns out, that Max didn't just vanish into thin air, he disappeared from our shores and ran into hiding. He knew he couldn't beat both Alessandra and Michel together. It had been close, he had almost defeated Alessandra after knocking Michel out and sending his soul flying, but when Michel reappeared in the basement, he knew he was done. He took the coward's way out and ran.

I had been asleep for exactly one week. Nobody could tell Michel why, the doctors and nurses he called in were at a loss. They said my body was fully functional, but my mind was resting. Michel had me connected to heart monitors, fluid and nutrition supplies and just waited. From the look in his eyes, it had been the longest wait in his life.

"So, Enrique and Stephen tell me you aided in the battle, after all, my dear."

We were sitting in the lounge of yet another of Michel's residences, where he'd had me resting after the fight. I felt a hundred percent, fighting fit, but he insisted we stay one more day before returning to the CBD. Looking out at the view over St Helier's Bay, there were lights of small watercraft twinkling on the waters and the dark shape of Rangitoto Island blotting the landscape. I couldn't tell if he was angry or slightly impressed.

"Stephen?" I opted to just ignore the tone altogether.

"Stephen was at the docks when you took out twenty vampyre in under a minute."

I spluttered, "It wasn't twenty."

"The number is irrelevant." Not to a hunter, but I thought I'd keep that to myself. "The fact that you did it is not."

There was a flash of something in his eyes. I couldn't quite grasp, it wasn't anger, but I couldn't tell what it was either. He was using everything in his arsenal to try to hide it from me. Even though I had got good at reading him, if he really worked at it, he could still hide his emotions from me.

The fact that he had to work at it at all said a lot about how much things had changed.

Well, the cat was out of the bag, so there was no sense denying it I suppose. "I didn't wake when you spelled me and left me locked in the chamber." I glared at him for that one, he simply looked back at me unmoved, waiting for me to continue. "It wasn't a dream, but something similar to what you create when you visit my dreams, it felt like that, but I could smell and hear and also touch and as you know, participate." My mind flashed briefly on Rocky, lying so still, so white. I had not participated then, other than to witness that horror, or intervened either. Of course I hadn't known I could intervene, but that's not the point is it? I should have tried. "No one could see me though, or sense me, or even hear my movements. It was as though I was a phantom. But I could kill. So I did."

I glanced at him to see if he found that repulsive, killing vampires when they don't even know you are there. It sounded barbaric, wrong, even to my ears. He must have been able to see the guilt on my face; it was too close to the surface and I hadn't even tried to hide it. Maybe I was slipping in that department too, because he reached out and took my hand and started stroking it. He didn't say anything, just gave me some warmth, when I had suddenly started to feel so cold.

"The first time, I didn't know what was happening, I just appeared at the docks in the middle of the fighting, but the second time, when I appeared in the club, I think I made it happen. I had woken up in the chamber and could hear the fighting in the club, but it wasn't until I felt you in pain, that I started to," I dared a glance in his direction, one eyebrow was delicately raised, "um, get a bit desperate. I panicked, I guess, I didn't want to hear or feel what I was hearing or feeling, so I just tried to not exist." It sounded all wrong, but it was really the gist of it. I had laid down on that carpet trying to block everything out, but when I felt the sense of nothingness approach, I had desperately grabbed it in an attempt to get away from everything else around me.

He sat forward and reached out to stroke my face. "What does it mean, Michel?" I asked. "I shouldn't be able to do this, should I? I haven't turned 25 yet, so if this is a power, which I can only imagine it is, why have I got it now?"

"I do not know, *ma douce*, I can only guess, but it is not something you should be afraid of. It is part of who you are, and without your interaction that night, the outcome may have been quite different."

"What can you guess it is then?" I was getting a bit desperate the more I thought about it. I had already been enough of a freak before, and I thought I had another two weeks, now only one week until I became more freaky and now this.

He looked contemplative then. I wasn't sure if he was going to tell me what he was thinking, but something shifted in his face as he said, "I have heard of one other Nosferatin, who came into some of their powers before they turned 25. This was a long time ago and I do not even know if they lived past their 25th birthday. But there were rumours of one in the Middle East. I had thought at the time, that he may have joined with the Master of Cairo, but she showed no signs of having been joined and still does not today."

A tingle of a thought went through me, just a brief glimpse and then it was gone. Something about what Michel had just said triggered a response deep within me, but it fluttered away before I could catch it.

"OK, but does it mean anything? It's not normal, does it mean I *don't* have to join?" Grasping at straws, but I had to try.

"No. The alliance between your people and mine is binding, conclusive. There is no way out. You will die if you do not join with us and the vampyre, as a whole, will lose their powers and become weaker over time if we do not have you by our side."

He didn't try to sugarcoat it, he had seen the hope in my eyes, but there was no point trying to run away from the inevitable, even though part of me still longed for it to be possible. I also knew I would have to make the biggest decision of my life soon, but I could delay it as long as possible, couldn't I?

I sat still for a moment digesting all of that. OK, so I had a nifty new power, one that I could obviously use now and at will, but one that came with a caveat, use only once during the course of an evening, or pay the consequences. Or, at least, I assumed that was how it all went.

Michel interrupted my train of thoughts. "I do think, however, that we should not advertise this ability, my dear. It would not be prudent to let the *Iunctio* become aware of this, it would - how shall I say? - cause quite a stir; I should think."

No surprises there. If vampires knew I could sneak up on them, unseen, unheard and not sensed, then there would be a riot for my head. I was now, probably, the most lethal thing in their world. I couldn't help grinning at that thought.

"How are you going to keep it quiet?"

He smiled slyly. "I have my ways." Then more seriously, "I have entered into an accord with Jock, Enrique and Alessandra."

My eyes widened at that. An accord, as you know is binding and vampires are usually very hesitant to enter into one with their own kind. It wasn't unheard of, but it was very rare. To do so was to tie themselves to what could potentially be a liability. There can be a lot of wheeling and dealing in vampire politics. An awful lot of duelling too, but mainly people just negotiate. They negotiate alliances, not accords, but fairly similar in its goal, and they align themselves with other powerful cities. The more allies you have, the more influential you are and therefore the more successful you will be in winning the city of your choice.

So far, Michel had been able to fight off any would-be pursuers of Auckland City, but the battle with Max had shown me that was not by strength alone. Michel was not as powerful as Max, but he had good connections. He was the perfect example of vampire politics in motion. He had manoeuvred himself into a position of power by aligning himself with the right people. I had no doubt in my mind that Michel was a devious and cunning mastermind when he needed to be.

So, although alliances are similar in their overall outcome as accords, they can be broken, which is a necessary evil in a world where wheeling and dealing can have drastic results. Michel obviously had alliances with Jock, Enrique and Alessandra, otherwise they wouldn't have come when asked for help, but now he had an accord with them too, and that can not be broken. Ever.

This also meant I'd be seeing a lot more of Alessandra. The bitch just wouldn't leave me alone, would she?

The length of time it took for me to digest this information had let Michel see I understood the ramifications. Michel had placed himself in a potentially dangerous position to protect me, but was it just because he cared? I doubted that completely. Did I want to confront him on that issue? Hell no. But I had to.

"Why would you do that?"

His lips curled slightly at the corners; even that small movement made his eyes light up with dancing swirls of every shade of blue. I could sink into those eyes if I allowed myself. "The end justifies the means, my dear. And as I have already told you, I will protect you no matter what. Forever."

He leaned forward then and cupped my face with both of his warm, soft hands. He took all of me in with that look, searching every inch of my face, as though he was committing it to memory, lest he never had the chance to gaze upon it again. "You are my kindred Nosferatin, Lucinda. There is no denying it, you know it as well as I. The connection between us is deeper than just simple attraction, although," his lips quirked, "that is undeniably a welcome addition to the mix, but it goes into the deepest part of us, it is as much a part of us as our own hearts." He started to stroke my cheeks, softly running his thumb along my jaw. "You may not be aware, *ma douce*, but not all vampyre have a kindred Nosferatin, some will live out their existence without such beauty in their lives. I have waited five hundred years for you."

His lips met mine, brushing against them in a slow, soft movement, then coming back to press more firmly, sending a shockwave of desire through my body. His tongue slipped between my teeth, seeking, searching, filling me with such longing I could hardly breathe. His hand now resting in my hair at the base of my neck, pulled my head back softly, exposing my sensitive neck to his mouth. The touch of his lips over my pulse made me shudder against him, he groaned softly against my skin and reached up with his other hand to caress my nipples, stroking softly against their already hardened tips with his thumb.

Heat was beginning to build within me, a luxurious flood of warmth starting down low and working up my body. It felt like every touch he made sent electric waves of pleasure through me. I was gasping and my heart had started beating in a rhythm all its own. Just when I thought I could stand it no longer, that I had to have him closer, had to have him naked against me, flesh on flesh, his head lifted suddenly away from me and he stilled.

"*Merde!*"

18
THIS CHANGES NOTHING

"I am sorry, Master. This cannot wait." Bruno's voice was even, but low, as though he feared Michel's response to his interruption. He wasn't looking directly at us either, but off to the side, as though eye contact would strengthen Michel's anger toward him. I had no doubt that it wasn't out of any sense of consideration of my dishevelled and lust-filled look. It was a survival mechanism, pure and simple. He was protecting his own arse, not my dignity.

Michel took a deep breath in, the power that had accumulated around him when he sensed Bruno's arrival was in check, but his eyes still flashed purple flecks in amongst the blue and indigo swirls.

"What is it?" Even, low and very scary.

Bruno hesitated, looking at me, then glancing quickly away. He was obviously unsure whether to disclose what information he had in front of me, but Michel hadn't moved from my side, his hands were still holding my arm and neck. So still and slightly more firmer than before, as though he was trying to control himself by staying connected to me. He hadn't even turned fully towards Bruno, which in itself was a statement that he was the boss and unafraid to have his back to the intruder. But by staying by my side he was saying more than just that, he was saying that anything Bruno had to say could be said in front of me. He was including me in his world despite him not knowing what blow Bruno was about to deliver.

Bruno cleared his throat slightly. "It's Maximilian, Master. He has been found."

The breath I was about to take in was forgotten, I tensed with unbridled fear. Michel began softly stroking my arm and neck and glanced over his shoulder to make eye contact with Bruno for the first time.

"Where?"

"Sydney, Australia." He paused then, only a fraction of a second, but Michel pounced. "Speak to me, Bruno!" The power that rolled off him let me know he had sent a command to his vampire, a not so subtle threat to obey. He was obviously losing his patience.

Bruno blanched when he felt the command's power hit him and hurriedly went on. "He has found a Nosferatin to join with, Master, they are joining tomorrow night."

Of all the things Bruno could have said I had *not* expected that. It's just as Michel said, there weren't that many of us around. I certainly knew of none in Australia, I could only assume he had found one somewhere else and had just taken them there. I hoped he hadn't found one of my friends from the website and was holding them captive, forcing them to obey.

"He *has* been busy," Michel said slowly, as he moved to sit next to me on the couch. Bruno relaxed visibly and came further into the room.

I wasn't dumb, I knew what this meant. With a Nosferatin by his side, Max would be unstoppable and I knew without a doubt that the first spot on his path to worldwide domination would be Auckland City and the little unsolved problem of me, and Michel.

"This changes things." Michel, stating the obvious. He sat still for a moment, obviously thinking things through. "Leave us, would you, Bruno. I will call for you when I am ready."

"Yes, Master." He was gone in a blur of speed, somehow managing to shut the door quietly, despite the fast exit.

I didn't like the look in Michel's eyes. I didn't like the way he sat there, so still. Not vampire still, but as though he was a tightly coiled spring about to unwind unexpectedly and scare the living daylights out of me. He sat there for a good two minutes. I didn't make a sound.

Finally, he spoke. "*Ma douce*, you know he will come here, with a certainty." Yes, I did. "You also know, I will not leave my city undefended." Vampires, by their nature, are territorial and proprietary, they do not give up something that is their's willingly. I had always known this about Michel. It was who he was, he couldn't help it, but, that also meant I knew what he was about to say to me and a very small, very tiny piece of my heart broke away and simply curled up to died, at the very thought.

"I cannot let you leave." In his mind, he owned me too, that much was clear and as such I was something he would not simply let walk out of his life, even if I wanted to. "And I could force you to comply. I could invade your mind and make you think that it is the right thing, the only thing to do. But I do not want to, *ma douce*." He took my hands then, they felt numb and cold, I could hardly feel the warmth coming through his fingers onto my skin. "Please do not make me."

He wasn't asking me to trust him, he was asking me to not make him break that trust, because basically, that's what it boiled down to. He could make me do this and I wouldn't even know he had done so until after the event. Despite my having a smattering of anti-vampire mojo skills and being more powerful than usual, Michel could do this. He is too strong and besides, his affect on my body would make his hold on my mind so much easier. I guess that's why when I do join with a vampire, they would no longer be able to do that, their powers having no effect over me unless I let them. I would of course hate him for it. I would never be able to trust him again and he knew this.

Now, I know what you're thinking. I'm going to have to join with a vampire before one month past my birthday anyway, or let myself die. Why not let it be Michel? He is charming, handsome, powerful and has way more light in him than dark, compared to most vampires. And I'll admit it, he pushes all my buttons, but if you have ever been forced into a corner by someone, forced to make a decision before you are ready to, then you will understand what I was feeling right then.

I stood up and walked over to the window, another large expanse of glass. I guess vampires get a bit sick of being locked in windowless chambers during the day; they seem to have an obsession with clear glass in their homes for the night. A cruise ship was slowly sailing past, heading out into the Hauraki Gulf. Small lights dotted the deck and deep sides and were reflected back on the surprisingly calm waters of the shipping channel. Right then, all I felt was how much I wished I was on that boat, heading off on some exotic holiday, no cares in the world.

He didn't crowd me, he stayed sitting on the couch, but I could feel him watching me, expectantly. Man, this sucked.

I am, if nothing, a practical person. I have always been able to break a problem down and work through its components to find a solution. It's just how my mind works. This was a little harder. Emotions were involved, even if I didn't really want to admit it. But the theory was the same. I thought about every detail that I knew. This was a decision I would have had to make in little under five weeks anyway, before one month past my 25th birthday, I just had to make it now, that's all. And the bottom line was this. Was I brave enough to walk away and die?

It's a question that has plagued me since finding out about this thing that I am. The one thing that I could not ignore or brush under the rug in an attempt to pretend it didn't exist. My ancestors had been brave enough, not only for themselves, but for their descendants, their children and grandchildren and great-grandchildren too. They had done something that took a tremendous amount of courage, I had at first thought it selfish, making this decision for their first borns, but I now realised they had been strong. Stronger than I think I could ever be.

Because as much as I can see the romanticism of the notion, sacrificing myself in order to deny the vampires power, I also knew without a doubt that I wanted it too. I certainly felt repulsed at the thought of sharing power with Maximilian, but when I looked at Michel, the pull or connection or whatever it was we shared was undeniable. I didn't want to die, I wanted him.

I turned to look at him, the window to my back. His eyes opened slightly at what was obviously a look of acquiescence on my face.

"This changes nothing, Michel. Nothing. You understand? It is just a joining of power." Don't ask me why, but that distinction seemed important to me. He may think he owns me, but he so does not.

He smiled his languid lazy smile, dripping in heat and sex and slowly glided over to take my hands in his. "Of course, my dear, of course. Anything you say."

As I was soon to find out, a joining is not simply an acknowledgement or alliance, it is closer in fact, to an accord. I couldn't just declare to the world that I was joined with Michel, it had to be witnessed and there had to be a sharing of blood. It was considered an extraordinary event, and vampires loved any reason to have a bit of pomp and ceremony.

So, despite my protests, word was sent out immediately to all vampires in New Zealand. I'm guessing a notice was put on the *Iunctio* too, even though it would alert Max to our plans, it was considered an important part of the wheeling and dealing of vampire politics. Michel was letting the world know just how powerful he was about to become.

Ordinarily the preparations for such an event would take several days, hence Max's not occurring until tomorrow night. He'd rushed it, but for whatever reason that was the soonest he could get it organised. Michel on the other hand, was prepared to cut a few corners and by 2 am I found myself in the main bar of a recently refurbished *Sensations*. Vampire tradesmen can reach a deadline in days, where regular humans would have taken months. The bar was unrecognisable. There was absolutely no evidence of what had happened just over a week ago, the place had been given an upspec too. New furnishings, now incorporating more reds, than golds and browns, and a slightly different layout. It looked good.

The club had been closed to humans and when we arrived there were already some fifty odd vampires in attendance, including to my utter surprise, Jock, Enrique and Alessandra. I thought they had left the country already, but they had to have been nearby in order to make it to the club within the few hours from the invitation being extended. Vampires can move at incredible speeds over land or water, but still.

We didn't greet them when we entered, Michel's entourage whisking us straight past those congregating in the club's main room, to the privacy of his chamber. When the door clicked shut behind us however, we were alone.

I was already nervous, but the sound of the door clicking just seemed to ratchet that up a notch or two. Michel came up behind me and placed his hands on my shoulders, pulling my back against the warmth of his chest , nestling his head into the side of my neck, smelling my scent.

"There are some things you should be prepared for, *ma douce*," he murmured into my skin.

Great. He'd been holding out. Why didn't that surprise me?

"Not all Nosferatin and their kindred vampyre have an attraction to each other, such as we do. The joining will create some sense of longing to be with each other for them, but it is purely designed to make them want to stay by each other's sides, to not stray. It will not make them feel more than that, unless an attraction later develops. For those who are attracted to each other from the outset, which we so undeniably are, the connection is somewhat more."

"Somewhat more?" I swallowed.

He had started kissing the side of my neck, up towards my ear and slowly taking my lobe into his mouth, nibbling, his breath warm against me, the sensation it created frustratingly intense. I felt my stomach contract and other areas tighten of their own accord too. "You may find it hard to resist at first, despite the surroundings, the initial rush of emotion can be overwhelming. It will subside, slightly, with time and you will get better at bending it to your will, but it may take practice."

"So...so, you're saying, I'll want to jump you as soon as the joining is complete, even if I don't want to?" This didn't change anything. I could handle it.

He chuckled against my skin, the sound of it sending further waves of pleasure through me. "It will not make you do anything more than you already wish to, my dear, it will merely amplify your emotions and desire."

When I stiffened, he turned me around slowly to face him and brought his head down to look me directly in the eye. His were swirls of blue and indigo, dancing and flashing in the light. I had a feeling that mine looked something like a deer's when sighted down the barrel of the hunter's gun. How ironic. "You will not be alone, *ma douce*, I too will be subject to its whim."

Oh, now that was just fine and dandy, wasn't it. I was the one who always pulled away from that final connection to him, he was always more than willing and ready to take it that further step. Why did the thought of him being unable to control himself around me make me scared and also send a shiver down my spine?

I was out of time now anyway, the decision had been made. I was just going to have steel myself and brace for the moment of truth. At least I could appreciate his telling me now and not just letting it hit me unawares in front of all those people. Forewarned is forearmed and all that.

We changed quietly, he allowed me privacy to do so, turning his back in the dressing room and concentrating on his own clothes. An event such as this required a certain level of dress, my normal attire of knee high leather boots, tights, mini-skirt and tee wouldn't cut it. A dress had been laid out waiting on our arrival. How Michel had organised so much so quickly and in the middle of the night was astounding. By the looks of the dress some designer had been hauled out of bed and made to open up shop just for me.

It was the most gorgeous deep blue, almost purple. Soft and luxuriant to the touch, it draped off my shoulders with a slight cowl neckline, baring my skin and neck. I didn't think that was by coincidence. The bodice was fitting, boned but not uncomfortable and the skirt flared out slightly at the hips. It fell to the floor in folds of draping fabric, pooling at my feet. I'd need either really high heeled shoes to avoid tripping over, or I was just expected to shuffle along like a slug, either way, it was making a statement with that amount of fabric, something along the lines of see, *I can waste expensive fabric, it means nothing to me at all*. There was no pattern on the dress, just an unrelenting shine that changed the hue of the fabric when I moved, making you think it was a moving picture, animated and alive.

My hair lay just below my shoulders now, but also spread out over them like a cape. I'd showered at Michel's house before we left, so it was dry and shiny and straight. The way it normally looked, but coupled with the fabric of the dress, you'd almost swear I had highlights in there, which I don't.

I turned to find Michel watching me. He was dressed pretty much as he always was, the only change was his tie, another blue, complementary to, but not matching my dress. That would have been too much. I guess his dress style was more fitting to the occasion than mine, no designer having to lose sleep outfitting him in the middle of the night.

His gaze was heavy, soaking me in, his eyes shone brightly. "You are beautiful, *ma douce.*"

My heart skipped a beat. Stop that! I chided it.

"Shall we?" He offered his arm, I paused.

"Just one more thing," I said as I rushed out of the room and over to my bag.

I rummaged in it for a moment, then came out with my silver knife in a little slim holder. A silver stake will kill a vampire instantly. If entered through the heart, a knife, while not as good, can cause enough damage for you to get away. I have disabled a vampire with a silver knife to the heart before, but only long enough to reach my stake and finish him off, just before he moved. It's not much, but I'd feel better having it on me. I may be *joining* into this vampire world, but I still know my part in it. I'm a vampire hunter and always will be.

I didn't waste time, lifting my leg up and resting my high heeled foot on the side of the bed and hiking my dress up to attach the knife to my upper inner thigh. I only just realised who I was doing that in front of when a warm hand was suddenly tracing the knife's holder and strap along my skin, sending instant shockwaves through me.

"If you insist on distracting me, my dear, we may never see this through." His voice was husky in my ear, the warmth of him enveloping me and pulling me towards him. I took a deep breath in an attempt to steady myself, only to immediately regret it, he smelled so good, so fresh and clean and like the ocean breeze. I sighed.

He pulled away, almost pained, and offered me his arm again. Here we go, I thought and walked out to face whatever destiny this life had in store for me.

The room stilled when we entered. A slight crackle of *Sanguis Vitam* around the edges, excited vamps can have some trouble reining themselves in sometimes. I'm guessing a few of these guys here were pleased their master was about to get a double load of power. Nothing makes a vampire happier than knowing they're on the right team.

A space had been cleared in the middle and we proceeded to its centre. I was finding it difficult to concentrate on my surroundings, the faces of all those vampires about me blending into one another. I could no further have told you where Shane or Bruno, or even Alessandra, was at that moment, than fly to the moon. My heart had started beating at an alarming rate causing my head to pound and my vision to blur even further.

Michel leaned in to me and whispered so only I could hear, "Calm yourself, *ma douce*, they can feel it."

He was right of course, every vampire in that room could taste my fear. It was not a good thing to show fear in front of a vampire. My anger and rage may be an aphrodisiac to Michel, but I was damn sure that my fear would go a long way to getting this lot excited too. I centred myself as best I could, concentrating on my heartbeat like I had done to enter the dream state that let me shift to the battles, but not allowing myself to seek out the nothingness that lay beyond. Within a few moments, my heartbeat was back under control and my breathing settled. Michel had waited patiently by my side doing nothing to assist me, knowing this was not something he could interfere with. I needed to show all those here that I could control my fear in front of them, that I didn't need his influence to protect me. They would find it hard to respect me otherwise, and as his Nosferatin, he needed them to.

Bruno approached then from the side. I hadn't seen him standing waiting there of course, but as soon as I had gathered myself he had started towards us. He too would have sensed just when I had myself back under control. He held a platter out to Michel, on it a stainless steel knife. It looked wickedly sharp.

Michel didn't hesitate, he picked the knife up with his left hand and sliced the palm of his right, turning it over and offering it hilt first to me. My lips were dry, my throat felt tight, but I forced myself to breathe and accepted it. My hand was only shaking slightly as I dragged the blade against the sensitive skin on my palm. It stung and started dripping blood onto the polished concrete floor of the room. The vampires around me visibly stiffening. Great.

Michel sensed it too and so didn't muck about. He reached for my hand and as soon as our palms met and blood mingled he shuddered visibly, standing almost rigid, his eyes closed with his jugular veins standing out starkly against the cream colour of his skin. He was swallowing hard, like he was fighting to stay in control, to handle whatever had poured from me to him. He tingled to the touch and blazed brightly, just for a moment, then opened his eyes and looked at me, a brief look of surprise crossing his features, then settling into his usual lazy-dripping-with-sex gaze. I almost pulled away, the purple was so intense... and then I felt it.

It started as a slow burn and soon erupted into an inferno. I couldn't take my eyes off him and suddenly found myself next to his chest. He hadn't pulled me to him; somehow I had taken the step necessary to put myself under his chin and against his chest. He smelt intoxicating. I found myself running my fingers across his chest, relishing the feel of his hard muscles under the material of his jacket and then I decided the jacket was too thick, so quickly fumbled with the buttons, determined to get the damn thing off him. He didn't stop me as I rushed to push the jacket over his broad shoulders. But as soon as the jacket was on the floor, my fingers had slipped inside his now opened shirt and were kneading his flesh with an urgent longing. I felt his hands come around me, touching me, moving up and down my back, over my bare shoulders and around to my collar bone and neck. The sensation his returning touch created was like lightning striking the earth.

Suddenly his lips were on mine in a bruising kiss, all hard passion and heated desire. There was nothing of the finesse I had come to expect from his kisses; this was pure demand and need and longing all rolled up in one. His tongue devoured me, and I wrapped one of my legs around his thigh, crushing myself to him, opening my mouth up and giving as much of myself to him as he was to me. All of a sudden he tipped my neck back and I watched as his fangs come out and down in one swift motion, his mouth was on my pulse before I could protest, his fangs piercing skin within an instant, his *Sanguis Vitam* filling the air and the pull of blood leaving me startling. I stiffened at the shock of what he was doing, I had so not expected that; he hadn't warned me, he hadn't even hinted that that was a possibility. Of course, he had mentioned that feeding could be pleasurable to the donor as well as the vampire, so I had assumed it would take some part in sex, but for the life of me, I had never really thought he would bite me.

And then, I wanted him to. I wanted this connection, this intimacy, more than I had wanted anything else in this world before and as those thoughts came pouring into my head I heard another's voice, whispering, pleading, insisting, "*mine, mine, mine, mine, mine.*"

Oh good lord, what have I done?

He stiffened, as though he had heard me. I did only say that in my mind, didn't I? Yes, because right now the only sounds coming from my mouth were whimpers and groans, not at all ladylike and absolutely no room for a coherent sentence in amongst them at all.

He pulled his fangs out and gently licked the blood that continued to flow, slowing it until it stopped altogether. He softly kissed the spot he had bitten, so tenderly, then pulled his head back and looked at me, his eyes blazing a deep amethyst, interlaced with pale violet - mesmerising.

"So, do you still think this changes nothing, *ma douce?*"

Oh, God in heaven help me.

19
SERVITUDE

I became aware of the stillness in the room. The vampires were all motionless, watching with fervent expressions, but as still as they could ever be. No breathing, no heartbeats, just a very unnatural obsessive-type look to their eyes.

Michel took my hand and turned us toward the crowd. "I present to you, my kindred Nosferatin."

The room, as one, went down on bended knee. The only vampires not complying were Jock, Enrique and Alessandra. Jock looked vaguely uncomfortable, Enrique's eyes glazed a bright intensity looking only at me, and Alessandra looked like she had swallowed a particularly nasty bug. But, the three of them approached as one, gliding across the room to stand in front of us.

All three bowed at the waist, hand fisted over heart. Even Alessandra. Curtsying not the thing for vampires then, huh? As they rose they said in unison - *had they practised this or what?* - "We pledge our undying allegiance to the Durand Line."

Whoa. What did that mean? They already had an accord, they didn't need to forgo their position of equality within it, but here they were, shouting to the world, that Michel was now considered as good as their Master too.

They hadn't finished yet - *no, of course not!* - they turned their attention to me and again in unison said, "We pledge our lives in the protection of the Durand Nosferatin" and bowed again.

What?

I glanced at Michel, but he didn't seem surprised at all. If anything his face told me he had expected nothing less. I was a little dumbfounded, to say the least.

Michel inclined his head and looked at me. *What, I'm supposed to say something?* I decided a nod should do. It did. They all relaxed then and started talking, the other vampires in the room got up off their knees and started mingling, catching up on battle stories and the like. Goody, must be party time.

Shane Smith sidled up to me, hesitantly. "Welcome to the family, Luce." What could I say? "Um, thanks, Shane." That seemed to be enough for him, so he smiled and went off into the crowd.

Enrique and Jock were in deep conversation about Max and how he didn't stand a chance now. Cocky didn't even cover it, and Alessandra was, well hot damn, she was flirting, all eyelids fluttering and breasts heaving with Michel. Bitch! He wasn't doing anything to encourage her, but he wasn't doing a damn thing to stop her either, so I decided I wasn't going to hang around and watch that spectacle and a drink 'round about now, would be mighty fine.

Bruno was at the bar, so I slipped into a seat next to him. He signalled to the barman, a vampire named Doug. Yeah, I know I laughed the first time I heard it too. And Doug started pouring me a *Bacardi & Coke*, my favourite. Guess the staff had been appraised of what I liked.

The strange thing is, I know I've said in the past that I wouldn't want to meet Bruno alone in a dark alley before, but lately, the guy's kind of grown on me. He's still a big nasty brute, all sly grin and fierce eyes, but he is the one vampire in Michel's entourage that I have had the most to do with. And although he still does the whole, *you're the Master's, Luce* thing, he also treats me exactly how I like. He knows I'm a vampire hunter and he respects that. No bull.

"Well that went well," I said a little sullenly into my glass.

"No more than to be expected, Luce."

"What do ya mean?"

"We all knew you were powerful; it was expected Michel would gain much from the joining."

All right, now he had me interested. I had sensed the power pouring into Michel when our palms were pressed together; I had seen his visible response to it, the way he even struggled to stay in control of it. But although I could sense a surge in his power level right now, I didn't think it was *that* impressive.

"Yeah, well he's doubled his power, we knew he would."

Bruno laughed. "You probably missed it, being all gooey eyed and all," I *so* resented that gooey eyed comment, "but he's more than doubled it."

I spun around in my chair and looked toward where Michel was standing with Alessandra, a slightly bored expression on his face, which funnily enough did perk me up a bit, but I couldn't see it. I couldn't see the increase in power that Bruno was referring too.

"I don't see it."

"Nah, he's taking great lengths right now to hide it." Why was Bruno telling me this, why all of a sudden did I get carte blanche in the Durand inner circle? Oh, yeah, that's right I've just *joined* myself to the boss. I am as good as one of them now. I wonder if that means I can't stake 'em now, when they do something wrong? An uncomfortable thought I'd address later.

I turned back to my near empty drink and drained it, holding up the glass and shaking it at Doug. He filled it in lightning speed and slid it back towards me. I took a large gulp. Then another.

"Why are you upset?" Bruno asked, without even looking at me.

How did I answer that? Could it be that I was upset because despite everything Michel still leaves me out of the loop? He expected to have more than doubled his power level, but he never let me know that. His right hand goon expected he would get more than double his power level, hell, probably the whole damn Durand line expected it, but I didn't. Suddenly the cocky comments between Jock and Enrique after our joining made sense. And, if I was truthful, what really worried me and I mean *really* worried me, was that I'm not sure how Michel will be with all that power. I had only just got my head around the fact that he would double his and now I had to take on board the fact that he had gained even more. Michel at full power was frightening, how much less human would he be now?

And there you have it. The crux of the problem, as they say. I'm a descendant of another race, but the blood of that non-human race is so diluted by now, that more than half of me is most definitely still human. Michel hasn't been human for over 500 years and now he was moving even further away from me.

I settled on, "I'm surprised, not upset. There's a difference."

"Well, you should be happy. This means you're likely to come into a shit load of power too when you turn 25."

And that was enough to stop my heart, right then and there. I didn't need this, I really, truly, most definitely did not need this. Does anyone even comprehend that it's been only a couple of weeks since I found out my weird and freakish anti-vampire/hunter skills were descendant from an inhuman race? Yet, still, they pile crap heap after crap heap after crap heap of new and frightening information over my head. I was drowning.

I never wanted power. I was happy I'd be faster, stronger. All those things that would aid me in hunting down scumbag vampires. I was even pretty impressed with my dream vision thing, as it enabled me to continue fighting when I wasn't even there. But gaining so much power, the amount that Bruno was alluding too, just made me feel cold.

I finished the rest of my drink and felt my world go a bit fuzzy. A bit of warmth returned to my extremities, I was even tempted to have another, but I never knew when I'd feel the pull and need to confront a vampire, so two glasses of alcohol were always my absolute limit. Besides, I had a sudden urge to be out of here. To be back in my apartment. To be surrounded by the familiar. To not have to pull my shields around me when faced with the *Sanguis Vitam* of so many vampires in the one room.

The only problem, my bag with my stake in it, was in Michel's chamber. And walking home with (1) no stake and (2) dressed in this beautiful yet cumbersome-for-fighting dress, was just not gonna cut it. I'd have to make a quick dash to the room, change and try to sneak out. Ha! Sneak out past fifty vampires; that would be the day. But a girl's gotta try, right?

I told Bruno I needed to pee; he just grimaced, and I skirted the club floor and slipped into the passage to Michel's chamber. It was open, so I partially closed the door - wouldn't want it to bloody lock me in here - and quickly ran over to my bag, grabbing a change of clothes and starting to strip.

Of course, I could blame the alcohol; I'd had those two glasses in under half an hour after all, *and* my stomach was empty, (I hadn't felt like much food this evening for some reason). But really, I was just so damn eager to get out of there, and my nerves were so frayed that I wasn't concentrating on my surroundings. So I didn't hear the door slowly open and then ever so slowly close and I most certainly didn't hear the click of the deadbolts sliding home, but I'm presuming they did because the first thing I heard was his voice and he was standing right behind me.

"Going somewhere, *ma douce?*"

I'd already slipped the dress off, it was lying in an undignified puddle to the side, so I was standing in just my knickers and strapless bra, one leg raised about to slip into some jeans. I stumbled at his voice, getting my leg tangled in the jeans and started falling backwards with a squawk. He caught me before I hit the ground and hissed at the shock his fingers against my naked flesh had received.

We landed on the carpet, one of his arms around the back of me, hot against my skin through the thin material of his shirt. His body above me, pressing down my side, moulding to me. His other hand already stroking across my stomach, following the ridge of my hip bones, then down to my briefs and flicking in under the lace at the top. I shuddered, I couldn't help it, the convulsion almost as good as an orgasm. His eyes blazed that new amethyst-with-violet-flecks colour and he leant in to kiss my neck, my jaw, up to my cheeks, eyelids, nose and then finally, thank you, God, my lips.

His kiss was divine, so hot and wet and everything my body craved at that moment. "I want you so badly, *ma belle*. I am fighting to stay in control," he whispered against my lips, his French accent thick, slipping his tongue in my mouth in between words, nibbling my bottom lip with his teeth when he finished. My hand had found his hair, scrunching it in my fingers as his kisses stoked the fire within, my other hand resting against his rock hard chest.

I pushed against that chest and rolled him over onto his back, straddling him, not caring about my near nakedness, relishing the feel of his already hard shaft pressing against me, fighting to escape the confine of his clothes. I leaned down, pulling his shirt apart, allowing the buttons to tear and pop off in all directions and began laying kisses all over his chest, up through the light curl of hair, to the hollow below his neck and then on around passed his pulse point to his ears. Biting, kissing, nibbling and loving the way he moaned and writhed beneath me.

His hands gripped me on the hips and started moving me against him, a slow, languid stroking of body against body, the friction creating heat that rapidly built threatening to consume me. Suddenly his hands left my hips and undid my bra at the back deftly, throwing it aside with what looked like offence at its obstruction. He reached up and grasped one of my now naked breasts, raising his head to take the other in his mouth.

I arched against him in response, little electrical shocks streaming through my body, a growing need creeping up from my centre stretching out to everywhere; fingers, toes, lips, right to my core. He responded with equal urgency; his hands covering my skin, every part of me he could reach, first stroking my back, then quickly moving to my arms, then down my stomach, up to my face, across my clavicle. It was as if he couldn't get enough of me; I knew how he felt.

Without even realising we had moved I felt the softness of the bed beneath me, the feeling of sinking into the covers. Michel was a blur; when he stilled he was standing in front of me in all his naked glory. He was beautiful. All lean muscles and long limbs. The cream colour of his perfect skin reflecting a slight sheen, a trickle of sweat making its mesmerising way down the centre of his chest, then his stomach, to nestle in amongst the soft curls above his sex. My eyes had followed its lazy journey down his body and were now resting on the sight of him. It lengthened slightly beneath my gaze.

He swallowed visibly, then moved toward me. Before I'd even

drawn a breath, he had removed my pants, somehow ripping them away without me even feeling it. He gently manoeuvred himself between my legs, holding the weight of his body above me with the strength of his arms. He ran his hardened shaft against me, covering the length of me, and then repeating it. I cried out in need, arching myself towards him.

He didn't give in, just continued to tease me in the same manner, leaning down to kiss me passionately on the mouth, gently biting me on the bottom lip, stopping to stroke my face and neck, then returning to teasing me again. The pressure building inside me was relentless, it couldn't escape, it wrapped around me, lifting me up on a wave and threatening to throw me off the other side, only to lower me gently back down again and then start all over.

I was writhing uncontrollably under him, gripping the sheets at my side, all but going crazy under his touch. Finally, I could stand it no longer. "Michel, please" I begged. I don't know exactly what I was begging for; to stop? To finish this? For release?

He moaned, a sound so vulnerable and raw, and thrust inside me in one motion; slowly pulling out and pausing, before repeating the action again, differing the speed, lengthening the pause, making me lean towards him, reach up to grasp his shoulders, trying to pull him to me and finally calling out in frustration and need. He laughed, a warm, throaty laugh, kissing me roughly on the lips and sped up his movements into me, taking me with him on a wave of pure bliss and hot need, higher and higher until we both could go no further and crashed back down to earth in the most delicious rainbow of colours.

He collapsed beside me on the bed, pulling me close and whispering sweet nothings in French against my neck, kissing me, smelling me, touching me. As though he never wanted this moment to end. My breathing was unsteady, and my heart was marching to its own beat, but all I could feel was the languid bliss and afterglow that flowed through me, the warmth of his body and breath against my skin, the touch of his hands and fingers over my hot flesh.

Finally, when the world stopped spinning, and the colours of the rainbow behind my eyes began to fade, it occurred to me that I had thought I could stop this from happening. Boy, had I been wrong.

Michel kissed my neck above my pulse, where he had bitten me earlier and reached behind to grab the covers, pulling them up and draping them over us, cocooning us in their warmth. The kiss to my neck had reminded me of what had happened earlier, how shocked and angry I had been that he had bitten me, I reddened at the fact that I had completely forgotten that thought and fallen so willingly into his arms. What was wrong with me?

"Why are you angry, *ma douce?*" he whispered against my cheek.

"I'm not angry." It was an automatic response, out before I had even comprehended his question.

"I can feel your emotions, all of you, you have no idea how impossibly intoxicating it was when I came in this room. When I touched you. Everything I was feeling multiplied by you, but more. It was *your* want I could feel, *your* desire that washed over mine. It almost drowned me. And I can feel your anger now too."

"You have got to be kidding me? You can feel what I'm feeling?" I turned my head to look at those impossibly blue eyes.

His lips quirked slightly at the edges, his eyes sparkling in the low light of the room. "A perk of the joining it would seem."

Oh shit. So, I wouldn't be able to hide a thing from him, well not at least what I was feeling. "You can't read my mind too, can you?"

He sobered at the sound of my voice. "No. But I don't need to; your emotions are so expressive, so vibrant, full of life. It is like a drug to me that I could never hope of quitting." He seemed pretty pleased with this turn of events. I was mortified.

I pushed his arm and the covers away, reaching down to the bag beside the bed to find some new underwear and slipping into them quickly before he could protest. He didn't stop me, he just watched, lying back on the bed like a well-fed cat, basking in the afternoon sun. I guess he was probably feeling pretty full right now. Full of my power. Full of my blood. And full of my emotions.

"Why are you so angry?"

I clenched my fists then forced myself to relax again. Shaking my head from side to side. Well, if he really wanted to know...

"Could it be that you hid from me the extent of power you would get in this joining? Or wait, maybe it's the fact that you bit me, without even warning me that could happen? Or, perhaps, I'm a little miffed that we just had sex, when I thought I had made it perfectly clear that that was off the menu? You pick, Michel, but if you give me enough time I'm sure I can think of more."

I snatched my jeans up off the floor and started pulling them on, my foot getting caught sideways down one leg, forcing me to hop around while I tried to dislodge it. Bugger. Couldn't even be ladylike when throwing a hissy fit.

His arm reached out to steady me before I threatened to topple over completely, visions of when he first entered the room washing over my mind and sending sparks along my skin. Of course, I hadn't even seen him get up off the bed. He turned me towards him, but I continued to do doggedly try to do my jeans up, the bloody zip catching and sticking. He gently reached down and took over, closing the zip with a soft *zzzt*, buttoning the top closed, but leaving the fingers of one hand resting on the upper edge, just inside, holding me still by that simple contact. His other hand reached up and stroked my bed tousled hair out of my eyes.

"I told you once before, *ma douce*. Your anger is my aphrodisiac."

He didn't try to kiss me, his lips curling in that sly grin, then stretching further into a beautiful smile that lit up his entire face. My breath caught in my throat, and I couldn't look away.

"Stop it," I whispered.

"Never," he replied and grinned further.

We just stood there looking at each other, me hardly breathing, heart stammering along, him calm and implacable, but warm and open.

"I can't go on like this, Michel. I'm going to need some space, time to think about all of this."

"What is there to think about, my dear? We are meant to be together, why do you fight it so?"

"You've practically taken over my life! I'm no longer Lucinda Monk. Bank teller and vampire hunter. I'm now Lucinda Monk immortal Nosferatin, joined to a kindred master vampire and about to come into an enormous amount of power. *And* unable to keep my bloody hands off you." He smiled further at that. "I need some space to get my head around all of this. I need to go back to my apartment."

He stepped back then. "Of course. I shall have Bruno drive you."

"Thanks," I said, a little unsure why he was agreeing so quickly.

"Um, what's happening with Max? When are we going to face him?" I may have wanted out of there, to be surrounded by only myself, but I hadn't forgotten what this joining had all been for. Max was always in the back of mind, sad but true.

He didn't smile; he just wore that mask he puts on when dealing with his vampire protégé; unfeeling, unmoving, un-anything.

"*We* are not going anywhere. I am."

My stomach dropped. "Like bloody hell!"

20

TRAPPED

"I will not be moved on this, Lucinda." Great. We'd made it to Lucinda already. "You would be in great danger from Maximilian, and I will not have it."

"You don't get to decide everything, Michel."

"Oh? Why would you think that? We are joined, and you are still an immature Nosferatin, yet you believe you can go up against a master vampire who has joined to a Nosferatin himself. A master vampire that will be more powerful than any you have faced before. You cannot imagine the power he will wield against you. Clearly, your abilities to judge the situation are lacking and therefore, I must do it for you. You are not invincible, Lucinda and I will not have you harmed."

I was not sure if that last sentence had been tagged on there just because he was getting a doozy of emotional anger rolling off me right then, I really wasn't convinced that he was *that* concerned for my safety. Sure I get killed he dies, but it's not the same as wanting someone's well-being because you care, is it?

Right now, I really wasn't even sure if he cared.

"How do you think you can stop me, Michel?" Huh! I had him there.

"My powers may have little effect on you, my dear, but Bruno's would. He will contain you until this is over." Oops. Forgot about that.

"This isn't right, Michel. I am a vampire hunter, I am capable of doing this, you need to have some more faith in me." My voice had sort of trailed off at the end there. I hadn't meant it to, it was just, well, I was kind of feeling a bit rejected and doubtful really. Rejected by Michel, whom I admit I did seek approval from - sucker that I am - and doubtful of my own abilities. If Michel said I couldn't handle it, was he right?

He just stood there, an odd look on his face, rigid in his body but such conflict in his eyes, like he was battling something inside. He shook his head and let a long breath out. His features softened a bit then, and he ran a hand through his hair. "I am not used to all this emotion. How can you live with this? It should consume you, rule you, yet you go from one emotion to the other without pause. I had forgotten how turbulent being a human could truly be."

I didn't know what to say to that. *Serves you right* seemed a tad babyish, so I just looked at him. If he was having trouble receiving all my emotions, then he should try living in my skin. On second thoughts, maybe not.

He sat back down on the bed then, looking a little defeated. My hopes rose, maybe he would meet me half way on this one. If we were going to work side by side for near eternity then we had to start trusting each other, right?

Unfortunately I'm not as good at reading him, as he is at reading me.

"I am sorry that you cannot understand that this is for the best."

Not I'm sorry for being a jackass, or I'm sorry for not believing in you, or I'm sorry I'm hurting your feelings and making you feel inferior and a child. No. That would mean he was something remotely like a human and Michel was definitely not. My life was spiralling out of control; I could hear the gurgle of it spinning down the plughole out of sight. If I didn't do something to stop this, I was going to lose complete command and Michel *would* be my master. I couldn't allow that to happen. I could not allow myself to be anyone's property. Hell, I'm a 21st Century woman, damn it. This is not the middle ages!

I just glared at him and shook my head sadly. I knew he could contain me; Bruno would hold me with just his little finger, and without staking him, which I reluctantly realised I didn't really want to do, there would be no way to get away from him. But, I could go along with this and then use my new vision shifting abilities to join the party, couldn't I? Somehow I was sure that I could shift to wherever Michel was, regardless of the distance between us. But, I didn't think it would be good to let Michel know how agreeable I was to this situation. He would know that I was hiding something and probably create an even harder cage for me to break from.

"I'm not happy, Michel."

"Oh, *that* I can tell, my dear" Good, if I could just hold onto that emotion, it's all he'd see.

"I don't think I can be near you right now," I continued. "I want to go home."

He really did look a little hurt at that briefly and then it was gone, replaced again by that mask; that horrible, stiff, controlled and unfeeling mask.

He stood and headed towards the dressing room, turning his back to me and throwing a final comment over his shoulder. "Bruno is ready for you outside." He shut the door to the dresser with a very final and resounding click. It sounded a little bit like the crack that had just split my pounding heart in two.

Nothing had changed in my apartment. Everything looked exactly as I had left it. The early morning light was starting to seep in through the windows. The sun would be well and truly up soon. I crossed the lounge to stand before the bouquet of roses on my table, unshed tears stinging the corners of my eyes. I grabbed the offending flowers and tossed them in the bin, then sat down and suppressed a shudder at what Michel's residual *Sanguis Vitam* signature was doing to my pulse. Damn him! Damn him for being what he was and damn me for wanting him despite it.

I'd been up all night but I wasn't tired, on the contrary, my roller coaster of emotions had just keyed me up, there was no way I could get any sleep now. I glanced up at the calendar on the wall of my kitchen and noticed that Rick should be at the gym early this morning. I'd long ago taken to keeping a copy of his roster; his hours were so chaotic I never knew when I could catch up with him.

Suddenly, I really needed to see my friend.

Despite his reaction to me just before the battle, I didn't even consider the fact that he wouldn't want to see me as much as I wanted to see him. We were mates, buds, the best of friends and had been from the first day we met. I needed to hear his voice, to have him joke with me, to make me feel like everything that had happened in the past 24 hours was just a bad dream. I needed the gravity Rick brought to my world; he made me feel stable, he steadied the spin when it threatened to suck me away.

I took a quick shower and dressed in my usual Gym garb; ¾ length yoga pants and a tight fitting tee, stuffed my bag full of all the necessary paraphernalia; stake, knife, change of clothes etcetera - everything a modern day girl should need - and headed out the door. The six-minute jog to the Gym was a nice warmup; people were already at the weights and running on the treadmills. The usual pre-work workout. Live in a city and exercise in a box. These guys wouldn't even know what it felt like to race through a paddock chasing little lambs, with the wind in your hair and the quiet of the country calming your mind.

Rick was punching a bag on his own, no client or class it would seem, just working out his muscles and loosening up for the day. He didn't hear me approach, I think my stealth abilities had improved lately, another vampire hunting bonus.

"Hey." I didn't say it loud, but he practically jumped right out of his skin. I smiled widely.

"Jeez, Luce! You damn near gave me a heart attack. Don't do that!" And then he stilled. He just looked at me, with this unusual expression on his face, like he was seeing me for the first time and he wasn't sure if he liked the view.

"What's wrong?"

"You look different. Like you have a glow or something. It's strange."

I tried to smile, but it sort of came out as a bit of a grimace. "Maybe it's something I ate?" I joked, but it didn't feel that funny.

He wasn't saying anything, so before it got too uncomfortable, I decided to ask the one question that had plagued me since I woke up from my sleep, or whatever it was.

"How's the Hapū? How's Celeste?" OK, so that was two, but you get the picture.

I had heard Celeste had survived; she'd been badly hurt, but had managed to escape any further harm once I'd left her. Michel had kept tabs on the Hapū while I was out of it and had also let them know where I was and what was happening. I had found that a little unexpected, I hadn't thought he'd have it in him, but I later found out Jerome had phoned twice daily for three days before Michel finally caved in.

Rick relaxed a little then, as though we were back on familiar territory. "She's doing great, she got up out of bed yesterday and spent the day out on the deck reading. She's tough; she's gonna be all right. It's Joe we're worried about. He misses Rocky."

Rocky, dear sweet, funny Rocky. I'd missed the Tangi, that was probably a good thing, I'm not sure I would have been welcome. The Hapū must be hurting right now; I made a promise to myself to go and see Jerome when this was all over, give him my condolences and thank him for his help. A phone call just wouldn't cut it.

"I'm so sorry, Rick. This is all my fault."

"Don't say that, Luce! It is Not. Your. Fault. Got it? We were proud to be fighting. You have no idea, it felt so right, like we had been denying ourselves this for so long. We are meant to fight alongside you and kill the vampires."

I was a little concerned at the vehemence in his voice just then, as though this was a pledge, not only to me but himself, to kill as many vampires as he could. Great. Just what I needed.

Just then his 7:30 appointment walked in, so he had to leave me. I spent the next hour punching my frustration out on a bag, kicking and hitting and throwing my full weight into it. It felt fantastic. I noticed Rick glancing over now and then, but he was pretty busy with his novice, trying to control the loose kicks and fly-away punches. When I felt I'd had about enough, I stripped my gloves off and went and had a shower in the female locker room.

When I came out Rick's client had disappeared, and he was tidying up the area, as though filling in time for me to come back. I took a deep breath, not sure what he was about to say. It was weird walking on eggshells around Rick; I wasn't used to this.

"Have you had brekkie? Wanna grab something at the café?" he asked, all bright eyes and familiar cheery face.

And just like that, I had my best friend back. I shouldn't have doubted him at all.

Coffee, that wonderful elixir, that giver of verve. Not everyone can make a decent coffee, but thankfully, the café at Tony's Gym has a philosophy. You're not going to want to come back for their healthy low-fat you're-eating-in-a-gym food, but you bloody well will for the coffee. It was bliss. I savoured every mouthful, letting it roll around my tongue like a lover.

"So," Rick said with a mouthful of blueberry non-fat low-sugar muffin. "What's with the glow?"

I glanced down at my hands. I couldn't see any glow. "What are you talking about?"

"You're glowing, Luce, even just sitting here, it's a pale violet hue all around you, but when you were kick-boxing before, it was an intense purple shimmer. Awesome, but freaky."

I cringed at the *freaky* comment, not my favourite word in the world. But, I also hadn't missed the colour choice of my glow. Purple huh? Now, I wonder why that would be? Bloody Michel, now he was making me glow.

"Do you think anyone else can see it?" I suddenly thought. Panicked that I wouldn't be able to return to work at the bank and a semi-normal life when my unscheduled leave expired.

"Nah. You've always kinda shined to the Taniwhas, I guess it's just the way we recognise you. But now, you glow. Kinda cool."

Yeah, if you want to walk around with a supernatural neon sign above your head announcing you're joined to a master vampire. Moment of truth time. Rick is my best friend after all.

"Max-has-found-a-Nosferatin-and-is-joining-with-him-tonight-so-I had-to-join-with-Michel-or-he-wouldn't-be-strong-enough-to-fight-him." It came out as one big non-stop word, all jumbled together and tripping over itself.

"Wh... why, what? Hang on a minute. You joined with Michel?" Figures he'd pick up on that little bit and gloss over the mega-master vampire doubling his powers and about to take over the world.

I took a deep breath. "You know I would have had to anyway. I really didn't have a choice." My little internal monologue chose that moment to pipe up and tell me, *but you weren't entirely opposed to the idea either, were you?* Shut it, I said back.

Rick's brow was furrowed, and he was biting his lip in deep concentration. I held my breath again, I'd never before questioned his friendship as often as I was now finding myself doing, but right now, I couldn't tell how he felt about all of this and whether he would just cast me aside as something for the too hard pile.

"Well, that's a bugger, isn't it?" I let the breath I was holding out. "Somehow, I just thought we'd find a way out of it, you know, there'd be time. I never really thought you'd have to go through with it. I mean, he's a vampire, Luce, he's one of the bad guys, and now you're tied to him for life."

"At least he's not as bad as some of them, Rick, he does have some good in him."

"If you think that, you've gone soft. They *make* you believe that, they trick you into being on their side, but they are nothing but evil, Luce, they feed off your vulnerability and they take advantage of your trust. I have yet to meet a vampire who is good."

I sighed, maybe this was a battle I couldn't win today. Part of me acknowledged that I had changed. I used to think that all vampires were bad too, some more than others, but all of them capable of treachery. And, it's not as though I don't know that Michel is capable of that too, hell, he's just proved it again this morning, but I see good there too. I see it, and I want to draw it out, I just can't help it. Maybe I've just got to accept that on this, Rick and I are not on the same page, hell, maybe we're not even reading the same book anymore.

I suddenly felt quite tired, and the thought of curling up in my bed was very welcoming. It had been a long night and also an emotional morning. I hugged Rick goodbye and slowly walked home, no energy to run, just dragged my feet and took my time, listening to the deafening sound of morning rush hour traffic, honking horns, voices raised and the general hub-bub of the city waking up and coming alive. The vampires missed all of this, all this activity, teaming with life. No wonder they were called the undead.

No one entered my dreams, and I slept solidly, undisturbed by neighbours coming and going or the gardener making his rounds of the property's lawns. When I woke up, the sun was about to set. I'd slept the rest of the day away but felt rejuvenated for it. I'd just exited the shower and got dressed in my usual evening wear ready for a hunt when I felt it. Or more accurately, felt the absence of him.

Michel was gone. It wasn't the same as before, when I was in my vision at the club and I could only sense a void when I tried to find him, now, I could still sense his life force, it was just farther away and getting further from me every second. He had left the city and was on his way to Max. I'd been stupid to think he would wait for me to come and say goodbye or even be there waiting to tell me I could come. I just hadn't thought he'd leave me after all. What an idiot.

And now all I felt was a threatening tide of panic at the thought of him not being near me; it made my palms sweat, my breath catch in my throat and my heartrate sky-rocket. The thought of him not being here frightened and alarmed me, more than I thought it ever could. I started shaking with barely contained fear, I could not lose him this way, I could not let him be alone when he faced Maximilian.

I had just decided what I would do when there was a knock on my door. Without thinking, I opened it and was met with the glowing red eyes of a vampire about to glaze me. I fought it as best I could. I mean usually I can fight the impulse, but not always and not when my heartrate was already motoring and my mind was not here, but chasing my kindred vampire across the seas.

"Invite me in," he said in his usual deep, gruff, no-nonsense voice.

I found myself saying it before I could even register the thought. "Of course, Bruno, won't you please come in."

As soon as he stepped over the threshold he hit me with another suggestion. "You will not rescind your invitation to me" and dug it in so deep I didn't even feel where he had buried it.

I always knew Bruno was a high-level master, close to Michel in strength, but not quite. He was more than capable of heading up his own family line, but he seemed very loyal to Michel for some reason and stayed. Tonight just proved how powerful he was. I'd never sensed this level of power come off him before; he had hidden it well.

Part of my mind was yelling at me that I was in trouble, the other part was calmly saying, *but this is Bruno, he won't hurt you*. Right then, as I watched him glance around my tiny apartment, making it feel even smaller than it normally was with the huge bulk of him, I wasn't sure which part was right.

"Nice place you got here, Luce? You decorate it?"

The breath I was holding went out and the cloud his influence had had on me lifted. The last suggestion still so deeply buried in my mind I didn't even register it. The thought of rescinding his invitation no longer existing as an option in my mind. I felt normal and this was Bruno, come to pay a visit. How nice.

"It's a rental. You get what you pay for."

"Hmm," he simply replied and went to sit on the three seater couch, taking up most of it. "Got any DVD's?" He had started flicking through the magazines and usual crap adorning my coffee table, searching for the remote control to the TV. Once he found it, he switched it on and started channel surfing.

"You're just gonna watch TV?" I asked incredulously. "When Michel has gone to face Max?"

He shrugged. "Enrique, Jock and Alessandra are with him. He'll be all right." And when I raised my eyebrows at him, he went on. "They're going for stealth. Small party, hit him when he doesn't expect it, at the joining, take him out."

"You really think it will be that easy? You're mad. Max will be unstoppable when he joins."

"He won't join. They'll get him before that." Then he chucked the remote down and said, "Crap. Nothing on the box. How about a game of poker?"

I was starting to get angry now, the fear of Michel being away from me quickly replaced with a white hot rage. How could Bruno sit here so calmly when Michel could be heading to his death? Did he not care at all?

"I gotta get some fresh air," I said and headed for the door.

For a big guy, Bruno can sure move. Of course, if he wasn't a vampire, I don't think he would possess that sort of agility, his body is made for brute strength, not speed. But because he is a vampire, he appeared in front of me in a split second and pushed me back towards the room.

"Don't even think about it, Luce."

I just glared at him and felt my fists shake at my sides. He sighed. "Don't make this harder than it needs to be. Michel doesn't want you going anywhere, so you'll be staying right here with me."

"I'm a prisoner then?"

"Nah, just think of it as temporarily detained." He went and sat back down on the couch.

Now, I know it was stupid, but I just couldn't help myself, I wanted out of there, so I had to try. I took a running leap for the door again, only this time Bruno's push when he appeared in front of me was a lot firmer and I went flying back towards the dining area and landed in a thump against the table and chairs.

"Ouch! That hurt, you brute!"

"You asked for it, Luce. I'm trying to be reasonable here, but if you insist on fighting me, I will fight. I could do this all night and not even break out in a sweat and you know it."

I actually pouted at that, it was just so unfair. "I could stake you."

"And I could just influence you again to not. You really want me in your mind, Luce?"

Arghh! This sucked and was so not right. "What am I supposed to do, Bruno, when I know he is about to face Max and may get hurt? What am I supposed to do?" I noticed the pitch in my voice going higher and higher as I said that, the panic returning slightly, crushing my chest and making it harder to breathe.

Bruno actually looked a little sad for me then. "I'm sorry, Luce, I've been given orders, there's nothing I can do."

"You could break them, you're strong enough. You're worried about him too, aren't you? You could let me go to him in my sleep."

He ran a hand over his face, a movement that took me so much by surprise I actually blinked back in shock. Bruno never came across as emotionally in turmoil. "It was a command, Luce." And then at the blank look on my face. "I could not ignore Michel's command if my life depended on it. He is too strong for me now."

And that was that. I knew then that I was trapped, that Bruno would fight to the death to contain me, to keep me awake and unable to enter the dream-state that would allow me to go to Michel. There was nothing I could do, but sit here like some sixteenth-century wife and wait for the noble knight to return, or not, from the battle. Of course, if he didn't return, I guess I'd soon know about it, wouldn't I? Or at least Bruno would, as I crumpled to the ground dead.

I stayed on the floor not saying a thing, just wringing my hands frantically in my lap. If you've ever found yourself in a situation you so desperately wanted out of, but were unable to achieve, you'd know what my state of mind was. Panic, fear, anger, desperation, hysteria - you name it, I had it.

After about half an hour of sitting there and feeling my backside get numb and my legs begin to tingle underneath me, I decided it was time to just join Bruno on the couch. He'd been skimming through a *House & Garden* magazine, throwing glances in my direction now and then. I damn well knew he wasn't getting any landscaping tips; he was trying to appear relaxed and at ease. Obviously, my silence and frantic hand-wringing had not gone unnoticed.

I slowly stood up and stretched my back, loosening all the knots that had festered there. I took a step towards him when I was hit by the most tremendous wave of pain, interlaced with adrenaline and a grim determination. I doubled over and fell to the floor.

Bruno tensed but didn't immediately get up to aid me. He was obviously thinking I was trying something on, but when I grunted and proceeded to dry retch, trying to heave up the non-existent contents of my stomach, he was at my side immediately.

"What is it? What's wrong?"

I heaved again, and again nothing came up. I stayed with my arms about my waist, leaning forward, waiting for the nausea to pass for a moment and then when it finally did sat back and looked at him, registering from the look of his widened eyes, just what he must be seeing on my face. Fear.

"It's Michel. He's in trouble."

21
DREAM WALKERS

"But, but he's so strong now. This should be a walk in the park for him."

I swallowed back bile. "Max is already joined. He must have done it as soon as the sun set, or even last night, but he's powerful. Oh God, Bruno, he's so powerful." I started shaking and a small sob escaped before I could stop it. Bruno looked tormented, unsure what to do.

"I have to go to him, Bruno. You have to let me sleep."

He just kept shaking his head back and forth, back and forth. "No. No. No. I...I can't let you, Luce. I just can't." Still shaking his head in protest.

"Arghh! This isn't funny, Bruno, he's being hurt, I can feel it. Everything. His astonishment, his disbelief, rage, fear. It's all here inside me too, I can't stand it, Bruno! I can't breathe."

Bruno just kept shaking his head, like one of those clowns at the Easter Show, you know the ones with their mouths open, waiting for a ping-pong ball to be thrown in, rolling their heads from side to side. Although, I didn't have a ping-pong ball and there was no big fluffy Easter bunny waiting for me to win.

"He'll be all right. He has Alessandra, Enrique and Jock with him. Three first level masters. He'll be all right."

"Jock's dead."

I saw it then. The realisation hit him that this had been a mistake. That his world was about to be upended and whatever it was that had kept him at Michel's side for so long; loyalty, love, affection, whatever it was, was tormenting him now. His master was in trouble and he couldn't help.

"I'll try, Luce. I'll try to let you sleep."

I breathed a sigh of relief and went to the bedroom to lie down on the bed. Centring myself again, blocking out the fever pitch of emotions coming from Michel and homing in on the beat of my heart. I felt myself start to drift towards that nothingness. That complete and utter blankness. I could feel it up ahead, getting closer, just within my reach. *A little further, just a little further. Almost there.*

And then I was being shaken awake by a big brute of a vampire with the most anguished and conflicted look on his face. "Can't let you sleep. Can't let you sleep. Can't. Let .You .Sleep."

I was so angry. I had been so close, almost there and now I was awake and feeling everything that Michel was feeling all over again. So far away from him and so close at the same time.

I reached out and grabbed Bruno by his stupid thick shoulders and stared him in the eyes. He met mine and didn't look away.

"You are going to let me sleep, Bruno and you will NOT interfere!"

He just nodded. "OK."

What the? He was getting up and walking out to the couch, sitting himself down and looking into space like a lobotomised bodyguard on sentry duty.

Bloody hell, I'd just glazed a vampire.

You see, here's the thing. A vampire can glaze a human. Duh. But he can't glaze another vampire. He can command a ghoul, no need for glazing, but he can't glaze another vampire. Oh, and did I mention, vampires don't get glazed. Ever.

Until now. *I can glaze a vampire.* Wow, this was big, but I didn't have time to celebrate. Michel although much more stable now, was battling hard, I could feel the effort required, the concentration it demanded.

His heart rate was up at an alarming speed and his breathing was rapid, too rapid. I could sense all of this as if I was standing right in front of him. He wasn't hurting any more, thank God, but he was working hard and I could also tell he was worried about Alessandra and Enrique, who were battling other vampires, trying to cover his back.

This sensing him was wicked, so vivid, technicolour in its imagery. I might as well have been sitting on his shoulder, I could see it all. But I knew I could do better than that. I could help him too.

I lay back down on the bed and centred myself, falling into that nothingness with such ease. I was suddenly standing on a street, the sun had not long set, I could tell it was still early evening. Sydney's a couple of hours behind us, but still, Michel must have tried to approach Max at twilight, maybe to get the jump on him. It hadn't worked.

I couldn't hear any signs of battle, but I pulled my stake out of my jacket pocket anyway. Always be prepared. I glanced around to get my bearings. I was in The Rocks. A part of Sydney near the Harbour Bridge. Tall terraced brick buildings stood like sentinels on either side of me. The typical red Aussie brick. The gables at the top of each building were arched, with a circle carved out in the middle of each one, some five stories up. There were surprisingly no humans around, but it was early and the whole area had a sense of foreboding to it. Maybe the vamps had bespelled the place to repel Norms. How considerate.

What do I do? I pushed my senses out to find Michel, but only got that void I do when I'm sleep walking, or whatever the hell this is, but I could sense Max, Alessandra and Enrique, plus about twenty other vamps nearby. I started heading in that direction. It was near the end of this first row of terraces, down a dark alleyway, how appropriate. I paused at the entrance to the alley and then slowly slid into the shadows and crept down. After a while I realised I didn't need to hide like a cat burglar, no one could sense me here, so I started jogging down the centre.

It came out into a courtyard with arches all around and covered walkways beneath. All brick of course, The Rocks is known for its old brick buildings. That and pubs and parties.

I could see Alessandra and Enrique battling all the vamps. So fast, so swift, working as a demonic tag team. One would go forward and make a strike, then fall back just as the other took point. It was fast and furious, but coordinated and controlled. They had established a rhythm and it was almost beautiful to watch, but my eyes had already left them and were fixated on the battle in the distance.

If I had been bowled over by the energy on display in the basement of *Sensations* or at that warehouse in Parnell, then I was dumbstruck and in utter awe of what I saw now. Not just a large, coloured ball of energy swirling and sparking and zapping in the air, but now tornadoes of colour spinning and striking and bouncing all over the place. Somewhere in amongst all that power and energy and mass of untold electricity were two vampires. Hadn't they fried themselves yet?

Bricks were raining down on them and then being thrust out at such a force they exploded against whatever they hit. The odd vampire taking the brunt of that force when getting too close. The roof had collapsed in one section, just off to the side and Max and Michel were simply dancing and spinning over the top of the rubble, creating gusts of mortar dust and brick splinters. The noise was deafening, cracking lightning and booming thunder, with a high pitched frequency that pierced the ears and threatened to burst the eardrums.

I realised then, there was nothing anyone could do to help Michel. This was a battle that only a joined master vampire could partake. Anyone else getting close to that inferno of a force would be incinerated in an instant. I didn't believe for a minute that my sleep walking self would come away unscathed. I couldn't help Michel, but I could help Alessandra and Enrique as I noticed more vampires enter into their fray and their dancing duet falter.

I started to take a step forward when a tall, thin human man walked out from the sidelines. I didn't think anything other than *are you mad, get outta here!* And then realised he probably couldn't see me. I stopped and looked at him, because he was just standing there, smiling. It wasn't a nice smile either; it was more a sneer mixed with a snarl and a whole lot of attitude. He was about 18 or 19 years old, thin, dressed in faded denim jeans with rips at the knees and over the thighs. I think they were more of a fashion statement than damage from a fight because his top kind of fit the picture. Black net singlet with nothing underneath, so his white flesh could be seen in the diamond pattern of the top, laced across with a series of silver looking chain. Along with his *Doc Martens* boots, the overall effect was definitely punk. He had three or four earrings in one ear and a stud in the eyebrow and one in the upper lip. Ouch.

I took a step sideways, intending to skirt around him and he simply countered the move, stepping sideways to block. I was stunned. His pale washed out grey eyes just looked at me, there didn't seem to be too much life in there, no spark, just the dull colour of water in a puddle on the side of the road. His jet black spiky hair had more life to it than those eyes. I started to get a shiver down my spine and not in a nice way either.

"G'day, Lucinda. You really shouldn'a come."

It was the broad Aussie drawl that gave it away. I know a lot of people think we Kiwis sound just like an Aussie, but there's a big difference. A Kiwi would never mistake an Aussie as a fellow countryman and vice versa. Theirs is all *Feesh & Cheeps*, and ours is more *Fush & Chups*. It's obvious, you can't be fooled. So, I knew who this kid was right away, but for the life of me, I couldn't figure out why he could see me.

"Come to join the fun, have ya, mate?"

"You can see me?" I know, it wasn't the best opening line I could have used, but I was floundering here.

"Bloody oath, mate! Been expectin' ya too. Took ya time, but."

Well this was weird. He could see me and none of the vamps could. He was clearly Max's kindred Nosferatin, one of my kind, so could I trust him? Only one way to find out.

"So, um, what happens now?"

"Strewth, mate, you really are a bit of a blonde, aren't ya. Now, I kill ya and in the process, I kill ya pathetic excuse of a vamp."

OK. Now I was getting mad. No one calls my vampire pathetic.

I shoved my stake into my left hand and grabbed my knife out of its sheath with my right. I could use the stake on the guy, but it's a bit of an overkill on a human, especially one that doesn't look like he had ever had any martial arts training at all, unlike me. We started circling each other, him with his nasty sneer, me with what I hoped was a *don't mess with me, buddy* expression. Just as I was wondering how many times we were going to go round in a circle looking at each other - because I admit, I was a tad reticent to make the first move on another human, vampires I have no problem with, but I'd never had a go at a human before - he flicked his wrist and a dozen vampires jumped down into the courtyard from the balconies above the arches. Crap.

I switched the stake and knife over. I can stake a vampire with my left hand, but my right is much more accurate and powerful. Now, I knew these guys couldn't see me, they had that blank look on their faces, staring vaguely in the direction of where I was, but looking right through me, but old Aussie Punk was giving them a stream of directions of where I was and how I was standing. Damn.

One vampire sprang out and I stepped quickly out of his way and watched him fly by, so Aussie Punk upped the ante and sent two in my direction. I managed to dodge out of the way by ducking down and rolling to the side, swiping out with my stake on the shin of one of them as he went passed. He howled in pain and outrage. Jeez, it was only a scratch.

Next Aussie Punk - I'm really going to have to give him another name, that one's beginning to grate - sent in six vampires at once. This was going to be more difficult. I tried to run to left and squeeze through a small gap, but the vamps closed in together, I spun around in a circle looking for a way out and felt well and truly alone for the first time in my life. I swallowed the fear; I was not going out without a fight. I ran directly at one of the vampires and staked him through his chest, turning to stake the next beside him and then spinning to do it again to the one after that.

I could hear the kid shouting orders, but the world was spinning around me so fast as I went on to one vampire after the other. Then reinforcements arrived, closing in in a rush, I tried to run at the nearest, raising my stake, but the vamps put their arms up at the same time, like washing lines, after a quick shout from twat features and one caught me in the throat and made me topple over backward landing hard on my tail bone and forcing an *oomph* from my mouth. All the vamps homed in on the sound and came at me. I scrambled to my feet, but it wasn't fast enough. A vampire had his arms around my body, crushing any air from my lungs in the next instant.

My heart rate tripled and panic exploded inside, sending spots of white dancing in my eyes. I fought not to scream, I'm not sure if I could have anyway, I couldn't get a breath in with the vice-like grip from the vamp at my back. I tried wriggling and struggling. I even tried to scratch his arms with my stake and knife, but couldn't get much purchase. I stomped on his foot, scraped my boots down his shin and tried to elbow him in the guts, but all of it was to no avail.

I suddenly felt very scared, and that's when I saw Michel falter. His mini tornado blurred and stuttered, I could see him now in amongst the still swirling mass of energy and light and colour, and then, I saw Max go in for the kill.

Somehow I must have got some air in because I could suddenly hear myself yelling, "No!"

The Aussie was coming towards me, an evil grin on his face. "I'm gonna enjoy killing ya, Lucinda." And then he started singing *Waltzing Matilda* but with my name instead.

From the corner of my eye I caught a flickering movement and then a man, about the same age as me, maybe slightly older, suddenly appeared. He was dressed in white linen pants with a flowing long-sleeved white shirt rolled half way up his arms, showing muscular forearms underneath, his dark brown skin standing out in direct contrast to the whiteness of the material. He had short black hair and high cheekbones with a fine nose. Far from looking feminine, he had the sense of nobility, the austere look of a fine middle eastern warrior.

Where the hell had he come from?

He turned to look at me, making direct eye contact with his piercing brown eyes and then a stake appeared in his hand. In the next instant he was airborne, slicing at the vampires in the courtyard, staking one then flowing on to the next, then the next and then the next; twisting and turning, dancing in the wind, his feet hardly touching the ground. He was poetry in motion. He was as beautiful, as stunning, as the sun. He was extraordinary. I couldn't take my eyes off him. Who was this man?

It took him mere seconds to kill all the vampires around me, the one holding me stiffening as he watched his comrades simply puff out of existence and blow away in the invisible flurries created by the man. Finally he was standing behind us and I felt the vampire's grip on me weaken and then disappear altogether in a cloud of dust.

Throughout all of this Aussie had just stood there with his mouth hanging open and a look of utter incredulity on his face. A bit like me really. We all stood still looking at each other for a moment and then the man simply threw a knife at the Aussie kid. It landed with a sickening thud in his chest all the way up to the hilt. The kid stumbled and fell forward onto his knees, his hands up to the knife, clutching it, but not pulling it out, his eyes wide open in surprise and a trickle of blood slowly running from his mouth.

There was a flash in the distance, over by Michel and Max, and I looked up just in time to see Michel ripping Max's head cleanly off in one smooth twisting motion. It went flying across the rubble and landed with a splat, then burst into dust. His body followed shortly after.

The air was still and silent. Enrique and Alessandra having chased the last of Max's vampires from the courtyard out on to the streets and probably all the way to the coast. I turned to look at the man next to me, mesmerized by his smile and the shades of copper and brown in his eyes.

"It is always a pleasure to meet a fellow Dream Walker, Kiwi."

He had a middle eastern accent I recognised immediately.

"Nero?"

"The one and only." He bowed a graceful movement, bending in the middle with his arm across his chest.

I just looked at him. I couldn't stop. He was gorgeous. Then I heard Michel groan. Suddenly nothing mattered except getting to Michel. I took a step towards him, then remembered Nero and turned back.

"We shall meet again, Kiwi. Soon." He nodded his head and flickered slightly and then he was gone.

Michel was on his side on the ground, panting, holding his stomach where his shirt had been torn right away. I raced over and skidded to a halt beside him, falling onto my knees in the rubble, not even registering the sharp shards of brick and rock piercing my skin through my tights. I reached out and touched his arm. "Michel?"

"*Ma douce*, you should not have come." His voice was ragged, his breath laboured. Naturally he'd tell me off, couldn't just be glad to hear my voice.

I started crying, slow tears streaming down my face, falling onto the ground, onto his arm. He reached up and brushed a tear away, his touch so soft, so perfect. Then it dawned on me, he shouldn't be able to see me at all.

"Can you see me?"

"No. I can sense you. I can feel you. It's almost as though I can see you." He sounded better, his voice stronger.

I reached down and moved his arm. The gash which had been so large moments before, was now just an ugly red mark, sealed and slowly fading.

"You're healing."

"It would seem your proximity, even as a phantom, brings me good health."

"So, it was just as well I came then, wasn't it."

I didn't wait for him to answer, I just leaned down and kissed him with brutal need. He had almost died, I had watched Max go in for the kill. I couldn't bear the thought of losing him, of this world losing him. He must have felt the same, because he gripped me in a tight embrace and began devouring me with his mouth, his tongue, his voice. Words in French and English, tumbling over each other, so fast and furious I couldn't make them out, but I knew what he meant.

I drew back, only because I needed to breathe, and then felt the beginnings of the blur before reaching into nothingness. Before I left completely to return to my body, I whispered, "Come home. Come back to me."

"Always," was his reply.

22
IS IT OVER YET?

I came to on my bed in the familiar surroundings of my apartment. I just lay there for a moment, staring at the ceiling and a particularly interesting mark just next to the light fixture. For some reason I felt a little queasy, maybe the distance I travelled when I shifted, no what had Nero called it? - *Dream Walked* - in my sleep had an effect. That was the furthest I had been outside my body. Previously, I'd just made it across town and in different rooms of the same building I was resting in.

Nero. Well, that was certainly a turn up for the books. How had he known I needed help? Because that was why he was there, wasn't it? He just appeared when all my hope had fled and got straight down to it. Puzzling. And man, couldn't he move?

And Michel, all that power, that tornado of colours: blues, reds, yellows, indigos; how beautiful he had seemed as he spun and fought Max. Frightening, yet beautiful.

My body ached slightly in every joint, through every muscle, but not too bad, more like I'd just had a hard and fast workout with Rick at the Gym. Like I'd really been put through the paces. I decided, as the nausea had now subsided, that it was time to get up and see if Bruno was still doing his lobotomised sentry impersonation.

I gingerly sat up on the edge of the bed, and when the world didn't tilt or begin to fade or anything, I stood and walked into the lounge. God, my body was sore, stiff and sore and tired. I hated hurting.

Bruno looked up as I entered, he'd been quietly flicking through a magazine.

"You're awake? How'd it go?"

"Michel's OK. Max is dead."

"Yeah, I figured as much, the Master's on his way."

OK. Vampires being in tune with their own and all that.

Suddenly, he sniffed the air and then he was immediately in front of my face, not a foot away, looking intently, running his hands over the back of my head, my neck, my arms. I tried batting him away.

"Hey! What the hell are you doing?"

"You are hurt. I can smell blood."

He actually looked panicked, like me being injured was going to result in something bad for him. It probably would, Michel had probably left specific instructions to keep me safe, this no doubt would not have met that criterion.

He had my jacket off before I could even protest and had started lifting my top up to peer underneath, but by then I had gathered myself enough to struggle with his too strong arms.

"Leave off, Bruno! You are not stripping me!"

"I must inspect the injury. You are hurt." He sounded a little like a demented robot with the last sentence. He stilled then and looked up at me. "Why are you hurt? You shouldn't be hurt."

I took the opportunity his distraction at why I was hurt had caused to feel my side. Sure enough, there was definitely a tender spot, bruising and when my hand came away, a small smattering of blood, not much, but it would have been enough for Bruno to smell. I stared at my hand. How had I got hurt? In the struggle with the vampire that had held me, perhaps my stake had sliced my side, but I couldn't remember it. All I remembered was the hopelessness descending on me like a shroud.

"I...I don't know." And then more surely, "It's nothing, though, OK? So you can drop the personal inspection. I get hurt like this all the time, Bruno; it's nothing."

Although part of me was a little shocked that I had been hurt at all and not even realised it. Or that I had been hurt while Dream Walking, I hadn't known that was possible, and now I was a little less enamoured with the whole thing. Still, it was pretty cool, though, wasn't it?

Just then Bruno turned into a statue, that good old familiar vampire calm and swung his head towards the door in such a quick movement it blurred. His right hand hadn't moved from my t-shirt, still lifting it slightly, his other holding my arm. He was standing so close I could feel the warmth of him radiating off his chest like an electric heater. The front door to the apartment sprung open and standing on the threshold was Michel.

His clothing was covered in dust with small rips in his hip-hugging black trousers; his black shirt had torn a little worse and hung in tatters here and there, showing his glowing cream skin and hints of rippling muscle. His beautiful dark hair was slightly messed, but it didn't detract from his beauty, just intensified it and his eyes blazed the most mesmerising shades of purple; sparklingly amethyst, deeply magenta, striking violet and lush mauve.

He smelled of ozone and slightly burnt toast. I couldn't place it for a moment, and then remembered where I had smelt that combination of smells before, by the Ley Lines. He'd travelled here on the supernatural superhighway of a powerful and deadly Ley Line. He must have been in a hurry to choose that mode of transport; that was for sure.

He had such a look of longing on his face that it stilled my breath. And then he growled, low and long, looking at where Bruno's hands were, at where he stood.

Bruno tensed even further, I hadn't thought that was possible, he had been so still and stiff already, and then in an instant, he was gone. Out past Michel and into what was left of the night.

Michel's gaze hadn't softened, he still glowed like an electric light bulb, bright and clear and intense, but behind that light was a deep hunger, barely contained, straining to be unleashed. Before I even had the chance to consider inviting him in - which of course, I had no way of not doing, my longing for him at that moment just as strong as his - he simply stepped across my welcome mat and glided towards me. The door slowly closing in his wake.

The first thing I registered was his hand in my hair at the base of my head, his mouth on mine and his warmth crushing me as he pulled me to him. I didn't fight him, I simply wrapped myself around him, arms and legs and anything else I could manage, holding on for grim death. He carried me directly to my bedroom and lay me down softly on the bed. Touching me, stroking me, devouring me with his mouth, his tongue, his breath. He had my t-shirt off before I even noticed and proceeded to cover my upper body with his lips, nibbling, kissing, licking, murmuring. His movements weren't his usual languid stroking but a more fervent and hurried action, as though he was scared I would disappear on him, and he needed to cover every inch of my body before I did.

I hazily realised that I had lost even more clothing, it should have concerned me that my clothes were disappearing at an alarming rate, but it didn't. I simply answered his movements with the frantic need of my own, unbuttoning what was left of his shirt and slipping it off to replace it with my kisses and touch. I couldn't get enough of him; I wanted it all. Heat had built inside me so quickly that it threatened to end everything before it had even begun. I gripped Michel's shoulders, digging my fingers in and vaguely heard someone who kind of sounded like me, whimpering and pleading to not stop, to go faster. I felt the cool air against the skin of my thighs, the softness of his naked flesh against the heat at the core of me and then just as quickly his hard length entering in a rush. I called out in surprise and then hunger, he didn't pause but proceeded to pump me with an urgency I had not ever believed could exist.

Within seconds I was airborne on a wave of pure bliss, his movements so strong, so powerful, my body shook from the invasion but clung to him with desire and need. I found myself giving direction in hurried, panting breaths; *faster, harder, longer,* all tumbling out and being met by his moans and whimpers and cries. Finally, we crested the wave, and I called out his name in a beautiful mix of colour and heat and tingling sensation that started at my centre and streamed out through every particle of my being, ringing in my ears and thundering through my pulse.

He collapsed against me, his breathing ragged and uneven, his sweat mixing with mine, his breath against my neck. For a while neither of us moved, just languished in the afterglow, then he started stroking my arms, across my stomach, hips and side. I tensed slightly when he grazed my side, where I had been hurt, and he moved his attention there, running his fingers delicately across the cut and bruises, followed by his kisses, so light and tender.

"I can heal this, *ma douce*, but you must let me in to do so." His voice was so husky, thick and low. It was the first time he had really talked, other than murmured words of passion and need. I relished the sound of that voice, letting it flow over me and ignite yet another fire within.

I took a deep breath and winced, realising I was still quite sore, amazingly having not felt a thing during our love making until now. I managed a nod and then let my shields down to let his *Sanguis Vitam* in. Immediately I felt the tingle that preceded a healing, felt the rush as it covered my body taking away the aches and pain and tiredness. When he finally lifted his head to look in my eyes, I was floating on a cloud of pure joy, unable to form a coherent sentence at all.

He smiled softly, his eyes still glowing with dancing lights of blue and purple, then his faced sobered slightly. "You had me worried, *ma douce*, I could feel your fear, your helplessness, yet I could not help you. It crushed me inside."

I didn't think he was being melodramatic, I could see the pain in his eyes, and I knew that if he had received my emotions when I had been Dream Walking, then he would have felt everything I did, probably even amplified.

"I didn't mean to distract you. I could have caused your death. All I knew was, when I could sense what was happening, nothing could have stopped me from being at your side. Nothing. And then, I saw you falter, and I saw Max take advantage of it. The last thing I saw before Nero turned up, was Max going in for the kill."

"Who is Nero?" His voice was even, although light, as though he was trying to show he really wasn't that interested, but I knew otherwise.

"He's a friend. Another Nosferatin who can Dream Walk."

"Dream Walk?" Again with the even but light voice.

"He wasn't really there; he appeared like I do and saved my life."

Michel took a sharp breath in. "I could not see him, sense him. I did not know he was there." I don't think Michel liked that idea; that there had been an unknown phantom helping me when he could not.

"Why do you think he came?" OK, I was starting to get a little concerned now at that even and light tone, not to mention the slight glow that now shone from his amethyst and violet eyes.

"I don't know; he just appeared right when I thought I was done for. Right when I realised I'd just signed your death warrant."

He softened at that, his whole body relaxing from his face to his breathing, to his firm but still hold on my side. He started stroking my hip, his thumb running circles along its edge, "*Ma douce*, I would not have let that happen. I had already mortally wounded Maximilian; I was simply waiting for the right moment to strike the final blow."

Now, I'm not sure if that was the entire truth, Michel was quite capable of lying to me, and part of me thought that perhaps he didn't want me putting too much stock in Nero being my saviour, that he himself would have been able to end it all and set me free. On the other hand, this is Michel, and even now after everything I had seen, I could not believe that he wouldn't have been able to overcome Max and save the day. He just had that presence about him, he always had.

He pulled me closer, wrapping his arms around me and covering us with the simple flick of his wrist, making the coverlet encase us in its warmth. He nuzzled in and kissed my neck, over the spot he had bitten me when we joined. It was as if he knew exactly how to find it, like it called to him.

"It is over, *ma douce*, you are safe. We are together, as we should be. Nothing can hurt you now." I kind of got the impression he was saying that as much to himself as he was to me, as though he needed that reassurance too.

"Of course, I am interested in how Bruno did not stop you from sleeping. Care to enlighten me how one of my own could refuse a direct command?" His voice was even, soft, he had started kissing me again. Was it to distract me from his true emotion to that question? I didn't know, all I knew was it was doing a damn fine job of it. Part of me registering that this could be very bad for Bruno, but unable to hide the answer from Michel at all. And really, what would be the point, he'd figure it out eventually anyway, by simply reading Bruno's mind.

"It seems I can glaze vampires now."

There's no easy way to say that to a vampire, is there? It's going to be a shock. How could it not be? They have lived millennia without having to suffer the indignity of another's influence. Sure, they have to obey the commands of their master, even if it means they would die, that's gotta suck. But no-one, or no thing, that simply passes them on the street, could have that sort of control over them, could invade their minds. To a vampire his ability to glaze humans is his crutch. How do you think they managed to feed in days gone by where consent wasn't even an option? It's not like they could bully a victim or kill every one they fed off, it would have led to their discovery in short time. So, they used their influence. And no matter which way you look at it, finding out a human and a Nosferatin who could kill them at that, has their sacred talent to glaze too, would not be welcome.

So, it did kind of surprise me that Michel didn't even stiffen, no short intake of breath, no power level flicker, no eyes glowing a different shade of blue or purple, not even a raised blood vessel in his beautiful face. He just kept layering light and delicate kisses along my neck. Oh, he was good all right.

"Interesting," he murmured, in between a few more kisses. Was that *the* understatement of the century, or not? "Two of your powers before your 25th birthday. It seems you really are an enigma, my dear."

I'd had enough of the Mr Cool attitude, so I cupped his face with both my hands and raised it up in front of me to look him in the eyes. He didn't blanch, even though it must have occurred to him by making eye contact with me now, I could have tried to glaze. He either trusted me or much more likely, was showing no fear. Gotta love that *show no fear* rule.

"You're hiding your true feelings to this, Michel. I can't read your emotions, like you can mine. Help me out here. Is this going to be a problem?"

His hand reached up to run the length of my face, softly stroking right down to my jaw. "Nothing you could ever be capable of doing could be a problem, *ma douce*. I always knew you were different from your kind, your potential unsurpassed by any other. I knew it the moment I saw you. Does it surprise me? No. Am I concerned you will it use it on me? Perhaps. Although we are joined, and I would assume you cannot."

That was a turn up for the books. I had asked if this was a problem, but I hadn't expected to get a straight answer, not really.

"Will it stop me loving you? Never."

Now, you may think I would have been prepared for that statement. I mean, I hadn't put into words what I felt for Michel yet, but I knew it was strong. Part of me believed the connection and attraction we had was all down to the joining, being his kindred Nosferatin and all. But I was also aware that I could not live without Michel in my life, and that was not a new emotion. I had felt that way before we even started dancing this dangerous, but delicious, dance. I was also acutely aware that it was just words and Michel is nothing, if not a good talker. He could talk his way out of a paper bag if he had to.

So, I didn't react to his declaration of loving me, I just nodded, kissed his forehead and rolled over to sleep. See? I can show no fear too when needed.

Michel paused, ever so slightly, anyone else probably wouldn't have picked it up, but I knew him pretty well by now. So, not always good at hiding his feelings then. But he recovered quickly and started kissing the back of my neck, my shoulder, my back and murmuring the odd word or two. It had been a long night, and I was tired through, I felt my eyelids droop slightly, despite me wanting to stay awake and listen to Michel's soft and low voice forever, feel it wrap around me and savour the sensation it aroused inside my soul. But I couldn't fight it, not in the warmth created by the blankets, by his body against the length of mine, by his breath brushing my neck. Before I even realised it, I had drifted off to sleep, so safe, so warm, as Michel softly stroked my side and kissed the curve of my neck, murmuring in a soft, slow string of French I didn't completely understand.

I woke to sun streaming in the windows; the curtains hadn't been closed at all. I panicked slightly that Michel might be lying in the sun, but when I reached out, the bed was, disappointingly, empty next to me. I rolled over and groaned, reaching for the pillow and the smell of him there. I felt something fall on my face as I pulled the pillow towards me and opened my eyes to see a single perfect red rose resting on the bed. I allowed myself a smile, this one I think I'll keep.

I felt surprisingly rejuvenated, flushed with a healthy glow, like my batteries had been recharged and my soul filled with happiness it almost overflowed. I could get used to this feeling, if this is what it meant to be joined to a Nosferatu, then it wasn't half bad. I had just come out of the bedroom, after showering and getting dressed, when I sensed someone was in my home. I had grabbed the knife resting on my computer desk, just inside the door to my room, before my eyes had even rested on the visitor.

He was sitting at my dining room table, all relaxed and quite at home. He smiled at me, all teeth and full soft lips, impressed at the smooth and fast movement of my reaction to the threat.

"You show such potential, Kiwi. It is exactly as I had hoped."

"Nero. What are you doing here?" Today he was dressed as casually as last night, this time his clothing, though, was all black. Similar in style, but the overall effect so very different. He oozed sexual appeal, like it was a dripping hot wax.

"I said we would meet again and so we are."

I recovered myself quickly, being around vampires so much, you learn to adapt to new and crazy situations with speed, lest you get yourself killed. "Yeah, but you said soon, and this is not my definition of soon. This is in a *couple of hours*, not soon."

He laughed and the whole room lit up with him. Low and throaty and so damn sexy. How dare he.

"Time is of the essence, as they say, and I could not afford to wait any longer. You were impressive last night, but you need further training. You lowered your guard by being distracted. A Nosferatin cannot afford that luxury. I will train you."

Huh. All the time I had known Nero, talked to him through the chat room on the website, spoken to him on the satellite phone, he had never hinted I could have training. Something I had longed for right from the start. He had left me to flounder and find my way, practically all on my own, offering a small titbit of information here and a glint of instruction there. He hadn't even told me what I was, until that last satellite phone call, where he had lowered his guard and been distracted and cut off. So much for not allowing himself the luxury of distraction. So, despite having had the contact with that small group of Nosferatin, I had always felt very much on my own. And here he was, all of sudden, offering to train me like it was perfectly reasonable and par for the course. Call me a sceptic, but I just didn't buy it. What was he really after?

"Why now?" My temper had risen slightly, I don't know exactly why, but I didn't trust him. So my sentences had become short, to the point, something that I needed to work on, as it had always been a clear signal to Michel in the past of where I was heading, even before he could read my emotions.

Of course, Nero sensed it; he had that strange aura to him that indicated he was more than just human, more so than me. He just seemed so otherworldly, as though he had lived a dozen lifetimes, to the one of mine. As though his wisdom, his knowledge knew no bounds. His gaze levelled on me and I noticed a flash of bronze in amongst the deep brown, it sent a shiver down my spine I tried to ignore. God dammit, what was with this man?

"Do you not wish to know more about who you are? About what you are capable of?" His voice was soft, silky, sensual.

"That's not answering my question." Another smile, another jump in my pulse.

"Very well, my little Kiwi." He said *my little Kiwi* as though he really meant it. No one other than Michel had ever used that connotation, that tone before. "I have long been watching you develop, marvelling at your success, your natural talent. None other, for so long now, has shown such potential. I had hoped I could wait until your powers came in full before approaching you, allowing you to adjust to them on your own. But things have unfortunately changed, and we are running out of time. You are one week from your powers; we will train every day until then."

OK, part of me so wanted this, the opportunity to hone my skills, to get some answers. I mean, Michel had told me everything he knew, but I got the distinct impression that there were answers that only

Nero would be able to supply and I longed for them. Besides, from what I had seen of Nero in that courtyard last night, the sheer beauty of his movements, the speed and grace of each step, each kill, I knew he had what I needed, what I craved. Perfection.

But he still hadn't answered my question. "All right, thank you, I accept." He inclined his head to me, in a slow nod, like he had done last night before he disappeared. "But I still don't understand the urgency. It's over; Max is dead."

He blinked slowly, those beautiful, captivating bronze and gold and deep, deep brown eyes holding me in their grasp.

"It is not over, Kiwi. It has only just begun."

Ah crap. I was so hoping he wasn't going to say that.

23
KINDRED

I had been standing in the middle of my lounge during this entire conversation, rigid, unmoving. I hadn't shifted, neither had Nero. He had remained in that relaxed and casual position, arm resting on my table, legs crossed but comfortable. I didn't think this was over by a long shot yet, so I decided to not show my discomfort or any reaction to his presence at all. I'm a big girl; I could do this. I just nodded and then walked into the kitchen to my coffee machine and began to get it whirring.

Nero watched my every move like a hungry predator. Jeez, I thought he was on my side? Turning his body as I walked past him to the kitchen, eyes never leaving me once. I could feel the weight of his gaze on me as I filled the bean hopper and set it grinding, then filled the portafilter with ground beans, tamped it and securely slotted it into its spot. Cup underneath, it began to force the hot water through the grinds and out into the waiting receptacle. The heady smell of caffeine beginning to permeate the room.

I didn't look at him, but said, "You're creeping me out a little. Your gaze is very intense." Fight fire with fire and all that.

He smiled, I think he liked the forthrightness, the challenge my words held.

"You are an enthralling creature. You fascinate me. It has been a long time since my interest has been piqued. I am enjoying it." Okey-dokey then.

I swallowed, I hadn't meant to, but *come on*, this guy just had a way about him. An intensity you couldn't ignore, as though every single thing he did or said was planned, was intentional and it was directed straight at me, hunting me like an eagle hunts its prey.

I chose not to verbally acknowledge his statements, though. I simply picked my coffee up and took a sip. I hadn't offered him one, he was Dream Walking, if he were anything like me he wouldn't have wanted anything to eat or drink. I'd been Dream Walking too, for me so far, the thought of food and beverage was just not right, so I was going with that being the same for him.

"*So, it has only just begun.* Please explain?" Mustn't forget my manners, even if I am forgetting to breathe.

"Maximilian was only one of many. They call themselves the *Cadre of Eternal Knights*. Their intention is to take over the night, to return it to the vampyre, to hunt with abandon unhindered by the Nosferatin, but aided by them instead. They would join with us and subjugate us, use our powers to further their own needs. It is not the first time this has happened. However, it is the first time we have been so weak, so outnumbered, so ill prepared. It was a mistake to hide, to weaken ourselves so; we should never have turned our back on our responsibility, no matter how noble the reason to do so was."

He had said all of this with his usual intensity, hardly pausing for breath. I had been so wrapped up with what he had been saying, how he had been saying it, I hadn't noticed that I had stopped drinking, stopped breathing, stopped everything, but had been pulled into that beautiful bronze and gold and brown of his eyes completely. He held my gaze. I was the first to look away.

Cadre of Eternal Knights. Michel had referred to a group of vampires who wanted to take over the night. This was them then; they had a name. Any group that thought so highly of themselves to use a name like *Cadre of Eternal Knights* were definitely confident bastards. And I was guessing, not one of them was less powerful than Max had been, but had Max been the only one successful enough to find a kindred Nosferatin?

"Have any of the others succeeded in joining?"

"No, thankfully not, but they are getting more and more desperate, taking risks and forcing our hand. You may not be aware, but Egypt is a powerful centre for supernatural power, we have several Ley Lines intersecting across our land, we are a magnet to the supernatural, a stronghold for those who seek power." He paused for a moment as if gathering his thoughts, sifting through them to pick out just what he wanted me to know and not more. "We also have a large number of Nosferatin, a community we have hidden from the world. The *Cadre* has discovered their existence, and they are hunting for them now."

Whoa. A community of Nosferatin. I had known my kind had gone into hiding, but I'd had the impression they had scattered in the wind, trying to make it harder for them to be detected. A community. Kin. People like myself, not having to hide who they were from each other. My heart suddenly ached for that familiarity, that closeness to something I had long been denied.

"How many Nosferatin?" It had come out in barely a whisper, my breath all but stolen from my lungs.

He smiled a sympathetic smile. "You are no longer alone, Kiwi, you shall never be alone again." He understood what I was feeling, the heartache that had now consumed me. "There are perhaps twenty of our kind, with extended family of course. Three mature, two immature Nosferatin. I am one of the mature."

Oh boy. Oh boy. Oh boy. This was too much to hope for. People like me. My kind. The emotion this created in me was overwhelming; I felt tears stinging my eyes. I hadn't realised just how alone I had felt, from the moment I had discovered what I truly was, realised my Aunt and Uncle, whom I loved as you can only love a parent, weren't the same as me. They'd had no idea who I really was and had denied me contact with those who did. The sense of isolation that notion had given me had more than once threatened to make me fall.

Then it dawned on me; they had mature Nosferatin, those who could only survive with a joining. They hadn't let their first borns die.

They had gone against the decision to hide, to deny the vampires power. They had done what I knew in my soul was the right thing to do. Although frightening, it was also so very, completely, right. I hadn't realised how much I needed that confirmation, that justification of my own decision to join. I had been chastising myself for letting my kindred down, for giving a vampire the powers we had so long denied them.

"You must have many strong vampires in your country if you have three mature Nosferatin."

"We have a family of vampyre, headed by one who is queen. Some of those of her line have joined with our kind, but not surpassed her. She is the strongest in our land. The most revered."

I knew the answer before I even asked it, but found myself forming the words all the same. "Who is she joined with?"

"Nafrini is my kindred vampyre." Pretty name, I vaguely thought, then felt an unexpected stab of jealousy. Where had that come from?

"So, you fear for your two immature Nosferatin?" I felt I was getting to the real reason he was here. He had hidden his community for so long, protecting it from discovery, I couldn't help feeling that disclosing its existence to another Nosferatin now, did not seem likely to be something he had ever done before. "You need my help."

"Yes. We need yours and your kindred's help. Nafrini is strong, but the threat is greater than even she can combat alone."

This was big. Vampires may be aware of each, even keep a close eye on each other, but those so powerful as Nafrini and Michel were unlikely to get too close. That territorial side of them unable to share. It just went against their nature to openly let someone as powerful as themselves, or potentially more powerful than themselves, in. The risk was too great. Nafrini must be desperate to have considered this, as was Nero for disclosing his community's existence. I suddenly felt like the power in this new found relationship I had with Nero, had shifted to me.

"Why has Nafrini not approached Michel herself?"

"It was thought more prudent to go through you." That didn't surprise me; somehow I thought Michel's response to this enterprise would not be positive.

I didn't relish the idea of approaching Michel on this. He could quite as easily decide that the joining of Nosferatin in Egypt with the *Cadre* was not a concern of his. Auckland may be a hot-spot for supernaturals, but it was also far enough away not to be on the *Cadre's* radar, especially as I was no longer available and Max was not around to exact revenge. There would be no reason for them to come at us when doing so would gain them little more than a location to control. Right now, their goal was immature Nosferatin, those capable of giving them the power boost they desired. Of course, by not helping to stop them, they would go unheeded on their path of domination, and when they had consumed all the power they could, they could then turn their attention to our shores. That was going to have to be the argument I used.

Because I already knew in my heart, that I wanted to do this. That I couldn't abandon my kin, as I had felt they had abandoned me.

"OK. I'll get him on board. We'll help you."

He rose then and came around the counter to face me, taking both my hands in his and raising them to his mouth to brush warm, soft lips against my knuckles in a silent kiss. I forced myself not to pull away and show the effect that simple action was having on me. His eyes met mine, and I knew I had failed miserably.

"I never doubted you would join us. I had not, however, expected you to be so captivating, so entirely enchanting." When I didn't say anything in return, he gave me one more of those devastating smiles, lighting up the room in the warmth of its glow. "I shall leave you now, as my Nafrini calls, but it is with the utmost regret."

I found my voice, somehow the thought of him dropping everything to run when called by his vampire gave my voice the strength that it had only just now lacked. "I have more questions. About what I am, what I can do."

"And you shall have answers, my little Kiwi. Tomorrow, I could not stay away any longer, than deny who I am." He nodded his head again, in that slow, measured movement, a ghost of a kiss on my lips and flickered out of sight, the warmth of his hands and mouth still lingering against mine.

It was difficult to think of anything else as I waited for sunset to arrive and the chance to talk to Michel. I decided to head towards *Sensations* early, making my arrival there right on dusk. There was a vamp I didn't recognise on the door; a big guy, similar in build to Bruno. With rosy red lips and a crooked nose; the nose didn't make him lose any of his handsome features, but instead just dirtied them up a bit, like he could be a bad boy if he tried and you let him. His hair was a mass of dark curls, cascading down his back, he was dressed in the obligatory black, tight jeans and an even tighter top. His muscles bulged everywhere. And I mean everywhere. There appeared to be a sudden influx of damn fine looking men in my world all of a sudden.

He had a strong *Sanguis Vitam* signature, level two I'd say, but he was reining it in, keeping it in check. I had no doubt this guy could be intimidating, but instead he just levelled his big baby blue eyes on me and inclined his head in greeting.

"Evening, Lucinda. I am Jett; it is a pleasure to meet the Master's kindred."

Well, I'll be. A polite vampire. "Hi, Jett. I haven't seen you around before."

"I am new to the family. Michel has kindly taken those of us willing, in Jock's line, under his protection. He has my undying support as does his kindred Nosferatin."

Oh, well that made sense. Although Jock had not been under the Durand line, he had an accord with Michel, making him a close ally at the very least. And because of Michel's higher power level, a subject to Michel's power at the most. As Jock had been killed, all of those vampires under him were now masterless, having to find their own way in the supernatural world without the protection of a family. Some of them, like old Jett here, would have been strong enough to branch out on their own, but political wheeling and dealing that is the vampire world, would have undoubtedly made Jett choose to align himself with Michel. Michel was powerful now, rather than step out on his own and have to perhaps combat Michel in the future for the snub his declining Michel's offer would have been; he chose the politically correct road. Join forces and keep Michel happy.

So, the family had grown. Why did that scare me ever so slightly?

"OK. Well, welcome to the family, I guess." He nodded and opened the door to the club for me.

It was early, so there weren't too many people around, but Shane

Smith was manning the door to the private area where I could feel Michel was, so I headed on over, taking a cursory glance around me. It never pays to *not* notice your surroundings when you're a vampire hunter. And despite being Michel's kindred Nosferatin and all and the hubbub that created, making all the big bad vampires offer up their undying whatever, I could never let my guard down. It just wasn't in my nature anymore.

Shane's face broke into its usual unguarded smile. "Hey, Luce. How're ya doing?"

I couldn't help it; I smiled back. Part of me wondered, though, if Shane wasn't as stupid as he appeared. He had the uncanny ability to make a hardened vampire hunter lower her guard with just a smile. What had I just been saying about that not being in my nature anymore?

"Good thanks, Shane. How about you?"

"Never better. The boss has given me a promotion." He said it with such pride, as though this was something he had been coveting for some time and Michel had just given him the moon. He said it as though he would do everything in his power not to let the faith the boss had shown in him down.

"That's great, Shane! What's the job?"

"Liaison to all the new vamps joining the family. I'm to help them settle."

Oh dear, poor Shane. He had no idea what he was up against. Some of those new guys would have his guts for garters, no two ways about it. The desire to climb the ladder in the Durand line would be too great and what better way to show the boss they had what it took to be at the top of the heap than prove their domination over another. Shane was a prime target. Why had Michel put him in that spot? Was he testing him? Was he tired of him and just wanted the problem that was Shane and his non existent power level, solved by someone else's hand other than his own? I only hoped Shane was a whole lot more clever than I had been giving him credit for all along.

"Well, that's, um, super, Shane. Good luck with that."

He just beamed at me and punched the code in the door that led to Michel's quarters.

I walked down the plush hallway with a soft smile playing on my lips. Shane just did that to me, plus I was about to see Michel, how could I not be smiling?

I had barely stepped inside his office, where I had felt his presence and sensed his *Sanguis Vitam* softly humming, when I felt a hard, unforgiving hand go around my throat, almost crushing it. My feet suddenly left the floor as my body was hoisted into the air and thrust hard against the wall at my back.

Oomph.

What the fuck?

24

NEVER PISS A MASTER VAMPIRE OFF

My stake was out and pushed against the chest of the vampire that held me in an instant. If I hadn't have been able to focus properly and see just who that vampire was, I would have slid the stake home without a second's pause, without any hesitation at all.

His grip lessened- I'm guessing in response to the tip of that very sharp silver stake - and I slid down the wall to land on my now extremely shaky legs. His hand stayed at my throat, the swirls of amethyst, violet and magenta battling in his eyes, his fangs flashing in the light of the room.

"What are you doing?" I croaked.

"You smell of another," Michel's voice growled. "It is all over you. You reek."

Charming. I stink, do I? "Well, you're the one adding to the Durand line," I said, trying to pry his fingers off my throat. He didn't budge, at least I could swallow, though. Oh, and breathe.

"This is not one of mine. I do not recognise the scent." His voice hadn't altered; it thrummed with unbridled menace.

Huh? "I haven't been near any other vampires, other than Jett at the door and Shane inside the bar. You're mistaken."

He growled, and I swear it sounded like a Taniwha or tiger or some other particularly big and scary and nasty wild animal.

Suddenly I couldn't swallow after all.

"I..I don't know who it is. I swear I haven't been near another vampire, Michel. Now. Let. Me. Go!" I had raised my stake back up to his chest, pushing the tip of it in through the fabric of his jacket, but not piercing his skin.

"Would you kill me and in turn yourself, Hunter?"

"If I had to, yes." I hadn't hesitated, not even flinched.

We stared at each other then. Michel searching my face for an answer he wasn't going to get. I was scared and angry; my throat hurt like a bitch, and I was damned if I was going to let him see any of that.

He slowly released his hand from my throat, I fought every instinct and desire I had to touch where he had nearly crushed me and just met his gaze and lifted my chin. His eyes travelled to the marks he had left on my neck, and I saw him hesitate as if noticing for the first time that he had hurt me.

"Someone has marked you," he said quietly, rigidly. "It is an intentional mark. They mean for me to notice it." His hand reached up and touched my neck then, tracing the bruises already forming there, his eyes still blazing, but not holding the menace of before. "I could have killed you. I wanted to."

My mind was reeling, he wanted to kill me? I had never seen that one coming and now the realisation of the world I had just married myself into, was slamming against my mind. What the hell have I done? Pushing that daunting thought aside, I tried to focus on the immediate problem. I hadn't been in contact with any vampires other than Jett and Shane today. I actually hadn't been in touch with anyone, I'd stayed in my apartment all day, catching up on laundry and housework, even a vampire hunter has chores. The only other being I had seen was Nero.

Nero. He had held my hands, kissing both them and me before he left. It didn't make sense, but somehow I knew that Nero had done this, had not been able to resist the urge. Could Nero fake vampire scent? Was it one of his powers?

Michel was watching me intently, he knew I had figured something out, hell he could probably sense my emotions. What was I feeling? Initially fear, anger and uncertainty. Now it was more like confusion, resentment and unfortunately, I can't deny it, awe laced with respect. Nero, you naughty, naughty boy.

Michel cocked a delicate eyebrow at me. Oh great, this was going to be fun. Not.

"Um, I had a visit from Nero today."

Michel stilled, didn't say anything but the implication of his rigid stance and continued raised eyebrows said *go on*.

"He wants to train me. Help me to develop my skills as a Nosferatin." I figured that was the least threatening thing to open with, mustn't upset the already borderline homicidal vampire. His fangs were still out after all.

"Why now?" Oh goody, short sentences. Maybe Michel was picking up that habit from me. He doesn't miss much, though, cutting right to the crux of the issue with those two simple words.

My throat was well and truly burning now; swallowing was damn near impossible. I could feel hot tears trying to pool in the corner of my eyes. Damn it all to hell; I was going to have to be the one to give in, wasn't I?

I reached up to my throat and managed a half croak; half whispered, "Ouch." Pathetic? Me? Nah.

He couldn't help it, I knew he was fighting it, but his lips quirked at the edges slightly and gave himself away. He reached up and placed one hand behind my head, cupping my neck; the other began tracing the bruises at the front and sides.

"Lower your shields," he said softly.

The rush of tingling his healing touch gave me came thrumming into my neck; I felt the ache lessen and my throat expand again, but it didn't stop there. He sent a wave of pure desire through me, hot and sharp and oh so sweet, making me gasp and collapse against his chest. I tried to raise my shields against the onslaught of hunger and need I was now forced to feel, but his *Sanguis Vitam* fluctuated, practically slapping them away, with a simple flick. He was proving a point or trying to mark me himself, either way, I was completely at his mercy.

I had forgotten just how intoxicating his power could be; when he wanted to, he could turn me into a puddle of molten goo begging for release. I hadn't had to think about it lately, just before we'd joined he'd been somewhat behaving himself and after we had joined, his power had no effect on me at all. Only when I allowed him to, like now, by lowering my shields. I swore to myself that I would rather be in excruciating pain for eternity than ever let him behind my walls again.

His mouth came down and claimed mine, kissing with a ferociousness I hadn't seen before. "You are mine," he growled against my lips before sending a spike of longing through me that made me whimper out loud.

His hand was still clutching my neck, the other now moving up and down my side, around my back, down to my rear and then back up to my breast. His touch, which normally would have sent uncontrolled shudders through my body anyway, simply burned me now, when coupled with his power stoking the flames. The longing and desire had morphed into a fervent need and ardent hunger so hard and strong I could hardly breathe.

I was clutching him and whimpering and moaning and making all manner of extremely unladylike demands, yet it wasn't enough. If I didn't get closer, didn't have all of him, I knew with a certainty that I would die. I was prepared to sell my soul for another kiss, murder a legion of innocents to feel his touch, and denounce all that is holy and light just to be near him.

Every nerve ending was so raw, screaming out to be satisfied, my world had shrunk to just the two of us, and he was denying me what I needed to breathe, to stay alive. The longing and need were interlaced with rejection and abandonment but still didn't stop me from wanting more. My body begged, my mind implored, and my words pleaded. *Please, please, please, please, please, please.*

Finally, somehow, he must have realised that what he was doing was wrong, or at the very least managed to get some of his anger under control and decided I'd had enough punishment for the day. Because this was definitely his punishment, even if it hadn't been my fault, that Nero had marked me without my knowledge or consent, to a vampire the result was where the punishment laid, and I had come to him smelling of someone else. His power level slowly diminished. The fervent desire and longing, need and hunger he had evoked within me, washing away, until finally, all that was left was rage. My rage, no one else's. It was all me, and I threw it out at him as hard and as fast and with as much strength as I could muster.

He stumbled backwards, with a look of surprise on his face, so I decided to give him more. I bundled up what hatred he had just created in me by forcing me to have those unwanted feelings, feelings that he could so easily have evoked in me with just his touch and words alone, and hurled it at him. Then followed it up with *disbelief, incredulity, resentment, disgust* and for good measure, so he could see just how much he had hurt me, *humiliation, powerlessness, fright* and finally *mistrust*. He had asked me once, not to force him to break my trust in him. It seems he hadn't needed my permission after all.

He leant back against the desk, panting. I hadn't realised I'd followed him as he'd continued to stumble back from the onslaught of my emotions. I was standing right in front of him, not touching but within reach. He looked ashen, slightly clammy. If I hadn't have known better, I'd have thought he was having a heart attack. Of course, vampires can't have those, unless you count the attack on the heart by a stake.

He reached a hand up towards me, I couldn't tell at first if it was in defence or to be a threat, but when he said, "Please, *ma douce*, stop. I am not used to so much emotion. Please." I realised the hand was to beseech.

I suddenly felt sick to the stomach. I had lowered myself to the level of a vampire and whereas they had an excuse, albeit a bloody flimsy one - being unable to help their basic natures when so aroused - I did not. I wasn't forgiving him what he had just done, he knows better, he has it in him to fight the dark, the evil that exists in all vampires, he just chose the wrong path today. But I was ready to admit, though, that he hadn't meant it as a personal attack, it was purely the basic response any vampire would have had and would have had to fight. He had just lost that fight today.

I sunk to the floor on my knees, suddenly so exhausted and bewildered and sad. I guess he was getting *regret* in spades right now because it was all that I could feel. He knelt down beside me and brushed my hair out of my eyes, stroked my cheek with his thumb, my jaw, then my neck.

"Forgive me, *ma belle*. It seems I have much still to learn."

I don't know why, I guess it was the fact that I had just let such raw emotion run freely through me so unchecked, but I started crying, small tears at first, quickly followed by great big racking sobs I couldn't control. My body shook as the pain washed over me and the tears streamed down my face. He held me tightly, rubbing up and down my back, kissing my face and neck, and murmuring his apologies against my skin. I don't know how long we sat there for, holding on to each other, unable to let go, but eventually I stopped crying. He didn't, however, stop apologising for quite some time more.

I may not have been angry at Michel anymore; I did understand what a vampire was like after all. Even if I couldn't completely forgive him for not successfully fighting this dark side of himself today, I was, however, unequivocally angry with Nero. What did he think he was doing? He had to have known what Michel's response to the scent would have been. He had to have known what danger he was putting me in. Why had he done it?

Michel had still been holding me, he had stopped apologising, he had even stopped kissing me; he was just holding on to me as though he thought he would lose me altogether if he let go, his head resting on my chest, his breath warm against my skin. I'm not entirely sure I wanted him to let me go either, despite what had just happened, the thought of being anywhere else, other than in his arms right now, was an impossibility. My basic need to be close to him over-rode all other thought or emotion. Why did being joined to a vampire have to be so hard?

"Why now, *ma douce?* Why does he wish to train you now?"

His question surprised me because I hadn't even realised he was gearing up for one, he'd been so still for so long; it came right out of the blue. I also know he knew the possible response he could have received to that question now. The man had guts or was just plain stupid. Actually, I'm thinking single-minded and downright determined, stubborn even, maybe obstinate. But there was no avoiding what I had come here for, so I swallowed any negative emotion his question stirred within me and relaxed my suddenly rigid stance.

"He told me about the *Cadre of Eternal Knights*, Max had belonged to them; they are hunting Nosferatin to join with, to give them the power to take over all vampires, humans, the world." I thought the best chance of getting Michel on board now was to make it sound really bad for every supernatural, including himself. *The world* kind of covered that. "There's a large community of Nosferatin in Egypt, where Nero is from, they have several mature and a couple of immature Nosferatin. The *Cadre* is targeting them."

The moment of truth. Michel hadn't moved, hadn't shifted at all, he was simply waiting for me to get to the hammer blow, which he undoubtedly knew was coming. "They want our help in fighting the *Cadre*; they don't believe they are strong enough on their own." Maybe if I appealed to his strength, this would work. A vampire hunter's got to try, hasn't she?

He sat back and leant against the base of his desk, still keeping one hand holding one of mine, his blue eyes swirling flecks of cobalt; but no purple, no amethyst or violet, just beautiful deep pools of blue. "Am I to presume he is Nafrini's kindred Nosferatin?"

I just nodded. "She has hidden it well then." He blinked slowly, raised a hand to the bridge of his nose and pinched. Do vampires get headaches? "So, he can Dream Walk, and he can lay a false vampire scent. What else can this Nero of yours do?" I understood the inference, *this Nero of yours*; he was warning me, letting me know he was aware. Nero was encroaching on what Michel believed was his property and he wanted me to take care. At that moment, I really wanted to take care too.

"He can fight, well actually he can really fight. I've never seen another human do what he did, the speed, the precision. It was remarkable." Hiding what I felt of Nero's skills wasn't necessary, Michel had already sensed my emotions and knew.

"He is not human, my dear. Not anymore, anyway."

"What do you mean?"

"If he is the Nosferatin I am thinking of, then he is close to my age, somewhere around 500 years old. Nafrini is older, 700 maybe more.

There were rumours of her joining when I had not long been turned. The world was abuzz with it. The rumours just as quickly disappeared, though, and since that day, Nafrini has never demonstrated anything other than first level master *Sanguis Vitam*. As I said, she has hidden it well."

I wondered why? Could it be she just wanted to protect her kindred Nosferatin and the community he held so dear? I couldn't see a vampire that long ago having that sort of compassion, that sort of care for another, especially someone who was in essence human. Vampires have modernised their natures since then. Michel is very forward for his power level status, he does have good in him, although I have had to question that recently. Still, for a vampire he is progressive. He lives in amongst humans and sets rules in his city for others to adhere, making sure humans are not hunted and therefore the vampire not discovered. But, centuries ago, it was different. Vampires still hid themselves, but they were more inclined to satisfy their cravings and to hell with anyone else.

All the while this was playing through my head, I couldn't stop thinking *Nero is 500 hundred years old?* I mean, I had always thought he sometimes sounded a bit old-fashioned, but wow, as old as Michel? That was just unbelievable; he seemed so human, so vibrant and alive. Not that Nosferatins aren't when they become immortal upon joining, it's not like their heart stops beating and they don't need to breathe like a vampire when it's changed, but still, *500 freakin' years old!*

I guess I had a lot to talk about with Nero tomorrow.

"So, what do you think? Do we help them?"

Michel smiled at me; it was a little more tired than his usual smile, but it did still reach the corners of his eyes.

"What would my Nosferatin like to do?"

I'm sure he was just playing me, buttering me up after such an abominable greeting, but I couldn't help thinking, *yes*! And doing a mental air punch.

"I think we should help them. If this *Cadre* group get power they could be unstoppable, they could come here. I don't want them in my city. I think we should stop them before it's too late."

"Then, we shall go to Egypt. I shall contact Nafrini myself." I knew why he wanted to do that, to send a message that he was the one in control, making the decisions, not me. But all I could think was, I was going to go to Egypt and meet Nero in person. I told myself it was because I just wanted to meet another Nosferatin, one that didn't want to kill me that is, but to be honest, it was all him, I just couldn't help it, I was curious.

Bad, bad, me.

25
AMBUSH

Of course, Michel set a caveat. We would not go until I turned 25, which was only less than a week from now anyway. Nafrini had accepted, I guess she understood that no kindred vampire would wish to endanger their Nosferatin when only a few days delay would alter the odds in their favour.

So, that left me with five days to fill in. It had been a tumultuous few weeks; I'd hardly had a moment to catch my breath, and part of me had felt like my world was spinning out of control. It certainly felt like my world was not my own anymore, but I was working through that. So, I decided to return to work at the bank.

Michel was not happy. I'm guessing having his kindred Nosferatin work as a bank teller just didn't sit well with his image or something, but I wasn't budging on this one. I love my job; it centres me. When everything else is crazy and unpredictable, counting coins settles my soul.

It was late on my first day back, about four in the afternoon, so I was in the mad rush of business banking that happens right before close. No shop owner wants to leave all that cash on their premises overnight, so the last hour before closing was always frantic for me. I loved it. I was so busy that I hadn't even noticed him. I have no idea how long he'd been sitting there, but he looked comfortable, relaxed. Reclining in one of the bank's trendy, but can't-possibly-be-comfortable bright blue chairs. He made it look like a luxurious bed, the way he lounged out in it. His long legs stretched out in front of him, crossed at the ankles, his arms behind his head as he watched me. Very comfortable indeed. But then, when had Nero ever not looked at home?

He smiled when my eyes finally saw him, that dazzling and wicked smile, all bright light laced with sinful deeds. I fought a blush and thankfully succeeded. I really had to stop acting like a lovesick teenager. But, it made the last quarter hour very difficult indeed. I found myself having to count customers' deposits two, even three times, my mind was so distracted by the presence of him. So I didn't finish bang on five, and my usually pleasant and friendly customers had begun to get frustrated with my slow pace and distracted conversation. By the time I balanced my float and had put it away in our large safe out the back, I was frazzled.

I couldn't see him when I came out from the staff room, changed ready for the jog home. Of course, he was waiting for me on the street when I exited the bank, that same sexy smile gracing his perfectly chiselled face.

"I shall walk you home, Kiwi."

"I like to run."

"Even better. Your training can start now then."

When I said I like to *run* home, I had meant a leisurely jog, following a direct path to my front door, but Nero had other ideas.

After we had been running at an alarming speed for 35 minutes, I began to think that Nero's idea of training was probably going to be different from mine. I can run long distances, I'm fit, I won't deny it. You have to be, to fight the never tiring, super strong, deadly killing machine that is the vampire. So 35 minutes is still a walk in the park, even at the speed that Nero had been insisting. I had passed that stage where your body burns and screams out obscenities at you and entered the dull but reassuring ache afterwards, sure that I could keep going if I didn't push myself. Unfortunately, for Nero, the first 35 minutes had only been a warm-up, and now the real running began. I was covered in a nice layer of sweat by now and a little annoyed I had a pack on my back. I had tightened the straps to stop the never ending bounce of it against my back and hips, but it was hot and clingy and the sweat pooling there was surely going to ruin it forever. You just can't throw a backpack in the wash.

We'd made it to Meola Road, and I could see Western Springs Park coming up. I got a sudden surge of hope, maybe we were going to stop there, it would be a good area for further training, and I could catch my breath. I knew I wasn't at my limit yet, I still had ample strength to get me home, but it was hot, and I was sticky, and I really needed to pee. Nero however, didn't even pause. I watched with dismay as we passed the pond and ducks, and then with mounting anxiety when the public toilets sped past and then we were on the footpath again, heading west.

We crossed the motorway at the Carrington Road intersection and continued along Mt Albert Road. OK, by this time I really was starting to wonder if Nero was just going to make me run all night long. He had that maniacal gleam in his eyes like he could do this forever. Our speed hadn't altered since we had started, any human running at this speed could only sustain it for a couple of kilometres, we had been running for over ten, and then he decided to up the ante. At first, I just let him pull ahead of me and momentarily enjoyed the sight of his back and butt as it strode away and then the competitor within took over and I dug deep.

By the time we had made it to Campbell Road and the large expanse which is Cornwall Park, I was gasping for breath. There was a sharp pain in my side and running down my right leg, and my bladder was about to explode. All of which was excruciatingly painful, but not nearly as much as the blow to the side of my head when Nero came to a stop in amongst some trees.

I spun away from him and crashed against a trunk. "What the hell?"

"Do you think you will not be attacked when you are tired, Kiwi? A vampire will not stop for you to catch your breath."

And then he came at me again, low, with arms open, ready to sweep me off my feet. At this point, he could have thrown me over his shoulders and dragged me off to his cave; I was in shock, pain and in no condition to fight back. I felt the air leave my lungs at the collision of his hard body against mine and then the sickening thud of my head hitting compacted earth and maybe an exposed tree root too. The world swam before my eyes, but Nero simply hauled me to my feet and started circling. He looked a bit fuzzy around the edges, and I think he was on a lean, or maybe that was me, but I could see him circling, I could see him assessing me and I was coming up wanting, that was for sure.

He struck out again with his open hand; I think he was holding back; he could have used a fist, but somehow my body reacted instinctively, and I jumped out of the way. He didn't connect, which was great, but I lost my footing and ended up landing on my side, straining to breathe, which was bad. He was on me in an instant; I rolled out of the way, but his foot had connected with my side, the one I had landed on and had the sharp pain in, so the foot was not welcome.

I somehow managed to reach out and grab his leg, tugging with all my strength, until he was on his arse. I launched myself up from the ground and pushed him back against the dirt, both of us losing our breath in a whoosh. He grabbed my arms pinning them to me and rolled us over, so he was on top now pinning me to the ground. Not a good position to be in and one I planned to remedy immediately. I brought my head up in a fast and swift motion, banging the top of my forehead against the bridge of his nose.

That just hurts like a bitch. I know, I've had a vampire do it to me before, and it was not fun. Blood started pouring out of Nero's nose, his eyes looked a little glazed as well and thankfully, his grip lessened, and I rolled out from under him. I scrambled away thinking I might just get a break and then felt him suddenly pushing me to the ground. My arms went out to stop the fall, the skin on my palms, wrists and forearms scraping in the dirt and bits of little rocks that littered the small clearing we were in. I felt the weight of him against me, his ragged breathing on my neck.

"Do you surrender yet, Kiwi." His voice was not quite the soft purr I was used to but strained and ragged with his breath.

But oh hell. Now he was taunting me. I wasn't sure how many more times I could use my head as a battering ram, but I couldn't think of anything else right then, so I tried to throw my head back against Nero's face. He had moved to the side, so I only got his clavicle and shoulder, sending a sharp pain right through my skull and making white flashes appear before my eyes. His weight had shifted, so I continued to go in that direction, rolling him over and throwing my arms out wide to free his grip. He scrabbled to grab me, but I was up and out of there before he found purchase and had turned to face him with a smile.

"*That* was the just warm up, Nero. Now we fight."

His bronze and brown eyes sparkled, and his face lit up with a smile. He was definitely having fun. We looked at each other for a moment and then we both launched at the same time. I landed a flying punch to his face, feeling my knuckles graze against his cheek, but he connected with a solid fist in my stomach, sending the air from my lungs and making me consider bringing my lunch up all over him. I staggered backwards, but he wasn't looking much better, he was shaking his head and panting, bent over with his hands on his knees.

I didn't fall for it. I came back at him with a side kick, jumping out of the way when he tried to grab me and turning round to land a high kick to his chest. He went flying backwards against a tree but bounced off and landed on his feet in a crouch. I was starting to think this would end in someone's death, but a part of me was pretty damn pleased with how I was holding my own with such an old and experienced Nosferatin.

Of course, I should have known better. I had seen him in action with those vampires in the courtyard in Sydney. I should have known he had been holding back with me all along just now. I should have known he was just toying with me, letting me believe I had a chance.

I should have known better.

When he launched into the air in a spin, arms out, legs evenly spread, I had a momentary vision of a sleek black cat sliding through the breeze, overlaid with the image of a strong muscular body of a ballet dancer, lifting off the ground and twirling through the sky. The impact of the blow sent a shockwave through my body and lifted my feet off the floor. I spun around and landed with a resounding splat on my stomach on the ground. This time I really could not breathe. I couldn't draw a breath; I couldn't move, and I couldn't stop the tears streaming down my face. I was paralysed in the dirt, my head and face turned out to one side, my hands by my thighs - useless - and my body screaming for mercy.

Nothing happened for an excruciating moment. If Nero had been a vampire, my head would be clear off my body by now, or my jugular severed. I was exposed and vulnerable lying there waiting to be killed. I felt like a failure.

His tan soft leather shoes were the first thing I registered in front of my face; then his head bent down to look at me, his hand lifting a strand of my hair which had fallen across my face, back into position over my shoulder. He looked happy, concerned and could that have been, impressed?

I finally found my breath and the strength to roll over onto my back. I still didn't think I could stand, but at least I'd see my death if it came calling, look it right in the eyes. I stared up at the darkening sky peeking through the heavy cover of leaves from the trees. It was still too early for stars, but I knew there would be some tonight, the sky was clean and free of the clutter of clouds. I sensed, rather than saw, Nero sit down on the ground next to me. I could hear his breathing; he still hadn't quite got it under control. Ha!

"Well, that was fun," I managed to get out in a semi-puff.

His hand came to rest on my shoulder, the warmth of it reassuring through the fabric. "You are truly sensational, Kiwi. You have no idea."

"I thought I pretty much sucked actually. You were holding back."

"Of course, at times. You are not fully matured, but I was not - how do you say? - going easy on you. I was fighting, and you held your own."

I appreciated the sentiment; he was trying to make me feel better; maybe he could even sense my emotions like Michel - who knew? I certainly didn't know everything there was to know about this man beside me, but I wasn't going to let him get away with that.

"You could have used that spinny thing sooner, finished me off right from the start. You were holding back."

He chuckled. "That *spinny thing* takes a certain amount of effort and concentration; it is not an easily acquired skill. One can be distracted enough not to able to achieve it. You had my attention in full; I could not have managed that move any sooner. You were... amazing." He said the last with a sense of awe.

Well, hot damn. I kind of liked the sound of that.

"So, are you going to beat the crap out of me every day this week, because if you do, I'm telling ya, I'm going to be a physical wreck by the time we get to Egypt."

"Your kindred vampyre can heal your injuries; you will not suffer long and the more we practice, the better you shall be."

I sat up abruptly at that and then cringed at the pain through my body. Through my *entire friggin' body*. I sucked in a sharp breath and held myself together with an arm across my bruised stomach.

"No." It was emphatic. "No way."

Nero turned to me slowly. "You would not allow your vampyre to heal you? Why ever not?"

I sighed. "Your little *message* yesterday made him lose his normally very nicely controlled temper. Which reminds me, I am extremely pissed off with you for that! What were you thinking?"

He looked a little abashed and then puzzled and then back to abashed. "I am sorry, Kiwi, truly I am. I had marked you before I had even realised it and it is not something you can then erase."

Why was this the story of my life right now, why was every man in my world constantly claiming me as their property and doing something wickedly horrible to hurt me and then apologising for it? It was a broken record I was beginning to resent.

"Where's your self-control, Nero? I thought you were ancient, been around the block, surely you could have stopped yourself from doing something so *stupidly, dangerously, insane!* I thought you would be better than a vampire."

He actually cringed at that, a momentary look of discomfort flashing across his handsome features. He had moved his hand down to my own when I had sat up, but he didn't remove it now, he had just stilled and was looking at me intently, a look of puzzlement now back on his face.

"For some reason, your approval is important to me." He shook his head at that. "I have let you down. I will make amends if it takes the rest of my life to do so." OK, so he was a pretty intense guy, but *the rest of his life?*

Could *my* life get any more complicated?

I shook my head at him. "Just promise me you won't do it again. I don't fancy having my throat crushed by a very jealous and possessive vampire."

He just nodded, a thoughtful look on his face. He hadn't been surprised by Michel's behaviour; he'd been around vampires for 500 years, he knew the deal.

"Why will you not have him heal you?" His voice was soft, back to its usual purr.

"It doesn't matter. I just don't like it. I...I don't like to appear weak."

I couldn't tell Nero; I couldn't let him see the struggle that Michel had to fight, the struggle that he had failed to win. Michel was mine to protect and even though I somehow felt more comfortable with Nero than I had with anyone since meeting Rick, I couldn't go there with him on this. I just couldn't. I would prefer him to believe it was out of some warped sense of pride, of vanity, on my part and not because of any weakness of Michel's.

"This is between you and your vampyre. It is your battle to confront." He said it matter of factly, in his usual intense way, part of me was relieved he was dropping the issue, the other a little sad. Even the all-knowing Nero didn't have an answer to my problems. I suddenly felt very alone.

"Can you stand, Kiwi? I must go, Nafrini is vulnerable when I Dream Walk, I do not like to leave her for long. Cairo is not the haven it once was for us. But I will not leave you if you are not ready to fight any vampyre that may cross your path."

"I'm fine, Nero. I just need to catch my breath. I think I'll stay here for a bit, take in the surroundings."

Nero glanced around the rather barren clearing in the trees we were in. I could tell what he was thinking. *What surroundings?* But he just nodded. "If you are sure?"

I nodded back and put on my best convincing smile of confidence.

His lips quirked. He wasn't fooled, but he was prepared to let me do this.

"Until tomorrow then, my little Kiwi." His hand reached up and stroked my cheek and then he was gone.

I took a deep breath in, it hurt, but it also felt good; the clean, crisp smells of nature all around. I reached over and grabbed my backpack - it had come off during the fight - and took my stake out. I might have been considering sitting here to catch my breath for a while, but I sure as hell wasn't going to be unprepared. I slipped it into the front pocket of my sweatshirt. The sun had set now, stars were beginning to shine, vampires would be awake.

I tipped my head back against the tree's trunk and let the sounds of the early evening in. The traffic in the distance, the sheep in nearby fields - Cornwall Park is farmed, strange but true - the rustle of leaves on the ground, the wind in the trees, the scratching of a small creature in the underbrush, the soft footfalls of someone approaching.

I was on my feet with my stake out in a flash. Even a bruised and beaten vampire hunter has quick reflexes.

His *Sanguis Vitam* reached me first, he was warning me of his approach. Michel slowly walked into the clearing and stood looking at me. He was dressed in his lovely thigh hugging black trousers and casual-for-him black shirt, not his usual suit and tie. The events of recent days having made him relax his wardrobe standards. I liked it. He could look so sinful in black.

I didn't loosen my hold on the stake, but I did lower it a little.

He cocked his head at me, eyebrow raised. "You do not look well, *ma douce*."

At the sound of his voice, so warm, so soft, I melted and slid back down the side of the tree to land in a mess at the bottom. I stuffed the stake back in its pocket and tipped my head back with closed eyes.

Michel walked over and sat down next to me in the dirt, no doubt messing up his perfectly clean and expensive pants. I felt him there, warm and still. This was familiar, wasn't it? And then again not.

"What have you been doing, my dear?" he said, as he took my right hand in his and began slowly stroking the back.

When I didn't reply, he just added, "I know you will not let me heal you. But will you let me take you home?"

I turned to look at him, his eyes so deeply blue, so mesmerising and beautiful. He smiled, and my heart missed a beat all of its own accord. I nodded then, and he stood, simply lifted me in his arms and we were gone.

I must have fallen asleep because the next thing I was aware of was being lowered gently onto my couch, Michel brushing my hair from my eyes. "I shall run you a bath, *ma douce.*"

I didn't fight him. I couldn't have fought a single soul. I had hidden it from Nero; he hadn't realised just how close to the edge he had pushed me. I had been hanging on by just the tips of my fingers.

Michel came back and carried me into the bathroom. He stood me up where I swayed slightly and stripped me off. He didn't try to seduce me; he didn't touch me in any sexual way, he simply handled me swiftly, but firmly and helped me into the bath.

It was warm and full of bubbles and smelled of mandarin. I love mandarins. I felt my head tilt back against the end of the bath, my eyes close and Michel begin to softly soap me up and wash away the dirt. My grazes stung, but he was gentle, my bruises hurt, but he took such care. I felt myself lifting one leg, then the other, one arm, then the other. My back being washed, my chest, everywhere and then he was towelling me off and carrying me to my bedroom.

He lay me down, wrapped the blankets around me, tucking me in like a child, kissed my forehead and said, "I will not disturb your dreams tonight, *ma belle*. When you are ready, come to me. I will be waiting. As always."

With that, he was gone, taking the very air, the warmth and the light of the room with him and leaving me so, so alone.

26

THE BOND

I woke to a world full of pain. White hot excruciating pain. I sucked a breath in and forced back a sob. Good Lord I hurt. I shuffled to the bathroom and took ten times as long as usual to get washed and ready for the day. By the time I made it out to the kitchen, I knew there was no way I was going to work, I'd have to throw a sickie.

I sat down at my dining room table and just sobbed; silent, quiet, little heaving sobs. My life really did suck. I wasn't quite sure what I was going to be able to do the way I was feeling right now, paracetamol had no effect, the hot shower I'd had before was pitiful, just existing took effort and hurt. This was not good.

I knew it had been a rough workout, but I had no idea the after effects would be so drastic. I'd had bad fights before, sure, I've spent my fair share of time at the Emergency Room, in bed all day, curled up on the couch channel surfing. But this was different; this was my body trying to tell me something and I didn't have a clue what it was. Other than *don't ever do that to me again you stupid idiotic twit!*

I was just sitting at the dining table staring into space, feeling like a useless piece of vampire hunter arse, when I felt it: a pull. Not the usual, evil-lurks-in-my-city pull, but a beautiful calling to my soul, a promise to make things better, a soft caress against my skin, a whisper that it will all be all right.

I don't know how because I'd never felt it before and he has never felt like this to me when I sense him, but I knew it was Michel, calling me to him. Without a second thought, I picked up the phone and called a taxi. No way I was gonna be able to walk all the way up there.

It was one of those extraordinary days in Auckland, blue, blue sky, sun pelting down, everyone in short sleeved tops, despite it being winter, pretending it was summer and smiling at strangers on the street. There's just something about a sunny day in the city. The noise of traffic, honking horns and screeching tyres, the low hum that resonates throughout, it all just seems to fade into the background when you get one of those days. A miracle that can't be ignored.

The front door was locked at *Sensations* of course, but the day crew were there, cleaning, preparing, keeping it safe. Humans that helped vampires. I was beginning to get used to it. They weren't surprised to see me, just opened the door with a short nod and turned back to their work. I was just wondering how I would get past the combination lock to Michel's private chambers and had my hand up above the keypad, about to wing it, when I felt a tingle in my arm and the door softly clicked open. It took me by surprise, so I did a little jump. There was no one there holding it open, so I settled my beating heart and just shut the door behind me and followed that now undeniable pull, letting it wrap around me and whisper to me, encouraging me on.

Michel's chamber was shut. The door didn't magically open. So I thought, to hell with this and just knocked. Nothing happened for a moment and then Michel appeared at the open door, in nothing but his black boxers, his hair a little bed tussled and with a strange look on his face.

"Lucinda, is everything all right?"

I was surprised he hadn't been expecting me, he was calling me to him wasn't he? "Um, I felt a pull, I had to come."

He didn't say anything for a moment, just looked at me with a quizzical look on his face and then his face lit up with a smile.

"The Bond," he said, pulling me to him in an embrace. His arms so warm, but the contact causing my aching body to scream and a whimper to escape my lips.

He quickly pulled back, holding me by my shoulders and scanning my body. I hadn't been able to put much on, it had hurt to raise my arms to pull a T-Shirt over my head, so I'd opted for short sleeved blouse and a simple short skirt. Not my usual black on black ensemble, this time white on white. It kind of looked like a poor attempt at a little rich girl's tennis outfit, but at least my tan looked good against the white and really, I couldn't have cared less. I had just slipped my feet into white trainers, no socks and had a small bag over one shoulder with my stake and knife and purse in it. That was it, nothing more, except a bruised and battered body that was making tears run down my cheeks right now.

Michel led me over to the bed, flicking his hand towards the door to close and lock it and helped me to sit down. He knelt down in front of me holding my hands.

"You are in such pain, *ma douce*, it is tearing me up inside. Is this level of pain usual?"

I just shook my head, sniffed a little and continued to cry. He reached up and stroked my cheek, my neck and sighed.

"Your Bond to me called you here; your body is trying to tell you to come to me, have me heal you. It's trying to help you to get better." When he saw the look on my face at the words *have me heal you*, he laughed a little mirthlessly. "It clearly does not know you as well as I."

He ran a hand over his face and let out a sharp short breath. "I don't know what to say to make you trust me, *ma douce*. I don't know what to do."

"Just hold me," I managed to whisper.

His head shot up, and he stared at me. "If you wish, *ma belle*."

Michel helped me lie back down on the bed, took my shoes off and set them down next to my bag, then slid into bed next to me, gently wrapping an arm around my shoulders and resting my head against his chest. He felt warm and smelled clean, like soap and sea spray, fresh and familiar. He started stroking my hair, and although he hadn't healed me, he wasn't trying to right now, my body relaxed more than it had done at any time previously that morning and the ache seemed to lessen in my bones.

"The Bond is something all kindred vampyre and their Nosferatin have, eventually anyway." His voice was low and soft, so wonderfully welcoming and full of life. "There is always a connection between them, sometimes starting well before they are joined, as ours did and growing stronger once the ceremony has been completed, but the Bond does not usually form until much later. And it certainly has not been known to form before the Nosferatin is matured.

"It is a very special thing. It allows us to find each other, no matter where in the world we are. To perform whatever is required to get to that person, overcome any obstacle. To talk to each other in thoughts, not read each other's minds, but send a directed thought towards your Bonded. It enables us to feed off the life force of each other, not in a negative way, but as a sharing of energy between two souls, making them almost as one. It strengthens our own powers, by simply using a fraction of our kindred's, the exchange is equal, no one member of the Bond getting less from the exchange than the other, it is the essence of our joining and something all joined wait impatiently to receive. I had not dared hope your Bond would awaken so early."

I was already feeling so much better, not healed but stronger, the aches had definitely lessened, the bruises still there but not as noticeable to me as before. Whatever the Bond was doing, being near Michel felt so damn right. But, I couldn't stop that small part of me wondering, is this thing making me feel something that I would normally not feel?

"Is it forcing us to be close, against our will I mean?"

"No, not at all, *ma douce*. The Bond is slow to develop in some kindred joining because the connection between them is not as strong. Had you joined with Maximilian, for instance, your Bond may not have formed for many years, maybe even centuries. It is an acknowledgement of your connection, and your connection is in direct response to your emotional state of mind, your heart's desire, so to speak. The Bond can not make you come to me against your will unless you wish it so."

He reached his head down then and kissed me softly on the lips, so slow and warm and inviting. He paused allowing me time to protest and when I didn't move; he kissed me again.

Against my lips, he murmured, "It tells me this is where you wish to be and nowhere else. It tells me you are mine as I am yours."

His tongue slid through my teeth, his teeth grazing my bottom lip and suddenly my body no longer ached, but was on fire. A beautiful lazy heat of fire flickering across my skin. I gave a soft moan before I even realised what I was doing. Michel chuckled against my mouth.

"You are always so responsive, *ma douce*, it is something I treasure."

He shifted slightly to start layering kisses down my cheek and neck, across my jaw and then back to my mouth. His kiss deepening and promising more and more with every stroke of his tongue, every brush of his lips. One of his hands started stroking my side, up over my stomach and then finding my breast through the material, tweaking my nipple. I arched towards him at his touch, and he gave a soft moan in response, his kiss becoming more possessive. I didn't fight it, my body, or Bond, or whatever the hell this was, just kept saying more.

I wasn't sure if this was at all real, but it felt real and part of me just thought, why not let this be real? Why not let myself have this wonderful, beautiful experience, allow myself to love this complicated but passionate man. With all my soul I wanted to be with Michel, I wanted him to win the battle against that dark side of him, I wanted him to come towards the light more than I had ever wanted anything in this world before. I knew that this was not going to be an easy relationship, being with a vampire couldn't ever possibly be called easy, but it was something that was so deep within me I could no longer deny it. I was meant to be here, by this man's side, with this man. I knew it with all my heart, body and soul.

His fingers were undoing the buttons on my shirt, reaching inside and stroking the naked flesh beneath. I hadn't bothered with a bra, unable to contemplate that difficulty and when his hand reached my naked breast he groaned, pushed aside the blouse and bent his head to take my nipple in his mouth, so wet and warm and delicious. His teeth teasing, followed by a tongue licking, only to be replaced again by a nip, a lick and the soft coolness of his breath. Little electric pulses had started radiating out from that spot, shooting down my body to more intimate areas, bringing with it heat and a wicked wetness. I rubbed against him in a natural movement, unaware of my actions and received a growl of appreciation in return.

Suddenly his hand replaced the thigh I had been pressing against, removing my underwear and returning to stroke the wet folds between my legs, dipping inside and moving back out to rub and tease and stroke. His eyes were shining a beautiful mix of blues and violets, flecks and swirls, lighting up his face and sending a shudder right through my body. He moved with that lightning speed he has and appeared between my legs, lifting my thighs and butt off the bed and burying his face in the soft curls at my crease. His tongue so sure and confident, lapping at me, teasing me, flicking that sensitive nub and sending shockwave after shockwave through my body.

I found myself groaning and calling out with each touch of that very clever tongue and then he started sucking, nipping and thrusting his tongue in as far as it could go and that was it, I was gone. On a wave of desire that had me clawing at his back, digging my nails into his flesh and scratching his shoulders as he devoured me, tasted me and pleased me. After what seemed like a lifetime of unadulterated bliss I broke the crest of all that delectable heat and screamed out in pleasure, letting the tidal wave of shudders rack my body and cover me with shivers.

Michel held me close, whispering to me, kissing me, comforting me and helping me come down from that impossible high. And then before my breath could steady, or my heartbeat slow at all, he positioned himself above me, stroking the length of me with his hard sex and with a look of strained control pushed inside in a delicious thrust of desire.

His movements weren't steady, the rhythm a staccato of hard and short motions, he was so close to the edge it was obviously taking every effort to hold on. His eyes met mine and I didn't want to ever look away. The need to be here with him so strong it stole my breath, so different from anything I had ever felt before in my life, it consumed me, it ruled me, it warmed and welcomed me, but most of all it shouted that this was right, so very, very right.

I could see he was having a similar experience, the look in his eyes intense, the violet flecks now mixing with amethyst, his groans and whispers fervent demands for *more, yes,* and *mine.* He became more frantic, moaning in amongst a ragged murmur of words. The sight of him sending me on another rising wave of delight, so much more intense than before, the fire building to a delicious roar, the shockwaves starting to come in such short succession I couldn't breathe.

I wanted to keep my eyes open and savour every second, every thrust, every feature of his fiercely hungry look; and I even managed it for a while. But as Michel's rhythm faltered even further and he let a cry of pure joy out, I crushed myself to him and rode the wave of rapture he had created to the very end, savouring the white noise and bright light of our coupling.

We collapsed in a tangled pile of limbs on the bed. The look Michel gave me one of utter surprise and delight.

"*That* was remarkable."

I was still breathless, I couldn't answer him straight away, but I knew what he meant. Sex with him had always been good, hell, *way* better than good, but what we had just experienced then, was in a whole different league.

When I finally recovered, my heart slowing from its desperate tattoo inside my chest and my breath had settled to a slightly more healthy rasp, I managed, "OK. You win. You can heal me now."

It was met with a low chuckle and warm arms pulling me close.

"*Ma douce*, I am already lost. I have the feeling I shall never win a battle with you, ever again."

27
SOMETHING MISSING

It was still only about midday when we finally emerged from the confines of our arms, Michel had healed me immediately, my heart rate only rising slightly at the moment of lowering my shields. All I felt now was bliss and an afterglow of warmth and comfort and hunger. I hadn't eaten since lunchtime yesterday, so Michel picked up the phone beside the bed and asked for a tray of food to be brought to his chambers. His vampires would all be out for the count, so mind-talking his request was not possible, he had to resort to the old *human* standby and actually talk to his servants. I'd said I would be happy to go out and grab something for myself, I felt so alive and healthy, like I could have run a million miles and swum right across the Pacific Ocean, but he wouldn't let me out of his embrace.

"You are *not* going anywhere today, or for a long time, my dear. I am not letting you out of my sight." He said it in a low growl, but it held a lightness to it, a challenge.

I could have bristled at what had sounded very much like a *fait accompli*, but something in me just seemed to purr, to acknowledge that I too had absolutely no desire to be anywhere else other than with him. My tray of food arrived, and Michel sat back on the bed with a lazy smile and watched me nibble on a bit of this and that from the assortment his staff had provided. *Sensations* has a small kitchen, not a full restaurant, but providing a nice selection of nibble-style foods for its patrons. The chefs had provided a selection across the menu, there was more here than I could have possibly managed to consume, but I was loving tasting a little of everything.

I glanced up with the realisation that Michel had not slept, being daylight most vampires do need to rest, only venturing out on sunless days and only if absolutely necessary, but I wasn't sure if rest meant sleep and if he was weakening himself or not.

"Do you need to sleep? Am I keeping you awake?"

He gave me one of his sensual smiles, full lips and knowing eyes. "You can keep me awake whenever you like, my dear, as long as it involves such sweet activities like this morning's."

I flashed him a look that said, *whatever*. He laughed. "I do not need to sleep, Lucinda, I am a level one *Sanguis Vitam* Master, but resting is good for the soul, is it not? And this," he indicated the bed and then me, "is resting."

"What about feeding?"

He sobered slightly, recognising the tone of my question. I wasn't sure I wanted to know the answer to this, but I needed to. He sat forward and took one of my hands in both of his.

"I shall need to feed, *ma douce*, when the sun sets. A vampyre does not do well to pass a night without sustenance."

I bit my lip and let a breath out. OK. I could accept this; it hadn't really been something I had thought about too much before. Well, I had kind of pushed it to the back of mind and ignored the issue altogether actually, but it wasn't like I hadn't expected it. I've been around vampires a lot now, they don't hide their feeding when it's just them and willing donors, no uninformed Norms about, and lately I had been at *Sensations* quite a bit out of public hours.

Michel had been watching me intently. Finally he said, "We have two options available to us, *ma douce*. I could feed whenever you are not here, or out of your sight and not advise you if you so wish to remain in the dark. Or, I could feed from you. I do not require much at my age and with our Bond, it would not weaken you should I feed daily." When I didn't say anything, he went on. "If it's any reassurance to you, *ma belle*, my choice is unequivocal. I could never desire to taste of another again."

Well, this was an interesting sensation, wasn't it? I was a little disconcerted, scared of having a vampire, even Michel whom I was only now realising I loved, feed from me. So long now I have hunted vampires who have fed indiscriminately on humans, without consent, without care. I have associated vampire feeding with the evil that lurks in my city.

But, then part of me was excited, excited by the prospect of being so close to Michel on a regular basis. Vampire feeding is very personal, very intimate. Of course, it can be horrible, torture, should the vampire choose, but for Michel, I could only imagine it would be the bliss of emotions he had instilled in me when he fed from me at our joining. The intensity of closeness thrumming right through to my soul.

And then, finally, there was the jealousy, unable to accept that another human could possibly feel any of that delicious closeness with *my* vampire, with my Michel. The jealousy was a living thing inside me, rearing up and shouting through my mind, *no!*

I realised belatedly, that I hadn't tried to hide these emotions at all and that Michel had sat absorbing them all quietly, waiting for me to come to the end of the roller coaster I had created. I looked up at him, he smiled ruefully at me, a little paler than normal, but hiding it well.

I licked my lips, his eyes homing in on that movement with a sudden look of desire. Which made me feel yet another emotion, one equally as heated as that now evident in his gaze.

"Would feeding from me daily result in us jumping each other's bones?" His eyebrows raised at that. I went on hurriedly, "I mean, not that I'm complaining, but, you know daily, that's like *every* day and I'm not exactly built like you, I mean, I know I'm stronger and all than a regular human, but I'm still human and every day is quite a lot and well..." I kind of ran out of steam then and felt a heated flush rise up my face.

Michel was fighting it, but I could see his chest rise in delicate chuckles until he could contain it no longer and burst out into delicious peals of laughter. He stopped when he saw the mortified look on my face, or maybe it was the emotion hitting him, in any case, he tried to school his features into a much more sober expression and said, "I would be delighted if it did, my dear, but it does not have to. I am not able to influence your mind, but I can control the endorphins that are secreted when I feed. To a certain extent in any case. It would be impossible for me not to relay the joy I would be feeling in being so close to you, but it would be your choice whether you should take that further and reciprocate. The experience, however, will always be enjoyable to us both, on more than one level"

I didn't know what to say to that. Getting turned on, on a daily basis, surely wasn't such a bad thing, was it? It wasn't like I hadn't realised what it would be like to be around Michel. Even without the feeding, it's an electric pot-pourri of heat and desire, lust and hunger. Why not throw that impossible closeness into the mix too? Oh boy.

Before I had a chance to answer Michel added, "You would have to be aware that I would still feed when in a battle. Should I find myself in one against human or a shapeshifter. It would be an impulse I could not ignore. It would be nothing other than a vampyre reflex, no other connotation than the means to an end. You understand?"

That, I could completely understand. That was a vampire through and through. To a certain extent, that's what the vampires did when I hunted them. They considered the hunt of a human and the feeding and sometimes killing of that human, a battle and once on that path, unable to stop themselves. Vampires suck blood. We all know it. It's what they are. They may feed for pleasure and sustenance in the modern day, but their basic nature is still so deeply rooted that not to feed when faced with an enemy was an impossibility. Somehow, I had no problem separating that type of feeding from what Michel does every evening to stay alive.

So, what did I want? Easy. I don't share what's mine. Michel knew the answer before I even opened my mouth, the wave of emotion so strong. He reached out and pulled me to him, kissing my neck, my jaw, my mouth.

"How is it that you can simply melt me with an emotion, *ma douce?*

You have captured my heart, do you know that? You hold it your hand. I am at your mercy."

Then he simply pushed the tray of food off the bed and threw me on my back and suddenly, I had a very amorous vampire climbing up my body.

His kisses were so sweet, so warm, so simply delicious. But he didn't want this to get carried away; he wanted to prove to me he could control himself, that I didn't need to fear his desire for me would rule his actions, no matter when. The kisses slowed, his touch more languid until he brought both of us back to just the warmth and a welcoming sense of safety.

However, Michel had not been joking when he said he did not want me out of his sight and when sunset came and duties called, his every move was with me in tow. Rather than carry out his meetings with members of his line in his office, as he usually would, he sat himself in the bar, in one of the private booths, but in a position where he could continue to watch me at one of the tables.

There was a jazz band playing tonight, entertaining the large crowd that had gathered at *Sensations* and the woman singing had a sultry, dusky voice, the music making me bob my foot up and down as it sat crossed over my leg. Whenever Michel was busy, Bruno would be at my side. Sitting himself down in a chair opposite me, having a drink and keeping up a string of jokes about the patrons, the new vampires to join the line and even the jazz band. I don't think I'd had a more enjoyable evening with someone other than Michel. Why had I not noticed just how normal Bruno could be?

The moment Michel had finished with a vampire, he was back, lavishing me with his attention, touching me with his hands. I wasn't opposed to reaching out and touching him either, the need to be close so strong. I have no idea whether the groupies were there, the young women who flock to his side when he's in the bar, as Michel's attention did not waver, it was only for me.

By early morning I was waning, however, tired from a long day and the terrible injuries from the fight with Nero. Despite Michel having healed me, my body refused to believe it was so and wanted sleep. Michel noticed my head drooping, from where he was sitting with Jett in deep conversation and rose immediately to come to my side. He said something to Bruno, I didn't hear and led me to his chamber.

Once he had me settled in bed, I said, "You need to go back out there, I'll be fine, I just need some sleep."

He smiled at me indulgently. "I will not be leaving your side, *ma douce*, today, or even tomorrow, the Bond requires us to be together. It is a desire that cannot be denied even if we wanted to. The establishment of a Bond is an important part of our joining. There is nowhere else I wish to be. I will, however, conduct my business from in here." He waved his hand over to a comfortable armchair and low table in the corner which had not been there earlier, a laptop already sitting out waiting for him. "No one will enter, I can communicate with my line, silently and from a distance."

I yawned and just nodded, having no desire for him to leave me at all. "There is however one thing you could do for me, *ma belle*."

I looked up at him questioningly.

"I am hungry, would you mind?"

Suddenly I was awake.

He smiled and chuckled. "Oh dear, you will get used to it, Lucinda, it will become as much a part of you as it is me, please believe me."

My eyes felt wide, my heart suddenly in my throat, my pulse beating at an altogether most alarming rate. Michel reached up and brushed his fingers against my throat, just over my pulse point.

"You do not make it easy, do you?" he murmured.

I swallowed the lump which had suddenly formed in my throat. Michel lowered his head and sighed. "I can feed elsewhere, but it would require me leaving you, as I cannot believe you would wish to watch." He looked up at me. "Is that what you would prefer, *ma douce*?"

I didn't hesitate, just shook my head, not breaking eye contact at all.

"As I thought, so I shall make this quick. Forgive me for the speed in which this happens, my dear, normally I would prefer to take my time and savour the moment, *especially with you*, but it might be best if we just - how do they say? - get this over with."

I bit my lip, I couldn't help it, I just couldn't stop my response to this; pure terror but also need so strong it ached. My mind was telling me to calm down, this is quite normal, a quite acceptable part of being joined to a vampire, but my inner monologue was shouting *get the fuck out of here!* I struggled to tell it to shut up.

Michel took my hand in his, turned it over and rubbed the wrist lightly, so softly with his thumb, right above the veins and arteries there. His voice was low and even. "I do not normally bother with the wrist, it is somewhat impersonal, but perhaps tonight it would be better."

He slowly lifted my arm up to his mouth, his fangs sliding out and down in a swift, smooth and quick movement. He didn't pull his lips back exposing teeth, as so many vampires do when about to go in for a bite, his mouth remaining so full and lush, his eyes met mine. And then before I could help myself, I reached up and grabbed his shirt with one hand, surprising him enough to loosen his grip on my wrist and then used the now free hand to pull his head down towards my neck.

He groaned, and I felt his fangs take hold above my pulse, his lips mould against my skin. His hands were gripping my shoulders; I could feel the warmth of his chest against my body, the firmness of his hip against my side. Then the slide of fang into flesh, creating a sense of sharp pain, which was instantly replaced with a sensation of acute ecstasy and intimacy so pure it rocked my soul. My eyes closed, even as tears slipped out past my lids and down my cheeks and all I could hear was Michel's voice in my mind saying *mine, mine, mine, mine.*

He fed for no more than 30 seconds, but it felt like the world no longer existed. I was weightless, drifting on a cloud of euphoria, swaying gently in a breeze of exhilaration, floating softly on a wave of pure joy. He did not let it become more; I felt no heat rise within me, no tightening of muscles that could send me over the edge, but only the reassuring sense of beauty and safety and... home.

He pulled his fangs out slowly, licking the blood that had pooled at his mark, kissing my neck, stroking my hand, brushing his fingers through my hair.

"Um." I don't think I had ever heard Michel say *um* before.

I looked into his face searching for something there. He was looking down not making eye contact, his face flushed, his pulse racing, his breathing rapid. He swallowed and I watched his Adam's apple, at the base of his throat, rise and fall.

Then deep amethyst and violet eyes met mine, and he said a little huskily, "Extraordinary. I have never felt anything like that before in all my years." And then his eyes lit up with the smile that had suddenly appeared on his beautiful face. "How is it that you continue to surprise me? I have lived a long time, Lucinda, it takes an awful lot to surprise me now, yet you," he paused to lick his lips, "you amaze me, you bewilder me, you enthral me, on a daily basis. *Tu es la raison de mon existence, ma petite lumière.*"

Wow. What could I say? Thanks just seemed inadequate somehow, so I opted for a kiss instead. Soft and wet and with everything I couldn't put into words but hoped he would understand anyway.

By the time he pulled away from my embrace he was well and truly dishevelled. His eyes glinting with sparks of amethyst light. He just looked down at me, in what I can only call awe. What was with this man? He seemed so much more human than he had ever appeared to me in the past.

We stared at each other for a moment and then I said, "I know I should be tired, but..."

He chuckled, that delightful deep rumble in his chest. "You need to sleep, Lucinda, would you allow me to help you, *ma douce?*"

I nodded and lowered my shields, letting his tingling touch wash over me, pulling me into a loving embrace and helping me drift off to the happy realm of sleep, with the knowledge I was safe and secure and home.

Just before I fell completely into that beautiful and familiar abyss, a thought appeared to me, I'd missed an appointment today.

Where had Nero been?

28
MEMORIES

When I awoke, Michel was sleeping next to me, his arm and a leg over my body, his face nestled against my neck. He was warm and soft, and for a moment I just didn't want to move but stay there wrapped up in his embrace forever. I turned carefully, so as not to disturb him and just took my time watching him sleep, soaking him in.

You'd think a vampire would go into that stillness, that absolute preternatural calm, when they sleep. There's no reason for them to breathe, they don't need to, or to have a beating heart for that matter either. It's superfluous to their needs. I'm guessing the younger vampires don't keep up that pretence, instead letting their bodies go to that place, wherever it is, that allows them to rest during the day. But for the older vampires, it's so easy. They've spent centuries pretending, so they could fit in, move amongst the humans without detection. For a vampire like Michel, even making your heart beat and your lungs work when asleep, would be second nature.

His face was relaxed, in a look I hadn't seen on him before. He's always so controlled when in public, even with me. I get the feeling sometimes, that every emotion or reaction that crosses his face is actually premeditated. Nothing Michel does is not planned, controlled, yet here he was with a softness to his features that made him seem just like a little boy. A beautiful little boy.

He would have been gorgeous as a child. I wondered then, what his life was like before he was changed. I realised I knew so little about him really, only his recent history here in New Zealand. I only knew he was originally from France, but where in France and what was his life like then? The enormity of what his age meant hit me like a blow to the stomach. Five hundred years old was a long time to live.

"Are you going to watch me all day, *ma douce?*"

He hadn't opened his eyes, but he had a little smile on his face, lifting up the corners of his mouth. Figures he'd been faking the sleeping too.

"How did you know?"

He opened his eyes then, so deeply blue and reached up to stroke a wayward few strands of my hair off my face.

"I felt your emotions. I think I may be getting used to them a little; I am starting to look forward to them. It is fascinating how many different emotions you seem to feel all at once. You flick from one to the next like a little bird in a tree, hopping from branch to branch. Fascinating."

"You looked so peaceful sleeping there, so relaxed."

"I am. I have you with me." He kissed my forehead, then my cheek. "Are you not at peace too?"

And here's the thing, I so was. Being with Michel fed my soul. I have always felt that returning to my parents' farm was where I charged my batteries best, being back with the lambs, feeling the wind come over the hills, the smell of the grass in the paddocks, the sound of the sheep in the fields. It had always been where I went to centre myself, to block out the craziness that had become my life when I moved to Auckland. But now, this sense of peace, of belonging, when I was with Michel, was so great and so, so very good. I could not imagine that returning to the farm would ever hold for me what it once did.

"Yes. Yes I am."

He pulled me close at that and just held me for some time. It became apparent, after several minutes of Michel not letting me go and me not wanting to be let go, that going to work today was not on the agenda. The Bond had other plans for us; wonderful, delicious plans, but not my normal routine, that was for sure. Part of me was very happy to oblige the Bond, but another part, that loud-mouthed insistent internal monologue part, kept telling me I still needed to be me, to not let this thing between Michel and me take over the person I once was.

I needed to be able to go to work, to have that very normal, very human part of my life to myself. No vampires, no vampire politics and definitely no vampire Bond. I also needed my apartment, my sanctuary. Staying here with Michel was bliss, my body craved it like a drug addict craves his next fix, but my mind told me otherwise. If I gave in to Michel and became his trophy kindred Nosferatin, trailing him and doing his every bidding, then I would never have any chance of equality in this relationship. Not that vampires are good at the whole equality thing, far from it, they tend to climb and crawl and claw their way to the top and once there, fight tooth and nail to keep it.

Michel may have strong feelings for me, and I think, possibly, maybe something a bit more. But he was still a vampire, and vampires liked to be master of their domain. His head might tell him I am an equal partner here, but the vampire within would want me to obey. I had never been good with authority figures; I wasn't about to change that character trait now.

Besides, I'd had quite a bit of time off work lately. That whole week after Dream Walking twice in one night, then several days due to fighting injuries and now the Bond. My boss may have been glazed into believing I had been there all that time, but my conscience had not. This could not go on.

But, for now, the Bond called.

As great as it was spending all day with Michel in bed, touching, kissing, exploring, breathing each other in, I also wanted to get to know more than just his body, as beautifully seductive as it was. I wanted to get to know him. That's only reasonable after all, isn't it?

"What was your life like before you were changed?" It was mid-afternoon, and I had just finished a tray of snacks and fruit juice brought to Michel's chamber by his staff, I was plucking the skin off an apple, nibbling little bits, bit by bit. Michel was in his usual position, reclining on the bed watching me, feasting with his eyes. He smiled when I asked the question, a lovely little curve of his lips, a small sparkle in his eyes.

"It was a long time ago, *ma douce*, I am no longer that person. You would not have recognised me."

I raised my eyebrows at him; I wasn't going to let him just brush this off. I wanted to know, and some part of me felt that the secret to Michel may lie in his past, and I couldn't uncover that secret unless he told me.

He let a soft laugh out at my expression. "You really want to know?"

"Yes."

"You may not like what you hear."

"I'll take my chances."

He put a hand through his hair, a gesture I was becoming more familiar with, one he only seemed to use in my presence.

"I have not talked of my life pre-vampyrism for some time."

He had started looking off into the distance, as though he was seeing another world. He sighed.

"I grew up in a small village near Lyon. A simple life, I was not of noble blood. My father worked hard to put food on the table, my mother even harder to make something of what little he could provide. We often went hungry to bed as children. I learnt at an early age, to have anything in life, one must fight for it."

A bitter smile. A small shake of his head.

"Prospects were poor in my village. My father died at a somewhat early age, and I was left to provide for not only my mother and younger sisters, but also my... family too. What skills did I have? I could fight. I had been fighting since I could walk. My life had consisted of one brawl and then another. I was not exactly feared in my village..., well maybe, by some, but I was well known for my skills in a battle. The new militia was seeking soldiers, so I joined. Sending every *livre* I could home."

He stopped then, still looking into the distance. I wasn't sure if he would go on, there seemed to be such sadness in his eyes. For some reason I hadn't thought that talking of his past life would cause him this much pain. How could I have been so cruel to have brought this up? I put my apple down on the tray and moved it off the bed, then came to sit in front of him. His gaze came back to me, from that place so far away, so long ago. The blues swirling their differing shades, a small shine to his eye I had not seen before. He reached up and stroked my face, obviously seeing the concern I felt for him there, feeling my compassion.

"It is all right, *ma douce*. I had forgotten so much."

"Don't say anything else. You don't need to remember."

"Remembering is not such a bad thing. It is cathartic, I think."

He leaned forward, his hand behind my neck and kissed my forehead. "I want you to know." His breath was hot against my skin.

"I was 32 when I was changed. I had not asked for it. I was a member of *la nouvelle* France's first standing army since Roman times. It was a heady time in our history. Political structures which would remain for centuries were formed. Absolute monarchy was the order of the day. Not being of noble blood, I started at the lowest of ranks, but I was an excellent soldier and rose to a command swiftly. My successes allowing for a position of rank usually only given those of certain birth.

"I had my detractors, of course, especially those of the aristocracy who resented my favour with the King. I had come to Charles' attention after commanding a brutal battle with the English. It had been a crucial victory in our expelling them from our shores. The turning point you might say. But despite my position as a favoured servant to the realm, I came under attack."

He paused then and sighed. It was the sort of sigh that broke your heart, it said more than that action alone should ever convey, it said the weight of the world had come to rest on this person's shoulders and would be borne there for the rest of his life. In Michel's case, that had proved to be many times the length of a normal human's. I could only imagine what that weight must have done to him in all that time.

"They came for my family first. I was under commission at the time, away from our village. Of course, I didn't know their fate until after the fact. I received word that there had been an accident and took leave from my battalion immediately, returning in all haste. It was a trap. But, thankfully the family had been killed swiftly. For such a harsh time in France's history, that was a small miracle. Those who would have me killed, however, did not dirty their own hands, nor rely on soldiers to carry out the order as they had my families deaths. They sent instead an assassin, someone they turned to for delicate matters. My death would not go unnoticed, it needed to be carried out with care.

"They did not know, however, that that assassin was a vampyre. Amicus used the opportunity to kill for a living, as a source of easy food. He had not expected I would fight so hard, that I would nearly succeed in killing him. I did not know what he was, so the deep cut to his throat and the knife to the stomach seemed sufficient, and I left. Determined to exact revenge on those who had killed my kin. Amicus needed to rest before repairing, but when he rose again, he hunted me down. I had not gone far."

This had all been said so matter of factly, with so little emotion, just a story being recited from a book. I had no doubt that it was to protect himself, break it all down to just events, not emotions. I was surprised that Michel was laying himself so bare to me, I had asked the question, but never dared to think he would open up so fully, let me see so much. Despite the sadness of the story, I couldn't help feeling privileged to be with him right now.

"What did you do?"

He smiled his usual knowing smile, the Michel I knew was back. "Amicus had seen my potential, he turned me, expecting me to be a strong servant to command. It took just over fifty years to surpass his *Sanguis Vitam* level and to exact the last of my revenge. The rest, as they say, is history." He smiled broadly at that.

I wanted to ask more, to ask what he had done for the 500 years since being turned, but I didn't get a chance. With a swift movement, just barely off that of a blur, Michel had me on my back, his body pinning mine, his mouth laying kisses all over my body.

"Now, enough! On to much more pleasurable pastimes I think."

Whatever happened to not having sex every day? God help me.

By the time we emerged from the tangled covers of limbs and covers and sweat-soaked sheets, the sun had set and *Sensations* was in full swing. Michel had Bruno bring me a change of clothes, so I was able to dress in my normal attire. I'm not a Goth, but I do like black. Hides better in the shadows and you never know when you may need to be hidden. I was sitting at the bar next to Bruno, Michel was at a table on the far side of the room, watching me, but dealing with his business needs, when I felt a tap on my shoulder.

By the time I had turned around, Bruno had Rick's arm in his beefy grip and was pulling it around behind his back. Rick grimaced but didn't complain, just growled a low warning to Bruno.

"Let go of me, vampire."

"Hands off. Lucinda is taken."

Great. Here's the ownership thing again.

"Let go of him, Bruno. He's a friend." I placed a hand on Bruno's arm to get his attention.

"No. You are not welcome here." Bruno directed that statement at Rick with an increase of pressure on his arm.

"What do you mean he's not welcome! Of course he is, he's my friend," I replied incredulously.

Bruno didn't let go but turned his face slowly to look at me with those fierce uncompromising eyes. "No, Lucinda. He is not welcome."

I got it then. He was receiving instructions from Michel, those silent orders spanning the airwaves.

"I'll deal with this," I said as I stomped off towards where Michel was sitting with another vamp.

He was deep in conversation, pretending he wasn't even aware of what was going on across the room, he wasn't fooling me. He looked up at my approach.

"Lucinda?"

Don't Lucinda me, buddy. "Tell Bruno to back off." I kept my voice steady, I was kind of proud of how it sounded.

Michel simply looked past me to the scene still unfolding at the bar, as though it was the first time he knew anything about it.

"Bruno is in charge of maintaining the standard of occupancy in the club. He is only doing his job."

"I'm sure he is only doing his job, but it's not to chuck the riff-raff out is it? Rick is my friend, Michel. I'd like him to stay."

His face clouded briefly, before returning to its usual mask of calm.

"Excuse me, Simon. I must attend my Nosferatin."

The way he said it sounded more like *I must discipline my wayward Nosferatin*, but the vampire didn't say anything, just nodded and left the booth they had been in.

"Sit, Lucinda." When I didn't make a move other than to fold my arms across my chest, he sighed and added, "Please?"

I slunk down into the seat opposite him.

"Tell Bruno to back off, Michel." Repetition, my mantra with stubborn vamps.

Michel sat looking at me for a moment, then scratched his head slowly. "We are in the middle of establishing a Bond, Lucinda. It is important we do not get distracted."

"OK. But, you can work and deal with your vampire stuff, talking to other vampires, isn't that a distraction?"

"It is merely business, my dear, nothing of a personal nature. Your relationship with the shapeshifter is quite different."

"He's a friend, Michel. That's all."

"So you say."

"What, you don't believe me?" He gave me a look then, one that said back off.

Neither of us said anything for a while, just sat there looking at one another. I had to hide a smile though when it was Michel who broke the silence first.

"What would you have me do, *ma douce*? My kin are aware of our Bonding, to allow the shapeshifter -" "His name is Rick." "- to remain would be an insult to my position, would it not? I cannot allow to been seen as threatened."

"Rick threatens you?"

"Of course." He said it with barely contained exasperation.

OK. This I hadn't seen coming. Michel being jealous of my friendship, yes, but to actually feel threatened, as though Rick *could* take me away, no – I hadn't seen that coming at all. Michel's always in control; this seemed to indicate an area he was not quite as sure of his control as he would have liked.

He reached over and took my hand. "Can you understand?"

Yes, I could understand, but to give in now would be to accept my position as the less powerful one in this relationship, it would hand Michel control of our interactions for a long time to come. In the eyes of him and his vampires, I would have toed the line, just like a good servant Nosferatin should. Also, Rick is my friend, why shouldn't I have that relationship with him? How could I ask him to leave, he wouldn't understand vampire politics.

No. I couldn't let Michel do this, I had to stand my ground.

I'd had my head down, staring at Michel's hand holding mine, biting my lip while I worked through all of this, when I raised it and looked into Michel's eyes, I realised he'd felt all of my emotions and knew exactly what my answer would be.

He closed his eyes and took a deep breath in. "I am sorry."

I didn't understand what he meant at first. Sorry he was acting the way he was? Sorry he had asked for Rick to leave? Sorry Bruno was being an over zealous Mafioso bodyguard? But then I heard Rick shout out, from across the room, "See ya later, Luce. Gotta Go."

I turned to see him wave and smile and simply walk out the door. It took a minute for my mind to catch up with that picture and then I saw the glow slowly fading in Bruno's eyes as he turned back to his drink at the bar and I felt the world turn a hazy shade of red at the realisation of what Michel had Bruno do.

Rick had been glazed.

29
YOU GLOW

I immediately took my hand back from Michel's and balled it into a fist, resting it on the top of the table between us.

"How could you?" It was low, even and dripping in anger.

"You left me no choice."

"There is always a choice, Michel. You just have trouble choosing the right one; it would seem."

He sighed. "I do not wish to fight with you, *ma douce*."

"No, you just want me to be your lap dog, to do what you say when you say. To not have a mind of my own, to not stand up to you, to not be independent. You want me in my place, right where you friggin' put me!" And OK, so my voice might have risen a little at the end there, but still, it was a pretty good speech, as far as speeches go.

Michel didn't seem to think so though, his eyes glowed their amethyst and violet swirls and he stilled, locking me with his gaze.

Then I was standing in his, now magenta coloured chamber, the warmth of his touch on my arms and side fading, my head a little giddy, looking in the face of a very angry, very unhappy vampire, but I had no idea how I had got there.

"Did you just glaze me?"

"No." It was barely a whisper.

"Then how did we get here?"

"I carried you."

"You went *that* fast?"

"Yes."

I had to admit I was impressed with that. I've seen Michel move in a blur, I've seen him look like he just appeared out of thin air, but I had never seen him move an object with such speed. I hadn't thought it was possible. I mean, he would have had to get out of his seat, grab me from mine, cross the bar to the private door, open it, get down the hall, open the chamber, close the door, and stand me there. In a split fraction of a split second.

"That's wicked!" I couldn't help it, it just was.

His lips quirked, just a bit at the edges, but I saw.

He let a big breath out - so did I, but I tried to hide it - and his eyes started to dim from their impossible glow that had lit up the darkened room. He flicked his hands and the lights came on, softly on the tables beside the bed, giving the area a more natural sheen from that of purple.

His hand ran through his hair; I was starting to like that motion, and he looked straight at me. "Why do you make me feel emotions I have never felt before?"

"Emotions? Like what?"

"Regret. Guilt." A pause. "Heartache."

"You can be better than what you are, Michel. You don't have to be an Amicus."

The understanding of what I had said poured off him, his eyes wide, his mouth slightly opened in a look of shock, his face slightly shattered. He recovered himself and turned toward the bed to sit.

"I am what I am, Lucinda."

I came to sit next to him, taking his hand in mine this time. "I don't believe that. I believe you could be so much more."

He leant his head against my shoulder; I could feel his breath against my skin through the thin sleeve of my top. "How is it you have such faith in me when I do not?"

I didn't know how to answer that, I just knew he could be better than this. The knowledge came from somewhere deep within, maybe the part of me that is all Nosferatin, the part of me that wants to lead him towards the light.

I squeezed his hand. "I just do."

We sat like that for a moment, just welcoming the warmth of the person next to us, not daring to break the contact. After some time, I took a breath in and said, "I won't be your puppet, Michel. When the Bond has been fully established, I'm going back to my apartment, back to work, to my friends, please don't stop me."

He didn't move for a moment, then finally when he pulled away and reached up to stroke my face with the backs of his fingers, looking at every curve, every ridge and line, he said, "I have always enjoyed a challenge, my dear, I just never knew you would be my greatest."

Right back at ya buddy.

We spent the rest of the night in his chambers, talking, cuddling and when the sun rose the next day, I felt whole. I knew the Bond had been completed, I felt connected to Michel like I had never been before. I could tell where he was and although I couldn't read his mind or even his emotions, like he can mine, I felt like I knew instantly what he was feeling, his moods; happy, sad, concerned, angry. It was an intrinsic knowledge that simply thrummed through my veins telling me my kindred vampire was safe.

I wanted to be near him, but I also knew I was able to walk away, safe in the knowledge of his existence through the Bond. I took the opportunity to return to my apartment, demonstrating my determination to lead a separate life. The actual moment of turning my back on him, as he lay on the bed resting and taking that first step towards the door of his chamber, was the hardest thing I had ever done. Although the Bond was happy for us to part, it was also making it very obvious that I'd be happier if I stayed. Just as well I'm stubborn.

I'd only been in my apartment about five minutes, managing a quick change and throwing some washing in the machine in the bathroom, when Nero appeared. I'd just walked back to the kitchen to switch the coffee machine on, and there he was.

"You could knock first."

"I was unable to reach you." He took a step towards me and stopped dead, his head cocked slightly to the side, his gaze intent.

"You have Bonded." He sounded, what? Disappointed?
"How can you tell?"
"Your glow."
"I have a glow?" This sounded familiar. I quickly glanced down at my body. Nope. No glow. "I can't see it."
"You will learn to recognise the glow of a Bonded Nosferatin in time."
"So, I only glow to another Nosferatin?"
"Yes." Good to know.
"What does it look like?"
"Bright."
"How bright?"
"Supernova." He smiled ruefully then.
I have a supernova glow. Figures.
"Do you glow?" I asked.
"Yes."
"How can I see it?"
"Concentrate on my aura. Look past my physical form; you will see a haze around me, look closely at that. Do not be distracted."

I tried, but it was hard. He was dressed in black again today, I have a thing for black. His linen trousers were down to just above his ankles, dark manly bare feet at the bottom, the trousers hugged his hips and thighs lovingly and didn't have a crease in them. How can he manage to keep linen wrinkle free? His top was a T-Shirt today, unlike the loose cotton shirts he had worn in the past, this black T-Shirt showed off every muscle, every line, every - well, I think you get the picture. Concentrating on a hazy blur around the sides of him was damn near impossible.

"I can't see it. How bright is it?"
"Not as bright as yours."
"Why?"
He smiled, a sexy smile as if to say, *I'll tell you, but you'll have to come a little closer*. I almost did. Damn, what did this man do to me?
"The brightness of a Bond glow is in direct relation to the connection you share with your kindred vampyre, but not just the mental connection of joining, it manifests the emotional or," a pause, "sexual,

connection between the vampyre and Nosferatin. My relationship with Nafrini is platonic love. She is like a sister to me. Our Bond glow is pale."

Oh. So, my glow was telling every other Nosferatin that I was doing the dirty with my kindred vampire. I felt a blush rise up my cheeks and started biting my bottom lip.

Nero just smiled more widely.

OK then. "Why haven't I seen you for a couple of days?" Change of topic time.

"You were with your vampyre. I cannot intrude at those times. Dream Walking does not allow for such an intrusion."

"But, you came when we were together fighting in Sydney."

"You were fighting. Not Bonding."

Oh. Another blush.

"So, what's on the agenda for training today? I'm guessing that's why you're here." Still trying for a change of topic here!

Nero came and sat himself down at the dining room table, his favourite spot. I guess it allowed him to see from into the bathroom off the kitchen, through the open plan area of the kitchen, dining and lounge and even a bit into the bedroom. It was probably chosen with care. I started making a coffee, training could wait.

"You are maturing in four days." Four days? Had the time really passed that quickly? "There is little I can teach you in the time left to us that would be of use. Your fighting skills are good, they will have to suffice, perhaps when you reach Egypt we can train further, but for today we talk."

"Talk?" I asked suspiciously.

"You must have questions about who you are, what you can do?"

Oh yeah, I had questions all right. I finished making my coffee and grabbed a muesli bar from the pantry, then slipped into a chair at the dining table next to Nero. I could feel his warmth from the small space that separated us. Man Dream Walking didn't dull a thing for another Nosferatin did it?

I was pretty sure that I had my head around where Nosferatins came from, how we had broken away from the Nosferatu and then how we had come back again, so I didn't want to waste the time hashing over that for now. What I really needed help with was my powers and what to expect when I came into the rest of them on the night of my birthday, at the actual time of my birth.

"I have received two of my powers already."

Nero's eyebrows rose. "That is impressive, Kiwi. I have not heard of another Nosferatin come into more than one before they turn 25." Michel had said the same thing.

"I can obviously Dream Walk, but when I did it twice in one night, I was out cold for a week. Why was that?"

"Dream Walking is perhaps the most powerful of Nosferatin powers, it is a power only a few of us possess. I know of only one other, for instance, who has this power right now, until I met you. It requires a large amount of our essence, our life force or our Vita Vis. We can easily handle one Dream Walk per night, but any more and it diminishes our Vita Vis too greatly. You are lucky to have woken again. Your vampyre must have stayed close to your side throughout, giving you some of his power to heal. Without that proximity, you may not have woken at all."

Michel was there when I woke, by my bed, holding my hand. His head was even resting against my side. I hadn't even considered that he might not have left my side at all throughout, it didn't seem possible at the time. Now I wasn't so sure.

"How does he give me some of his powers?"

"His proximity alone would allow for the exchange. It is an intrinsic part of a joining, but is not limited to after the joining ceremony is complete. If a vampyre and their kindred Nosferatin have connected on a most intimately basic level beforehand, it is possible to use the power of both for a necessary task. Be it healing, protection warding, or enhancing strength and the like."

"Protection warding?"

"To ward a property or a person. A protection ward can be carried out by a vampyre or Nosferatin to a certain extent, but to significantly boost that ward, a sharing of powers is needed. Although the sharing is intrinsic, a kindred vampyre or Nosferatin can intentionally choose to use the power from a sharing for enhancement, should it be for the benefit of both. However doing this intentionally before they have joined, creates an even stronger connection, one that does not allow the other party to pull out of the joining so easily. There should always be a choice to join."

I felt the chair and ground go out from under me, the realisation of what Nero was saying hitting so hard. Michel had warded my apartment before, I knew this, I knew it was possible and I didn't have a problem with it, he was keeping me safe in a way that I found acceptable. But he had also warded the holiday home in Taupo and to such an extent that he was adamant that Max could not find us. Yet, when I challenged him on how that was possible, he refused to tell me. Now I knew why. He didn't want me to know he had crossed the line, using my powers to boost the ward and thereby making it damn near impossible for me to refuse to join.

Was anything I felt for Michel even real?

"Are you all right, Kiwi?" Nero was leaning forward and looking intently in my face, his hand was on my now shaking shoulders, his thumb gently rubbing where it lay.

I took a moment to steady my heart rate, calm my breathing, allowed myself just to concentrate on his touch. After a few seconds I felt the world right itself, but hell, my head hurt. So did my heart.

"I'm fine." It was quiet, a little shaky, I have no doubt he didn't believe me. He didn't remove his hand, just continued to rest it there, so warm and calm and safe.

"Will you tell me?" His voice was soft and low like he didn't want to frighten me.

I just shook my head. Another thing for Michel and me to battle in private. This was not Nero's to fight.

When I didn't answer, he sat back, removing his hand, but the warmth it had created remained.

"Your ability to recover from two Dream Walks in one night will improve after your powers arrive and as time passes. To start with, two Walks in one night will probably only make you sleep for, let's say, three days, not seven and that may become less as time goes by. However, it is not something I would recommend you attempt unless absolutely necessary, the risk to your safety when you sleep is obviously great, even with your kindred vampyre nearby."

Well, that made sense and besides, I couldn't think of another occasion that would necessitate me to do a double Dream Walk in one night. I certainly hoped not anyway. I couldn't think of anything else I needed to know about Dream Walking, I thought we'd covered it enough for now. That just left my other nifty early power.

"My other power is glazing vampires."

I'd realised it was a pretty cool power when I first used it, I had never heard of it ever happening before, vampires just don't get glazed, but I was sure Nero would have known all about it and would offer up some wisdom. Some tips, maybe tell me about how many there actually were like me out there, glazing up a storm.

"You can do what?"

I guess I was wrong.

"Glaze vampires. I made a vampire who had been commanded by his master to detain me and not allow me to sleep, let me sleep so that I could Dream Walk."

Nero was still, no emotion on his face and then just a twitch in the corner of his mouth, then another and then he was laughing. The most amazing, full bodied, throaty and rich laugh. The whole room felt wrapped in its brilliance.

"You are phenomenal, my Kiwi. Truly phenomenal."

"So, I guess that's never happened before?"

"Not to my knowledge." And then he sobered. "I do not think this is a gift you should share with too many. It would not be safe. The vampyres would feel a little threatened I think." He laughed again, then looked me in the eyes, his a swirl of cinnamon and copper. "You are amazing."

He stilled there a moment, then cleared his throat and looked away, as though he was uncomfortable with the comment, or the proximity to me, all of a sudden.

I felt a little sad at that; I'm not sure why.

"Well, that's it. They're my powers so far. I guess I'll come into more in a few days time."

"From present evidence, I do not doubt it, but I am afraid I could not tell what they will be. It is different for each of us. Most Nosferatin will feel them arrive, it is not a shock, just a little tingling sensation. Initially one or two, then over a period of months, the rest. They do not all arrive at once, only improved strength and speed are a certainty from day one, but what you will receive, I could not say. I can only assume it will be monumental, as far as you are concerned, Kiwi."

Well, that's great. I'll just have to be patient. Not exactly one of my best qualities. At least it will be a subdued affair, a slight tingling I can handle.

"Is there any of your kindred's powers you wish to discuss?" Nero asked.

I was pretty sure he was trying to sound me out on how powerful Michel had become, maybe to relay the information to Nafrini. Another joined master vampire coming into her territory would be of a concern, but I wasn't going to give too much away. I'm not stupid, I wouldn't put Michel, or me for that matter, in that position, but I was curious about how Michel's abilities to read my emotions could be handled. Him always getting the drop on me by instantly knowing what I was feeling was beginning to give him power over me. Power I didn't want to relinquish just yet, if ever. If I could learn to hide my emotions, then so much the better. Maybe Nero knew how and besides, this power didn't seem like a strategic battle secret or anything.

"Michel can read my emotions. Do you know how I can hide them from him?"

"Why would you wish to hide them, Kiwi?"

"He can always tell what I'm feeling, even if I don't want him to. And -" Yeah, and here's the thing. I had really hurt him with them once, used them like a weapon. The effect on him had been so strong, so devastating, it had broken my heart in two. I never wanted to do that again. "- I can hurt him with them. Throw them out at him. I don't want to do that." I couldn't say *again*.

The last had been said in a whisper; I'm not even sure how Nero had heard. But he took my hands in his and turned me to him.

"It is a gift. Not all kindred vampyre will receive."

"A gift? It's a nightmare!" My voice was breaking as I said it.

He reached up and brushed away a tear which had started down my cheek, his hands a little rough and hardened, a warrior's hands, but so warm and soft despite the small callouses there.

"Far from it, Kiwi. This is the gift that will bring your kindred vampyre back towards the Light. How can he not be affected, changed, by what he now must feel?"

30
CHANGE

Nero didn't stay long after that, and when nightfall came, Michel appeared at my door. I really wasn't sure how to face him. I was still so upset about the warding of the Taupo house and the fact that it would have had an effect on my choice to join with him. Not to mention him having had Rick glazed. How could I look him in the eyes? How could I spend the entire evening with him?

Luckily, it wasn't necessary. He was distracted, an issue had arisen in Wellington that he had to attend, one of his line requiring his assistance. The thing with vampire families is, when a vampire is made by a master or chooses to be absorbed into a family line, they swear their allegiance by blood to that master, prepared to do anything he commands. What do they get in return? Safety, protection and the backing of a level one *Sanguis Vitam* master when needed. Half of Michel's business dealings were with his line, sorting out problems, keeping them in line and on occasion, like tonight, assisting them with his power and presence. It takes a lot of time and energy to be master of a line and Michel's had recently nearly doubled. He was busier than he had ever been before.

Part of me worried about that. I didn't like to see him distracted or tired, but there was nothing I could do. Vampire families and vampire politics are what they are. That's probably why power and strength are so important in the vampire world.

"It will take all night, *ma douce*. I won't return before sunrise, and I will have to sleep tomorrow. This night is likely to be... busy."

We were sitting on the couch, not long after he had arrived. Michel had manoeuvred us there as soon as he walked in the door, not even registering my discomfort when I opened it to him, he was that distracted. Weird.

"Is everything all right? It's not dangerous is it?"

It's surprising how the reality of fear for someone's safety overrides all other thought because suddenly I didn't care about the protection ward in Taupo or Rick. I was sure I would get back to those though, just give me time.

"It will be fine. I will be fine. It is just an urgent matter that cannot wait. I will see you tomorrow evening, and I swear I shall make my absence up to you then."

That last statement was said as he nibbled my ear, sending a delicious wave of pleasure down my neck and body. I felt myself relax into him, a reaction so instinctive, so natural, I could not have controlled it. He just had that effect on me, despite my brain telling me otherwise. I think even if I was really, *really*, super mad at Michel, he would still elicit that same response, right in the middle of me throwing a temper tantrum. Damn.

"I couldn't leave without first saying goodbye. I missed you today." Now his lips were on my face, my cheek, my jaw, my mouth. His words interspersed with kisses and nips and licks.

"I thought you didn't have much time." There was no denying it, my voice was shaky, a little breathless.

He pulled away slightly, looking a little flushed himself. "You are right. I am getting sidetracked."

"Sidetracked?" I lifted an eyebrow at that.

He laughed. "OK. Deliciously sidetracked. Is that better?"

"Acceptable."

He stood then, ready to leave and I felt an absolute sharp sense of panic. It rippled through my body, sending adrenaline racing through my veins. I racked my brain for something to say, something to stop him walking out my door. I'd never felt this absolute terror before, fear for his safety, fear for him leaving me. I felt a little small at that. I'm a big girl, I don't rely on others for my happiness, but right then, my mind and body was telling me otherwise.

He stopped immediately, feeling the emotions rolling off me and turned to come back to my side.

"*Ma douce*, please do not worry. I will return."

"Why am I so scared?" My voice was pitifully small. I cringed a little at it.

He kissed my forehead, leaving his lips against it as he said, "It is the Bond. It has not fully settled. It will get better."

"I don't like it. I don't like being this way. This is not who I am."

Michel pulled back, holding me by my shoulders and looking me in the eyes, his so blue and indigo, so deep and mesmerising.

"I know who you are, Lucinda, and the Bond does not alter that for me. You are the strongest, most capable human I have ever met. The fire that burns within you is a blaze. You will learn to control the Bond, trust me."

I hoped he was right. I hoped I could win this battle because if I didn't, my life as I knew it would be over. Why did it feel like I was constantly fighting for me?

Michel sensed I had calmed and gave me a quick kiss on the lips, then straightened up and walked out the door. It was only later that I realised, he hadn't fed from me tonight. And man, didn't I just love the emotions that rolled through me at the thought of that.

Work the next day was normal, no surprises, no supernatural events, just a great day with normal people who genuinely cared. A few of my workmates, who were about the same age as me, were teasing me about my upcoming birthday and getting older. How little they understood the repercussions of my ageing. How turning 25 only a few weeks ago had meant just another year, but now it meant so much more.

I've never been one to make a big fuss, I mean, it's just another year over, isn't it? And to tell you the truth, it only reminds me of my parents. You know, my real parents, my biological parents. I wonder what my mum was like when she was pregnant with me, was it an easy birth, was I a good baby for her those first few weeks she had me and I had her? And my father, my Nosferatin father. What had he been like? Would he have cried at my birth, knowing I would not live past my 25th birthday, because of the choice he had made? Did he regret having me?

Yeah, birthdays aren't big in my life, especially since I moved to Auckland and found out so much about who I am. Part of me is unbelievably happy that I did make the move. Country Hick to the big city. If I hadn't have, I would have simply fallen over dead in the paddocks with the lambs one day, a full moon cycle after turning 25. My Aunt and Uncle would have had no idea why. I would have simply just ceased to exist. I didn't want to die. I love life. Despite how crazy and out of control my life has become, I am glad I moved to Auckland.

I changed into some black leggings and a loose T-Shirt after work, getting ready to jog home. The lowering sun was making shadows dance along the tall buildings on the street when I came out of the bank, changing the façades from grey, to gold, to a soft red. I was greeted with a whoop of delight and suddenly ensconced in the arms of Rick.

"There she is! My favourite vampire hunter."

I couldn't help it, I laughed. He was laughing, too, and spinning me around, making a right scene on the side walk. An over exuberant Taniwha was exactly like a big puppy; you just couldn't contain them. Finally, he got himself under control.

"I'm taking you out on the town, girlie. Just you and me. We need to catch up, just like old times"

Yeah, it hadn't been like old times for a while now, we used to hang out regularly, but lately things had changed. I understood what Rick was saying; he wanted his friend back too.

"Where's Celeste?"

"She's working late tonight, I'll catch up with her later. So, what do ya think? Shall we start at the *Red Hummingbird* and move on from there?"

"OK, but I've got to change first."

"No worries, I'll race ya home." And with that he was off.

Taniwhas are all speed and grace, even in their human form. It has always been fun training and running with Rick. I don't have to hide who I am; I can run fast and hard and know he won't be surprised or judge me. He's not a push-over either, he's got his competitive side, so what should have been a ten to fifteen-minute jog, turned into a six to eight-minute sprint. We'd hardly broken a sweat by the time we arrived.

I had a quick freshen up and then changed into my uniform for the night; you know, the short black skirt and top, with a lightweight black jacket on the top. Stake and knife secured, ID and credit card in a pocket, some flat black slip-ons on my feet - I may be short, but I never feel the need to wear heels; who could possibly outrun a vampire in heels! - and I was set.

The sky was still clinging onto its blue and indigo and crimson glow, steadfastly refusing to let the night in, so it was a pleasant walk back into the city and towards the Sky Tower where the *Red Hummingbird Bar* is. It's at the base of the Tower, so there's no need to go up the escalators and pass near the casino. And it's also decked out in a lush and extravagant setting, all deep rich reds and golds, purples and greens. There are different areas to sit, stools or the bar, chairs and padded bench seats with tables or circular seating with cushions like something out of an Arabian palace. We chose a corner hidden by deep, thick green foliage in the largest indoor garden setting in a bar I had ever seen. The seats weren't super comfortable here, but the sense of privacy was always nice. I'm not too good in large crowds.

Rick went and got our drinks, he's a *Coruba & Coke* kind of guy, me, I like *Bacardi & Coke*, but tonight I was having wine. A nice chilled, crisp and slightly fruity *Sauvignon Blanc*. Bliss.

"So, only a couple of days to go, what's it like to be getting so old?"

"Ha, ha! You're older than me, Rick. You tell me?"

"My kind doesn't age as quickly as humans, so I couldn't tell ya." He winked at that, then sobered, probably suddenly realising I wouldn't age at all from now on either. It did kind of make me stop and consider too, come to think about it.

We both fell silent for a bit then, but I didn't want us to be talking about all that today, I was here with my best mate, I wanted just to enjoy myself, enjoy his company.

"So, how's it going with Celeste?"

It was obviously the right thing to say because his face lit up and his eyes shone brightly. I could suddenly see the younger Rick, the Rick I knew but had not realised had been missing of late. I guess it went into hiding at the time of the battle at the docks when Rocky was killed, and Celeste got hurt. I couldn't blame him; I had changed a little too since then.

"Pretty good really." And then he blushed slightly. "Um, I think... I think I might ask her to marry me."

His head had ducked down, the flush deepening, he clearly wasn't sure about what I would say. Me? I just squealed and wrapped my arms around him.

"That's fantastic news! I couldn't be happier for you both. Have you got it all planned, the proposal? The Ring? Oh, what ring will you get her?"

"Calm down, Luce, calm down!" But he was grinning, grinning like the cat who had got the cream. "I haven't got the ring yet, and I've got no bloody idea how to ask her. I was hoping you'd come up with something."

"Oh, no way! This has to come from you, from your heart. You know Celeste; you know what she would like. Anyway, I'm too much of a practical person, for me, it doesn't have to be wine and roses, romantic candlelight settings with a string quartet in tow, I'd far prefer an intimate moment, a private place, somewhere that means something to both of you and a proposal from the heart. Nothing fancy, just the honest to goodness truth of how that person feels. That's what I'd like."

"Well, for someone who didn't want to offer any advice, that's pretty good and thorough. You've thought a lot about this haven't you?"

Had I? I didn't think I had, I mean I am only 25 and I have a career and a hobby that keeps me fairly busy, a deadly dangerous hobby, but still, it does take up a lot of my spare time. So no, I didn't think I had put much thought into it, don't all girls just naturally know though?

And then of course, I'm immortal now, how could I ever think of marrying someone in the same light again? No human marriage would work, they'd grow old, I wouldn't, they'd have to know what I was, which isn't too scary a thing, well, maybe just a little. But, it just wouldn't work. And vampires? Well, they don't marry, do they? It's not like I'd seen a lot of couples in my somewhat limited exposure to their kind.

But, it did make me pause for breath, yet again another perfectly normal part of my future that had now been turned on its head. I really am a freak, aren't I?

I didn't tell Rick any of this though, I just said, "Every girl's dream, isn't it?"

He looked at me a bit funnily then, I'm not sure if he believed me or not, but he just smiled and took a sip of his drink.

"So, any idea when you'll do it?" I asked to break the silence.

"Soon. I don't think I can contain myself much longer. It's making me jumpy, and she's picked up on it. Hey! I don't suppose you'd be my best man, would ya?"

I laughed out loud at that. "Jeez mate, you'd better do better than that when you do ask Celeste to marry you! *I don't suppose* is not a good way to start it off. But, yeah, I'd love to be your best man."

I felt all warm and glowy inside. This was great. My best friend was getting married, and he wanted me there with him, right there. I'd thought maybe Rick and I were growing apart. He'd started dating Celeste and me, well, I had started getting involved with a vampire, even if I didn't have a choice. Right then, though, I couldn't have felt any happier, being here, having fun with my best friend.

"Anyway, that's enough about me, what about you? You haven't told me how every thing's going with the Nosferatin thing. We didn't get much time the other night at *Sensations*, I had to leave."

He looked a little puzzled then and I'm not surprised. A deep glaze from a vampire can do that to you, and as it was Bruno who had carried out the glazing, I'm betting he planted it deep.

"It's OK. A bit crazy at times, but what can I do? I've just got to get on with it, haven't I?"

"You're not scared? At all?"

I thought about it then, was I scared? Hell yes, you don't just stop being scared, do you? It's not like you wake up one day and say all those evil dark horrible things that keep happening to you are just a phase, they'll pass, it'll be all right. Even if I am a Kiwi and our perpetual saying is: *she'll be right, mate*. I knew this life I now lead would never be right again, but being scared was not going to change a thing, other than make me jittery and unable to protect myself when needed. So, no, I was still scared, I just wasn't going to let it rule me.

"It's not like that, you don't stop being scared, but you do have to face that it's there and then not let it take over your life. I'm still scared, Rick, I just work my way through it."

"How can you be around them, Luce?"

The question took me by surprise. What on earth could he mean? I had to be around them; I'm a vampire hunter by birth, I don't have a choice. It calls to me, and I have to answer. I thought Rick knew that.

"What do you mean?"

"Well, they're evil, aren't they? And yet you seem to be spending more and more time with them. Aren't you worried?"

"About what, Rick?"

I didn't like where this was going; he had that look in his eyes again. That wild eyed look of someone on a mission, I just wasn't sure I wanted to know what mission Rick was going on right now.

"About being hurt! About being their food! About becoming one of them!" He'd really raised his voice on that last one, a vein had started throbbing in the side of his head, I couldn't take my eyes off it.

"You know it's not like that; Michel is not like that." I tried to keep my voice soft and level, non-threatening, trying to get a bit of cool back into the heat of the moment.

"Does he feed from you?" His eyes bore into me as he asked that.

"That's none of your business!"

"So, that's a yes then. Jesus, Luce! You're just dessert to him. Something to keep him alive, if you can even call what he is *alive*." The last was delivered with grimace and spit.

"I am not dessert." My soft and non-threatening voice had vanished. I was all low and barely contained fury now.

"Oh come on. I've seen the way he looks at you, the way they all look at you. Like you're dinner, or a particularly tasty pudding. They devour you with their eyes, Luce and if you can't see it, you're blind."

"It's not like that, Rick, you don't know."

"Then try and explain it to me, Luce, because I'm having a real hard time understanding how you can be so close to a thing that kills, that controls other people against their will with just a look, that takes what he wants and never lets go, that walks all over you and then sucks from your vein. Tell me, because I just don't get it. He is not alive, Luce, he isn't even human!"

I was shaking, I could feel it, a small shudder through my entire body, but my voice was still even and low. "I'm not human either, Rick. I kill. I can control others with just a look. I'm not sure I can let go of something that is mine and who knows, when I come into my powers in a few days time, maybe I'll suck from a vein too. What does that make me? What do you think of me?"

He looked at me in a mixture of shock and disbelief and could it be? Disgust? He was trying to hide that last one, but I saw it, I know I did. Then he simply downed the last of his drink and headed to the bar.

My heart was stammering in my chest, my breathing was uneven, I'd fisted my hands and could feel my nails digging into them. Small tears had filled the corner of my eyes and I dashed them away angrily. Of all the people to turn from me I had not expected it to be Rick. Sure, I could stay here and try and win him back, butter him up, tell him lies. Tell him that I wasn't going to see much of Michel again, that I wouldn't let Michel feed from me, that I wasn't changing, becoming more supernatural than human, that I was still me. I could have done all of that. He was a friend after all, and you fight for your friends and their friendships, don't you?

But I didn't. I just picked myself up and walked out the door, straight through the busy atrium of the Tower and out to the night. My night. The darkness wrapping around me like a familiar friend, one who didn't judge, one who didn't ask those difficult questions, one who just said, *hey, I'm here for you and always will be.*

So much for getting my friend back.

31
PARTY TIME

I hadn't been aware of where my feet had taken me; I thought I'd been heading in the direction of home. But when I came to an intersection and looked at the street signs, Mayoral Drive and Queen Street, I realised I'd been heading towards *Sensations* without even knowing about it. I hesitated. Did I really want to go up Queen Street? I could just turn around right now and head home, curl up on the couch and pretend this night never happened.

Part of me wanted to, but a bigger part, the part that makes me get up off the ground when a vampire's knocked me down, or run towards the danger when my fear is screaming no, that part of me said, no. Don't hide who you are. Don't try to be something you're not just because someone wants you that way. If Rick couldn't see that I was still the same person inside despite everything that was happening to me, then he could go to hell.

Right now, I needed friends and as weird as it was to say it, those vampires at *Sensations* were my friends. I started up the hill.

Jett was on the door again. Seems Bruno had moved on to greener pastures. As to be expected, he was dressed in black. The same black jeans and tight black T-Shirt I'd first seen on him. He wore it well. His long curly hair was tied back at the base of his head today; it made the features on his face stand out even more than usual. The nose so much bigger and uglier, with its slightly crooked bend, but the smile he gave me was genuine, and it lit up those big blue eyes and made you not want to look anywhere else. I chided myself for looking. Michel may not be able to glaze me any more, but other vampires still could. Best to be more careful.

"Hey, Jett!"

"Hey yourself, Lucinda."

"You know, you can call me Luce, all the others do."

"The master does not."

"Yeah, well, the *master* calls me whatever he damn well likes, but you, you can call me Luce. OK?" I hadn't meant that to sound so rude, really I hadn't, it just kinda came out that way. "Sorry, that was a bit rude. I've had a rough night."

"There is nothing to apologise for." His face was even, neutral. I think he meant it. I think.

"So, is it busy in there tonight?" For some reason I just wanted to be prepared, a big crowd of dancing humans just wasn't my cup of tea this evening.

"Private function."

OK. "Can I go in? Or will they chuck me out without an invite?"

"This is your home, you can come and go as you please."

"Um, it's not my home, Jett. I have an apartment."

He just looked at me as though I was the one who was crazy. Jeez, vampires!

"Your home is with the master. The master lives here."

This was so not going anywhere. "Right. I'll go in then."

He nodded, that slow short incline of his head he seems to do and opened the door to the inside.

I was immediately met with a mixture of vampire *Sanguis Vitam* signatures, differing power levels, tingles and pinpricks along my skin, more so than usual and with a cursory glance around the room, I recognised the scene. No Norms. The only humans here were groupies and willing donors. The vampires were partying tonight. I wonder why?

It was kind of like a scene from a movie. Seriously gorgeous people lounging around on sumptuous furniture. They were all dressed to impress too, latest fashions, stunning outfits, flawless make-up and hair. Some were openly feeding, others getting a little too familiar for the public setting that it was and still more hiding in the shadows doing God knows what. I didn't want to look too closely; those were images I could gladly keep from repeating in my dreams.

There was a heady scent in the air too, intoxicating even, it sent shivers down the spine. Did vampires give off pheromones when en masse like this? It wasn't quite an orgy, but I didn't doubt it could turn that way in a flash. This was so unexpected. I'm not a prude, but I'm not a swinger either. I don't frequent those sorts of places where they dress up in leather and wear whips and chains like jewellery. *Sensations* had always had a little zing to it, the dark furniture, lush surroundings and low lighting screamed indulgent behaviour, but this? This was something else entirely.

I scanned the room for a familiar face, but couldn't see anyone other than Doug behind the bar, and he was busy, orders flying off the counter in that vampire preternatural speed. Whoever was footing the bill for this bash was gonna feel it. I decided I'd just head in the direction of the Private area, when a vampire stepped in front of me, barring my way.

He was tall, really tall, so I had to crane my neck back to look up at him. That's not saying much, I have to look up at most people, but still, he looked like a tree. Strong arms in a casual dress shirt of deep red, over tight form fitting black trousers. I'd got so used to vampires wearing black lately that my eyes lingered on the shirt, taking in the broad chest, thick arms. I shook myself and kept on tipping back to get a look at who this guy was. He obviously wanted my attention, but I wasn't going to step back and show fear. That would have been a dead giveaway, emphasis on dead.

He was, of course, handsome, I don't think there would have been an ugly vamp in the room tonight, Jett with his crooked nose was about as bad as it was going to get and he was standing outside. He had slightly unruly blond hair, but it had that staged look about it like he'd spent an hour gelling it into place. His eyes were a piercing blue, an intense azure; it made his lightly golden skin stand out. Vampires don't get sunburns, unless by accident right before they *die*-die, but if they had tanned skin when they were turned, it more or less stays that way in the undead life as well. I'm picking this guy was from a sunny country, maybe Greece or Turkey? His mouth was full and currently curved in a beguiling smile. It finished off his features with an all mighty full stop. This guy was simply dazzling.

"Can I help you?"

"Absolutely, you can," he drawled, American, wouldn't have picked that.

He reached out to touch my hair running a hand through the strands, then rested his hand at the side of my neck, stroking over my pulse point.

"What are you doing?"

He cocked his head at me, a little surprised I was asking that question. "What does it look like I'm doing? Savouring my meal."

Oh great. I was so glad Rick was not here to hear this.

"I'm not on the menu."

"All the humans here are for our enjoyment. Be that physical or nutritional. Which one are you?" His voice was husky, inviting.

His hand at my neck had tightened, the other one now gripping my left arm slightly. Where was everyone tonight? None of Michel's guys would have stood for this. Where was a decent bodyguard when you needed one? Guess I'm on my own. Again.

"Neither. And I suggest you remove your hands before you get yourself hurt." Best to come out guns blazing with a vampire holding your neck.

He laughed at that, actually threw back his head and laughed. Didn't loosen his grip though, did he?

"Perhaps you could be both. First my meal, then my entertainment. I've always liked my fun with a bit of bite."

At that his fangs slipped out and down and his lips drew back in that definitely not-sexy move some vampires have. If only they practised in front of a mirror, they'd get a hell of a lot more pussy that way, I'm sure.

I really didn't think I should stake someone on Michel's property, in the middle of a private vampire function. The repercussions would be too great. God knows who was running this party and how they would react, and really, I had no idea how Michel would either. Neither thought was comforting.

So, where did that leave me? His fangs were getting closer, I could feel his hot breath against my skin, the world had squeezed into just him and me, those fangs and my bare skin. Time had slowed, but not stopped, in too short a space of time his teeth would pierce my flesh. Nobody in the room had come to my aid, some had noticed, but had simply turned away, the vampires uncaring, the humans too weak to show support. God, why was I always ending up in these situations?

Out of frustration, I shouted *Michel!* in my head. I was angry that he hadn't been here to greet me, that he hadn't sensed I had arrived, that he didn't even know that some Neanderthal vampire in his bar was now about to chomp down on my neck and then do God knows what to the rest of me. Where the hell was he!

The door to the club opened with a resounding bang. I couldn't see who had done it, I was facing the wrong way and kind of in a bind, but I could sure as hell feel it. And then everything happened so fast. Michel appeared beside us with eyes blazing the most amazing array of purples; violet, heliotrope, amethyst and amaranthine, sparkling like diamonds around the room. In the next instant, the vampire was flying through the air and landing in a heap against the bar, breaking wood and glass and sending patrons flying.

He was on his feet in an instant, but as soon as he saw who his attacker was, stilled. A look of shock and outrage on his features.

Surprisingly his voice was very calm when he said, "Is there a problem?"

Michel just growled and slowly walked towards him. His *Sanguis Vitam* was electrifying. Vampires in the vicinity were scrambling to get out of the way, as far as possible out of the way. Humans were being discarded, left where they had been dropped; they too were making desperate escapes, but somewhat more pitifully. I felt Bruno come up and stand beside me more than I saw him, my eyes too transfixed by the display that was Michel. He glowed, the most stunning shade of blue and purple, it made him seem so godly, so terrifyingly beautiful. It didn't seem possible that he was of this world.

The vampire realised then that things were not going well, but I could tell he was struggling to understand why. I almost felt bad for the guy and took a step forward to say something to Michel. Bruno's hand came down on my shoulder, not hard but firm, halting me in my place. I understood, this was not something a human, albeit vampire hunter/kindred Nosferatin should get in-between of. So, instead, I threw my thoughts out to Michel. I wasn't sure if he'd hear them, but it felt right, and I had nothing to lose. *He didn't know who I was, Michel, he thought I was another human groupie, a donor. He didn't know.*

Michel hadn't paused, still making that slow and determined walk towards the vampire, who was by now every shade of green, sick with fear. I wasn't sure if Michel had even heard me or not, his gaze so intent, his step so sure. He growled a low, threatening sound that rumbled around the room and made several of the humans whimper. I didn't blame them; I would have whimpered too if I wasn't trying so hard to get Michel's attention.

Michel stop! You don't need to do this. He didn't know. Please, for me.

Somehow that got through to him. Wow. I don't know if it was *what* I was saying in my thoughts to him, or if it was the fact that I had just been sending thoughts non-stop throughout all of this and finally they had broken through his anger and rage, but he stopped advancing on the man, and his glow slowly diminished. His eyes still blazed, but he had schooled his features into that neutral mask vampires wear around each other.

"It seems my kindred Nosferatin is prepared to forgive your transgression." The vampires eyes widened alarmingly and he slid a quick glance to me and then back to Michel. "She has more compassion than I, however, as the infringement was made against her, I shall allow her to mete the punishment."

What?

So, *now* all eyes were on me. Before they couldn't even spare me a glance, but *now* they were transfixed. Super great.

"Lucinda?" He hadn't turned towards me, he was still staring intently at the vampire, but in his mind he sent the thought, *come stand with me, ma douce.* At least he was lucid enough to use my pet name, I thought weakly, as I came to stand next to him.

The vampire had started apologising then, almost drivelling in his rapid flow of words, "Sorry, I had no idea, had I known... You were so beautiful," he received a small growl from Michel then. "It's just I couldn't understand why you had not yet been taken. I'm so sorry; I'm so sorry, so very sorry."

I'd raised my hand then to tell him to stop making a fool of himself, but he'd kind of run out of steam anyway and seemed to look as much like a vampire as a pussy cat right now.

What am I meant to say? I asked in my mind, directing the thought at Michel.

He is yours to punish, you choose, came his cool reply in my head.

What punishment could I give him?

I was hoping for a stake through the heart. I heard it then, the lightness in Michel's thought, he was enjoying this. Typical.

I don't want to hurt him. Who is he anyway? This mind talking could prove very helpful.

A visitor, come to pay their respects. It seems word of my power increase has reached the furthest corners of the Iunctio and those who wish to strategically align themselves with us have started calling. And then there are those who just want to come and see if it is true.

Which is he?

Michel smiled at me then, a small turn of his head towards me, his eyes lifting to meet mine. *The former I think. I believe he is the representative for the American Council of Families. They have long been requesting a meeting, some of their business interests have much in common with mine. However, their methods of arranging that meeting have been - how should I say? - blunt.*

There's a group of American Families with a representative? Now was not the time to be sidetracked, so I hadn't flung that thought out to Michel.

So, where does that leave me now? Do I tell him to leave and piss off America? Or is that what you want?

The look Michel gave me was unexpected, surprise, a sort of astonishment. *You would consult my wishes?*

Of course. I'm your Nosferatin. And, yes, I hadn't sent that little titbit of information flying through to his head. But it was how I felt.

We were in this together, even if sometimes I didn't really want to and sometimes I wondered whether I had even been cornered into this deal without any chance of escaping from the start and sometimes he did things that made me mad. The truth was, I was here now, and ever the practical person that I am, I knew I couldn't do this without Michel. So, I wasn't going to fight it anymore.

Tell him to leave. The American Families will take the inference that it is. I will not be bullied.

I couldn't imagine that Michel would ever be bullied, but maybe the American Council, whoever they were, were bigger than even him. It wasn't a reassuring thought.

I turned back to the vampire who had been watching us intently, all too aware that we had been communicating telepathically, yet another confirmation of the strength of our relationship. Only those Bonded could do this, and we shouldn't have been Bonded just yet.

"Well, you've kind of put a dampener on my evening. You see, I've already had a shit of a night and I'd thought coming here would change all of that. But, you're just one more supernatural to piss me off. So, here's the thing. Get out of my city and get off my land."

He stared at me incredulously, his mouth gaping open, his brow slightly furrowed. Michel stepped forward and in a low growl said, "I believe she has evicted you. I suggest you not waste time in obeying her command. She is incredibly beautiful when in a rage, but I fear you would not win."

The vampire took one look at me, then back at Michel. "The Families shall hear of this."

"Oh, I do hope so," Michel said evenly, then flashed his fangs.

With that the vampire vanished, a blur of colour as he raced from the room. Bruno, a flash as he followed with several others of Michel's clan, no doubt to ensure the vampire left as requested and didn't come back.

"Well, that was fun, my dear," Michel said turning to take my hand. "Shall we retire?

The music started playing again and the vampires in the club visibly relaxed, the humans not so much, but the chill had definitely left the room.

We walked towards the private door to Michel's quarters and I said softly, "So, are we at war with the Americans now too?"

He laughed, that lovely rich, deep rumble in his chest I've come to love. "So it would seem."

Oh crap.

32

FLIGHTLESS BIRD

Michel threw his jacket on a chair in the corner of his chamber, took his shoes off and undid his deep blue on blue tie, leaving it hanging around his neck in strands that caught the light every now and then and shimmered slightly. He grabbed a bottle of Merlot which had been left out on his dresser with two glasses nearby and filled both, then turned to hand one to me. He looked tired, really tired. That took me by surprise.

I've only ever seen Michel tired once before, in Taupo, after the battle with Max. He'd lowered his guard, that façade he keeps on most of the time and sat sprawled on the couch with his hand over his head. It was a sight I hadn't expected to see again, Michel's power level has increased tremendously since that time, I couldn't imagine what would tire him now.

He came and sat on the bed beside me, stretching his long legs out in front of him and resting back against the copious gold and brown cushions. He levelled his gaze at me. "Why are you looking at me like that, *ma douce?*"

I hadn't realised I had been looking at him in any particular way, but now he mentioned it, he did make it feel like I had been staring and maybe there was a look of worry there too.

"You look so tired. What's happened? What's wrong?"

He smiled his lazy smile and motioned for me to come and cuddle in. I didn't need to be asked twice. The need to be near him still so strong, it was the dominant emotion in my body right now, one I had no intention of fighting. He felt warm and soft, the smell of him now so familiar, fresh and clean, like when it has just stopped raining. He wrapped his arm around my body and I rested my head against his chest, listening to his heartbeat steadily thumping, feeling his chest rise and fall.

"It was a long night and day, *ma douce*, I have only now just returned with Bruno."

I sat up a little at that and turned to look directly at him. "I didn't realise you weren't back. I mean I sensed you were OK, but I hadn't even picked up you weren't in Auckland." I was a little worried about that, was there something wrong with our Bond? *Did it matter if there was*, my little voice asked. I ignored it.

"Perhaps you did not try to seek me?" His eyebrow was slightly raised, his voice light, but I thought I noticed a small muscle twitch in his jaw, a sure sign that he was not impressed and trying to hide it.

"I...I don't know."

He reached up then and stroked my face. "It is all right, my dear, it means the Bond has settled. I thought that would be welcome news to you, to not be so ruled by its whims." And he was right of course, I couldn't help the sense of relief that flooded through me. The Bond had allowed me to have a normal day, a normal day that turned to custard, but not because of the Bond. I was happy, I was hopeful, this could mean a return to some form of normality for me. This was what I had wanted. Then why did I also feel a little let down?

I had begun to think our Bond was special, unique. Different from those of others. Stronger, more powerful. I hadn't realised I wanted that, a strength of connection to Michel and dare I say it, power. What was I becoming?

I settled back against his chest; my failing moral standards could wait for analysis at a later date. He was home, he was safe and we were together.

"So, why so busy all of a sudden?"

Michel took a sip of his wine before he replied. "My line has increased dramatically in a short period of time. Provision for that number needed to be arranged. I have established a base in Wellington. It was... not quite as straight forward as I had hoped."

"How hard was it? What happened?"

"Nothing for you to fear, *ma douce*, just politics as they are." For some reason I didn't believe him. He was hiding something. It wasn't anything overtly obvious, just a gut reaction. I'd been around Michel a lot lately, I had a kindred Nosferatin connection to him, a Bond, but this was all just good old familiarity. I knew Michel, or as well as anyone could know a master vampire, and I knew he was hiding something.

"You know I don't believe you."

"Yes, I can tell."

"Then why won't you tell me? We are meant to be together, side by side and all that crap, aren't we?"

He cringed. "*All that crap?* How eloquent, my dear. For something so sacred and revered as a kindred joining and Bond, it really does not do it justice."

"You're stalling."

He smiled. "Could it be that I wish to protect you, Lucinda? Keep something of the horrors of my world from you for a little longer? Would you begrudge me that?"

"No. But I think it's more of a case of what you think I *need* to know or not. And I'm guessing this is a need to know."

He looked at me for a full minute, not dead still, vampire still. He was breathing and his heart was beating, he was just taking me in, I think. Searching for a reason to give into this argument. He sighed.

"I have no doubt you will send me to an early grave, *ma douce*." I seriously doubted that, but I'd allow him his moment of melodrama if it meant he'd open up about this. "There have been some vampire killings in the South Island. Not many of my line venture that far south, but some have recently felt the need. The killings have now crossed Cook Strait and we had a few episodes in Wellington last night." Seeing the look on my face; worry, surprise, amazement, he continued. "I believe it to be an isolated event, but, nonetheless, I have arranged an investigation by some of my best. Establishing a base in Wellington seems prudent for more than just accommodating increased numbers in my line."

He reached out and brushed my hair from my face, where it had fallen forward over my eye and tucked it behind my ear. "It really is nothing for you to worry about. My men have it in hand. Besides, we have more pressing matters to attend. I have heard from Nafrini."

That got my attention. We hadn't expected to be in touch with the Cairo vampire until we landed, her contacting now could mean only one thing.

"The *Cadre* have struck in Cairo. Capturing one of the immature Nosferatin. She requests our presence urgently. Nafrini is holding the rest of the *Cadre* off, but seeking the stolen Nosferatin is of utmost importance, they have not been able to follow the trail. She has requested we assist in the hunt."

"Can they spare any of their own to assist us?"

"I believe they are cornered. The fight is quite intense. They cannot leave their compound at present, hence they cannot follow the trail."

That was unheard of. If the *Cadre* could hold down a powerful joined Nosferatu and her kindred Nosferatin, then they were stronger than I had imagined. Way stronger.

Michel could feel my understanding of what he had said, the consequences of what was happening. "This is not good news, *ma douce*. They are indeed stronger than we had expected. But I will not endanger you by leaving before your 25th birthday. Nafrini will have to hold them off."

Hold them off. But, by the time my birthday came around in another three days time, the immature Nosferatin could be joined and where would that leave us?

What did we know about the *Cadre*? They were a group of vampires hell bent on taking over the world and they saw the Nosferatin as their means to achieve it. They believed it their right to hunt humans unhindered, that their status and power put them in that rightful place of *on top*. Max had been a member of that group and he had come to New Zealand specifically to get me, when he had heard of my success, my exploits you might say. There's not too many of us left, so we do stand out when we kill a few of their kind. He had intended to join with me, to give him the power needed to vanquish those vampires who opposed the *Cadre*. Those vampires like Nafrini and Michel.

And now what was left of the group seemed even stronger than Max. Could it be that they were just more organised? Or that there were just more of them than Nafrini's line could handle? Could there be that many?

Or was it something else? I was beginning to get that creepy feeling between my shoulder blades, hair on end, shiver down my spine. Like someone had walked over my grave. This didn't feel right and my body was trying to tell me to stay the hell out of it, but I knew I couldn't. We couldn't leave Nafrini and Nero to their fate, it was not in my nature. If I could do something to help, I would. Besides, what would happen if the *Cadre* did succeed? It wasn't worth thinking about.

We needed to know more about what was happening in Cairo though, otherwise we could be walking into a trap.

"Did Nafrini say anything else?"

"Communications were cut off. She did not have time."

"Cut off?"

"Her end, not ours. I'd say the *Cadre* were preventing her from calling in reinforcements from other vampire lines."

A thought suddenly occurred to me, the land lines and even cell cover may have been cut off, but not satellite. "I could use my satellite phone to get in touch."

"You have a satellite phone, *ma douce*? Why would you need that?" His eyebrows were raised in a questioning manner. He looked genuinely intrigued, like he hadn't had any idea at all that I had one. OK. So, Michel hadn't left the satellite phone on my bed, but who had? And if Michel hadn't have left the phone, entering my apartment when he shouldn't have been able to, then did he even leave those orange roses? But then, the roses had a card with his writing on it, so it had to have been him that time, right? But the phone, that was obviously a different matter.

Now wasn't the time to get bogged down by it though, we needed answers, and we needed them quickly. Going home to grab my phone would take too long, but I knew another way to find out what was happening.

"Forget the phone, I'll Dream Walk." I was already laying myself down on the bed, having quickly placed my glass of wine on the bedside table. Michel was above me in an instant.

"No, you will not!"

I sighed. "Michel, we need to know what's going on over there. We need to make sure we're not walking into a trap."

"I can handle whatever we are presented with; you do not need to endanger yourself by Dream Walking."

"I won't be in any danger." - I wasn't entirely sure about that, I mean I knew I would be invisible to other vampires, but Nosferatin could see me, that was kind of the point though. I wanted to talk to Nero, but also, I had been captured by vampires when I Dream Walked in Sydney and that thought hadn't entirely been swept under the rug just yet. - "I'll pop in, get an update from Nero and pop back out. It'll be only a few minutes. I promise."

"No. I cannot protect you when you Dream Walk," Michel replied agitatedly.

"I don't expect you to."

"You are vulnerable without me there."

"I can take care of myself."

"I need to be there! You need protection!" All but shouted.

I didn't get this. I'd Dream Walked before and granted Michel hadn't known about it until after the fact, but he hadn't seemed too upset by it, well not really. But there was something else going on here. His eyes were wide, his pulse at the base of his neck was thundering, his breath rapid and face slightly flushed, if I didn't know any better, I'd have said he was truly scared. But even that didn't make any sense. Michel had not interfered when I hunted locally, he might have followed me more closely recently, turning up when I hadn't expected to see him, but he still hadn't appeared as desperate as he did now.

"Look, I don't know what the problem is," - then feeling his tightened grip on my shoulders and even more desperate look in his eyes - "but, this is what I do, Michel. It's one of my powers for a reason and right now, we *need* to know what's happening over there. Trust me. I can do this. Please?"

He looked a little strangled there for a moment, he didn't move, just kept staring at me with an unusual look on his face. He was obviously battling something deep within, but I had no idea what it was. We were running out of time, we needed to do this now.

Slowly he rolled off me and sat rigid on the side of the bed. "Be quick," was all he said and it was barely a whisper at that.

I settled myself back down and worked to clear my mind. It was a little difficult after seeing such emotion fluttering across Michel's face, but I had to block that out. I concentrated on my breathing, my heartbeat and then felt myself relax into that black nothingness, then once surrounded by the thick deep darkness, I sent my senses out to Nero. It was easier than I had expected. I had never really consciously sought another while Dream Walking until now, but it seemed to come instinctively.

I found myself appearing in a large room, the walls were all made of stone, whitewashed and bright. Fabrics hung along the lengths, making what would have been a stark setting, warm and comfortable. The pictures were of ancient Egyptians, the type of images you see in text books talking about Pharaohs and the Sphinx, white loin clothes, brown skin and cobra-like headdresses. Cushions were scattered at my feet; bright reds, blues, yellows and greens, tassels tickling my legs. I had landed right in the middle of them and they nearly made me lose my balance. At least my landing would have been soft, I thought abstractedly.

There were groups of humans all around, hugging each other closely, crying and shaking, trying to sooth the younger ones, cringing at the noises coming from the bordering room. There were no windows here, but a skylight let the hot sun in, shining down on those gathered beneath, making their white clothing and brown golden faces stand out in stark relief against the coloured wall hangings. It was daytime, but I could feel vampires fighting nearby. Why were they fighting in the light? This was not good.

It seemed, naturally, that the humans; elderly, middle aged, even children, couldn't see me, so I left them where they were and headed towards the only door at the far end of the room. I didn't hesitate, just wrenched it open and jumped through, stake in hand. I was met with a scene from hell.

Vampires were fighting hand to hand, flashes of power dancing off windowsills and walls, a kaleidoscope of colour from amber to rose, apple green to aqua, blue-violet to burnt orange, it was a melting pot, blinding and yet so compelling, it was difficult to look away. I could smell burnt fabric and a much more acrid smell underlining it of burnt flesh. I swallowed and tore my gaze away from the strobing lights.

Dust was swirling in the air, chunks of stonewall and no doubt vampire, every movement a person made sent the dust motes dancing up off the ground. If the light wasn't blinding, the dust certainly threatened to be more so, blocking all vision from within a foot of where you stood. I stifled a cough and tried to get my bearings. It was fairly obvious which vampires were Nafrini's, they were all dressed similarly to how Nero does, linen trousers and loose linen shirts, tanned skin and dark hair, where in comparison, those of the *Cadre* were dressed in commando black. Tight fitting, dark and sleek, like the way they were moving. Their hair a mix of colours, their features a snarling grimace of hatred, their skin slowly smoking in the rays that caught them through the windows, here and there. I didn't think they would be able to hold out much longer.

Nafrini's vampires were composed, but determined, their beauty still so obvious whilst in the fray, but they were weakening too, a few showing signs of sun damage. I spotted Nero across the room. He wasn't spinning, but he was moving with lightning speed. I guess he had been holding back on me when we fought after all. Figures. He was moving with such grace, a small strike here, a swift step there. A parry, a thrust, he wasn't using a sword, but his stake might as well have been one, it was like a long extension of his arm, a part of his body, he seemed so in tune with it.

I noticed too then, a couple of other humans, Nosferatins, fighting beside Nero. These had to be the other mature Nosferatin Nero had talked of. They weren't quite as graceful or as fast as Nero. They had a style of their own, it was efficient and seemed to be successful, but it wasn't that beauty I saw when I watched Nero. That utter brilliance of his motions, the way his body slid through the space around him, like a sleek mountain cat jumping from ridge to ridge.

The *Cadre* had Nero and the other vampires cornered, they had them moved back against the far end of the corridor we were in. The windows along its length to the left of me, the wall to the room I had just exited to the right. I wondered why some of the *Cadre* hadn't just broken off and gone for the humans in the room, who were clearly Nosferatin family. That's why Nero and the others were fighting so hard, to protect them, but Nero's group were keeping them busy, not allowing for any to break away. But, I was beginning to worry they were about to lose this battle. Step by excruciating step, the *Cadre* men were advancing and step by ever more excruciating step, Nero and his side were retreating. Despite the sun, the *Cadre* were determined to finish this now.

I had to stop them.

I know I had promised Michel I would pop in, take a peek and pop back out again, but I couldn't turn my back on them now. They were about to be defeated and those poor humans, those Nosferatin, in that room, were about to be killed and used by these creatures. I couldn't let that happen.

No one had noticed me, the vampires of course couldn't, the Nosferatin too busy, so my position of advantage had gone unchecked. I was behind the *Cadre's* men, they were between me and Nero, they didn't see what hit them.

I decided for a random attack, rather than starting at one side and moving across the line of vampires there. I ran at my first victim on the right, slid the stake home and somehow managed a spin through the air across the corridor by pushing off the wall with my feet, by the time the vampire had burst into dust, I had staked another by the window and was already rolling back past one in the middle of the rear guard. I slashed out at that vampire, just as he was turning to see who was attacking them and missed his heart by a millimetre I should think. Enough for him to yell out in pain and also fling his arm up instinctively to protect himself. I went flying back down the hallway and landed in a heap, feeling my breath come out in a rush.

I rolled onto all fours instantly. Training with the Taniwhas had taught me that, it was so second nature, you tended to just do it before the pain set in, no Taniwha wants to bare its stomach to the predator's claws.

The vampires couldn't spot me and were looking around uneasily at the back of their group, the rest continued to fight, trusting their buddies behind them to cover their backs. Not for long, I thought bitterly and launched myself at one of the more confused vampires standing in a crouch. I staked him through the back as I launched over his shoulders in a somersault and landed next to another looking alarmed, I didn't waste time but sunk my stake home. The dust cloud created blinded me for a minute, so I didn't see the arm that came out and punched me in the face, sending me spinning around and crashing to the ground. It was a lucky punch, the vampire had just aimed for where he thought someone would have been standing when they staked his comrade, I had just been too slow to move out of the way and ended up getting caught.

I mentally kicked myself, shook my head and rolled away from where I had landed, getting tangled in the feet of another vampire, making him come down on top of me, arms and legs flailing and then registering the shape beneath him was solid, despite not being able to see it and attempting to crush me in the grip of his arms. Luckily for me, I had already raised my stake, so when he pulled me in for bear hug to end all bear hugs, my stake took hold and pierced his heart.

The dust from that one did choke me and I coughed and spluttered as I crawled out from under it on all fours. Dust clung to me; my hair, my skin, my shoulders, my clothes, I could feel it stinging in my eyes, gritty in my mouth. I spat out a fair chunk of greyish blue gunk from the back of my throat and tried to swallow away the rest, only to start myself coughing again as soon as the wet dust hit the back of my throat. God this was just lovely, wasn't it?

Somehow I had managed to keep crawling through all of that and even though I was coughing and spluttering, the vampires had been unable to pin down my exact position due to all the confused shouting and cursing that was now ensuing from their midst. I staggered to my feet, dusted myself down - a reflex action when covered with vampire dust - and straightened my shoulders. These guys just weren't taking the hint, were they?

Only two more were facing backwards towards me now, the rest fighting tooth and nail against Nero and his team, good odds, but I was tiring. My breathing was rapid, my heartbeat a little erratic. This had to work, I needed to finish this or I'd end up making a mistake that would cost both myself and Michel our lives. The thought of Michel made me momentarily pause, but I pushed it aside, no time for sentimentality in a fight. Concentrate and get it over with.

I decided to go for the larger of the two, he looked more threatening and he was against the wall of the corridor, the other one was in direct sunlight and suffering for it. So without hesitating any further, I ran towards big dude and at the last moment, when he must have heard me gasp and tensed for an attack, I slid between his legs, came up behind him and stabbed him in the back. I didn't stop for the dust to settle, but spun around in front of the final vampire waiting and ended up in his face, the stake already inside his chest right up to my hand. I saw his eyes widen, then he disintegrated into dust.

The remaining vampires swivelled at the fall of their last back-up and fled through the windows into the day. I crumpled to my knees gasping for breath and feeling every bruise and graze keenly. Nafrini's vampires had already begun to secure the building, I didn't even see them move, but they were gone, I could hear them shouting orders and moving around behind me down the corridor. I saw a tall swath of brightly coloured fabric zip past, noticed a pretty face and long dark hair flowing down the back and then the corridor was silent and still.

I opened my eyes to find Nero kneeling in front of me. He didn't have a strand of hair out of place, his clothes were immaculate, no rips or tears or crumples or dust, his face a shining glow of sweat, but that was the only indication of him having fought. He laughed, his smile bringing such joy to me I was momentarily shocked at my body's response to it.

"So, little Kiwi. It seems you really can fly after all."

33
CAIRO

I couldn't imagine what I looked like, but I had felt better, I knew that much. I struggled to get to my feet, only to find my knees crumple under me again, then Nero's arm wrapped around my side. I wanted to let the blackness in, flow towards that nothingness and Michel, but I needed to know what else was happening here, what to expect when we arrived. So, I took a steadying breath in and slowly released the tension from my body. It kinda worked, well sort of.

"Better?" Nero asked, his arm still held around me, his warm body up against my side.

"Yeah. Sorry, I was late."

He laughed as he led us over to some seating that had miraculously remained intact. I could still feel the warmth of his touch even when he pulled away and sat down next to me, not touching, but almost.

"I should say you were right on time, Kiwi. Perfect in every way." His eyes were shining brightly, the gold flecks dancing in the cinnamon swirls within. Wow. I realised I'd been staring at him a little longer than I should have and quickly ducked my head. So much for remaining cool under pressure then.

He sat back in his seat, winced a little and let out a sigh.

"Are you all right?"

"Nafrini will heal me; I will be fine." He looked up sharply then and said, "I see you have let your kindred heal you too, these injuries are all today's." His hand reached out as if to touch my cheek, but stopped mid-way, a look of uncertainty on his face. I had never seen Nero look uncertain before, intense, not uncertain. He rested his hand back at his side. I think he may have even sighed again, but I'm not sure.

"What happened, Nero? How did they get so close?"

"They outnumbered us, 3 to 1, not impossible odds, but they appear to be well prepared. That was not their first wave today. The attack began at sundown, first a group of twenty, then when we had dispatched them, another group similar in size, then again another and so on and so on until now. This, I think was their fifth group."

"That doesn't make sense. If they had that many vampires, why not hit at once and overpower you from the start."

"I am not sure." He paused, thinking it over, then added, "I think they were targeting the unjoined vampyres, they would fight myself and Nafrini off and our two other joined pairs, but not attempt to kill us, but they would kill the other vampyres in our line, those who have not yet joined. I didn't notice it at first, but in reflection that seems to be the case."

"So, they're intention is not to wipe Nafrini and you out." And therefore also not me and Michel. "But, instead to capture you?"

He looked at me, then a slow look of comprehension lit his eyes. "I had not thought of that. Why would they?"

Despite the gravity of the conversation, I couldn't help feeling a sense of joy at Nero asking for my opinion. Here was this amazingly talented Nosferatin, old beyond my years, intelligent, clever, had an answer for everything, yet asking me a question with such brevity and intent, expecting me to be able to contribute an adequate reply. How is it when I was around Nero he made me feel big and yet when I was around Michel he sometimes made me feel small?

"I'm picking there aren't enough of us, the Nosferatin, for them to carry out their plans. We're precious, important to their success; they can't afford not to have us on their side."

"Surely they would know we would not join them?"

"Could they make us? Hold something of ours as ransom, force our hand?"

Nero's face darkened at that. He ran a hand through his short black hair, somehow making it tidier than not, the golden brown skin on his muscular forearms rippling with the movement. I found myself licking my lips and had to force myself to look away. What was wrong with me? Nero was sex on a stick to be sure, but (1) He lives in Egypt, (2) He's joined to a mega-old, no doubt mega-powerful vampire and let's not forget (3) Michel! *Stop it!* I shouted in my head. *Behave yourself!*

When I chanced a look back at Nero he was watching me, a small smile on his face, he held my gaze for a moment and then glanced away, with a slight look of anguish replacing the smile and then it was gone.

"They are depleted today but will return this evening. I must attempt to locate Amisi, our stolen immature Nosferatin. I shall use the daylight to my advantage while I can."

"If they come back tonight, will you be up to it? No sleep?"

He smiled, one of his light-up-the-world-with-a-sunbeam smiles, eyes all sparkling, white teeth gleaming.

I sighed. "You know, you really shouldn't use that unless you mean it."

His eyes flashed with wickedness. "What makes you think I don't, my little Kiwi."

I just shook my head, when I looked back at him, he had schooled his features into the intense look he usually wears. He wasn't looking at me but had his head down looking at the floor; his hands were also scrunched into fists at his side.

After a while, he said, "Thank you for your help, Kiwi. It shall not be forgotten. We will see you soon, I hope."

He wouldn't look at me again, and I got the distinct impression that the conversation was over. Sometimes I just couldn't quite figure Nero out. One minute all sexy smiles and flirtatious looks, then the next minute back to his distant intense self. All these mood swings were making me dizzy, but I guess it was just who he was. Complicated. Crazy. Beautiful. Huh.

I didn't reply, just let myself fade into that intoxicating nothingness and reach out for home.

Michel was hovering when I came to, a look of pure relief flooding his features when I opened my eyes. "Thank God, *ma douce*. You said only a moment; that was more than half an hour. You have no idea what this is doing to me." He stilled then, just a second, then quickly began to remove my clothing.

"Hey! Hey! Steady on! Ever heard of foreplay?"

"You have been hurt. Lucinda! What did you do?" That last was said in a very impressive growl, making the hairs on the back of my neck stand up and my little internal monologue whimper, then run away and hide. I knew Michel wasn't going to hurt me; he was angry sure, but not hurt me. But that voice he sometimes has? Hell, it can scare the living daylights out of you without even trying.

"I'm fine, really, stop fussing." I was trying to flap his hands away, but failing miserably. Everything hurt like a bitch, but suddenly I didn't want him to know. I didn't want him to fuss and worry and wrap me up in cotton wool. Dream Walking was part of who I am; I had this power for a reason. And if I hadn't have gone to Nero, they may well have been captured and most of their line dead by now. I had this gift. I was not going to be put in a gilded cage and never be able to use it.

"Michel. *Michel*. Michel!" It took three efforts and me holding his face in both of my hands and bringing it to mine before he stopped trying to ascertain the extent of my injuries. I looked at those beautiful deep blue eyes and sighed. This man was going to drive me crazy, but I couldn't stop loving him. I pulled his face towards mine and brushed my lips across his; he stopped trying to lift my top off me and stilled. I tried again for a light touch, then followed it up with a nip on his bottom lip. This time I got a small stroke over my skin, a swirl of a thumb across my hip. I deepened the kiss and forced my tongue between his lips, putting as much of myself into the movement as I could, letting him know I was here, safe, with him. I had come home.

He moaned softly against me and then pulled back. What? "You are trying to distract me, *ma douce*." His voice was husky, soft. "It will not work." Now, that was a challenge if ever I heard one.

And I had every intention of proving him wrong. I pulled him down further and started laying kisses against his face, down his cheek, across his jaw. He didn't resist, just moulded into me like a silky blanket draping across my body. I found his pulse beneath his skin on the side of his neck and gently sucked. The response was most promising, so I did it again, this time eliciting a low groan.

He reached a hand up under my top and stroked my nipple, tweaking it erect, then started laying kisses of his own over my face and neck. His lips were so soft and warm, his touch sending shivers through my body. How is it he could make me feel so alive?

He seemed quite interested in my own pulse point then, lavishing attention to that spot with his lips and tongue, whilst managing to send shockwaves of pleasure through my body with his hand. The sensations battling each other for my attention, writhing inside me like molten lava, swirling around me like delicate feathers, touching my every nerve ending, everywhere.

I arched my back up towards him, my hands digging into his shoulder and back. He wrapped one arm around me, sitting me up in a swift move, so I settled across his lap. His other hand caressed my hair, down my back and across my shoulders, then back up to my neck, tipping my head back to expose my pulse. I knew what was coming, but it was still a small sharp shock, as his fangs entered my flesh and he began to draw. The sharp sting of his teeth was soon replaced by a wave of absolute joy, laced with pleasure and dripping in desire. He wasn't holding back tonight, but letting me feel everything that he was feeling, testing me to see if I could cope.

If sensing my emotions was anything as intense as this was for me right now, I couldn't believe Michel had handled it all so well. This was blinding in its purity, crushing in its intensity, driving right into my soul. Suddenly I couldn't get enough of his skin against mine; I needed to feel flesh on flesh, to run my hands up his muscled body and sink them in his beautiful long hair. I started unbuttoning his shirt while he continued to drink me in, somehow managing to concentrate on each button, each button hole, until I had the shirt open and could finally feel the smoothness of his chest, down to the coarseness of his light curls leading to the darker area below.

He flipped me back on the bed, allowing me access to his chest, all the while not removing his lips and fangs from my vein. I'm not sure how long he had been sucking on me, it had felt like time had slowed, but I knew he normally wouldn't continue for more than 30 seconds. This just happened to be the longest, most delicious, most beautiful 30 seconds of my entire life. Finally, he withdrew his fangs and licked the trail of my blood running down my neck. I felt a little bereft at the fact he was no longer connected to me in that way.

He looked into my eyes, his a mesmerising swirl of indigo and blue laced with sadness I had not seen before, his hand cupping my neck, the other stroking my hair. "You have no idea how worried I was, *ma douce*. How helpless I felt. I have not felt such helplessness since I was turned." He paused to lay a kiss on my cheek, my jaw, my lips, then returning to look me intently in the eyes. "I do not know now how to stop feeling it; it is eating me up inside."

I understood that depth of emotion, one that threatens to consume you. As a human, or in my case, part-human, I have had experience learning to digest them, label them and file them where they need to go. For Michel, this was not the case. 500 years of being a vampire can make you forget. He no longer had the coping mechanisms a human would rely on in this situation. I wasn't sure how to help him, this was all part of his return to the light, but I thought perhaps I could try.

"Maybe we need to replace that emotion with something more pleasurable?"

He watched the curve of my smile, heard the challenge in my voice. I was rewarded with the most dazzling sparkle in his eyes and a slight twitch of his mouth.

"Maybe, we should."

His head bent down again, and full lips met mine, warm and soft, ducking his tongue in between my teeth, lavishing wetness and warmth inside my mouth. One hand had started moving over my stomach, round my side and then resting on my hip, rubbing circles with his thumb, the other hand was wrapped in my hair, tangled in the mess that had been created, trapping me where I lay. I didn't fight it; I had no intention of being anywhere else. I reached up and ran my own hand through his hair, the feel of it so soft and silky against my skin, the colour so deep in the low lights of the room. My other hand rested on his chest, not pushing, but lightly tracing the lines of his muscles, trying to commit to memory the feel of his hot skin.

Michel lifted his eyes to mine, the soft indigo and blue mixed now with a darker amethyst and magenta, colours that used to frighten me, but now only made me lust for him more. There was still a haunted look in those eyes, one that reached out and sang softly to me, called for me to soothe him, to replace that look with something else. I pushed against his chest, and he let me roll him over. I ended up straddling him across his hips, my short skirt riding up high on my upper thighs, his hands finding natural holds on my hips, just under the fabric of the skirt. I quickly lifted my arms and took my T-Shirt off over my head, leaving my skin bare on my upper body except for my bra. He didn't waste any time and quickly began stroking my flesh across my hips, stomach, ribs and up to my bra, one hand pulling me down slightly while he deftly removed the last item of clothing on my chest and discarding it over the side of the bed.

His hands found my breasts within a heartbeat, his thumb roughly rubbing over my nipples and sending a shock of desire through my body, heating me up from the inside out, sending a luscious wave of craving down my spine. He looked so gorgeous lying beneath me; his hair had come loose from its usual clip at the base of his neck and now lay dark and striking around his face, fanned out over the pillow, framing him. I took my time soaking him up with my eyes. His face was slightly flushed, the haunted look of only moments before was beginning to seep away, being replaced with a look of hunger, need, desire, that sent further warmth and heat through me, tightening muscles in much lower and more intimate places. His bare chest was impossible to ignore, I couldn't stop running my hands over every inch of his well sculptured physique. He was still wearing his white shirt, but it was open and hanging loosely to the sides, giving me free access to explore his broad chest and chiselled abs. What was with this guy? Five hundred years old and he was divine.

I tore myself away from the wonderful view of his upper body and shuffled down his legs until I was able to undo the button and zip at the top of his trousers and begin to slide them down. Michel simply placed his hands behind his head and watched me with half closed eyes, taking in everything with a lazy sexual gaze. He knew what was coming and had no intention of stopping me. That heated look, filled with such confidence and satisfaction, made me even wetter. I could tell he had noticed as a small shudder went through his body, making him close his eyes momentarily and take a deep breath in. I waited for him to open his eyes again and then took hold of him firmly in my hand.

Our eyes stayed locked on one another, his length swelling beneath my touch, his breathing coming a little more raggedly, but he was determined to keep hold of my gaze. It was me having trouble concentrating, not him. Finally, I could stand it no more, and I bent my head down and took him in my mouth. Warm and hard, yet so soft and wet, he responded with a quick intake of breath, his body going rigid, then slowly relaxing and tensing, one after the other, as I continued to lick and suck and nip and taste all of him.

It was hard to think of anything else; I was so consumed with the thought of pleasuring him, teasing him, creating any response I could, anything to make him forget that feeling of helplessness and replace it with something else. I did not want to ever see that haunted look in his eyes again if I could help it. It was only because he touched me, gripping my shoulder, that I became aware he had been saying something, so intent on what I had been doing.

"*Ma douce*, if you do not stop now it will be all over." His voice low and breathy.

I pulled back and glanced up at him then and was rewarded with the most amazing look of craving and yearning and need in his eyes, not a glimpse of the torment he had shown me before.

"Mm, well," I licked my lips, he groaned a little under his breath. "I think my work here was done anyway."

He gave me a look as if to say *not in this lifetime* and launched himself at me; we went tumbling over the side of the bed in a tangle of limbs and sheets and sweat soaked bodies. I let a yelp out only to be replaced with a moan as his mouth found mine and his hands began to work their magic over my body.

"Now, I think it is my turn, is it not?" Michel flashed a mischievous look at me before starting to kiss the side of my face, down my neck, over his mark where he seemed to be able to elicit the most delightful sensations from and on round down my throat and clavicle towards the dip between my breasts. His hands finding my rear and then round to my thighs, stroking, teasing and kneading. He somehow managed to skip kissing my breasts, the obvious exclusion of them making me only want his attention there even more and suddenly he was down at my belly button, lavishing attention there. *Who would have thought a tongue in the belly button could be so erotic?*

Michel laughed. I must have said that last bit aloud, but I was sure I hadn't.

"You are throwing your thoughts at me, it is most delightful, *ma douce*. Please do not stop."

I felt a blush creep up my face, but it was soon forgotten because Michel was on a mission to find as many erogenous zones as he could. He'd moved on from my belly button to my hip and then so slowly, kissing and licking and nibbling his way down to the crease at the top of my thigh. I sighed, I couldn't help it, it just felt so damn good. He paused there a little while to make sure I was getting the attention I needed and when I let a little moan out, he simply moved away, further down my thigh, towards the inside of my leg. So close to my wetness, but never actually nearing it enough to satisfy the sudden urgent hunger for him to be there.

I squirmed slightly, not even realising I was trying to get myself into a better position for him to go where I wanted him to be. He stilled my movements with a hand to my stomach and then continued to move away down my leg. I let out a stifled moan of frustration, but he just laughed and carried on, on his predetermined mission. Damn him; he was just trying to tease me to frustration. And it was bloody well working too.

His hand had started softly kneading the bend of my knee, which for some unknown reason sent me into a writhing mass of frustrated anguish, I couldn't even begin to understand why my *knee* would have such an effect on me. He seemed to like that response, so flipped me over onto my stomach so he could lavish kisses there instead. By this time I was putty in his hands. I could no further have got myself off that bed and relaunched my attack on him than fly to the moon.

He was relentless in his pursuit of teasing me. The fire that had begun to burn so intensely inside of me had all but taken over my entire body. I was a slave to the sensations Michel was creating, unable to stop moaning or thrashing about beneath his touch, his kisses, his soft nips and licks. He seemed to know exactly where to touch me to get the best response. I guess over a period of 500 years you pick up a trick or two.

Finally, when I thought I simply could not take it any longer, I felt his weight and warmth against the back of me, his breath against my neck, brushing through my hair, he lifted me up slightly with one hand and positioned himself between my legs. Then after a brief tease at my entrance, the hardness of him sliding through my wettest place, he pushed inside slowly, allowing me to feel every movement of his penetration, allowing me to stretch to fit him, but not so fast that it filled the gnawing need to feel him deep within. I moaned and heard someone who sounded vaguely like me saying, "Michel, please."

"Tell me." His voice was husky, barely contained.

"I want..." I paused, he had stopped moving, just stroking my hip with his thumb where he was still holding me up, his full bodyweight on his other arm.

"Tell me."

"Don't stop! God, don't you dare stop!" I was breathless, I could feel a small bead of sweat trail down my back, between my shoulder blades, but the overriding thoughts in my body were: *Don't stop. Deeper. Faster. Now!*

He groaned as he began moving inside of me again and I heard his thoughts as he threw them at me, *That is better, ma douce. Let me hear you. Let me be with you. Don't ever shut me out.*

So, I didn't. I let my mind open up, and felt the flood of emotions and feelings and sensations and thoughts go tumbling out towards him. And felt a reciprocal wash of the same back from him at once, almost taking my breath away at the raw hunger and need from within him. My body was riding a wave of pure desire, every nerve ending on fire, every craving I had begging for their fill, every bit of tension he had built in my body pleading for release. He moved faster at my insistent cries, his own thoughts tumbling in a maelstrom of words; *Beautiful. Perfect. So perfect. Mine.* And then as his rhythm began to falter and my eyes started seeing bright flashes of lights, our breathing coming in uneven gasps, he switched to French, I don't even think he realised what he was doing. *Ma petite belle lumière. Ma belle fille. Tu es parfaits, si parfaits.*

I may not have understood every word he said, but I felt all of him at that moment. Nothing hidden, nothing contrived, it was all of him, and it filled me up with such a beautiful sense of peace, such a wonderful sense of belonging. I felt tears roll down my face as we crested a wave of heat together and came floating down the other side.

We only allowed ourselves a few hours entangled in each other's arms, whispering sweet words, basking in the afterglow of our lovemaking, there was no time to enjoy the moment any longer. Although getting light out, we had a plane to catch. Cairo was waiting.

After being huddled into one of Michel's heavily tinted vehicles, driven by one of his day crew, we headed out to his private hangar at the airport. Bruno had been left in charge of the family business here in New Zealand while we would be gone, no one else was to accompany us. We both felt the less, the better; together we would face this.

The time of the flight was not unimportant; it would mean we landed in Cairo right on their nightfall. The family jet, a *Gulfstream G650*, was fully enclosed in the hangar. As soon as we arrived the hangar doors were closed behind us blocking out the early morning sun which was still trying to make its way up over the horizon, and we made our way on board the blacked out jet. Inside, the windows were all completely shielded, operated automatically at a console beside one of the large leather seats. The interior was exactly as you would expect, soft cream leather, mahogany and maple wood trims, marble-like tiling and polished gold fixtures. The carpet a lush cream and gold design, a small dancing dragon imprinted in a coat of arms, you wouldn't even have noticed it without looking closely, but it was there.

I sunk into one of the seats on the large couch and felt the softness wrap around me; I failed to stifle a moan. Michel laughed as he came to sit next to me, pulling me to him, so his arm was around my shoulders and my back was against his side. I loved being this close to him, feeling his warmth, the rise and fall of his chest. I rested my head back against him and savoured the contact.

"Why don't you sleep, *ma douce*, it is a very long flight and you will need your energy, I think."

Sleep sounded about right then and with his warmth around me and the softness of the leather I was asleep before the plane had finished taxiing and lifted in the air.

I'm not sure how I managed it, but I'd somehow slept so deeply I hadn't felt Michel move me at all. I was no longer wrapped in Michel's arms, but my head was instead resting in his lap. His hand was absently stroking my hair while the other held a small tablet computer with a magazine or newspaper displayed on its screen. He hadn't moved when I opened my eyes, but I knew he'd know I was awake, feel my emotions, notice the change in my breathing.

"How long have I been asleep?" I stretched then, lengthening my legs and arms and arching my back. When I looked up at Michel he had a look of such tenderness on his face, it made it hard to believe this man was, in fact, a vampire. Oh, how the times are changing.

"We are almost there, *ma douce*. You have slept well."

I rolled myself into a sitting position. "The whole trip?" God damn, I must have been tired.

Michel just smiled. "You clearly needed it; I did not think it wise to disturb you, despite the desire to do so on many occasions. You did not even stir for our refuelling stops. So, waking you for my desires seemed unfair."

I rolled my eyes at that and received a staged look that shouted, *what?* in return.

"How long until we land?"

Michel was about to answer when one of his staff entered with a tray of food for me, fresh fruit, toast and jam and coffee; sweet, beautiful, aromatic, freshly ground and brewed, coffee. I could have kissed him. The guy, a human, nodded and quickly left. Michel settled back to watch me eat, sometimes I think it might be his favourite pastime, well maybe his second, anyway.

"We should land in an hour."

Good that would allow me time to eat and freshen up, use that gorgeous, well-appointed bathroom I had spied in a brief glimpse earlier. Nothing like landing after a full day's flying to feel all sweaty and gritty and not at your best. I'm sure vampires can manage it OK, but not little old vampire hunters, that's for sure. The thought of disembarking from this little slice of airborne heaven into the heat that was Cairo at this time of year wasn't appealing.

As I munched on my yummy breakfast, I asked, "What's the plan when we land?"

"We shall try to contact Nafrini. From what you said, they had a respite from the *Cadre*, thanks to your involvement." He no longer looked like he was going to have a coronary over that, but he did stress the words ever so slightly. "They may have been able to move their kin to safety and can now work with us to locate their lost Nosferatin and perhaps organise an attack against the *Cadre*. It is Nafrini's soil; I will have to adhere to her wishes."

Yes, can't upset the powerful joined Nosferatu, we were visitors in her land, albeit invited and allied for the moment, we would still need to be careful how we went.

I freshened up in the bathroom after that, relishing the multi-headed shower facilities and smelly lotions and shampoos. I was sure I'd smell like a florist when I stepped out of the stall, but it seemed subtle, even in the smaller room. The plushness of the jet was just as obvious in here, lovely fittings trimmed in gold, with cream and gold tiles, once again sporting the dancing dragon discreetly here and there. I'd have to ask Michel what the dragon meant; I hadn't seen it anywhere else, just here on board his plane.

I dressed quickly; I could feel the plane begin to descend, my ears needing a stretch of my jaw to pop them. It was a slow decompression, but a sure signal we were approaching Cairo International Airport. From my Dream Walking experience yesterday I knew it would be hot. I had opted for a lightweight three-quarter length sleeve blouse in a light dove grey with close fitting Capri pants, covering my knees, in black. I wanted to blend into the shadows to keep from being seen by the creatures of the night, but I also didn't want to attract any unwanted attention from the Norms either. Dressing appropriately for Egypt made sense.

When I came out of the bathroom, Michel had also changed, not too dissimilar from his usual attire, all black and totally sexy. He was sitting back down on the couch looking relaxed, not at all concerned about what might face us. "I have organised a car to meet us on the tarmac; we shall just have to head directly towards Cairo city centre and try to locate Nafrini there."

"Do you have ideas on where to start?"

"It shouldn't be hard, she will sense me as soon as we land. She will no doubt come to us if able."

Oh, I had forgotten that master vampires of Michel's and Nafrini's level could sense each other. Michel was always aware when someone powerful had entered his city. Handy, I guess if you want to keep hold of your territory from encroaching vampires.

The plane touched down lightly and after a couple of minutes came to rest away from the main Cairo terminals, near hangars which were obviously an area for private jets and the like. I had expected us to be met by customs or something similar, but when the door to the jet was opened, there was just a solitary limousine on the tarmac and a lone figure waiting beside it.

We came down the stairs and walked towards the car. The heat hit like a solid wall; it felt like I was pushing my way through thick molasses. But at the sight of who was waiting for us, I couldn't help it; I couldn't keep the smile from my eyes, or the idiotic grin from my face. He stepped up and took my hand, bending over at the waist and laying a light kiss across my knuckles. His eyes danced in the artificial lighting, his smile blinding all on its own.

"Kiwi. We finally meet in person and you are even more beautiful than I could ever have imagined."

I didn't get to answer, because anything I could have or would have said, was drowned out by a long, low and menacing growl at my side.

So much for diplomacy.

34

HELIOPOLIS

Nero didn't even react, just slowly lowered my hand, never breaking eye contact with me. Eventually, he did let go and turned to bow to Michel.

"Welcome, Michel Durand, to Cairo. Nafrini Al-Suyuti welcomes you to her land."

He said all of this whilst still bowing, head low in respect. He rose now and looked Michel in the eye, never even blanching at the slight glow of magenta and amethyst that had taken up residence there.

"It is kind of Nafrini to provide us with a driver." I'm quite sure that Michel had meant that statement exactly how it sounded. He knew damn well this had to be Nafrini's kindred Nosferatin, but he was also making damn sure Nero knew he wasn't impressed. Men.

"So, what's the plan, Nero?" I thought I'd better get us back on track or we'd end up having a duel right here. I didn't fancy Nero's chances against Michel, but then again, Nero did have some wicked moves.

Immediately Nero shifted his full attention back to me with another of his dazzling smiles. He had been all serious and lacked any facial expression, other than polite welcome when addressing Michel, but now he lit up like a Christmas Tree, all light and happy glow. What was he playing at, antagonising a vampire who had come to help him? Was he seriously that reckless?

I tried to ignore the look he was giving me and knew that no matter what was happening on my face, no matter how good I was at schooling my features to a pleasant mask, Michel had already registered my emotional response to Nero. This was so not going how I had expected it. What had I thought would happen? Well, I admit, I kinda forgot all about the emotion reading thing and just was looking forward to meeting my Nosferatin idol. Because that's what Nero was, I decided, someone I truly looked up to, someone who could teach me so much. I put as much of those thoughts into my head as possible, hoping my emotions, or perhaps a stray projected thought would reflect that instead.

"We have relocated our family and have been awaiting your arrival to mount an attack."

"You know where they are?" I was surprised and amazed he had accomplished so much since I had last seen him in the Dream Walk.

"Yes, I shall brief you both on the way, there is not much time to waste." He seemed very pleased with the news he was relaying, I couldn't blame him, this was exactly what we needed. We all climbed in the back of the car, which had a driver all of its own, that no doubt Michel had been well aware of when he made that little remark. A human's scent and heartbeat stand out quite easily to a nearby vampire.

Nero briefed us on what they had uncovered today as we drove through Cairo's streets heading towards her city centre. Everywhere I looked out of the windows I could see Date Palms swaying in the evening breeze, nothing like our quasi-palm trees back home, the Nikau Palm, these were the real deal. I was also surprised to see so much sand, a reminder of how close the desert was, but interspersed with that sand was a lushness, beautiful greens, like an oasis, right on the side of the road as we zipped past.

The buildings became more impressive as we headed away from the airport, sand coloured, thick set structures, with arched windows and faux balconies, the sidewalks crowded with colourful swaths of cloth. I had expected to see only light coloured clothing, tans and whites, similar to what I had seen Nero in before, but the colour was cheerful and vibrant, quite different from my imaginings. They turned the mono-toned buildings into a backdrop fit for an opera, the coloured clothing making the people stand out in stark relief. There was, of course, a lot of people in whites and pale colours, but they simply blended into the crowd, lost in a kaleidoscope of colours.

Market stalls swam past us as we slowed to negotiate traffic and pedestrians. I glimpsed even more colourful tablecloths with bright blue and green and red Hookahs for sale. Followed on with tea houses, street side seating overflowing with faces, some drinking coffee, others just laughing and talking and more still smoking their Hookahs. It occurred to me that most of those I witnessed were male, but I didn't have time to consider this further as we had arrived at Nafrini's new residence.

Even I felt the wards as we passed under a heavy archway into a cobbled courtyard within. I could see figures surrounding the area, some half-hidden in the shadows by the columns supporting more arches, some up higher on balconies and even more at the entrance securing the door behind us. All reeking *Sanguis Vitam*. Nafrini hadn't taken as large a hit to her entourage as I had expected.

All around the courtyard were windows and doors decorated in ornate carved wooden designs. Beautiful intricate arches, with circles set in relief inside, they looked like a stencil, so pretty and perfect, lay them down on a sheet of paper and trace a pattern through the holes. They were stunning and so unlike anything I had ever seen before in my life.

The door to the limousine was opened, and we all stepped out into the heat of night again. Michel took my hand as soon as I exited behind him, it wasn't an unusual gesture, but I had the feeling it was premeditated, for Nero's benefit. Nero didn't show any signs of noticing and simply led the way into the building itself.

We were greeted by further vampires and in amongst them a large number of humans, all moving around doing their own thing. The sense of community I felt from them was astounding. Vampires were talking to humans with respect and vice versa. There was no overt use of powers here, just one being talking or interacting with another. A part of me realised the rest of the world could gain a lot from what Nafrini and Nero had achieved here.

The inside of the building was as beautiful as the out, lovely furnishings, similar in design to those I had seen in the Dream Walk. Bright colours and rich tapestries, ornate furniture and comfortable covers, pillows upon pillows and a slightly fruity smell in the air. Cinnamon mixed with apple, I think. There was a lot of marble and wood and smooth white sandblasted walls, all of which lent itself to the plush furnishings gracefully, interspersed here and there with delicate statues on high plinths.

Despite having to move so quickly, Nafrini had somehow secured a palace for her people in just under 24 hours since I had last been with them. Influential, she clearly was.

Finally, we entered a smaller room, decorated much the same as elsewhere, cushions on the floor to the side, a desk with comfortable chairs surrounding it, bookcases behind filled to the brim with brightly coloured leather bindings. Standing at the far end of the room was an elegant, beautifully clothed woman, she was perhaps almost six feet tall, with fine features on her deeply tanned face, high cheekbones and delicate long fingers in her hands. She had long black hair down past her waist, loose and shiny and shimmering in the candle light of the room. She was dressed in the most beautiful shade of purple, amethyst mixed with pomegranate, long sheaths of fabric, folding over themselves and draped perfectly over her shoulders, showing just the barest hint of smooth skin beneath.

Her eyes were alight with colour; deep amber laced with cocoa and a hint of copper flecks. They were heavily made up, with shades of copper and cinnamon elongating the roundness of their shape. She looked stunning, there were no two ways about it, she was a queen.

As soon as she spotted Michel, her face broke into the most hypnotic smile. There was no power there, just sheer natural brilliance, lighting up her face and eyes even further. She glided towards us with her hand extended. Michel took a step away from me and bent at the waist in a bow similar to Nero's, all grace and practised movements; he took her hand in his. Bent his head and placed a lingering kiss on her smooth skin.

Part of me wondered if his actions were in response to Nero's at the airport, giving as good as he got, but all hopes of that were dashed when Nafrini spoke in a low and sultry voice thick with eastern African accent, against his ear, loud enough for everyone to hear.

"It has been a long time, my love, you should not hide yourself away so. You have been missed."

What the...? *Did they know each other?* For some reason, I hadn't seen this coming. Despite knowing how old Michel is and how old Nafrini is and how vampires didn't just stay in one place but moved around the globe. Despite knowing Michel would have a history I wasn't privy to, that he'd had a life before even coming to New Zealand, before me. I had never once stopped to think he would know Nafrini. Stupid. Stupid. Me.

And then came the anger. Why had Michel chosen not to mention this? Once again he had omitted something that might just have prepared me for this moment. Was it intentional? Did he hope to get a response from me? To what avail? I realised I'd just been standing there staring at the exchange between them, stock still, like a statue, my hands fisted at my sides. Michel would have felt the emotions rolling over me, Nafrini would have sensed my hitched breath, my increased heart rate and Nero, well Nero was just watching me with steady eyes. No sympathy, no sadness for the position I now found myself in, just a steady gaze of interest. Did *everyone* want to see me throw a fit?

Well, they obviously don't know Kiwi girls then. We're hard and tough and have a bloody great sense of pride. There was no way I was letting them see me crumble. I don't know what protocol called for in situations such as these. Do you wait to be introduced? Curtsey? Grovel at her feet? I really didn't care, so I took a step forward and put on my most dazzling smile, stuck my hand out and said, "Hi, Nafrini. I'm Luce. It's a pleasure to meet you finally."

Out of the corner of my eye, I saw Nero smile, just a brief touch to his lips. Nafrini removed her hand from Michel's and turned her gaze on me. I'm not sure I was receiving the same startling amber and cocoa look as Michel had, this time they seemed a little daunting, a little scary around the edges, rather than beautiful, but she smiled and shook my hand anyway. Whew!

When she had removed her hand from mine her eyes lingered in an appraising slide over my body, without looking away she said, "She is intriguing, Michel. I understand now why you chose New Zealand. Why you sacrificed your lifestyle in Paris. I had always wondered what would cause you to give up such a position."

Michel stiffened slightly next to me, it wasn't anything overtly obvious, just a slight twitch to his arms. I don't think Nafrini would have noticed, but I'm getting good at sensing these little pauses in his shields, these moments that he simply can no longer hide from me. He didn't like where this conversation was heading; there was something here he didn't want me to know. I didn't turn to look at him, just kept my pleasant face and steady gaze on the Amazon woman to my front, but in my mind, I sent out the thought, *Paris*?

He ignored me, I hadn't expected him to answer, but I knew he had heard me. This was something we would have to cover later. Instead he decided to take control of the conversation himself, a typical Michel tactic.

"You have found yourself a lovely home, Nafrini, at such short notice, it is commendable."

She laughed openly at that, acknowledging his rebuff. Her laugh was musical, like the tinkle of a wind chime, it didn't sound right with her low and sultry voice, but somehow it still suited her. I wondered if it was practised.

"I have friends in the President's Cabinet; this home is on loan, a small unused section of the Heliopolis Palace. We have, of course, made improvements." She was referring to the wards, they weren't normal, I just wondered what she had done to create such protection, how much of Nero's power was she using?

"Now come and sit down, friends, we have much to discuss." Nafrini indicated an area to the side with low cushions, she sat herself down in a fluid motion, all grace and sleek movements, settling into the cushions like the queen that she is. Nero was next and looked just as graceful, well practised at slipping onto the floor with style. Michel didn't falter, but followed suit, equally as elegant, ending up looking stunning against the backdrop of the colourful cushions. That just left me. I haven't sat on the floor on cushions since I was at Kindergarten, my style hasn't improved much since then. I just thanked my lucky stars I wasn't wearing a short skirt after all.

Nero produced a map of Cairo. Heliopolis was actually a suburb, just east of the city centre where they had been when I Dream Walked to them last night. This was not a usual area for vampires, they tend to entrench themselves in the middle of a place, so they hoped that it would be overlooked, but with the level of wards on the place, any stray vampire would have difficulty breaching the security as well. Of course, the level of power needed to maintain that protection could also attract unwanted interest. It was a catch 22. They had hedged their bets with the location but solidified with wards. I hoped it paid off.

The *Cadre* had ensconced themselves near the city centre; a suburb called Coptic Cairo, part of Old Cairo itself and Nero had managed to do a quick reconnaissance of the building and sketched up what he had found out. There were some 80 of the vampires left, and he proceeded to show us where they were located around the complex, including where he thought Amisi was being held. The plan was to head out immediately, leaving a small contingent of Nafrini's vampires to guard the rest of the Nosferatin community. We made quick plans of attack and our intended approach to the *Cadre's* stronghold and then rose to head to the vehicles that had been assembled in the courtyard.

Nero pulled me aside while Nafrini and Michel were discussing further features of the plan. "There is time for you to meet the others if we hurry. It will only be a short visit, but I thought you would like the opportunity to meet some of your kind."

Somehow Nero always knew what to say to me, what was important and what was not. Not that I'm saying rescuing the stolen Nosferatin and destroying the *Cadre* were not important. It's just the thought of more of my kind being so close by, so near and if things did go against us tonight, I would not have had the chance to see them, to greet them, to be with them. This was a piece of me that I had felt missing since learning of my kind, where I came from, who we are. It felt like a huge hole in the centre of my chest, gaping and gnawing at my insides.

I managed to cover it with my feelings for Michel, dim it slightly with my contact with Nero, but never really fill it; it was always still there.

I forced myself not to let it show, but I wasn't fooling him. He gently brushed my cheek and nodded to Nafrini, having obviously sent a silent communication to his kindred and led me by the hand from the room. I'm not sure if Michel noticed, or if he was too busy with his *old friend*, but he didn't stop me, he didn't come after me, he didn't even send me a thought.

We ran down a corridor, then another and another, somehow ending up well inside the building, away from the courtyard and the cars, somewhere to the rear and off to the right-hand side. We burst through double doors into a light and airy room, the smell of fruit in the air, from the Hookahs in use to one side. All the eyes of the people gathered there turned to look at us as we entered.

Men were off to one side, smoking the Hookahs, the women and children on the other, talking and laughing and preening their young. They looked happy and content. However there was an undercurrent of anxiety, hidden behind the friendly faces that greeted me. I had seen it when we banged through the door. Once they spotted Nero and his hand in mine, his face smiling, they had relaxed only then.

"This is my Kiwi. I have told you of her, family. She has come to help." He turned to me then with a gorgeous smile painted on his face, the full lips curved deliciously, his eyes shining brightly, cinnamon and coffee swirling in their midsts. You could not have been affected by Nero's smile. Besides, I've always loved coffee.

The people began to gather, to hug me, kiss my cheeks, to hold my hands and in the case of the children, to pull on my pants and shirt. It was a little overwhelming. They were speaking mainly in Arabic, a beautifully musical sound, words I couldn't understand, a lot of Ls. But some of them were speaking English, and I heard the odd word or two, "Prophecy", "She lives", "Seeker". It didn't make sense, and I was about to ask Nero what they were saying when we felt a large shift in the tiled floor and heard a rumble come towards us from the front of the palace like an earthquake rolling out from its source.

I stumbled, along with the mass of people about me and only just managed to not tip over on top of them. Nero had stilled, cocking his head to the side. "It is Nafrini. The *Cadre* have found us, they have come."

"They can't breach the wards. They can't get in." I said, but not quite managing to hide my alarm and concern.

I was already running after him, he had shouted in Arabic to a few of the men in the room, who were blockading the door behind us as we sailed through. "They already have," came his reply.

We started heading back the way we had come, but the corridor had fallen in on itself, so we backtracked and took another hall off to the side. This one led further towards the right hand rear of the building, away from the Nosferatin community and not towards the fight, where Nafrini and Michel were no doubt battling.

"We're going to have to go outside and come back around the front of the building; there is no other way through," Nero shouted above the noise of cracking concrete and shattering walls. We slipped out of the side of the building, Nero moving his hand over the door and muttering a few low words in Arabic, or maybe Latin, I couldn't be sure. I felt the ward give way and then he paused on the other side and resealed it. I knew we had powers to place protection wards on buildings, but I had absolutely no idea how this was carried out. Watching Nero now, it looked like some sort of spell or charm. I realised I had so much more to learn about who I was and what I was capable of doing. I only hoped I lived long enough to find out.

We slunk along in the shadows made by the palace walls, hugging the side of the building to stay out of sight. By the time we made it to the front of the palace it was obvious the fight had been taken inside. Dust hung in the air like an early morning fog on the farm, unmoving in the still of the night. I was about to take a step towards the entrance, intending on attacking the *Cadre* from the back, similar to what I had done last night, when Nero grabbed my arm.

He looked torn, when I turned to glance at him, anguished and slightly pale. "What is it? What's wrong?" It could be anything, Nafrini is hurt, Michel?

"This is not our battle tonight, Kiwi. We must fight elsewhere."

"What do you mean, Nero? Of course this is our battle. Michel is in there. Nafrini. The others."

He shook his head. "Amisi is not with the *Cadre*, she is still at their base, we need to act now, before it is too late. Nafrini has asked us to rescue her. There is not much time."

He saw the dawning look of horrible comprehension on my face, his only looked sadder.

"She doesn't think they'll make it, does she? She wants us to free Amisi before it all ends."

Nero reached up and touched my face softly, wiping away some dust and stonewall grime.

"Our lives are not such a bad exchange for a young innocent, are they?"

I don't know, I kinda liked mine.

But, I just took a deep breath and nodded, the last thing I did before we tore through the nearby streets and away from the battle at Heliopolis was to send a thought out on the wind....

Michel! I love you!

I didn't get a reply.

35
THE COPTIC

We had run down several streets before Nero stopped by a sleek black *Alfa Romeo* car parked next to the kerb. I thought it must have been one of theirs, parked away from the palace as a backup, but when he ran his hand over the car's lock and muttered a few words in that other language, I realised I was wrong.

"You're stealing this?"

He flashed me a smile as the door clicked opened and simply slid into the driver's seat, reaching over and unlocking my door. "Get in, there is not much time."

I guess Nero wasn't opposed to Grand Theft Auto then.

The car was fast, but Nero seemed to make it fly through the streets away from Heliopolis. We swerved past pedestrians, still out socialising as the night wore on, bumped over uneven roads and screamed around corners barely on all four wheels. The engine sounded rich and throaty as Nero put it through its paces. I silently reached for my seatbelt and secured it in place.

The colours all around us seemed to be flying past in a blur. At one stage I couldn't tell if it was people or late night market stalls that were making the rush of colour streak past my window, I had to close my eyes and force my uneasy stomach to settle.

"I am sorry if my driving is upsetting you, Kiwi, but the Coptic is a fair distance away, we must proceed with all haste."

I just nodded, not trusting myself to comment. He reached over and squeezed my hand to reassure me, just as we came to a surprisingly tight stretch of road. The side of the car screeched against a parked vehicle, swiping our wing mirror off right by my side, sending sparks into the air and finger-nails-on-chalkboard sounds down my spine. Suddenly, I found I could talk after all. "Two hands on the wheel! Two hands on the wheel!"

Nero's attention returned to the road with a look of grim determination. We made it through that impossibly narrow road only to come out into an over-crowded square of some description. People were not only milling around the sides in large groups, but crossing the divide casually. When they heard our car horn frantically beeping, they began to jump and dive out of the way, but part of me knew there was no way we were going to make it across the square without connecting with someone. Nero slammed on the brakes, and the car fishtailed wildly, nose down and tyres screaming, and we finally came to a stop right in the middle of the square.

No loud thumps. Thank God.

And then I felt the bruise; the seatbelt had already started making, blossom across my shoulder, chest and lower abdomen. Oh God it hurt, I sucked in a breath, but that only made it worse.

Nero was trying to get the car started, but we had gone over some part of a market stall as we entered the square and obviously done some damage, smoke was starting to filter out around the bonnet in front, small at first and then thickening as I watched transfixed by it.

The people in the square were shouting and raising their fists at us, rocking the car from side to side, banging on the roof and doors. I didn't blame them, we had almost killed someone here tonight. Finally, Nero shouted, "We will have to go on foot from here, it is not much farther."

He began to get out of the car, and I grabbed his arm. "What about the crowd?" But he had already gone and was pushing through the people on his side of the car to get to me. My door suddenly got wrenched open, I hadn't unlocked it, but when Nero opened his driver's door, mine had automatically unlocked. Damn central locking. I was pulled out of the vehicle by large rough hands, a dark-skinned man started shouting in Arabic at me while shaking me like a leaf.

I couldn't focus properly on the people around me; my head felt like it was going to be snapped off my neck by the force of this man's arms; the world was just a crazy cacophony of noises; loud, jarring, booming noises. Then I realised I could fight. This might be a human, but I know how to fight, and right now, this man was threatening me.

I brought my arms up in front of me and then roughly swung them out to either side, snapping the man's grip on my upper arms and threw his arms wide. He didn't stumble, but he was in shock. I don't think he realised a woman would fight back. He recovered himself quickly then and with a look of anger on his face he came at me, fists bunched, ready to strike. By this time Nero had arrived and he clamped a hand on the man's shoulder, saying something harshly in Arabic.

The man's head swivelled towards the new threat, but he stopped. He shouted something back at Nero, which I had no way of understanding, looked at me long and hard, then back to Nero, who nodded and then the man simply left. The group around us also dispersed with muttered grumbles and sideways glances, not all of them friendly, but some I noticed were in surprise, and could that be? Awe?

Nero grabbed my arm, right where it was sore from beefy feature's grasp and tugged me into a run away from the now somewhat silent crowd. I gasped at his hold over that tender spot, and he moved his hand down to hold mine, still tugging me forward. I finally found my feet and pace and fell into rhythm beside him.

"What was all that about? What did you say to stop him?"

Nero looked at me quickly, just a glance, then back towards the street we were running down, his face was hidden, a mask of concentration. I didn't think he would answer me, but he said, "I told them you were a *Child of Nut*."

I skipped around a group of people and rejoined him in the middle of the road, keeping pace with his long strides. "What does that mean?"

"My people have a legend, that Thoth, the God of Wisdom and Knowledge, once prophesied a child would be born to Nut who would become Pharaoh after Ra." He stopped talking to negotiate another group of people, then rejoined me and ran silently for a few paces. I was about to ask, *what the hell does that mean?* When he continued. "It is told that she had five children, Osiris was the first born and it was proclaimed to the heavens on his birth, 'The Lord of All comes forth into the Light!' We are the children of the Light, Kiwi. We force out evil and banish the Dark. To my people, we are the *Children of Nut*."

"How did *that* stop him, it's just a legend."

"To my people, it is not."

I didn't know what to say to that. It was just a legend, but it had got us out of a tight spot, so who was I to complain?

"Why did he believe you?" Another dodge around a group of younger people, loud and boisterous. They have teens in Egypt too then. Huh.

The streets had become more narrow, the buildings so much older. There were parts of walls bisecting alleyways that looked as old as time itself, or at the very least perhaps Roman in their origin. It was a rabbit warren of paving, low walls and crooked buildings. At any other time, it would have been a lovely place to stop and take photos. Why is it on my first trip to Egypt I don't even get to be a tourist? I had no doubt I would not be seeing the Pyramids anytime soon.

He shrugged, a simple yet elegant movement on him. "It is easy to see with you."

That didn't make any sense at all, but just as I was about to voice that, he took hold of my wrist and steered me into the shadows, slowing our pace down to just a creep.

"We are almost there. Let us be cautious."

"What's the plan?" I whispered as we were hunkered down behind a low wall some ten metres from The Coptic Museum. The *Cadre* hadn't settled for a simple dwelling as their hide-out, they had commandeered The Coptic Museum, a beautiful old sandstone building engraved with arched designs and delicate mouldings along its roof line. The main entrance was a squat building, compared to the rest of the museum around it, with a flat roof. The glow of master vampire eyes obvious, now and then on top of the entrance building, standing guard. Between us and the main entrance was a courtyard with two perfectly square green grass areas, each planted with a mini palm tree, and a large expanse of paving. Not an ounce of cover anywhere to be seen, crossing the courtyard unnoticed was going to be impossible.

"We go in from the top. Take out the guards there and enter through the roof access."

It was good as far as plans went, the buildings on either side of the museum were the same height as the outer buildings of The Coptic, which were all higher than the entrance building. If we could enter one of those and jump from their rooftop to The Coptic and then down to the entrance building, we might just be able to do it. Nero started moving off, back away from the entrance and towards the building on the left.

The neighbouring building was made up of various shops with what appeared to be apartments above. Nero ran his hands over the door to one shop, muttering his magic words quietly and the door clicked open. Dark inside, we negotiated our way past touristy objects, brightly coloured materials, Hookahs and small figurines of Pharaohs and Sphinxes, with the odd Pyramid or two.

At the rear of the building was a store room, a workshop and kitchen facilities, I guess for making morning tea and to the left a stairwell leading up into darkness. We quietly stepped on the stairs, expecting them to creak, but they remained silent as we ascended past the closed door to the living area. A T.V. could be heard, passed unattended bedrooms above and finally reaching the door to the fire escape and roof access.

Another muttered word from Nero and a wave of his hand over the door knob, and we were out on the external fire escape and climbing. The final steps to the roof top surrounded by dry heat and the noises of the city settling for the night.

Nero crouched at the edge of the building, trying to remain unseen. I knew we would have to move fast, the vampires guarding the roof would sense us well before we approached. Initially, they would assume our heartbeats belonged to the occupied buildings surrounding The Coptic, but once we landed on that building and made our way towards them, they would know an attack was on. There was just simply no way to sneak up on a vampire.

We both looked at each other, Nero's eyes shining in the dim light of the streets. I couldn't see their colour, but I knew there'd be gold and cinnamon and maybe coffee flecks dancing there. Right now they looked big and dark and endlessly deep. He reached up and ran the back of his fingers down my cheek, resting his hand at the side of my neck.

"Whatever happens here tonight, Kiwi, it has been an honour and delight to have finally met you."

I smiled, how could I not? He was warmth and light and everything good in this world; I couldn't imagine a world without him in it. He leant in and lightly dusted my lips with his, a soft, warm meeting, too brief, not enough.

"Let us do this." And then he was over the edge of our building and running full speed across The Coptic's roof.

I launched myself after him, feeling my heartbeat rise and knowing the alarm bells would already be ringing through the vampire guards' minds and probably on to those inside as well. Vampires can communicate telepathically, it was a given we had just ruined our element of surprise.

Nero made contact first, rushing straight at the first vampire to greet his approach, he launched into the air in a spin and sailed past the guard leaving him a trail of dust behind. He paused only briefly to prepare for the next and began his spin again. I pulled my gaze away from him towards the vampires coming from the side. They had spotted Nero and were heading straight for him, they hadn't registered my heartbeat or presence in the storm that was Nero right now. I took advantage of their distraction and lunged at the back of one of the stragglers.

My stake slid home with a satisfying squelch; then dust coated the air and everything in it. Two vampires who had moments ago been hell bent on getting Nero spun around and came for me. Oh goody.

Their eyes glowed eerily in the night, and we circled each other briefly. It wasn't long before one came at me from the front and I rolled out of his approaching grasp slicing my stake across his stomach. His growl was low but controlled, a minor gash that would heal almost instantly. I had come to a stop in a crouch but didn't stay there long, launching myself at the other vampire and managing a strike to his upper chest, that bounced off with the flick of his wrist. Unfortunately, I went spinning too at the tremendous force behind that casual movement.

I landed in a heap to the side and glanced up to see Nero had stopped spinning and was now battling hand to hand with three vampires. More were coming out through the rooftop access; I could only hope we lured them all outside and managed to kill off the bulk of the guard on Amisi, even before we entered the museum itself. If there were still the same amount inside, then God help us.

Two more vampires joined my attackers; the odds were rapidly depleting on my side, but Nero wasn't doing much better. Had he realised there'd still be so many here at their hide-out? Did he care? He certainly wasn't showing any shock at their approach, just a single-minded concentration and an increased look of dogged determination on his face.

I had already moved from my position and now found myself facing off with two vampires in the front and the other two circling around the back. I did not want them to make it there, so I struck out quickly to the vampire on the right, gashing his arm and receiving a shriek in return. I spun around behind him in a move I didn't even know I was capable of, flying through the air and watching the horizon spin slowly around me and landed a blow to the second vampire across his neck. I needed to get more accurate, none of my strikes were connecting where they should, but these vampires were fast, super fast and I just didn't have Nero's speed.

I continued to move in that slow spin aiming for my next victim and praying for a just a little break in my luck. But as my arm came out to land the blow, stake tip already resting on the vamp's back, right above his heart, I felt an excruciatingly tight grip on my wrist and a sudden pull of my body as I went flying through the air only to be hit by the bulk of a solid wall. The solid wall turned out to be a vampire, and he didn't waste time in getting a boot into my side as I lay at his feet. He was pulling back his size 12 shoe, ready to go in for the next rib cracking hit, when I stabbed my stake through his other foot and watched the blood begin to well around its tip.

He screamed out a curse in Arabic, but by then another vamp had hauled me to my feet and was attempting to strangle the life out of me, his face inches from mine, his red eyes blinding in their intensity. I had not been able to pull the stake out of the other vampire's boot and was trying alternately to grab my second from inside my shirt and also pry his fingers from around my neck. Neither was working, my breathing was shallow, my heartbeat pounding, my head had started thumping, the pulse in the side of my neck sending shockwaves into my skull with each ever increasing beat. Flashes of bright white interspersed with strobing black had already begun their deadly dance before my eyes. All of this happening in less time than it takes to think it, I was running out of time, and that meant so was Michel.

I was only too aware of what Michel was feeling right now, somehow the nearness of my death made me more in tune with him. I could feel his efforts in the battle he was fighting, his determination to win at all costs, the desire to protect me from death so strong. He was not concerned for his own safety at this point, only in so much as his death would mean mine. He was fighting like a man possessed, holding his own, as none of those around him had even remotely his power level, but despite this, the numbers were vast. The *Cadre* had been so much bigger than we had expected, those facing Michel and Nafrini amounted to over 50 still, and yet there was already so much dust. The chances of overcoming those odds were slim, yet Michel never wavered. His only thought to preserve his own life so that I would not die.

I was struck by the sheer selflessness of his emotions, he was taking a beating, but only because he was holding back from placing himself in a position that would mean my death. The overriding thought in his brain was of me.

I couldn't let him down. I tried to think of what I could do to get out of this situation. *Get a stake and stab him.* I couldn't feel my fingers, couldn't even tell if they were near my shirt, near my stake, if they could grip around it. *Pry the vampire's fingers off my neck.* Yet again my hands weren't working, I now realised they were lying limply at my sides, my arms just tingling, but not able to follow the commands from my brain.

I could feel my heartbeat faltering, my chest was so tight from lack of air; the world had grown dim, and a sense of fear laced with stillness had begun to envelop me. I couldn't remember why I was here, what was happening. Nothing made sense anymore, but I knew I should be scared. Strange, though, I wasn't.

What was I doing here?

Why am I so tired?

Maybe I should just let that blackness that's coming in arrive; maybe I'm meant to sleep. That's it; I'll just sleep. Sleep sounds so good right now.

Fight back! Don't give up!

What was that? It sounded so far away. Can't be important.

But sleep is, back to sleep. I want to sleep.

Lucinda! Fight!

OK, I heard it that time, and it really was a voice. A loud and demanding voice, but also it wrapped me up in warmth and light, then slapped me in the face.

I opened my eyes and stared straight into the depths of hell, two red glowing orbs hovering in front of me. I took what little breath I could and croaked, "You're going to let go of me now."

Nothing happened, he just continued to grimace and sneer and kept on with his pursuit of crushing my windpipe and throat to smithereens. So, stubborn girl that I am, I repeated it, and this time I really meant it.

"LET GO OF MY THROAT, NOW!"

He immediately released me and the air came rushing in my mouth and down my sore throat like a wave of burning fire. I doubled over trying to catch my breath and was immediately grabbed from behind by another vampire. The first was still staring at me, slightly puzzled, so I shouted at it, holding his gaze, "KILL ALL THE VAMPIRES. DO IT NOW!"

And with that he was off, racing around in that vampiric speed, ripping one head off after the other. It was only after he had left me in the grip of vamp number two that I realised I should have commanded him to help free me.

Number two wasn't wasting any time, he wrenched my head to the side with one hand, whilst still gripping me from behind with the other and then I felt his fangs pierce the skin at the base of my neck and the immediate drain of blood being sucked. It was torturous, like every vein, every nerve ending was being pulled out as he sucked. I could feel the nerves straining and tightening and then simply retracting, all the way up my body. The threads of agony from each line of nerve went from my toes, up through my legs, over my entire torso, my arms, my chest, my neck and tearing out through his mouth. I heard myself screaming, but it only seemed to make him more determined, his grip tightening and the sucking sensation deepening. Oh God, this was it. It had to be it; he was taking so much more from me than Michel ever had. This was going on too long.

I couldn't glaze him; he was behind me, his face buried in my neck, covered by my sweat soaked hair, I couldn't look him in the eyes, something that was essential in order to be glazed. I fumbled for my stake, I could feel it, against the skin of my stomach, stuck down the sheath in the waistband of my pants, but I couldn't grip it. My shirt was in the way, or my trousers were, or his arm, or something, but I simply couldn't grip it. And now the lights were back, dancing a pretty pattern in my face, a mesmerising duel of colour, not just blinding white and strobing black, but glinting greens, blazing blues, rushing reds, and sunshine yellows. It was beautiful. It spun and ducked and dived and weaved, it twirled around me and wrapped me in its glow. *So beautiful.*

I don't remember what happened next. The colours all came closer, surrounding me, bathing me, they were everywhere and nowhere, they were so dazzling and so welcoming, but I was ripped from their warm embrace and thrust instead into cold darkness.

So deep and black and complete.

36
DEATH BECOMES YOU

I came to lying on the hard bitumen smelling rooftop of The Coptic, the concerned face of Nero looking down at me, the stars shining brightly around his head, striking against the deep blackness of space. He looked a little worse for wear. His clothing was torn, revealing deep gashes along his shoulder, blood was oozing out of the side, making a slow track down his chest, my eyes followed its progress, until I could see it no more beneath the white linen of his shirt.

He smiled, that all encompassing, brightly beautiful, smile. I sighed. I felt extremely light headed. Even lying still on my back on the flat and level surface of the roof, the world was slowly spinning, but the blurriness that had at first rimmed my vision was fading and I noticed too, that the spinning was becoming more apathetic, more lethargic in its twirling of the world.

"Did we win?" My voice was barely a whisper, my throat still dry and sore from the strangling, my strength almost non-existent.

"Only because of you, my little Kiwi." Nero looked at me a little strangely then, as if seeing me for the first time, his eyes devoured my face, his hands stroked my arm and cheek. "You were amazing. If it were not for you, we would have succumbed."

Huh? I just had the crap beaten out of me, nearly died, twice, and I saved the day? How was that possible?

I felt my eyebrows furrow, I frowned at him and managed a very ineloquent, "What?"

He chuckled, still stroking my arm, but now raising me slightly into a sitting position. I leaned against him as the world swam and then slowly stilled again. His mouth was against my head, right above my ear, I could feel his warm breath as it traced the line of my neck, down, so softly. His words were soft against my ear. "I thought I was lost. There were too many of them, I had led us into a trap. I was barely holding my own and then a vampire started running through the midst culling out one after the other. They had barely realised what was happening by the time he killed ten of their men. They rallied, more coming out from inside. My hopes were again dashed and then I saw you. In the arms of that vampire," - he stopped, took in a deep breath, then let it out so very slowly. I could feel him shaking slightly beside me. - "you were so pale, so white, your eyes were closed, you were no longer fighting. And then, and then you started glowing, all these colours, so bright, so vivid, so beautiful and after a moment that light started dancing around you, through you and then suddenly out from you in every direction and where it landed on a vampire, they simply turned to dust. I have never seen or heard of anything like that."

He pulled away from me then and looked me in the eyes, his so serious, so intense, swirls of gold and cinnamon dancing in their depths. He looked like he was going to say something, then quickly changed his mind, giving a small shake of his head.

I didn't know what to say to that. Who would? I was going to get a reputation for glowing in ever more bizarre and completely brilliant ways. Part of me wondered numbly, if I might just blaze myself out one day. I had no idea what had happened, I was sure it had been someone else who had come to our aid, someone like Michel, swirling around in colours of light so blinding, so perfect. But now this. It was all too much to comprehend.

"Where's Amisi?" I decided the best course of action was inaction, as far the glowing was concerned, getting us back on track seemed like much more steadying ground.

"I have not been inside, I came straight to you."

I pushed him away and stood up, the movement momentarily making the world go black and I reached out instinctively to steady myself. Nero grasped my hand and held tight.

"Are you all right, Kiwi? Do you wish to rest, I will go and get Amisi. I do not think there are any more vampires, no more have come to the rooftop in the past few minutes."

I took a breath in to calm myself and chase away the cold sweat that had broken out against my skin. I hated feeling faint, it's one of those sensations that rip right through to the core of you, taking away any sense of control.

"We don't know that. And I'll be fine." I glanced around and spotted my stake, the one I had lost in kicker's foot, it was now just sitting lonely in amongst the dust. I managed to get over there and bend down and pick it up without vomiting or falling over, so that was a bonus.

"Let's do this, Nero. Let's get her out, now."

He nodded, that quick, short nod that he does, a slight look of concern on his face, but he offered no argument.

We entered through the roof access, down a short flight of stairs. The corridor they opened up onto was brightly lit, quiet and bare. Nero fished the schematics out of his pocket and quickly familiarised himself with where we were.

"This way," he said, setting off at a trot.

We had rounded two corners without incident, when we came face to face with a vampire. He hadn't expected to see us, maybe he hadn't got the memo yet that we had just dusted over thirty of his buds on the rooftop, but he recovered himself instantly and thrust a hand at Nero's neck.

I had my stake over his heart in a flash, he stilled. "If you don't let go I'll push this home."

"You'll push it home anyway, Nosferatin, why should I release my grip?" His accent was thick, but understandable. You don't get to live 200 years without picking up a few languages along the way. He spoke English well.

He also had a point. I had no intention of not staking him. Who was I kidding? So I just went ahead and did it anyway. When the dust settled and Nero was left standing there with his head cocked slightly to the side and eyebrows raised, I just shrugged my shoulders and turned back towards our goal.

Finally we came to the room we believed Amisi to be in, there were no guards at the door. What did that mean? Had they moved her? Was she already joined? Had they killed her thinking it was the only recourse left them? Only one way to find out.

Nero ran his hand over the door and then when he obviously didn't detect any protection wards, another ominous sign, he wrenched it open and we stepped in. There was no mad roll to the side, like you see in the movies, no stakes out drawn and ready to fire, well they were out, just not held in a teacup grip pointed at the ground like a movie cop, we just simply walked in knowing this was not a surprise entry, knowing that we were quite expected.

The room was full of display cases along the outer edge, old and broken pieces of pottery and objects delicately sitting on black cloths and felt covered plinths within, the walls were adorned with mosaics, some still brightly shining with flecks of gold, others so worn you could hardly make out the Pharaoh it depicted. There was a deep sense of history in this room, that these things in here had seen more of the world than I could ever imagine, and I wasn't just talking about the museum pieces.

Down the end of the widened central walkway was a vampire, tall and well built, dressed immaculately in a close fitting black suit and deep blue shirt and slightly lighter blue tie. He was light skinned, a hint of cream to his toning, had short black hair which shined in the down lights from above, his face was nondescript really, handsome, but not a face you would remember. He simply would fade into the background in a crowd. His eyes were a pale distant sky blue.

Beside him was another vamp holding a young girl, maybe eighteen or nineteen years old, definitely Amisi, she looked like Nero in so many ways. Long black hair, dark skin and delicate facial features. She was scared, but hiding it well. Go girl, good for you.

I could feel the presence of more vampires in the room, fanned out around us, maybe four, two on either side. So, an even half dozen, not entirely bad odds, but the vamp holding Amisi did have a knife to her throat. That kinda ruined any advantage I might have felt.

Old dark suit smiled openly at us and spread his hands in greeting. "Welcome, Lucinda and Nero, we have been waiting." He had a cultured English accent, rather like Queen Elizabeth, it was strong and masculine though, it purred a little across my skin. He was being subtle, his *Sanguis Vitam* well contained, but I didn't doubt for a moment that this man was powerful, so very, very powerful.

"You were both impressive, your antics on the rooftop quite entertaining." He called the killing of thirty of his vampires entertaining, like it had been a programme on T.V. and the ads were now on and he was having a nice little chat with his guests about what had just been screened. Smooth.

Nero and I hadn't said a word, we hadn't moved, we knew a trap when we saw one. The vampires on the roof were a mere delaying tactic, not the real thing, a distraction to wear us down, to make us lower our guard. It had worked. Nothing we could do now would improve the odds on us getting out of here alive, of us freeing Amisi unharmed.

"We have been following you a long time, Nero, you have remained very elusive, even in your own country. I am so glad we finally meet." He'd been looking at Nero directly, a warm look on his face, but he turned now to me, giving me the full force of his attention. His eyes glowed a slightly darker shade of blue, with a short swirl of crimson and I nearly staggered under the weight of them. "You, however, have been a most pleasant surprise, my child." He laughed then, a really creepy chuckle, he might as well as been screaming, *mwah haw haw!* for all it sounded like. I felt a chill dash down my spine. "You, I believe, are special." He paused then, tapping his finger against his cheek, as though contemplating something. I really wasn't sure I wanted to know what though.

"Come!" he said and the crimson in his eyes flashed. I found myself taking a step forward, Nero reached out to take my arm, to stop my progress, "Luce!" It was the first time he had called me that, I thought, then brushed him off and kept walking towards Death. Because that was what he felt like, I understood completely what this thing was, he was Death and he wanted me to know it.

I stopped just in front of him, swaying slightly, like a sapling in a breeze, but there was no breeze in here, just the chill that had seeped into my bones, that made me shiver ever so slightly.

I realised my body may not be under my control, but my mind was and I could talk. I wasn't going to just let Death stare me in the face and not do anything about it. I may not be able to fight with my fists or my legs, but I could show no fear in my voice.

"Who are you?" It was steady, even, neutral. I was thrilled at that.

"My name is Charles." As soon as he said his name, a barrage of images flashed before my eyes, as if the name alone held power enough to control me. Charles covered in mud, dressed in furs and animal pelts. Charles standing in a field the colour of blood, holding a severed head up and receiving a battle cry from those around him. Charles riding a horse, chasing someone down, impaling him with a staff. Charles laying waste to a village, from one ramshackle hut to another, nobody spared; men, women, children, his fangs glinting in the moonlight, the cries of those he assailed flying away on the wind. One image blended into the next in a collage of colours and smells and sounds making my head pound and my stomach churn.

"Stop it." It wasn't steady, even or neutral, it was a pitiful whisper, a plea. He'd made his point.

The images faded into black, then colour slowly seeped in as reality enclosed me once again in its grip. I was still standing in front of him, swaying, but upright. His gaze was fixed, a hardness to his features, I couldn't tell if it was the real him or a mask.

He looked at me intently, cocked his head to the side and smiled. "You have joined. Such a pity. You would have made a fine prize. However, you shall not be wasted."

He reached out his long thin-fingered hand towards me and I knew, without a doubt, that I did not want this thing to touch me, at all, ever. My internal monologue started hammering away in a frantic high pitched voice; *Get out! Get away! Run! Spin! Light up! Don't let him touch you! Back up! Drop! Hide! Roll to the side! Do anything, anything at all, but do not let him touch you!*

I kind of sympathised with it, I didn't want him to touch me either, but I couldn't move. I couldn't breathe. I think my heart had thumped its last beat, it was so still. Then his cold hand cupped my face and for a moment nothing happened, and then pain. Such terrible, crushing, excruciating pain, through my cheek, where his hand was touching, right through my body and all around me. A fire so hot I thought I was melting, my skin peeling away from my bones, a stab of sharpness that made me want to double over and protect myself, but my body wouldn't do what I was telling it, a blindness so complete that all I knew was pain. Nothing else.

And then a pull. Not of my body towards him, but something so much deeper, so much more a part of me, who I am, what I am, it was more than a corporeal shell, more than just blood, it was my essence. I had a sudden realisation he was stealing my soul.

In my mind I heard him laugh, a cruel and vicious sound. There was no light in this thing in front of me, just unending black and I could see it, hear it, feel it, all. All of him and it had no end. Somehow, I don't know how, but I managed to speak through the haze of pain, my teeth gritted, my breathing rapid and my voice nothing more than a whimper, but I spoke.

"You have no light. You have never known light."

He heard me though, even with my voice so weak, he heard every thing I thought or spoke or whispered. "I have no need of light child, I am Death. And Death becomes you too."

At that, the pull ramped up a notch, and I did collapse to my knees. I was vaguely aware of noises behind me, fighting, scuffles, sounds, but Charles and I had only eyes for each other. He would not let me look away, I was to face Death with my eyes wide open, it would not let me cheat it.

I will give you light. I have no idea if I said that aloud, if I was capable of it still, or if it was just a thought, but his eyes widened slightly and then the room began to glow. A rainbow of colours, prisms of light, a resplendent spectrum from violet, to indigo, to blue, to green, to yellow, to orange and to red. It swirled around us, through us and across us. It felt warm and safe and light and right. Part of me thought that this was really weird, that something otherworldly was happening right now, but another part, the insistent voice I'd been hearing since I moved to Auckland, that part just kept saying, *keep going, it's all right, you're OK, just keep going, you're doing fine.* It was comforting, it wasn't bossing me, or shouting at me, or urging me in its frantic life-on-the-line way, it was celebrating me, congratulating me, welcoming me. It was strange.

And it kept me going. I don't know for how long, but I knew if I stopped too soon, all would be lost. So I kept focusing on that light, on the good in the world around me, on the beauty that exists in humans, in their love for each other, their compassion, their strength of courage when faced with so much dark, their ability to get up again when struck down, their kindness in small acts, their sacrifices for what they believe in, their unfailing desire to keep moving forward, to keep learning, expanding, growing. *There is so much light in this world, we only have to open our eyes to see.*

I was feeling very tired now, so very, very tired. The light was still shining brightly, but the world was starting to tilt. I fought it, with absolutely everything I had, I clung to it, I held it tight and I would not let it go. *I must keep the light burning. I must keep the light burning. I must keep the light burning.*

I became aware of a noise, soft at first, then more persistent. It wasn't my internal monologue, but something above me. I tried to shift my head up but it hurt too much to move. The pains in my skull were like a hot knife of steel, they shot down neck and through my body making me convulse. I could feel my body tighten in a rigid arch, then loosen against the floor, then tighten again, and loosen and tighten and loosen and then repeat the motion all over again and again. Finally my body must have had enough, I know I had, and it slumped back down against a cold hard floor. The colours dimmed and the world threatened to fade to darkness, I think the darkness actually won for a moment there. The only thing stopping me from sinking further was a voice saying over and over again, "Don't you die, Kiwi. Don't you dare die. Don't you die on me!"

I blinked in the surroundings and felt someone pushing against my chest, lips against my mouth, a push of hot air filling my lungs.

"She's awake! Stop! She's awake, Nero!" A light voice, a young woman's.

"Lucinda?" A male this time, filled with concern.

I took a steadying breath and felt my stomach roll, I went with it and up chucked all my breakfast all over the floor next to Nero.

"Sorry." It was small, a little weak.

Rough arms grabbed me up and wrapped around me, a hand through my hair, a stroke down my back.

"I thought you were dead. I thought I had lost you."

I sighed and leaned against the warm expanse of his chest, savouring the smell of him, the feel of his muscles, the shape of his body against mine.

"Did we win?" It still didn't sound like my voice.

"Yes. You won. You did it, Kiwi. It's over."

Good. I thought I'd said it aloud, but I'm not sure, the blackness came then and I let it take me. It didn't scare me like before, it just wrapped around me and promised peace.

I woke to the constant sound of humming, an engine, air conditioning, something like that. I felt the warmth of a body holding me, the soft wrap of a blanket over me, the slide of leather beneath. It was so comfortable, so safe. My eyes blinked open, a dark material in front, a shirt, a man's chest. He smelt nice, like spring mornings on the farm, fresh and bright and promising such wonders for the day. I tilted my head back and looked into the most startling indigo and blue eyes. So full of something, warmth? Light? Happiness? Relief? All of the above.

I couldn't help it, I had to reach out and touch that perfect skin, the golden touched cream, so smooth and faultless, classical.

"Beautiful," I whispered, then felt the pull of sleep calling. As I sunk back down into its feathered bed of safety I felt a kiss upon my forehead and murmured words against my skin.

"Je t'aime trop, ma douce. Je t'aime trop."

EPILOGUE

I slept the entire flight back to Auckland only waking briefly as we transferred to a waiting car. It wasn't until the next day, some 72 hours after leaving for Egypt, that I finally stirred from my sleep completely. I'd woken a few times, even managed to eat something and have a shower, but sleep kept luring me back. Now I felt the final edges of its handle slip away and glanced around my surroundings, taking them in for the first time in days. I was in Michel's chamber, at *Sensations*, the room lit lowly by candles, the smell of mandarins in the air.

When I looked around there was a table with two chairs, a dinner setting, candles, a red rose, something smelt divine. My mouth watered and I licked my lips.

I heard a low chuckle. "You are hungry, *ma douce*? Or perhaps you would like a bath first, I have drawn one for you. It is your birthday after all, you should get to choose."

He was sitting in an armchair reading from his tablet computer. Legs crossed, dressed in his now trademark black trousers and casual black shirt, open at the neck, sleeves rolled up. His eyes shone a beautiful shade of violet, with deeper hints of blue, he looked relaxed, he looked well. He looked gorgeous.

I thought about his question for a moment and decided I really didn't want to sit at that beautiful table setting in a crumpled T-Shirt, which is what I appeared to be wearing right now. "A bath first."

He smiled, a little wickedly. "As you wish, *ma douce*."

Before he had a chance to accost me, I sat myself up, made sure the world wouldn't tilt and then headed to the bathroom. The bath was still steaming; he must have run it only moments before I woke up, probably sensing my sleep pattern, my shift towards consciousness. It was filled with an enormous pile of bubbles, they covered the tap and spout, I knew when I stepped in the water would overflow. Exactly how I liked it.

I stripped down and sunk into its welcoming warmth. I felt myself relax and let out a soft sigh. Michel came and sat next to the bath on a small chair. "Would you like me to scrub your back, *ma douce?*" He had that little boyish look to him, all sweet innocence and charm. I knew better.

"Let me just soak for now."

He leaned back and stretched his legs out in front of him, making himself comfortable while I luxuriated in mandarin bliss.

"So, tell me, what happened?" I'd closed my eyes and tilted my head back, but I didn't want to sleep, I wanted to know what had happened after I'd passed out.

"Well, it seems, you burst into light, twice, dusted about thirty vampyres and a very powerful Master vampyre by the name of Charles, all in the space of a few hours. Quite impressive really."

I found myself biting my thumb nail while I digested that little piece of information. "Are they all dead?"

"Yes, the *Cadre* is no more."

"How did it go for you and Nafrini."

He leaned forward then, rolled up his sleeves a little further and grabbed the soap and sponge from the side. Lathered them up and began to wash my arms and legs, moving onto my back when he gently pulled me forward. Soft strokes and circles, warm and smelling so nice.

"We worked well together, *ma douce*. It seems Nafrini was impressed. We may choose to form an alliance, one that will be beneficial to us both in the future. We left with her best wishes. I think, I could be wrong, but she is a little scared of you, my dear. They all are."

"Of me?" It came out as a squeak, I hadn't meant it to. How could that powerful, beautiful, regal woman be scared of me?

Michel laughed, making it impossible not to smile with him, so warm and welcoming. "Well, you can hardly blame them. You were a right little tinder box, from all accounts." He was washing my feet, taking his time, not rushing, making sure every toe was individually cared for, my arch, my instep, my heel. His focus was absolute. It made me smile even more.

He glanced towards me, raised his eyebrows. "Are you scared of me?" I asked.

He sat back, the sponge still in his hands, his arms resting on the side of the bath, letting the water drip back inside. "Yes." He was serious, it surprised me. "But, not for the same reasons as Nafrini." His voice was soft when he said that, tender, as if he couldn't bring himself to say it any louder, as if it was already too hard to admit.

He reached back and grabbed a thick white towel from behind the door and I stood and let him towel me dry, wrap me in it and then pull me to him. His arms wrapped around my shoulders, his chin resting on my head. I used to think I didn't like it when men did that to me, I'm short, I don't need reminding, but there was something so close, so precious in this moment, that I had no desire to be anywhere else at all.

"Come, you must eat." I dressed quickly and when I came out he was removing the metal covers to my dish. Lamb roast, baby peas, carrots and potatoes, with a delicate sauce on the side. Perfect.

He drank his wine while I ate and then when I couldn't possible fit another bite in - oh maybe just one more baby potato - then he rose and came round to my chair, taking my hand and flicking his wrist, making music come out of the very walls. I couldn't see any speakers or a stereo for that matter, but it was soft and sweet and so romantic.

"May I have this dance, *ma douce?*"

How could I refuse? Michel danced with the practised grace of someone who had danced for centuries. His steps so fluid, his body moulded to mine. I didn't need to think, or act, but simply allow myself to curve to him, letting him lead around the room. It was magical. A more perfect birthday I could not have imagined.

The song came to a stop, another starting straight away, but Michel stilled us, tipped my head back gently with his hand on my chin and let his mouth brush against mine, then deepened it into the most exquisite kiss, all lips and tongue and heat and desire and promises of so much more. It was wet and warm and oh so lovely; I never wanted it to end.

But that's not how my life goes, is it? Nothing ever goes the way I plan it. Even as he was kissing me, stroking my arms, my back, up into my hair, holding my neck, I felt a slow sense of humming in my mind. It started out as a musical whisper, almost in tune with the music playing through the room, then surpassed it and took over all other sound. The crescendo of noise wasn't awful, far from it, it was clear and crisp and beautiful and pure and so full of light. And that's when I noticed, there was light, every where. Not like when I lit up the vampires on the roof or when I faced Charles in the museum, but within me, through me, it felt so contained and yet so powerful. I felt like I could reach inside me and pull it out, mould it, use it, give it away.

I looked down at my body and noticed it glowed. All the times I had been told by others - Rick and Nero - that I had a glow and could not see it, finally I got to see. And it was spectacular; fresh violets, majestic purples, comforting mauves, and dazzling amethysts. All blending together to create a shine and light not exactly blinding, but so intense it made you blink.

The colours began to thrum in time with the crescendo of whispers in my mind. I felt a surge of power shift through me, making me stumble forward and collapse against Michel. I blinked and tried to stay focused, but the noise and colour were so distracting, so all-consuming, I couldn't see anything else. It lasted a good five minutes, not at all painful, but unfamiliar and a little scary. I was finding it hard to catch my breath.

So much for a little tingle then.

Michel was holding me in his arms when the glow diminished and the buzzing stopped, the look on his face when my eyes met his, said it all. This is what he had been waiting for, this is what he had expected all along.

I felt crushed.

Then I was distracted again by the power accumulating within my veins, it filled every corner of my mind, every cell of my body. It was calling to me, caressing me, enfolding me, in such a rich blanket of sheer brilliance it blinded.

I became aware of something else then, a sense, or perhaps just an awareness of power and not just any power, but *Sanguis Vitam*, near me, in the city, through the country and I realised with a start, throughout the world. It was as if the more I followed that source of power, the more I could see. Initially, I was confused; it just didn't make sense, why was I sensing all this power? But then it dawned on me, I was actually *seeing* all the vampires throughout the world. I could *seek* them and find them all and it was... frightening.

There were more vampires than I had ever considered possible. They were spread around the globe and growing.

I knew without a doubt that although we may have eradicated the *Cadre of Eternal Knights* from our world, evil still lurked within; festering, growing, kneading at humanity. I could see it; I could feel it. It was a tangible entity right before my eyes.

But what to do with it?

I forced myself to breathe, to let that *Sanguis Vitam* flow back into the world, away from me, away from now. I looked up then, into the softly glowing indigo and amethyst eyes of the man in front of me and shook my head. I could see it there, but I didn't want to believe it. He had planned this, to what end, I did not know, but he did not look surprised and that alone scared me.

Despite his beautiful smile, his soft caress of my cheek, despite the kiss he rested on my lips, I was scared of what this power would mean to him, of what it would do to him. Despite everything we had been through I still wasn't completely sure he would turn toward the light.

I took another deep breath in to steady my nerves.

"This changes nothing, Michel, nothing at all." If I said it aloud, perhaps it would come true.

He just smiled at me, that damn knowing smile of his, and leaned in to kiss my forehead.

"Of course, my dear, of course. Anything you say."

MICHEL'S POV
Kindred: Chapter 2

READ ON FOR A SNEAK PEEK AT MICHEL'S VIEW...

It never fails to amaze me the lengths certain vampyres will go, to prove their idiocy. I lean back in my chair and force myself to reply to the idiot on the other end of the line.

"Manuel, you know as well as I, that my interests do not stretch to your land. Why would I be interested in America, when I have the South Pacific to myself?" I pinch the bridge of my nose in an effort to dispel the headache forming behind my eyes. I feel out of sorts this evening, an unsettling that is making my vampyre-within growl.

"Michel," Manuel's Hispanic-American accent drawls, "Tomas is not concerned that you may have interests here, he considers your attempts to dominate the market... intriguing. He merely wishes to remind you that any ventures into our land should be sanctioned by the King. You would not want to alienate the King, *amigo*."

I force myself not to let the growl, threatening to explode from the back of my throat, out. Instead, I reply calmly, "I am not interested in your lands." How many times and in how many different ways must I say it?

There is something here I am missing. The American Families

have never shown this much interest in my business pursuits before. They have never set foot on my land. But, all of a sudden, I hear reports of American vampyres travelling our roads. Why now? Why me?

Manuel drones on. "Tomas would merely like to remind you, *amigo*, that together you could accomplish much more. He would like to increase his offer to 1.2 million. I believe this should satisfy you that his intentions are only to aid in your expansions."

"1.2 million is an embarrassment and you know it, Manuel," I reply, unable to contain the growl any longer. I am sick of these quasi negotiations. America is not interested in my plans for expansion. I know this, but I cannot pin-point how I do, or what is leading me to this conclusion. The only thing I have to go on are the hackles rising on my back. My vampyre stirs restlessly within, he is also disagreeable tonight.

"You leave us little choice, Michel," Manuel says with a forced sigh. I say nothing, let him dig his hole. Then from nowhere, "There are rumours on the *Iunctio* that others have noticed your land."

A chill runs down my spine and I sit forward in my chair. "My land? Or my business interests?" Just where is he going with this and why are my fangs suddenly itching to descend?

"You do not believe your departure from Paris was not noted by those who watch these things, do you, *amigo?*"

My departure from Paris? That was 95 years ago. "It has been a long time since I left the *Iunctio*, Manuel. I am sure if interest were to have been garnered, it would have happened before now."

His cold laugh reaches me down the line. He knows more than he is saying, but how?

"The great Michel Durand leaving his position and life on a whim? How is *that* not going to gain notice?" My fangs flick out and down, my heart stops, I am barely breathing. I have no need to, but the vampyre on the other end of the phone would pick up on my lack of breath if I stop completely. He may already be aware my heart no longer thuds, but I can do little to prevent that now.

A whim. No one, other than close confidantes, are aware of why I came to this country. No one else should have knowledge of what called me here. But this... cretin, this poor excuse for a vampyre, implies otherwise.

I waited over 70 years for *her*. Seventy years of not knowing whether I had made a mistake or if my patience would be rewarded. Seventy years of yearning for something I was not sure would even exist. And this vampyre is aware. A part of me, long thought controlled, rears its ugly head. My fingers clench around the first object they can find, my Visconti pen. In a split second it is dust. I painfully release my grip on the remains - one finger at a time - and force my dragon back down.

"My interests in this land were varied, Manuel," I say in a surprisingly bored voice. "But my desire for a change of scenery cannot be of that much entertainment for the masses."

I wait for his chuckle. So predictable. Perhaps my boredom is not entirely feigned.

"I appreciate the effort Tomas is putting into his offer," I continue, before he has a chance to reply. "But, he is wasting his time and you know it. My answer will not change. The Durand line does not require American assistance, now or ever." That last was perhaps overkill, but this has gone on long enough.

"You are making a mistake, *amigo*."

"So be it," I reply and return the phone to its cradle, disconnecting the call.

I sit immobilised in my current position. Neither reclining in the seat nor perched on the edge. Somewhere in between. They know about *her*. They know why I am here.

Ninety-five years and just when I am so close to the end, so close to gaining what I have desired for so long, it is threatening to explode in my face. I will not let it. I will not let, what I have nurtured and cared for and coveted for so long, be taken by another. *She is mine.*

I stand and start pacing, distractedly send a thought out to one of my line and return my mind to when she first arrived. I knew the instant she had come. Several months before her birth I felt her. I didn't follow that call, I sat in stasis for weeks, awaiting the proof to materialise. Too scared to consider I was wrong.

But she did not fail me. She was born in the New Land, just as they said she would be. And then that night, that cold, wintry night. I don't know what made me go there. I had to use the Ley Lines to get there quickly, something I don't usually consider. It is not safe, but the need to be there for her was astounding. I stood and watched in morbid fascination as they drove the family's car off the pass. I watched in horror as they forced her father to avoid their vehicles and consequently careen down the side of a cliff.

I have never moved so quickly before in my life. Nor have I since. In a fraction of a moment I was beside the tumbling car, the colours of the occupants' clothes blurring as the momentum of the vehicle picked up. I could see her, in the back seat. Strapped securely in a baby capsule. She smiled at me. Actually smiled. Even as the car tumbled like a discarded toy tossed from a cot, her parents' screams reverberating around the vehicle as the metal crunched and windows shattered and the inevitable crashed towards us all.

Without a thought for the amount of *Sanguis Vitam* it required, I pulled her from the car. My ability to move objects without actually touching them is sound, but such a task under such circumstances has its disadvantages. The car tumbled on as we slowed down and then silence reigned.

I collapsed beside her quiet figure, still strapped securely in the capsule and allowed the world to spin around me for a moment more. I could hear the slowly dwindling creaks and groans of the crumpled metal below. I could not sense any life. But above me, coming down the ravine, were others. Heartbeats frantic, breathing rapid and hoarse, the scent of victory on the air.

With the last of my strength I shielded her. I wrapped my conscience around her precious body and hid her from their sight. I used what little reserves I had to summon the sound of emergency vehicles, conjured an image of the baby several metres from the wreckage and prayed to whatever God would listen, to a Dark soul like mine, to make them believe what they saw.

They must have, because I cannot remember what happened in the next few moments, my consciousness only returned when one of my line arrived. The sun was threatening the horizon by then and my kin's urgent demands for both our safety finally reached my ears. My last memory of that scene was watching her watching me. So peacefully, so warmly, so unafraid.

We left as the emergency vehicles arrived and only barely made it to shelter before the day dawned bright and clear.

I glance up now, returning my attention to my immediate surroundings and the vampire who had crossed my office threshold and stood waiting for me to acknowledge his presence. He did not say anything. He did not indicate any concern for the fact that he had been standing there several seconds before I realised his presence at all.

"Dillon."

"Master. How may I help?"

"What have you heard of American interest in our land?" I return to my side of the desk, I need the illusion of control it will give. I am not in control. If Dillon senses it, he wisely doesn't show concern.

"There have been some visits, but nothing that would raise alarm. Merely curious travellers. Nothing more."

I don't sit, but pause to consider his words. "How many curious travellers?"

"Perhaps a dozen."

My gaze shoots up to his, he blanches. I don't know what he sees on my face, but it is enough for him to gauge how precarious his position currently is.

"I will immediately investigate further, Master. A dozen is an increase I had not recognised as a concern. My apologies."

He bows low, hand fisted across chest. He doesn't stand up again. I don't encourage him too. He has overlooked an obvious threat. It is not like him, but it is not acceptable either. I watch him for several minutes and realise distractedly, that my hand is rubbing my chest, above my heart. I stop the motion and stare down at my torso. A heaviness has descended inside. A squeezing that threatens to crush my body, shatter my ribs and pulverise my heart.

She is in the city. She hunts. I sit down in my chair stunned, this is not the first time I have sensed her hunting, but lately, it has become more acute. As though time is running out and if I do not make her mine soon, I will be lost. I swallow past that uncomfortable feeling, that sense of lost control. No one, not vampyre, not human, has ever had the effect she has on me.

"Tomorrow you shall start investigating their interest further," I say quietly to the still bent vampyre before me. "There is more to their presence than we are aware."

"Of course, Master," he replies automatically. I wave my hand and he springs upright again a small grimace flashing over his face and then a blank mask.

I notice, from the corner of my eye, he is watching me, intently. It is only then I realise I am rubbing my chest again. I force my hand to my lap.

"Leave," I command, lacing my voice in *Sanguis Vitam*, ensuring he cannot return to the club tonight. I don't want him to be aware of her approach. To put two and two together.

He nods, bows again and leaves. I lean back in my chair and allow my hand to return to my chest. I need to get control of this motion, but for now I seek solace in the movement and let myself *feel* where she is.

She is fighting. I have no concern that she will win. I know how good she is at what she does. But still I ache to be at her side. I sigh and force myself to detach from the sensations she provokes. *Merde!* She is not even before me and I feel so much.

I send a thought out to one of my line to fetch her. But to only announce his presence when she has finished with the rogue. I know she would abhor interference of any sort. A small part of me wants to tease her, to turn up there myself. I feel my lips spread in a smile.

My vampyre acknowledges my request and I sense his retreat. I send directions on where to find her. I can trust him. Others would not think so, he appears less than he is, but Shane will not overstep the mark, he will follow my instructions to the letter. He is more than others see.

Now I must wait. Without even being aware I find myself straightening my suit jacket, making sure there are no creases, that the tie is sitting just so. I curse myself, she couldn't care less how I appear. She barely even registers anything other than the shade of my eyes or the Dark within my soul. She is a Hunter, through and through. And I wouldn't put it past her to attempt to stake me should I cross that Darkened line. Somehow that settles my nerves.

I clear the remnants of my shattered pen to the trash can and pull a duplicate out of my desk drawer. Grabbing a sheaf of paper I begin to write nonsense. Anything to appear busy. Several minutes pass and I feel her at the front door of the club. Bruno opens his mind to me and lets me hear their conversation.

"Lucinda Monk, long time no see," my Second says, allowing his gaze to wander the length of her body, he does it for me. "Good to see you," he adds, purposely instilling a gruffness in his voice that pales humans, but not her.

"Yeah right, Bruno. Wish I could say the same."

I laugh at her response and then glance down at the paper I have before me. I cringe. My writing has produced evidence of my insanity. I crumple the paper before anyone has the chance to see how lost I truly am. Throwing it in the trash can beside the desk, I see line after line of her name taunting me from its crinkled corners.

I roll my head on my shoulders and adopt my usual mask. I force myself to not close my eyes as she approaches, a sense of calm flowing over me with each delicate step she takes down the hall towards my door. If I could give in to what I desire right now, I would already have her skin beneath my fangs. My jaw aches to let them down. To make her mine and no one else's.

I pull on every reserve I have. I am the Master of this City. No one can get the better of me.

The door handle shifts beneath her hand and her scent invades my nose. Candied apples and sunshine, honey and Spring. Before I can even stop myself my *Sanguis Vitam* is across the office floor and caressing up her body. My heart no longer beats, but I have never felt more alive than I do right at this second.

She strides into my domain, pushing valiantly against my power, making me instantly hard with carnal thoughts.

"Knock it off, would you!" she demands and my vampyre purrs within.

"Ah Lucinda, ever the lady I see." My gaze covers her body in a second, I should take longer to drink her in, but I now must play the game. "I thought you may have missed me and needed a little reminding."

God, she is beautiful tonight. Her hair is a little untidy, no doubt from the recent fight. She hasn't bothered to smooth it flat, she doesn't care what I see. I mentally shake my head at her lack of interest, then I chide myself at my desire to twist the strands of that glorious hair in my fingers, to nuzzle my face into the crease at her neck. I surreptitiously clear my throat and return my eyes to her face. Not a hardship.

"Very funny, Michel, but could you can it for a bit? I can hardly draw a breath."

She. Is. Perfect.

I pull my *Sanguis Vitam* back reluctantly and without its distracting pleasure against her skin, I notice what I should have noticed as soon as she arrived. She is injured. She is hurt. That fight with the rogue has harmed my Lucinda and I was too busy seeking my own pleasure to have picked up on it before.

"You are hurt." I vaguely recognise my own voice, then I am beside her in an instant. I don't remember moving, but this close her scent is intoxicating. It takes every ounce of my self control not to give in and bite.

I reach up before she has a chance to react and stroke her cheek. Fire burns through me and my vampyre growls in response. I ignore its desires and concentrate on the bruising developing on her beautiful face. If she hadn't already have killed that rogue, I would be doing right now. Slowly. Painfully.

Without realising what I am doing both hands begin to trace each and every blemish that vampyre has made. From her cheek, down her long neck, past the fractured ribs I can sense beneath her rapidly rising and falling chest, to finally rest lightly, reverently, above each hip. I have stopped breathing. I have stopped thinking. I am just responding to the moment with dawning fear.

"Wh..what did you do?" she stammers and well she might ask.

I have no idea how I have done it, it is not a talent I have had before. Nor do I believe it is one I could call upon for any other. But somehow, my connection to this Nosferatin has elicited a healing response. My desire - in the moment I recognised her pain from those injuries she had sustained - to heal her was all consuming. So much so, that my body acted of its own accord.

This is bad. Very bad.

"You were hurt, my dear. I could not have that," I manage, hearing the cursed French lilt to my words.

"You heal people now?" she asks, stunned. I can't blame her, I'm a little stunned myself.

To heal her before we have joined can only mean one thing. If I do not complete this joining before too much longer, I will begin to fall. Somehow the gods have decided that I must join with this woman, but it is not enough for me to already agree with them. They have to make it a death sentence too.

I vow she will never know the consequences should I not join with her now. It is irrelevant. I *will* have her. She need not be aware that I will slowly die, if she denies me this. I will not make her suffer that at all.

"Only when the desire is strong, it would seem." I finally answer her question and then turn to move to my side of the desk.

I make sure the movement is predatory and sleek. I may not want her to know what rides on the outcome of her accepting me, but I will be damned if she doesn't see what she will miss should she say no.

When I resume my seat, I can't help myself, but my gaze follows the contour of her body again. This time taking in the crumpled blouse, stretched thinly above her breasts - I strain to see if her nipples are erect - the line of the jacket, hiding silver I am certain she could reach in a flash, to finally her short skirt. It hugs her hips, the exact same hips I recently touched, albeit through the material of her clothes. I fantasise at what furry delight lies beneath her skirt. My fingers flex in response to where my thoughts are heading. I'm glad I'm sitting down behind a desk and she cannot see my immediate response.

"So, you requested my presence. Here I am." I smile at her bravado. She has no idea how much of her life I control.

"Have a seat, my dear. We have much to catch up on."

She hesitates, as though she has a choice. Funny girl. She makes me smile further.

She launches herself at the seat in front of my desk. The movement sensual and unbelievably erotic. I don't think she intended it that way. For someone so petite, she appears as though she is ten feet tall. Her legs, ribbons of hypnotic muscle - which I have visions of wrapped around my waist - fold in on themselves as she lands on the chair seat. Graceful, but in such an unintended way. I know she does not see herself as such, but to me, she is the picture of supple beauty. Exquisite. Divine. Perfection. My God, I want her so much.

I reach for a bottle of wine and glasses from beneath my desk while she is distracted by the feel of the chair. I had it changed from the one she has sat in before. I wanted her to be enveloped in beauty the next time she sat before me. I smile to myself at her response, the chair fits perfectly. I couldn't have envisaged a better reaction than this. If only she knew the lengths I would go, to make her happy.

Her hazel eyes open and pierce right through my heart. I reach for the wine in an attempt to hide my reaction, confounded that she has this effect on me at all. She is so pure. So *not* what I have been attracted to in the past. She is innocent and Light, full of promise and hope. I am jaded and battle-worn, fighting the Dark within on a daily basis. If I allowed myself, right now, to let that Dark in, what would she do? I let a little of my vampyre peek out from behind the closed doors, magenta washing the space between us. She doesn't react. I think my heart just shattered.

I stand and bring the glass to her, attempting to brush my fingers against hers. She avoids the contact like a seasoned pro. What is wrong with me? I am acting like a love-sick teenager.

I return to my side of the divide, perhaps space is the answer. The more I place between us, the more I can actually behave like a five hundred year old vampyre and not some besotted imbecile. I curse my reactions and pull on the Dark within to fortify my resolve.

And then I see her watching me, her hazel eyes devouring the length of my body, a small roll of her bottom lip between her teeth. *Mon dieu!* She could have me now and I would gladly die the final death for just one taste. The Dark I have called on makes me incline my head, let her know I have seen her interest, reveal how much I am aware of her reactions to my body.

"So, what did you want to catch up on, Michel?" Her words bring us both back from the edge.

I take a sip from my glass, to stall and gather my thoughts. There is a reason, other than my fervent desire to be near this woman, that I called her to my side this night.

"How was your evening?" I ask, calmness returning to my façade. It's all an act, if only she knew.

She smiles and the room lights up with her. "You're asking me about my evening?"

I can't help responding to that light, letting my voice reach out and touch every visible point on her skin. And then some. "I would like to know, my dear, that you are well and happy. I'll start with your evening and then progress from there. Or perhaps you would like me to - how do you say? - cut to the chase? If so, then why not come a little closer, there's room enough for two on my chair."

Please say yes. My body craves your touch.

"Very funny. It was eventful, how was yours?"

My disappointment that she won't play the game is overshadowed by the knowledge of why she has had an eventful night. I must not let her know I am aware of her hunts this evening. To do so, would be to invite her disdain of what I am. I cannot allow for her to pull away. Not now. Not ever.

"Eventful, how?" I ask.

She gives up on the wine, I smile. I hadn't thought it possible to relax her with alcohol. My Hunter has more sense than to fall for that trap.

"I killed three vampires who were preying on innocent lives. One was a level four Master."

"The bruises and fractured rib," I offer, determined to distract her from my true desire right now. To reach across the desk and make sure the injuries have in fact disappeared. I curl my fingers around the stem of my glass and will my vampyre to retreat. He is as protective as I.

The urge to let him loose is all consuming. He growls inside me - with the strength of a dragon - to be released. He whispers to me that she is still hurting. That I haven't, in fact, healed her bruises. That I must touch her again to be sure. It takes all of my formidable will power to ignore his suggestions. Not because I know it is unnecessary, she no longer pains, but because I want to touch her with every fibre of my body and mind.

"Is there something you're not telling, Michel? What's with all the activity lately? The lack of manners on your turf?"

The vampyre-within wins the battle momentarily, magenta bathes the room and lands upon Lucinda. The sight of her washed in my vampyre's shade is enough to make me startle. She has not only picked up on my distraction, she has formed a reason for it that is untrue. Can she not see I am upset because of her nearness? Not because of some vampyres who threaten to enter my land.

I think of an adequate answer, it is better she does not know how she makes me feel. A distraction is required, one that will refocus both of us on the reason why she is here. My *Sanguis Vitam* flows out from me with infinite ease and care, I ignore the guilt I feel at using this on her and concentrate on the reasons behind it instead.

"What I am about to tell you must not leave this room, Lucinda. Do you understand? Not even to your shapeshifter friend and his kin."

"Of course," she answers, a slight crack appearing in her voice. I don't allow myself the luxury of showing any sign of the pain I feel at scaring her. To act as anything other than the Master of this City with her would invoke suspicion. I cannot have her second guessing my desires. Not yet.

I remove my power and force regret into my features. I don't regret showing strength, I do regret that I cannot confide in her yet.

"There has been some rumblings in the *Iunctio* of late. At first I thought nothing of it, but it has traversed the seas and landed upon our shores. A group of vampyre who flout the rules, who wish to take over the night completely."

I let my words sink in. She needs to be aware of how much danger she is in. I would move Heaven and Earth to protect her, but even I have limitations. She is capable, I must trust with fair warning, she will be able to defend herself.

"The revolt was thwarted in London, a similar one barely got started in New York. I had thought we were far enough from the centres of power to avoid attention, but it seems even I cannot keep some things hidden from the *Iunctio*."

I briefly visit the *Iunctio* now, to ensure nothing new has been posted there. The rumblings I had spoken of were happening everywhere. Not just my land. That was reassuring, to some degree. If it was happening elsewhere, then maybe Lucinda was not in as much danger as I thought. I shake myself and return my attention to the woman in front of me. An impossible wish, who would not covet my Hunter?

I had not wanted to admit so much to her yet. I had wanted to keep her in the dark a little longer. But time is no longer on my side. For one, the rumblings are an indication of something much more insidious encroaching on our land. For another, my call to her has just clicked into overdrive. I must join with her soon. I must play this just right.

I wasn't sure if she was ready yet. I wanted fervently to apologise for the pressure I was about to exert in order to get what I wanted, but the Dark inside swelled and my resolve settled into marble and stone. All concern for hiding how in-tune I now was with her, thrown out the window.

"You should be careful for a short while, my dear. Take extra precautions. Now would not be the time to rush with foolhardiness down dark dead-end alleys."

She looks momentarily alarmed. "This is your war, Michel, not mine. I've still got a job to do, no matter how many rogue vamps enter the city, they can't just chow down willy-nilly on my neighbours." I wince at her reaction, cursing my Dark within.

It only roars with delight. I am at its mercy now, as much as Lucinda. I will make her mine. I will taste her soon. But not today. Today she must be prepared to fight.

"It is you they seek, Lucinda. It is you they hunt."

Made in the USA
Columbia, SC
29 November 2019